Pro

In a cream-coloured room wit
well-travelled filing cabinet a
was told he was dying.

Mr Slater used a tone whi
his message was as bleak as
some papers then leant forward on the desk as to
brief intimacy, momentarily looking Daniel in the eye. He was
sorry to be the bearer of such bad news but unfortunately
nothing could be done.

Daniel became weirdly aware of the hairs protruding from
the man's nose and ears, of the glare from the unshaded
lightbulb and the smell of disinfectant. His stomach began to
cramp, the muscles in his legs were tightening and, of its own
accord, his index finger burrowed through the knit of his
jumper. An old cast-iron radiator was making the room
oppressively hot and he felt a bead of sweat slipping from his
temple.

There would be no miracle, then. This was the end of the
road. He was facing an horrific stumble towards death. He had
seen others in the clinics and knew that soon he would need a
wheelchair and oxygen cylinders and twenty-four-hour care.
He would be fighting for breath, every day and night.

A trolley rattled down the corridor as rain battered the
window and an ambulance passed outside. Mr Slater paused
for a sip of water. Daniel had stopped listening anyway…

That night, he kept the bedside lamp switched on and,
helped by half a bottle of whisky, he drifted into and out of a
sleep in which broken dreams opened once again the blinds of
memory. He shuttled back to another existence – his only
escape now – to that time when life had been endless and
intoxicating, when the island of Serifos offered him such
vistas. He had arrived there first as a young man…

That day! When the vehicle door at the rear of the ferryboat
dropped open, his eyes were forced to adjust, squinting after
the dimness of the car deck on which he stood. Sunlight
sparkled off the deep, deep blue sea. Reversing to dock, the
Ferry Boat Kyclades juddered; water churned white and

mooring lines were thrown ashore. The fumes from the three trucks behind him cleared and he could taste salt.

The tannoy crackled: '*Se líga leptá to karávi tha ftásei sti Sérifo! Sérifo!*'

In his room, half awake, his tongue ran along midnight-dry lips…

He and half a dozen other backpackers trooped down the metal ramp, blinking in the blinding Greek sun, the scorching midday heat. People bustled round, but beyond them the quay was remarkably empty. Fishing boats rocked in the harbour and the bay was fringed with sand and bamboo. A small, shining white town looked down from a hill. In his head he heard bouzoukis, like in old movies, as if the island vibrated to an ancient rhythm.

He smiled, already loving this place where he had just happened to land.

Weeks later, he carried back precious memories of Serifos to his tiny terraced house in Leeds: a magic that came from beyond the beaten track, from sleeping on the beach with beautiful young people from all over the world; the clear bays teeming with fish; local women bathing on Saturdays in vast swimsuits, long gloves and corrugated cardboard hats; old men with gat teeth and deep wrinkles and old tales to retell over thick sugared coffee in the *kafeneíons*; and nights that lay over everything like a comfort blanket, the warm black sea inviting you to come and play.

The island summoned him year after year – not least because of the girl who became the centre of his life there and whom he adored: Helen, who had set him on fire. He knew her spirit would be entwined with his on Serifos forever, that he would die still amazed by her, still under the spell she cast, dancing before him under the stars.

Yet, when he woke to the cold winter morning, still sensing her, still loving her, he knew she had been lost long ago and Serifos was far, far away now and that he was dying, alone and afraid.

Circles on the Sand

Keith Brindle

Circles on the Sand

ISBN: 9798345846483

Cover design by Keith Brindle and Helen Swansbourne

For my wife, Christine,
whose love, support and guidance
have been invaluable

1979

Chapter 1

Jeanette perched on the rock beside Helen and the sea washed quietly over their feet. As so often, the breeze had dropped once night fell; the slapping of the waves and a shoosh as they lapped against pebbles on the sand were the only sounds.

The girls were in a secluded spot beneath the hill at the very start of the beach, with just darkness ahead of them and across the water. Above, the heavens were customarily wonderful. There was a sickle moon and the stars but intermittent showers of meteors too, stunning white streaks which burnt across the sky to disappear in an instant.

It was warm enough for strappy tops and short skirts. Helen was almost content.

'Greece is beautiful,' said Jeanette.

'Yes.' Helen swept back her hair.

'It was a good evening.'

'Yes.'

'And you had time with Daniel.'

'I did.'

'But..?'

'But?'

'Still no progress then?'

'No change.'

Jeanette leant across to her.

'He was whispering in your ear.'

'He was trying to make me laugh.'

'He did it several times. I was watching.'

Helen dipped her fingers in the water and bit her lip.

'He did. He was telling me about Mike.'

'Ah… What's new? Mike's got a part in a sequel to *The Wicker Man*..? No? He'll be disappointed. A primitive sex cult would fulfil his every fantasy… What he wouldn't give… So, come on…'

Helen couldn't help herself, even though she'd been told in confidence.

'He was telling me how much Mike fancied you when we

all first met.'

'That's when you were laughing.'

'It was. I was.'

'Quite rightly! I had a lucky escape. Not that he ever stood a chance.'

That awful Santorini night on Kamari Beach was recent and still vivid to both of them. Helen remembered her friend close to tears, telling Mike what he could do with his drunken breath and groping hands and Mike berating her for enticing him – and, yes, he'd called her 'frigid' – before he stumbled off into the pitchy darkness and gusting wind, no doubt seeking some other poor girl to satisfy his needs.

'We both know why he gave up... Daniel's still apologising for him,' said Helen.

'Because he's decent... But we all understand Mike well enough... Thank god you picked the other one, girl.'

Helen knew she'd got it right. Daniel might not be perfect, but he was desperately close. He was steady, reliable. If only he'd been more discerning in his choice of a travelling companion. They tolerated Mike because he was Daniel's friend and for no other reason. He was not as awful when he was sober, but had become the grit in an otherwise blissfully smooth-running holiday. His crude streak was an annoyance that neither could abide.

'Daniel's a bit slow.'

Jeanette had to smile. 'Desperately slow. But nice. He didn't lick your earlobe even?'

'Jeanette!' Helen flicked water at her but without malice.

'I'll tell him to try that next time.'

'Please don't.'

A couple were making their way along the beach, wrapped around each other, dark shapes occasionally stopping to kiss. The girls watched them go. Helen wished Daniel was with her. Her head was ridiculously full of hope and she had moments of surprising breathlessness when he was near. She thought perhaps, just perhaps, he might be the one to set her free from those terrible years.

It was a pity Jeanette had wanted to leave the taverna earlier but there was only so much of Mike she could stand.

She couldn't let her go alone; though if they'd stayed and Jeanette had walked back with the others, Helen might have had Daniel to herself and it might have been the night when he kissed her and held her and told her he loved her. He did love her, didn't he? Yes, she knew he did.

'Have you ever been happier than this?' he'd whispered earlier in the taverna as he poured her wine from the tin jug.

'Never.'

'I'm the same.'

Right then he'd be ordering another beer, laughing at the conversation, perhaps perplexed about why she'd left. Maybe he'd be rubbing his chin, like he did. Carina and Phil would be picking out any girls that walked past as likely targets for Mike's ever-hungry libido whilst Daniel would be above it all, the special one...

'You can pop back to him if you want.'

Jeanette could read her mind.

'Remember I've had eighteen years without him.'

'And...?'

Helen swung round so that her feet were clear of the water.

'And therefore I intend to lie on the sand over there out of sight... perhaps going ever so slightly out of my mind...' She laughed. 'But I'll watch the sky and begin to decide what to do with the rest of my life. Maybe my happiness is not dependent on Daniel. After all, he's just a frill.'

She'd once been a convincing liar, but that was no longer the case.

'He's more than that,' said Jeanette. 'He's exactly the thrill you've been needing.'

It was a cliché, but Helen always said that Jeanette had wisdom beyond her years.

****

Having climbed the steep track from the harbour to the top of the headland, Daniel paused to savour the velvet night. Almost all the scattered buildings on the hillsides ahead were shuttered and closed. His eyes adjusted after the thin illumination from the handful of tavernas down at the port, the line of cast iron

6

lamp posts and occasional yellow bulbs strung along the seafront. Gradually, the shapes of the hills became identifiable against the other blackness of the sky, with galaxies wheeling across from horizon to horizon, and for the moment his worries lifted. The air was sweet.

He slithered his way down the stony footpath to the beach and set out along its six-hundred-yard curve. He'd seen nothing of the girls. He felt stupid not to have gone with them when they left the taverna because he could have been with Helen at that moment, touching her, tasting her...

Five bottles of Fix had mellowed him. He hoped he'd find her. He wanted to tell her he'd do anything for her. Anything.

However, half way round the bay his reverie was interrupted. The loud voices of figures round a driftwood fire fifty yards ahead were puncturing the peace.

'Hey, hey, Erica! Fuck, Erica..!' a man screamed. '*As fuck... As fuck*!'

There were often fires on the beach, but rarely noise, apart from guitar chords and singing. This was very different.

Approaching, Daniel realised it was just two men and two women, but they'd been drinking heavily and from a distance had sounded like many more. They were not far from where he and Mike slept, their place marked by their rucksacks and sleeping bags. Mike's towel remained where he'd laid it out on the sand to dry before the sun went down.

Daniel sighed heavily. There was no Helen to be seen and this noise meant he wouldn't be able to sleep either. He knelt beside his rucksack, watching, deciding what he should do.

The men were perhaps twenty-two or twenty-three years old and Greek. One was tall and broad, the other thin, and they hollered and chanted as they downed their beer. Meanwhile, the women, in tight tops, were as loud as their companions, sharing the alcohol, sometimes squealing, filling the night with a bizarre mixture of German and English.

'*Zuerst singen wir und später tanzen... und* then, *zusammen*, we *ficken*. Oh, yes, yes, yes... We fuck, we fuck. *Alles zusammen*. All togezzer. You – *beide zusammen*,' shouted the larger and louder woman, to the men and the vastness of the night. She held the smallest man in one arm

7

whilst her free hand waved a wine bottle back and forth.

'*As fuck..,*' he shrieked again.

It was approaching midnight. Daniel didn't need this. He didn't want to spend hours lying almost beside them, fixated on the sex that was bound to follow.

With resignation, he pulled out a bottle of water from beneath his rucksack, took his sleeping bag too and retreated thirty yards along the beach, determined not to be annoyed. These people would not ruin his mood. Finding a rock-free spot on the sand, he swilled his mouth, hoping to freshen it after the food and the drinks, took off his tee shirt and shorts and stretched into the sleeping bag's sheet lining.

Lying back, his head on his small heap of clothes, he breathed in the natural scents: grasses, shrubs, the smell of the beach itself. Not far away, their fire was crackling but the smoke wasn't spreading in his direction. His skin felt stretched from the day's sun and the sea was shifting just yards away and the Milky Way was beautiful and this was why, every year, he came back.

He might have been totally relaxed, but he worried about what Helen might be doing and as soon as he closed his eyes his gnawing torment returned: Dianne would arrive in only three days. Dianne, who'd been his girlfriend for twelve months, who was sharp and alive and athletic in bed, who had the looks and hair of a young Marilyn Monroe... and as long as he lived he would never forget the night after that party in Camden. He should have been excited that he'd soon be seeing her again after their weeks apart. And yet, and yet... he'd got things so badly wrong.

'I can get a fortnight off work. If you like, I can come and join you,' she'd said, her eyes sparkling, way back in February. 'I can book my flights now...'

He couldn't tell her he went to Greece for the summer hoping to meet new girls. Ever the coward and a fool, 'Yes... Great...,' he replied.

He wanted the best holiday he could manage after leaving university and before knuckling down to turgid employment for ever, and there was never a certainty he'd pull in Greece anyway, so he'd convinced himself she could be his insurance policy. It would be perfect to have her there at the end of his holiday. They'd make love on the sand, under the stars…

But meeting Helen had changed everything.

What to do..? What a mess…

And he was still too close to the drunks. The big woman picked up a guitar and began to strum, filling the air with a guttural contralto. It was not entirely tuneless but the words gave it away as Dylan's *Ze Times, Zey Are A-Changing*.

She sang verse after verse until after what seemed an eternity her rasping ended, and the two men – perhaps inspired by the lyrics or relieved the rendition was over – became yet more energised. The taller one threw wood on to the fire then dragged the other into the sea, both bellowing as they went. They came back for the women, who initially fended them off. The men persisted, in Greek, whilst the women resisted, in German, before finally removing the few clothes they were wearing and, screeching with laughter, submitted themselves to the waves. The men watched them strip before tearing off their own wet things. Naked and shrieking, all four splashed together.

'Freedom,' shouted the large man, the one with the fullest beard, the longest hair and the deepest voice. He stood up, spreading his arms as if trying to embrace the ocean itself. 'We have freedom. Freedom… Freedom…'

They hugged and howled.

Daniel closed his eyes once more. They would surely move to the inevitable couplings soon and the volume would reduce. He was settled and tired and didn't want to trek further away.

He could doze. He just needed to think of Helen, who was so different, who moved like a soft spirit, like some goddess running half-clad through his dreams each night, slim and chestnut brown. He imagined her beside him, leaning over him in the moonlight, her hair touching his chest, her breasts touching him lightly too, soft and firm, her hand stroking his cheek before moving so her body was tight against his…

His eyes fluttered half-open.

It took him a moment to make sense of what was actually happening.

The big man from the quartet was lying beside him. Still

naked and wet, hirsute from top to toe, he was stroking Daniel's head, leaning on one elbow, looking down. He'd been smoking but brought with him another smell too, a sweetness like a Greek bakery. His hand moved rhythmically as it smoothed Daniel's hair. He was all bulk and a huge erection.

'Hey,' he said, in a voice that had turned sonorous. 'My friend, we have freedom. So come, come, my friend, you come join us. Dance, drink, make peace, fuck. I am Yiannis. We have freedom, my friend... Freedom...'

He continued to toy with Daniel's hair, as you might pet a cat or soothe a lover.

'Yiannis. I am Yiannis..,' he intoned.

Daniel had not heard anyone talking about love and peace since he was a kid and though he approved of the sentiments he definitely did not welcome this physicality. This was bizarre. This wasn't something he wanted. Yiannis could have been smothered in the big German woman or impressing himself upon the smaller one, instead of doing this. Instead of... doing... this...

He knew how Mike would react. Mike would use his fists. But the man wasn't threatening violence. In addition, Daniel was in a sleeping bag and had never been a fighter and the man was over six feet tall and Daniel was not; he was impressively muscled, and Daniel was not.

Almost all the Greeks Daniel had ever met had been loud but gentle, yet this one could be the exception, so Daniel said nothing, closed his eyes and kept them closed. Like a child, he was desperate for the monster to go away.

'Freedom, freedom, my friend,' repeated Yiannis.

He was extremely inebriated and, in contrast, Daniel felt very, very sober. This had to stop. He had to do something.

In his first term at university he'd studied Buddhism and now, desperate to avoid bruising or maybe even worse damage, he opted for what his tutor labelled 'religious passivity'. It was all he could think of. In one movement, he rolled from his back on to his right side, so he faced away from his unwanted suitor. Yawning significantly, as if courting sleep, he curled into a defensive ball and lay still. He could think of no other ploy. He tried to keep his breathing steady.

'Hey, hey. *Ti écheis?*'

He didn't understand the man's words but the touching stopped.

There was perhaps a minute of still and silence, then it worked.

'*Ai gamísou...*' Yiannis got up, noisily cleared his throat, spat and staggered back to his friends.

Daniel was mightily relieved. As soon as he judged it safe, he rose too. To his right, the four party animals were re-united, stretched out with feet in the sea and arms in the air. Apart from them, no one else was around. There was still no sign of Helen, but at that moment his pressing need was simply to put some distance between himself and his unwanted suitor.

Back along the beach was a gully in the sand where a stream must have run down from the hills in winter. He headed for that and some seclusion. Further up its course, Carina and Phil had set up home when they could no longer cope in their mosquito-trap of a room in town. He didn't want to invade their space, so stayed nearer to the sea. Although the depression was shallow, he hoped it might help reduce the noise from drunken four. He settled himself against its side in his sleeping bag, wriggling as sand slid down and over his shoulders, and he closed his eyes again.

But he was only moving from one problem to another because, predictably, stepping out from the shadows in his head, Dianne reappeared. He used to think her face was serene, but now, each night, it twisted with bitter disappointment then betrayal and anger until he managed to force it away.

Helen was the girl he wanted. He could picture her in the water, lying on the sand, spinning and laughing after wine, dancing, slender. She was deep and troubled, but, oh, those brown eyes... It was crazy that he'd not yet dared to kiss her. He'd not been so reticent since his mid-teens, when Alice, she of the long black hair and sultry gaze, had beguiled him for months until her father stepped in and ensured Daniel would not be loitering outside their house again.

Now, he was far from home and knew that on a beach in the sunshine you only see the best in someone, yet he was convinced that a lifetime with Helen could never be enough. When he died, he wanted to be in her arms.

Mike would say that was a fucking big thought, so he hadn't told him exactly how he felt. He didn't tell Mike everything.

He knew, too, what his parents would have said about it all. He thought of them less than he used to as his memories faded, but still he always ended up picturing his uncle's burnt-out Austin Maxi at the side of the motorway, the flashing lights and emergency services and, awfully, their bodies. He hadn't been there that night, but knew all about the collision and the explosion and the fire. It pained him that they'd never have the chance to disapprove of the way he was letting down Dianne or to know about Helen.

He sighed again and pulled his sheet tight round his neck. It might as well have been a noose. The clock was ticking. Mike knew Dianne would be with them soon; but he'd no idea how truly terrible her arrival might prove to be. Only Daniel knew and each day brought him closer to that reckoning. And whatever transpired when he met Dianne and offered to carry her pack, his friendship with Helen – idyllic, platonic for now, a romance forever, whatever it was – would be doomed.

He was desperate for a way out. He wanted Helen, not Diane. He wanted Helen, no-one else.

After what seemed an age, he finally slept.

****

Mike's day began with his bowels grumbling and the soles of his feet burning, as usual. Since stepping barefoot off a sand dune into gorse bushes on Agia Anna Beach on Naxos one very drunken night, he'd worked away each day with a needle, digging out thorns as they came to the surface. It wasn't easy, because his feet were hardened after nearly a month walking around bare foot or in sandals, but the probings had become a routine part of his life over the past fortnight. It simply meant he experienced soreness all the time.

The procedure had been made more difficult because the mad girl had stolen his glasses on Santorini and, stupidly, he'd not brought his contact lenses with him for fear he might lose them. However, he considered himself adaptable and could locate thorns by pressing and squinting, so he was managing his daily gougings well enough. He assumed that the salt water was helping the healing process. Like everyone else, he spent much of each day in the sea.

He peered around, his back slightly stiff, and registered the fact that Daniel still wasn't beside him. If he'd spent the night with Helen, that was good, though. After all, Dianne was coming and Dianne was pretty special and had that face and that body; and if Daniel was absorbed with Helen, Dianne would be available soon, which suited Mike perfectly.

He was desperate for things to improve. Identical days were dripping by. Santorini and Naxos had a tangible buzz in the evenings and many more girls, so there had always been a chance of getting laid, but on Serifos nothing memorable happened. Phil, their new friend who liked Steppenwolf and brown ale but tried to sound literary, had said they'd all become like the Lotus Eaters because time was passing with no points of reference. He loved it. His girlfriend Carina loved it. Helen and Jeanette loved it. More than anyone, Daniel loved it. Mike didn't.

Last evening had been another crushing disappointment. His stew had been excellent, even though he guessed he was eating veal; and the drink had been as plentiful as ever. But there were still no available women. The Scandinavian girls who'd arrived on the beach earlier and raised his hopes drank ouzo all night but then just put their arms around each other and kissed each other's cheeks and seemed to have no interest in anyone else. Such a waste.

Helen had breezed into the taverna and out again, with Jeanette in tow, and had smiled at Daniel but not at Mike. Jeanette had scowled at him too, as was her way. He wasn't sorry about that. He found it difficult to even be civil with her.

He grunted: the day was becoming hotter and last night's food had worked through his system so he needed to move. He pulled on his shorts, found his flip-flops, and located the toilet roll in his pack. He noted that Helen was asleep at the back of the beach with Jeanette, not Daniel, but spent no more than a moment wondering where his friend was before heading up the hill to find a quiet spot to have diarrhoea.

As secluded as he could be, a clump of gorse on his left and a rock in front of him, he crouched and considered his life. He knew he wouldn't be spending another summer drifting amongst the Greek Islands. Daniel didn't notice the strips of wind-whisked toilet paper and old carrier bags caught in the thorns on the bushes at the back of the beach; he didn't mind scraping a shallow hole to bury his shit every day or using a faeces-coated squatty toilet in a taverna at the port; and he didn't mind going without a proper wash, happy so long as the baby oil was helping to roast his skin-deep reds and browns. To Daniel, living on these beaches for weeks was utopia. But this was Mike's first backpacking holiday and he preferred comfort.

He dreamed of a hotel with a pool and with a room affording some quiet and shade, next door to a bathroom with a shower – yes, Daniel, imagine that, a bathroom! He wanted privacy into which he could bring a lovely French girl, who'd be happy to spend all day and all night enjoying his skin and the exercise and employing her Gallic skills, a girl who'd smell soapy clean and not just of sun oil and who might wear perfume and jewellery. Hopefully, nothing else. Just perfume and jewellery.

He was a long way from all that. Instead of sating his desires, he had all the free time in the world to dwell on Callaghan and Thatcher and the national political morass they'd all face when they got home in a couple of weeks, and to fret over the fact that he hadn't yet found anywhere to live for the next twelve months at university.

The state of his feet and his bowels wasn't improving his mood.

He shouldn't have committed six weeks to sleeping around the Greek Islands. Yes, Daniel was right, you could afford to eat and drink well because everything was so cheap in Greece; and Serifos was away from any tourist route so it was cheaper still and he spent little more than a pound a day. But he knew he should really be climbing out of bed at his parents' in Stoke and getting on with reading for his PhD. He had books stacked and notebooks ready. He'd even bought a portable typewriter; he should be learning to type. Or, at the very least, he should still be labouring in the pottery, making money to tide him over when he needed to travel to do research. He'd have been earning for another couple of months if Daniel hadn't lured him away, tantalising him with tales of naked beauties and crystal seas.

He loved the beauties and appreciated the seas but he knew two weeks would have been enough. Apart from anything else, he needed regular sex and it hadn't happened. Greece had turned out to be more like a scout and guide camp than the international orgy he'd been promised.

Beneath him now, at the bottom of the hill, he could make out movement. He couldn't see clearly, but the routines were predictable so it was bound to be the usual raggedy man who came along the beach each morning, using a thin switch to tap forward his emaciated donkey. It would be bearing two panniers, probably full of water melons.

It was a hard and simple life on the islands. Even the man seemed starved, so the animal could expect no favours and presumably was used to the flies and the open sores on its hide where its wooden saddle and burdens rubbed.

This was nothing like the holiday Mike had enjoyed last year in Torremolinos.

A lizard skittered past his feet, startling him. It was a monster – green, of course, but perhaps seven inches long. He jerked upwards and his right thigh threatened to cramp. He'd remember to have more salt with his evening's chips.

He balanced himself more comfortably, squatting with his weight on his left foot.

Out across the sea, there was what looked like thick black smoke. The ferry was approaching, though it might still be thirty minutes away. Maybe it would deposit a new assortment of attractive young women seeking an intellectual rugby player who might not be able to see well but had an excellent sense of touch? Within the hour, they might be finding a spot on the beach to call home and he and Daniel would have new neighbours and he would have a new purpose in life. He was assuming his friend would return from wherever he spent the night.

He thought again about the relatively imminent arrival of Dianne too: elfin face, slender, altogether perfect. She could change his entire outlook on life if Daniel was busy elsewhere. Mike's holiday would be salvaged if the possibility of copulation raised its scented head once more and demanded he fondle it, kiss its lips, admire its legs and run his hands and then his tongue gently towards their apex.

He finished, stood and squinted down the hill. Someone was swimming. He might join them.

****

Daniel woke at the bottom of the gully. The sun had risen above the arm of land opposite, across the bay, and it was so hot he had to unzip the sleeping bag and then, soon afterwards, struggle right out of it and on to it. He checked his watch. It was approaching eight o'clock.

Everything was quiet apart from the occasional wash of a wave and the relentless cicadas. Even the goats on the hills were silent for once: there was no bleating, no jingling of bells. There was no breeze, no cloud, and, of course, no sound of traffic. The world was fresh and clear and still. He closed his eyes again against the brightness.

He knew, without looking, that along the beach figures would be stirring, sitting up and watching the ripples on the shifting waters, anticipating the arrival of the first ferry. The locals would already be busy scraping a living around the harbour, but real life hardly touched the beach.

He extended his legs and arms, rubbed his sandy hair and got to his feet. Helen and Jeanette were away to his right, in their sleeping bags by the bamboo. He was pleased because it suggested Helen had not spent the intervening hours with anyone else.

He headed back to his rucksack to find his swimming trunks. Mike's sleeping bag was there, in a heap, but there was no sign of his friend. Then he saw him, a hunched figure limping slightly as he climbed the hill behind, stepping carefully round bushes and crumbling dry stone walls.

The four drunken figures at the end of the beach were long gone. Daniel had a memory of voices passing in the night.

He waded into the sea, to clear his head and empty his bladder. When he was thigh-deep, he lowered himself carefully, gasping at the change in his body temperature as the cold rose to his chest. He felt perfectly cool now. It was another spectacular morning to be alive. He dipped his head under the water where small silver fish were sliding around the rocks, part of a world that never stops shifting. He turned on to his back, floated at first, then kicked languidly, drifting out over the patch of weed in the centre of the bay. Thousands of feet above, a plane seemed to be hardly moving as it cut its way across the sky.

Perhaps all would be all right in the end? Maybe Dianne would miss her flight or perhaps she would have found someone new…

That was a ridiculous fantasy, but for just a while longer he was living in the make-believe of the moment.

****

As Mike returned to sea level, Daniel emerged from the water and picked up his towel, watching the Ferryboat Minos as it approached the bay. Few of the young people on board, if any, would disembark at Serifos. Most would be returning to Piraeus from the busier islands to the south: Mykonos, Ios, Paros and Naxos. Mike could picture the lifeboats full of sunbathers trying to relax against the uncomfortable wood, whilst the decks would be covered in sleeping bags and dozing students. Beautiful bronzed girls from all over the world were en route to the airport and home.

He stood beside Daniel. 'What happened to you last night? You were there and then you weren't.'

''Morning. Oh, enough was enough. I gave Phil what I owed to pay my share of the bill. It was time to sleep.'

'And to find the delightful Helen?'

'Mm. But she was nowhere around. I've no idea where they got to.'

'And I've no idea how I'll explain all this to Dianne when she turns to me for sympathy and succour.'

'You will say nothing.'

Mike shook his head. 'People think badly of me – no, don't try to deny it, I'm well aware of the calumnies that swirl behind my back – but I can't think why I am so frequently their target when you are so much worse than me. Years ago, they'd have called you a cad.'

Daniel offered no defence. They gazed together towards the ship. Mike casually nudged two bottles by their feet.

'These yours? You brought beer back...?'

'No. They belonged to a friend of mine. You're going to be jealous... Romance blossomed whilst I was alone. It's all down to my natural allure, I suppose. I was almost taken in my sleep by a handsome Greek hunk, an Adonis with an erection that put me in mind of the Leaning Tower of Pisa.'

'A man, eh? A change for you... But a tower...? And leaning? He was leaning? It was leaning? Leaning much?'

'From what I remember, it was much too large to stand properly upright.'

'Impressive. And sad too, in its way... Still, leaning or not, it's tragic that you turned him down. *Carpe whatnot*, as the poet said. You did say no? I bet you did. Never one to seize the moment. Or the proffered tower, evidently. And it could have been a whole new beginning for you too. He might have whisked you off to Mykonos. You chickened out?'

'I did. We all have our moods... Besides which, I am not just an easy lay, you know. I was not going to throw myself at the first man to come along...'

There was more smoke from the boat as it slowed and its bow waves set off for the beach.

'It'll be Dianne arriving in a few days. I'll have to find myself a new mate for what's left of our stay. The two of you won't want me around.'

'The longer this holiday lasts, the more I am certain I would prefer never to have you around.'

'Thanks a lot…. But seriously, mate, what are you going to do? Helen… Dianne… You're going to end up in hospital – though goodness only knows where the nearest Casualty Department is… Have you checked? Somewhere on the mainland, I guess?'

'I am well aware of my plight.'

'And you always pretend to be the good guy...'

Daniel offered no reply, then, 'Well… Breakfast soon?' he asked. He nodded towards Mike's stomach. 'How are things?'

'I'll get by.'

'How many times? Just stop eating and drink only water for a day and it'll clear.'

'Yes, mother. But I fancy eggs and coffee… I'll go for a swim first…' Mike paused. 'But get this girl stuff sorted, eh? You're going to have to start being honest with these birds. As it stands, you're heading for disaster, mate. There'll be blood on the rocks.'

The sea looked inviting. He waded in.

****

Eventually, Helen emerged from her sleeping bag. Tired or not, she had to cool down. She adjusted her vest and knickers and wriggled out into the fresh air. Jeanette was lying beside her, already wide awake.

'And good morning to you.'

Helen stretched.

'Good morning, Jan. It's turned out nice again... Do you know, we've been in Greece over a month now and haven't seen a single cloud. Ever pine for Lancashire rain?'

'Nope.'

'Me neither…' Helen ran her fingers through her hair, her nails scraping sand from her scalp. 'So – what shall we do today?'

'Ideas?' said Jeanette.

'I thought I might do some clothes shopping, maybe get my hair done and then go watch a movie…'

'Or we could just stay on the beach and swim? Since there aren't any clothes shops or hairdressers and there's no cinema…'

'We could lie by the pool?'

'If there was one…'

'Ok. You win. Beach, for a change.'

Jeanette unzipped her sleeping bag all around and lay back with her hands behind her head, eyes closed, visibly content.

Helen wondered whether to cover herself with a towel against the sun, but decided she was fine for the moment. 'Wow. This heat. Even this early. It's burning already. You know, you're lucky to have black skin…'

Jeanette raised her head and nodded sagely. 'Yeah, girl. 'Course we don't burn. So grateful for dem years in de cotton fields. Us blacks've had nuthin' but good luck.'

Her eyebrows lifted as her mouth stretched into a cynical grimace and they both spluttered into laughter.

Despite that, the old man with the donkey passed them without a glance, eyes fixed on the animal's flank.

'They're amazing, the Greeks, aren't they?' Helen said, watching him plod away. 'D'you think they just pretend we're all not here? Or maybe hope we'll all go away soon and never come back?'

'Guess it's all pretty strange for them,' said Jeanette. 'You know what I mean… Here we are, all on a jet plane hurtling towards the end of the twentieth century, but when the modern world lands on their shores, the locals are still in the – what…? They're like out of another age… somehow still struggling along. It must be hard for the old.'

On Tinos, they'd watched ancient ladies crawling off ferries on their hands and knees and up the steep hill to the church of Panagia Evangelistra. Inside was a blackened icon, a disappointing old painting in a jewelled case, reputed to have healing powers. This was a momentous moment in the pilgrims' lives but the whole redemptive experience was a long, long way from day-to-day life in industrial northwest

England.

'Here we are now,' Jeanette continued. 'That old guy's working and I'm sunbathing; you're lying there like that and I bet he's never even seen his own wife half undressed.'

'You reckon?'

'I do. I wouldn't be surprised if she gets her clothes on and off behind a screen. They could be centuries behind the rest of the world. And there you are, shameless. You're an attractive girl, stretched out half naked: I bet he won't have seen his own granddaughter in her underwear…'

Helen's face clouded: 'Maybe that's as it should be.'

She blinked, hurled back to a small bedroom in a terraced house in Darwen on a wet Sunday with church bells ringing outside and Brian Matthews' *Easy Beat* on the wireless downstairs in the kitchen. The familiar acrid smells were in her nostrils, that taste in her throat.

Jeanette bit her lip. 'Oh, Helen. You all right? Sorry. Shit. That was insensitive and some, wasn't it? I didn't think.'

'I'm fine. Don't worry. You shouldn't have to think. It's not your problem. You didn't say anything wrong.'

Jeanette gave her hand a squeeze.

'Soz anyway.'

'No problem…' Helen paused, then consciously lifted her mood: 'I'm with you, though: I do like them – the Greeks. The younger guys can be a bit pushy and I know the women don't have much freedom, but the older men are lovely. They're so very… decent, aren't they? You have to love that.'

'I do. And the men are all handsome…'

'All? Well, they're swarthy…'

'Yep... They'd do anything for you…'

Just for a moment, she seemed distracted.

'*To you*, you mean? Not *for you*. They'd love to do things *to you*.' Helen poked her leg. 'Just be careful, lassie. They're nice, but they're men. All it takes is the slightest encouragement…'

'… Said the young girl, lying like a Siren under the open sky… with her hand down her knickers…'

'Oops. Yes. Just ignore me, Jan. I didn't think you'd notice. I hope to god the old man didn't see anything. It's the sand again… It's amazing how it gets everywhere, isn't it? I mean, absolutely everywhere. Crevices… I'm not going to sort it without a good soak... I need to go in the sea…'

Jeanette levered herself on to her elbow. 'You can go join the gang. The boys have beaten you to it.' She nodded to their right.

Helen propped herself up and squinted against the sun. Mike was heading into the water, Daniel watching him go. As if sensing their eyes on his back, he turned to the two girls, paused a moment and then waved. Helen raised a hand in response.

'If only Danny wasn't with Mike...,' said Jeanette.

'You've not even begun to get over it, have you?'

'I never will. He's a bully and he's sexist and no one talks to me like that. No-one.'

'They shouldn't.'

'There's not even been an apology.'

'Maybe we should have gone off on our own right away. We could move on even now. Kithnos, perhaps? Or we could try to work our way over to Leros. Not many go there. Or down to Folegandros. Remember that guy we met? He said sometimes there's no drinking water, not even any to buy, but we've got water purification tablets. And you can shower from a well in the middle of a farmer's field. Proper primitive Greece. I'd love that.'

Even as she spoke, Helen knew she didn't want to go anywhere.

'Chlorine tablets. Yeuk! And I'm not sure I want to shower under water hauled up in an old olive oil can as I stand there among sheep droppings… Not that we can wash here at all, of course… Do you remember that shower at the taverna on Santorini? Wonderful… But, anyway, we can't leave. What about Danny…?'

'Oh. Yes.' Helen glanced at him again. 'But you're more important...'

'That's kind. If not absolutely truthful. You want to stay and I'm happy. There's something about this island. And the people. I'm having a special time.'

'Me too. Still, just say and we can get the next ferry.'

'Thanks, Helen. You're really good.'

Helen felt another sharp pain.

'Oh, god. Have I done it again…? I'm having a bad morning…'

Helen bit her lip and put on her positive face: 'Look, forget it, forget it. I'm sorry. I guess it must be like walking on eggshells, being with me. Stop fretting, Jan. He used to say that… and it's all been on my mind again recently. It's the disturbed nights. Bad dreams. Maybe it's because of my brain's prolonged exposure to sun or the endless alcohol. But it'll pass, it always does. I'll squash it all away again. Don't be afraid to say anything. We're closer than that, aren't we?'

'Yep. We certainly are.'

'So: swimming?'

'I'm enjoying lying here and taking in the new morning. You go and wash out your sand. Danny's waiting for you, girl.' She was still watching him. 'Bless him – he's not going to come over if you're still in bed. Which you are, more or less… What a gentleman.'

Helen put her towel over her thighs and slid on her bikini bottoms, then her top. She tucked what she had slept in into her pack, turned her sleeping bag inside out, shook it for sand and insects and spread it neatly over her rucksack. Only then did she go to join Daniel.

The two of them stood in the shallows as Mike front crawled across the bay, with the tiniest fish darting around their toes and a baby crab turning over in the wash.

She flicked her hair over her shoulder and it touched Daniel's arm. He didn't react but was no longer focused on Mike either; his gaze seemed to be on the horizon and it was impossible to guess where his mind was wandering. He rubbed his thin beard.

She studied his profile: 'Be still my beating heart' and all that nonsense. Her pulse was racing again. The feelings she got around him were still new and scary. She wanted him to put his arm around her, to hold her. It was always like this when they were together. And there were his lips… She hadn't felt like this before, with anyone. Several nights before she thought he was going to kiss her and her insides somersaulted, but he stopped and she didn't know why and didn't know what to do next.

Of course, her friends had been through all this years ago. They'd talked about it at school. She'd listened and pretended and gasped with them as if she were normal and her experiences were like theirs, even though they weren't.

So, here, on a Greek island, maybe she was beginning to catch up at last. She wondered if she loved Daniel. Could you be in love with someone you hadn't even kissed? She definitely trusted him, but knew she was like a thirteen-year-old mooning over pictures of David Soul.

She'd no idea what she'd have done if Jeanette had wanted to float away to another island and she'd been forced to leave him behind. Life without the promise of Daniel was unimaginable.

****

Standing beside Helen, Daniel's turmoil worsened. He wanted to take her hand and pledge to love her forever, but Dianne was on her way. He'd been a fool not to tell Helen about her at the beginning and how could he explain now? So he did nothing and said nothing and the water washed around their feet.

'Good morning, Helen,' said Mike, pushing the hair from his eyes as he waded out. 'You are looking tasty enough to eat this fine morn.' He swept the water off his arms and chest.

'Thank you, Mike… You look…' She paused. 'You look particularly wet…. My turn to swim, boys. I'll see you later.'

'Yes.' Daniel watched her go. She was just as perfect from behind.

'How does she remain immune to my charm?' asked Mike. 'I wonder.'

'And when will you inform her about Dianne?'

'What?'

'When will you inform her that Dianne's coming?'

'Oh. That. Soon.'

'That? There's something else?'

He couldn't tell him. He knew how Mike would react if he told him about the disaster: how the condom had split; how Dianne had stared in disbelief whilst he'd felt a horror he had never experienced before; how she had rushed to the bathroom and done what she could, though they both knew that it was lap-of-the-gods time. There'd been no recriminations, just dismay.

It seemed a lifetime ago, but it had only happened a couple of weeks before he left for the islands. Dianne drove him to the airport and kissed him in Departures – affectionately, even desperately, he thought; there had been lingering goodbyes and 'fingers crossed's; and then he was two thousand miles away and for a while didn't have to worry. Whatever was happening, it was at the other edge of Europe. For nearly a month he'd been free to enjoy himself: in Greece he could be a different person and they hadn't even spoken because phone boxes on the islands never connected to England. What could he do?

Yet over the past week his concern had been multiplying like a virus. He was too young to be trapped, too young to be a father.

'Come on – is there something else?'

Mike could never know. Unless it turned out the worst was happening...

'No. There is nothing else to tell. Like what?'

He could feel an insistent gaze, but resisted the urge to turn towards him. Instead, he watched Helen's careful breast-stroke move her slowly away from the beach. He wanted to wait for her but needed to move Mike on.

'Breakfast time, then? Eggs?' He shouted out to Helen: 'We're going to eat. See you there?'

She stopped to tread water, then waved. He and Mike headed back to their packs to change from trunks into their shorts.

****

They meandered along the beach into town. Daniel wore his big floppy hat so his ears escaped burning but Mike had no such protection and, in addition, behind his cheap sunglasses he needed to screw up his eyes against the glare.

'You need a decent pair of glasses.'

'I had decent ones and expensive prescription glasses too, you'll remember. Jeanette took them. Both pairs. You know that.'

'As if.' Daniel sighed. 'We keep having the same conversation. You were drunk. Considering the state you were in, you could have done anything with them. That makes sense to me. The girls insist you were paralytic and lost them. Jeanette is not evil.'

Mike stopped, aggravated yet again. 'The truth is, that girl couldn't deal with the fact that I didn't fancy her. When I didn't give her the seeing-to she was after, she took her revenge. She wanted sex and I didn't so she wanted to make me suffer. Women are like that. And before you begin to suggest butter wouldn't melt in Jeanette's pretty little mouth, remember how many times in my life I've been drunk and haven't lost my glasses. This time it was different. They were taken and hidden, probably buried. Out of spite. Case closed.'

Mike continued to smoulder: yes, he'd been drunk, but not that drunk. He could remember almost everything.

They climbed the hill and descended to the harbour. In the shade of the taverna at the bottom, Phil and Carina were perched on a couple of broken chairs, watching the last trucks and pedestrians making their way from the ferry. The Minos had been tied up for some time. The vehicles juddering past were battered and old and might have come straight from North Africa; two old people were trudging along, laden with carrier bags; and six backpackers were standing across the track, apparently discussing what they should do next, speaking rapidly in Italian.

'This is your moment, Mike,' said Carina. 'Four girls, two guys and they're all pretty. If the girls aren't interested, you could give the boys a try... The one with the moustache is gorgeous. *Parliamo Italiano*?'

Mike liked Carina. She was a Geordie with no pretence, long blonde hair, a slightly lived-in face, a nineteen-fifties' hour-glass figure, acid banter and the ability to drink like a fish: tremendous.

Phil, the man in her life, was grinning at her as usual: 'Careful, pet. Remember you're taken.'

He was from Newcastle too and not unlike Billy Connolly, with big hair and a beard and eyes that spoke volumes when called upon. However, it was as if his face had been scraped with a Bowie knife. Because he was red-haired, his skin was sensitive and his face was permanently burnt because he never used enough sun cream; and it was always peeling and looked worse because of the mosquito bites.

'There are some neat bodies over there, though,' he said. 'Plenty to go at, but. They don't have Carrie's quality, of course. If you see them side on, they've not got the front elevation…' Helen and Jeanette would have berated him for his crude sexism but Carina just smiled as you might at a toddler. 'Have I ever told you I fell in love with her first of all because of the size of her tits?'

'Yes…'

'Often…'

'You see, Phil, you're boring everybody again.' Carina smoothed his hair. 'Never mind, lover. At least I don't fancy you just because of what you've got. Let's face it, you've nothing for a girl to get excited about. It's hard enough to find most of the time. But I do feel sorry for you, and our togetherness will continue to grow from my well of pity…'

They'd been a couple for several years and were going to get married.

Daniel had told Mike he envied Phil's security and Carina's patience, but he needed a girl with smaller breasts.

'Like Helen.'

'Yes.'

'Or Dianne.'

'Yes.'

'Your loyalty does you such credit…'

Through the banter by the harbour, Mike had been watching the Italians.

'So,' said Daniel, 'are you going to go over and chat, or… shall we move on?'

Mike considered his options, but before he'd made any decision, the clean-shaven Italian came over to him.

'Hello. Can you tell where is beach, please? For sleep.'

'You need to go over this hill,' Mike said, waving his hand in an up-and-over gesture. 'That way. It's not far.'

'Ah, *si*. It is here. Thank you. *Grazie, amico mio*.' The Italian smiled at him appreciatively and went back to tell the others.

'You attract waifs and strays because you radiate such empathy, such sympathy,' said Phil.

Mike could take it.

One of the girls, tiny with long black hair and the shortest and tightest shorts, was turning to stare at him as they set off up the rough path over the hill.

'Aren't you going to offer to carry her pack for her?' asked Daniel. 'She's craving your attention.'

Mike thought the same but wasn't going to perform to order.

'Piss off...' he said. 'Come on: breakfast. She'll keep....'

'Bloody hell,' said Phil.

They followed Mike along the waterfront, laughing at his unaccustomed reticence. The locals were sorting out their boats after the night's fishing and a man was hanging squid on wires outside the fish taverna.

Phil was still thinking about the Italian girl: 'A chance gone begging. You'll regret it. That backside, man...'

'We'll see. We'll see.' Mike felt supremely confident; he was going to be lucky this time.

When they arrived at their favoured breakfast and cake bar, they sat at a table under a tree, in shade. The red and white chequered plastic table cloth had just been wiped clean.

Phil shifted his attention to Daniel, his tongue pushing into his cheek as was his way.

'I was just thinking.... No Helen today? Aphrodite's abandoned you?'

Unlike the others, Mike knew that the shit would be hitting the fan shortly and wasn't surprised by Daniel's furrowed brow. The game would soon begin. When she learnt about Dianne, Helen would view Daniel as being unforgivably in the wrong – which he was – and would sympathise with Dianne, and see her as a victim – rightly so. Dianne had never been abroad before and was trailing out to the Greek Islands on her own, all because of Daniel. She wouldn't forgive him: there was no way this could end well. She would certainly need someone to comfort her. Splendid.

Mike pulled out his knife and fork from the basket of bread that had arrived, ready for *choriátiko psomí,* fried eggs heavy with salt, and coffee. He smiled broadly at the world, which was showing signs of turning at last and was smiling back at him. Maybe, after all, everything was going to be as fine as fine could be.

****

Helen laughed as loudly as the others when Daniel regaled them with the story of his brush with Aegean manhood the previous night. She and Jeanette were installed at the next table but missing nothing.

'So, what did this guy look like, Danny?' asked Carina, wiping the yolk from her plate with the last piece of bread.

Daniel might have been trying to decide where to start the description, but then half-spluttered. 'Shit. Like that… He looked like that… That's what he looked like… looks like… There. That's him… Yiannis. That's Yiannis…'

Helen turned round. They all stared at a man strolling by, black-bearded, handsome and tall, in a billowing shirt and tight jeans. He seemed not to notice. Their chatter paused, then began again once he'd passed.

'You really missed out on that one,' said Carina. 'He's gorgeous. Is he a Greek god?'

The girls were watching his bottom heading up the street. Helen was silent but impressed.

'Steady, Carrie, my angel,' said Phil, wheeling out his usual mantra. 'Control your hormones.'

'He's bloody gorgeous. But I still love you.' She gave him a peck on the cheek and Helen thought it was sweet. She wondered if she would ever be that comfortable with Daniel.

Across from her, Jeanette had finished her yoghurt and honey and was immediately restless. She was as far from Mike as could be, under the circumstances, but Helen knew she was never relaxed in his presence.

'I'm off round the bay.' Jeanette inclined her head away from the harbour. It was an escape and she headed there regularly, away from everyone, to stretch out on the sand under a tree beside the old rowing boats with just a book, a bottle of water and sun cream for company. She liked the solitude, she said.

Helen's desires were different; when Jeanette left, she pulled up her chair to Daniel's table.

In his customary way, Stavros, the small but effusive owner, was trying to help them decide exactly who should pay what. He spoke little English and his wife none at all, but he was all luxuriant Hellenic moustache, spreading belly, enthusiasm and broad smile. They liked him, and the affection seemed to be reciprocated. He hugged each of them every morning when they arrived, and in the evening if they called for coffee and cake. ('*Yássas .... Yássas, oi fíloi mou...*')

His business was not large, really no more than a snack bar with a scattering of tables, but he was supported by what seemed an army of small children who ran around helping to clear the plates and bottles and glasses and wandered on to the unmetalled road in front of the occasional vehicles. They were there from first thing in the morning until last thing at night. Jeanette said it was cruel. Mike pointed out that they survived. Helen gave them spare drachmas.

The man had steady custom, a loving family, the sea across the road and apparently endless sunshine. Helen envied them their life. They would probably be there forever.

Finally, the bill was settled. 'Once more to the beach, then?' said Phil. 'Before the tide goes out...'

There would certainly be no long walks in the sunshine: Daniel and Mike had tried that and almost died of thirst. Some days before, they'd set out for the next village, Ramos, but didn't know it was just a couple of houses and pressed on past them, over the hills and far away along the cliffs for several hours through the middle of the day, and became desperate enough to call at the lighthouse to ask for water, but no one was home. Unable to even find a way down to the sea to cool themselves, they were forced to doze away the afternoon under a solitary bush beside a small water-hole on a hillside. When they woke, covered in ants, they drank from the pool because they had no alternative, scooping up water from beneath the green algae – hence the bad stomachs. Daniel's had recovered but still Mike refused to be sensible.

They'd found a return route back over the hills, following the sound of ferries' horns, but everyone had become more circumspect. Now, they simply lay on the beach and swam in the sea and were content – all except Mike, and no one cared what he thought.

When Phil and Carina stood to leave, Mike joined them.

'Daniel? You coming?'

'I'm having another coffee. Helen..?'

'Yes, I'll have another too.'

Phil winked at Daniel as Mike led them away.

****

Helen was alone with Daniel, who was sitting opposite her. The atmosphere changed, immediately. Everything was awkward.

'Helen…'

'Yes.'

'Nothing…'

The coffee arrived but their silence continued. The air was hot, concentrated. Her breathing became shallower. She should say something, anything, but nothing came. She fixed her eyes on a tiny white boat moored out in the bay.

She wanted and she wanted.

The silence extended.

Finally, without speaking, Daniel inched his chair round, beside hers. He fidgeted, moving his cup, the cheap silver serviette holder, the salt. Then he rubbed the back of his neck and his light beard, then laced his fingers together and stroked his palm with his thumb.

They both gazed out into the morning.

She hoped and she hoped.

Stavros was back with his proprietorial smile. 'Anything? You want more?' he said.

'*Ochi. Efharistó*,' said Daniel, shaking his head. But Helen hoped he was lying and that he wanted much more.

She found her courage. 'That's a first. I've not heard you speak more than one word of Greek at a time before. You're virtually fluent.' She laughed and felt she was tumbling deep into his eyes. So she looked down.

The most immense longing.

He took her hand and gazed at it, whilst she waited, not knowing anything, not daring to wish any more. And then he leant over and kissed her.

It wasn't a lingering kiss, but it lasted long enough for her to know his lips were unexpectedly gentle and his moustache and light beard were soft and set her tingling and were not like the hard, rough, scraping bristle she'd known before.

Instantly, she responded. There was a heat right through her body and she shook. She was struggling to control herself and put her hand on his thigh, to steady herself as much as anything, and if her eyes had been open, she guessed her vision might have lost all focus.

Quickly, it seemed, the kiss was over. They sat back again and then, what might have been a few seconds or many minutes later, without even knowing what she was doing she leant across and kissed him in return.

This time they kissed slowly and it was intimate and her tongue touched his and she felt moist and relaxed and tense all at once and as if everything might explode inside her and outside her and beyond them both. His arm was round her shoulders and his hand was in her hair and her own hand tightened on his leg, on the skin between his shorts and his knee, gripping as if she might never let it go.

Then, it was over and she sat back, amazed at herself and at what had happened.

She looked around. No one seemed to be paying any attention. It was the biggest moment ever but no one else had noticed.

Daniel was breathing deeply right beside her and watching the boats again and she stared at him and realised that her life, her proper life, was happening at last and nothing would spoil what had just begun.

'It was straight out of a Mills and Boon book,' she said to Jeanette later, 'and it was fabulous.'

Chapter 2

The late afternoon light was always the best. The blistering heat had gone and richer colours saturated the land, which seemed less parched. Rocks on the hills turned softer, rusty and green. There were still bodies in the inky blue sea, but they were lazy ones and no one was playing games. The beach was relaxed, waiting for the evening.

Daniel and Helen had spent the last hours together, quietly, where the Germans and the Greeks had cavorted the night before.

He was on his towel, propped on one elbow, watching her lying beside him. She seemed to be asleep, but he didn't need her to do anything. Just being there was enough. Amazingly, they had time to themselves: Mike had gone off over the hill to the nudist beach with the Italians; and Jeanette had not yet returned from her sojourn round the bay. Carina and Phil might have been somewhere drinking.

Leaning across, Daniel pushed a hair away from Helen's closed eyes. They opened, then closed. He kissed both her eyelids. She licked her top lip. He kissed her slowly and deeply. Her back arched slightly as she put one arm around his waist and one hand against his cheek and then she kissed him back with all the meaning in the world.

'I'll always need you more than want you, Helen... and I know I'll always, always want you,' he whispered.

'Glen Campbell's *Wichita Lineman*,' she said. 'You can be more original than that, surely.'

He didn't mind.

The cicadas chichichichiched behind them somewhere in the sparse vegetation, rarely pausing. A warm but freshening breeze came across the bay which meant the melteme was on its way: the August winds were arriving at last. That was fine. That, he thought, was as it should be, and he was where he should be.

Her eyes were still closed but she was smiling and her hand casually stroked the underside of his thigh, beneath his shorts, toying with the light hair there. Truly, he'd never been this excited. She could have no idea of the effect she was having. He wanted to make love to her more desperately than he'd ever wanted anything in his life.

Yet all the while, there lurked the same shadow. He had to force Dianne from his mind again and again and again.

****

When Daniel left her to get ready for the evening, Helen had time alone, to think, to collect herself.

She began to empty her rucksack. Anyone who knew her well wouldn't have been surprised, because she always tried to cope by organising things. It was her way of re-establishing some degree of order in her life.

She began by sorting out her clothes, spreading her towel on the sand and arranging neat piles: three clean tee shirts, two dirty; two pairs of shorts, badly in need of a rinse; a sun dress and a skirt; two bras and three clean pairs of knickers and, examining the rest more closely, six pairs demanding a wash…

She put everything away again and sat wriggling her toes in the sand, watching the sky transform to a stunning red and orange wash. It had been a life-changing few hours. Everything was different now.

'I've met a man.'

She jumped. Jeanette was standing behind her.

'You've..?'

'I've met a man.'

Helen blinked. 'You've met a man…'

'Yup. A Greek man. On the beach.'

'Yes… You would. I suppose.'

'He's called Kostas. He's nice. He wants me to meet his mother.'

Helen spluttered and put her hand to her mouth.

'Oh, Jan. I'm sorry. But, no. Not that. He doesn't, does he?'

'He does.' Jeanette was grinning too. 'And his sisters…'

Helen was speechless.

'I know, I know…' Jeanette knelt beside her. 'But he's

lovely. You'll have to meet him. You'll see what I mean… He wants us to get married.'

'Jan!'

'Just like that.'

Helen gasped. 'And you've only met him today?'

There was a pause. 'A few days ago.' She might have known what Helen's reaction would be. 'I know. I should've said. It just seemed… I don't know… a bit unreal. I didn't think he'd be there the next day… Or the next…'

'Some secret, that… How could you not tell me..?' Her friend's face fell. 'But you've told him he's got to be joking?'

'I've told him I'm flattered. I've said I'll think about it.'

'Jesus, Jan. Good god… After a few days? You know what he's after?'

'Of course. What could be more natural. However… I gave up my job to come on this holiday.' Jeanette held out her hands, as if weighing possibilities: 'Handsome man, well-to-do family, life in Greece and what he wants might just be what I'm after too… On the other hand, there's a small room in my mum's council house in Bolton and life as an unemployed shoe shop girl… Tricky one… I mean, think. Do you really want to go back to another job in another café? Do you? Honestly?'

'Leave me out of this. And I was a junior chef, as you well know. Meanwhile, you were an assistant manager… But there's more to it than that… You sound like someone trying to decide whether to go out for a drink on a Friday night, not commit your life to a guy who's chatted you up a couple of times… He says he's well-to-do?'

Jeanette nodded. 'Sort of. Not quite in those words, but yes.'

'But… but… is he lying? What do you know about him? I mean, actually. And you met him two… three days ago?'

'Four or five.'

'And you've just been together on the beach…?'

'And in the taverna…'

'Shit! Well, that makes a difference, of course... You can trust anyone if they've revealed their inner depths and past life over a Greek salad… Jan, you can't do it! You can't want to marry him. You're supposed to be in love for that. This is crazy. He's a man. He'll say anything. Come on. He's Greek. Think!'

'What have you got against Greeks?' Jeanette sounded unusually sharp. 'It's a bit like labelling people because of the colour of their skin, isn't it..?'

Jeanette was right and Helen was chastened.

'Yeah… Ok.' She took a moment. 'I'm sorry. Point made, Jan. Really sorry.'

'No probs… Actually, I've decided he's rather special. He doesn't smoke either, which is amazing over here. And how long does it take to know somebody? He gave me this necklace.'

She leant towards Helen. It was delicate, made of tiny shells.

'Beware of Greeks bearing gifts!'

'You'll meet him and you'll see for yourself, girl.'

'Bloody hell. You're serious. Really serious… Will the marriage be tomorrow?'

'No.'

'I just thought, at the rate you're moving…'

'Not tomorrow… If I say yes, there'll be the church and stuff… Greek Orthodox…'

She did her best to look angelic and Helen couldn't help laughing.

They both went quiet, sitting side by side as the colours over the hills shifted to purples.

'My mum gets back from her latest honeymoon today,' said Helen.

'It's a shame you missed her wedding.'

'Yeah. But I went to the others. I'm sure it wasn't much different.'

Still uncontrollably pleased with herself, 'Love is in the air,' sang Jeanette, quietly.

'Beautiful rendition. John Paul Young, eat your heart out…'

Obviously, Helen couldn't let it all slide by. She began again. 'Jan, you're almost engaged… It's quite, quite ridiculous.…'

'Oh, it's fabulous… It's been… such a day…' Jeanette was soaring. But then her face fell as she came down closer to earth: 'Oh, god, I'm so bound up in myself that I'm forgetting all about you… Sorry, sorry, sorry. It's just not often I get a marriage proposal on a Greek beach with a man down on one knee… Yes, honestly!' Her face went dreamy for a moment. 'So – please forgive me. Go on, tell me: how was your day?'

'It's been a bit special all round, I guess. Not just for you. I love Danny.'

'I know that.'

'He kissed me.'

Jeanette's face somehow brightened still further. 'Good. About time… How was it?'

'Indescribable.'

'Excellent. Of course it was.'

She beamed at Helen and Helen leant across and smoothed back her hair. Wow. She thought her friend had lost her mind, but it was hers to lose. Why go to Greece if you weren't going to go crazy?

They sat together, contented and holding hands.

****

When Mike woke the next morning, he stretched and yawned and an immense sense of satisfaction coursed through his body. Even his bowels felt better. Even his feet weren't so painful. He didn't care so much that he still couldn't see clearly. The world was magnificent again.

The previous day had been unforgettable. After breakfast, he'd helped the Italians clear their chosen spot in a slight hollow at the back of the beach, shifting rocks, burnt wood and stray thorny branches so they could erect their two small tents. He didn't know how they'd all fit in them but imagined it would be great fun.

In return for his efforts, they invited him to join them for the afternoon, over on the nudist beach, where Gina, she of the short shorts and dark eyes, the silky black hair and the promise of athletic sex, had given him all her time. She giggled as she wriggled her fingers through the hair on his chest and smeared Soltan on his back and finally ran off to join the others in the sea, where they splashed together, totally naked. She was even more lovely without clothes.

His appetite was well and truly wetted; Italian love-making was on the menu.

He was as full of anticipation as the time when he stood outside a brothel in Montmartre while on his school trip to Paris. Unfortunately, he'd been just sixteen and his 'O' Level vocabulary book had none of the important words and phrases he was sure he'd need. How would he negotiate the price for a blow job or, better still, the full sex thing, in a foreign language? Also, he hadn't the faintest idea how much he'd be expected to pay, even in a comparable place in England. Did he have enough francs? Would they just laugh at him in a whirl of scented feather boas?

He was also terrified he'd catch VD and be forced to have antibiotics injected into the end of his swollen penis while his parents watched and told him that he was getting what he deserved for being disgusting and bringing shame on them all, that he'd let down everyone who cared about him, especially his Great Aunt Harriet, their barometer of moral righteousness.

He'd turned from the red lights and the raven-haired girl at the entrance and hastened back to his sniggering friends and regretted his cowardice for years thereafter. Sex was different when you were an adult though. There was nothing to fear and everything to gain.

Gina had stayed beside him all day. She spoke little English, but he was fine with that, because if he wanted conversation, he had Daniel. What she did possess was a beautiful body, olive skin and Mediterranean beauty. She had wound her hair into a pony tail, wrapped round with an elastic band, and it was the only thing covering any part of her. You could never get a similar experience in Stoke.

The evening ahead promised much. And he was increasingly coming to believe he might make it with Dianne soon too because, finally, Daniel was cosying up to Helen. After weeks of disappointment, the world was becoming his oyster and Serifos was a cauldron of expectation.

'Mike, Mike,' Gina shouted, waving for him to join them in the waves.

Unfortunately, he couldn't move immediately. He needed to bide his time because his excitement had got the better of him. In fact, he'd been forced to lay a towel across his lap.

He attempted to think of anything that was not female and brown and bare, until he decided he was not too swollen to look indecent. Then, trying not to focus his mind on the lithe girls, he slipped off his trunks and ran over the hot sand and pebbles towards Gina, who was hopping up and down, waiting for him. As he got closer, her breasts were bouncing rhythmically and he tried desperately not to embarrass himself before he was safely covered by the waves.

She laughed as he splashed towards her and could control himself no longer. He wrapped his arms around her and she nuzzled against his neck, slid her hands to his groin and held him firmly and then rubbed playfully as he grew still bigger and he slid his hands down her back to her cheeks and between her legs.

Nobody seemed offended. Nobody even seemed to notice.

Much later, Mike broke with tradition and dined with his new friends who had settled in the restaurant by the jetty, under the old tree that grew in the centre of its sandy terrace. When night fell, there were lights among its branches.

Disregarding his troubled stomach, as usual, Mike drank several beers that were needed after hot hours on the beach, and also a large percentage of the four or five jugs of wine the Italians ordered during the meal. They didn't seem to mind and welcomed his high spirits, then accepted the money he pressed upon them when the bill arrived, which prompted them to order ouzos and more ouzos. Mike usually softened the aniseed-tasting liquid with the lemonade-like *nkazóza*, but they just added water and ice in the Greek way and he went along with that.

They all got very drunk.

The boys became loud and then almost affectionate, giving up any attempt to speak English. The tallest, Roberto, leaned close and might have been inviting him into some mafia clan for all Mike knew; Carlo put an arm round him as if he were a

40

long-lost brother. He seemed to be trying to convince Mike to grow a matching moustache, but it was impossible to say with any certainty.

The girls laughed together endlessly and although he didn't speak Italian Mike could tell that he and Gina were central to the conversations and jokes. She mustn't have minded, because she laughed and held on to his arm or rested her head against his shoulder. This, he felt, was how holidays should be.

Later, happy and relaxed, he let Gina lead him away and lead him astray.

'Come, come, Mike,' she said, pulling him along beside the sea. 'There is little place. Quiet place. Here, here. Come, come.' She checked behind them to ensure the others weren't following and giggled and guided him behind a low dune. It was as secluded as anywhere on the entire beach. She lay on the sand and raised both her arms and he took hold of both her hands, then dropped with his knees either side of her.

She reached up. Her fingers dug into his hair and held tight. She went completely still.

He was acutely aware of the silence and stillness all around.

'Please, Mike, yes,' she whispered.

'Yes?'

'Yes, I think. Yes, please.'

'Yes, please, Gina. Yes, please...' he echoed, quietly.

The alcohol was coursing through their veins. He was never going to refuse. She made clear exactly what she wanted. Further words were unnecessary.

She had a flexibility that was truly remarkable and he decided there was much to be said for the Common Market. If her light, supple body made him seem leaden and stiff, he was more than happy to be her clumsy plaything. She toyed with him for what could have been an hour. Finally, she straddled him and pushed back and forth rapidly then more rapidly until they came simultaneously in an explosive climax the like of which he'd rarely experienced.

It was sensational and afterwards, alone in his sleeping bag, he slept blissfully.

By seven o'clock next morning, he needed his daily trek up the hill, but it was not as urgent as before, despite all the alcohol. His insides were sorting themselves out. Quite simply, everything was improving.

On his return, he found Daniel still with his eyes closed, not really stirring. He lay beside him and relaxed.

It was Gina who brought him back to life.

'Hello. Yes, for Mike,' she said. 'And for you, Daniel.'

She was standing in front of them in her skimpy clothes, with two small glasses full of coffee which the Italians had made on their camping stove.

Mike smiled at her, remembering everything. He had run his hands over every inch of that body. Everything about her was immaculate.

The rest of her group was clustered together at a respectful distance, waving and shouting their good-mornings.

Daniel didn't react.

Mike compensated. 'Good morning! This is great,' he said. '*Grazie*, Gina.' He waved back at her friends and took the proffered drinks: '*Bella* coffee.'

She was so *bella* too. He knew he could have fallen for her, head over heels, had it not been for the fact that Dianne would be packing her clean underwear and bikini this very day. In all probability, somewhere in North London she had already bade a fond farewell to her comptometer and the accountant who employed her.

It would be a wrench to switch to a new amour, but he calculated that he might have to consign his Italian beauty to history, despite all her charms. He'd been there now; and if Danny chose Helen – surely he would? – Dianne would be devastated and need a sympathetic shoulder to cry on and a more steadfast friend to shield her from the cruelty of the world, and he had to make the most of things whilst the dice were rolling for him. And, after all, he would be going home in a fortnight and Dianne lived in the same country. It would be unreasonable of anyone to suppose he could keep popping over to see Gina in Napoli each weekend; London, on the other hand, had pubs and clubs and proximity to recommend it.

Gina was so, so pretty, but when the time came to cast her aside, he hoped she would understand. Quite simply, his charisma would be needed elsewhere.

****

Helen and Jeanette had headed off along the beach before anyone was stirring.

'Let's go and see what you make of my man…'

For once, Helen welcomed the early departure, but as soon as they were on their way Jeanette was in her ear again. 'I'm not going to give up: what did happen last night? You'll have to tell me eventually.'

'I've said: nothing much.'

'What wasn't?'

'Anything. Nothing. Nothing was anything much. There is nothing to report.'

Jeanette stopped and waited.

Helen tried to remain calm, despite the pressure from her friend.

'All right. If you won't, I'll start…,' said Jeanette. She put on her business face; Helen feigned interest in a dead fish washing around at the edge of the sea. 'You've decided you're in love… Danny is the one you've spent your life hoping for… Your eyes were all misty yesterday and last night you chose the pair of lacy knickers you were saving for a special occasion…' Helen looked up. 'Of course I noticed – and why shouldn't you..?

'I've never seen you like that: "How's my hair…? Is this top ok..?"

'So… we went out and you spent most of the evening gazing in adoration at your beloved while he salivated over you… You left the taverna hand in hand with him, long before the rest of us moved… You strolled into the twinkling night… Then..?'

'Nothing happened…'

'You're not good at being coy. Tell me. Now.'

Helen sighed again. 'Nothing. Nothing really… Well, we kissed and things but…' She faded away.

'The things I can guess.' Helen felt her face redden. 'So, what about the 'but'?'

'We didn't actually... I mean, not the whole way... But afterwards he was different. I don't know.'

'Things like that happen with boys...' Jeanette paused. 'But I am surprised. I thought you'd be spending the night together. I mean, I know it was kind of your first date, but even so... I thought you'd both want that.'

'Yes... Well, we didn't.'

'Obviously... So how are you feeling now?'

'Messed up, Jan... I don't know what I did wrong. I don't know why he went off like that. Now I wish I'd never...'

She wanted to tell Jeanette everything but it was just too private.

Jeanette stopped and put an arm around her. 'That's silly. Everyone knows what he thinks about you. He can't have changed just like that.'

'But he didn't even want to talk to me...'

'Hey, it can't be that bad. He'll tell you what it is. He will. In his own time. Boys are strange.' There was another silence. 'You've no idea..?' Helen shook her head. 'It'll be nothing. You'll see. Whatever it is, it's not going to ruin everything. Trust me. Danny's not going to give you up now.'

They reached the bakery and the morning scrum for service. Even at eight fifteen the shop was loud with a cacophony of large Greek women, most wearing widows' black. They demonstrated their practised competence in demanding the attention of the women serving and levering hesitant foreigners out of their way. When the girls eventually managed to get to the front, Jeanette pointed to the feta cheese pies and indicated that she wanted two. '*Thýo, thýo parakaló.*' The grim woman behind the counter pushed the pies into a paper bag. From the fridge, Helen added a large carton of orange juice to their order. After the total had been written down by the shop assistant, who was communicating much more effectively with everyone else and probably telling them that she was far too busy to cope with girls who didn't even speak Greek, Jeanette shuffled together some notes and coins to pay, then they edged their way out and sat on the much calmer jetty to eat breakfast.

'That was hard.'

'It was,' said Jeanette. 'But think how much we're saving by giving the breakfast place a miss… My mum would be proud of me. Maybe. If she cared.'

'We're quite a pair, aren't we?'

'Scintillating backgrounds… But we're getting by pretty well.'

'I've not asked you about your mum all holiday, Jan.'

'She said she was heading back to see the family. Barbados calling… She might stay… She told me I mustn't worry about her…'

They finished the pasties and the juice watching the locals in their boats, then brushed the flakes of puff pastry from their tee shirts.

'Still no story?' said Jeanette.

'Not right now.'

'When you're ready… At least we've had food to sustain us through any trials that might lie ahead, eh? So, to Kostas and beyond. One small step, and all that. God, I hope you like him… Come on.'

She led Helen out of town, around the bay to where there were few buildings. They left the unmade road and paddled along through the warm shallows. Behind them, a ferry began sounding its horn to announce its arrival. The increasing breeze swirled dust and gusted through the expanse of bamboo over to their left.

They said little. Helen was worrying about Daniel and what happened; she imagined Jeanette was focused only on Kostas.

'There he is.'

Under a small tree along the shore, Helen saw a dark-haired man, maybe twenty-four or twenty-five, in a blindingly white shirt, sharp trousers and polished black shoes. He was flipping komboloi beads back and forth across his fingers. As they approached, he broke into a broad smile, revealing a gold tooth.

'Jeanette!'

He took her hands and kissed her on both cheeks. His gaze lingered on her, then he turned to Helen.

'Eleni,' he said. 'I am honoured to know you.'

'It's nice to meet you, Kostas.'

Delicately and briefly, he took her hand then kissed her lightly too, on her right cheek, then her left. He smelt of aftershave.

His eyes were soft and he radiated charm. She could see why Jeanette was so taken with him. He came across as a kind and gentle man.

'And so, now,' he said, 'as you promised, you will come to visit my mother...'

'Now? You mean today?' Jeanette's brow furrowed.

'If you will. Oh, yes, please.' His appeal was impossible to refuse. 'And Eleni, of course, you come too. My sisters are waiting, and my grandmother.'

With a sweep of his arm, he gestured for the two young women to lead off down a narrow track at the back of the beach. It took them through the bamboo and was just wide enough for a car. Indeed, there were tyre tracks in the dirt. Kostas walked respectfully just behind Jeanette's shoulder.

This close to Kostas' family, Helen put her troubles behind her for a moment. She was aware that the coming meeting could prove very difficult. She and Jeanette had not seen another black person on the islands – either visiting or living there. How in the world would these people react to Kostas' black girlfriend? She herself rarely saw Jeanette's colour but she'd been beside her friend in school and outside. The racism in England could be terrifying. They'd both joined the Anti-Nazi League and naturally the people there were fine, yet on marches Jeanette had faced blazing hatred from the right-wing thugs they were facing down.

And Greece was totally white. Historically white. Stunningly white. They'd got used to it, but Jeanette got stares wherever they went. She hoped with all her heart that Kostas had prepared the ground well for their visit. She couldn't ask.

And there was no escape now. They were meeting his entire family, it seemed, within minutes. Daniel would not yet have eaten breakfast.

****

Mike went off with Gina to rinse their empty coffee glasses in the sea and Daniel was relieved to be alone. A terrible, terrible evening had been followed by a largely sleepless night which had now transformed into the torment of the morning. For once, he wasn't spending his time looking about for Helen. He was suffering and needed to see the extent of his injury but was frightened to find out just how damaged he was.

He'd said virtually nothing as they sipped their coffees, trying to maintain the pretence of being sleepy, hungover. It had given Mike and Gina the opportunity to get on with their flirtings, Mike appallingly self-satisfied and she all playful flutterings. They'd paid him little attention, bound up in their own games. Normally, the performance would have entertained him mightily, but he was in a very dark place.

And after the bitter drink, he now had to face the bitter truth. He needed to know the worst.

Sitting on his sleeping bag with his knees raised, he glanced around, to make sure he was alone, then slid his hands down and delicately touched his penis. He winced, even though there was no new discomfort – just the awful soreness and the throbbing that had been there for many hours. In the darkness, of course, it had been impossible to discover how bad it was.

He took a deep breath and eased back his foreskin, managing not to groan despite the sharp stab of pain.

His eyes watered. He glanced down, braced.

As he had feared, there was a cut under the foreskin, perhaps an inch long and deepest in the middle. It ran up to the big blue vein, which, thankfully, was intact, but he had bled. The head of his penis was red and sore, maybe because it had reacted badly to the Savlon cream he'd smeared on during the night.

What should he do? What could he do? How the fuck would he cope in the unlikely event that he got an erection? Or an infection?

Even though he was totally consumed by despair, he suddenly sensed an audience. Immediately behind him, Mike was back – thankfully on his own – and regarding him with considerable interest.

Daniel immediately jerked his legs straight and lay on his back, covering himself with his sheet sleeping bag and shifting his arms down by his sides. His embarrassment was acute, humiliation ladled on to his discomfort.

Mike said nothing at first. He sat beside him and toyed with a couple of pebbles. Daniel expected him to laugh, but he was splendidly controlled.

Finally, though, he had to comment.

'OK, mate. My stomach's a little easier this morning and I'll be having a dig at my feet shortly, to see if there are any more thorns still lingering. My eyes are as the same as ever. That's my update. Now, moving on to you…

'With Helen finally falling under your admittedly somewhat dubious spell and the gorgeous Dianne due to arrive shortly, no doubt with her womanly needs craving to be met, tell me… and please be honest now… why would you need to lie there playing with yourself? It's an odd question, I know. One I've never asked before. But right now it seems appropriate. Were you… just practising? Checking everything's still in working order? I know it's been a while… You don't have to answer, of course. It's all down to you…'

Daniel closed his eyes. Where to begin?

Mike waited, unusually patient, though Daniel knew he was relishing every moment because Mike was Mike.

'I have got a problem.' He wanted to curl up and die.

When he reopened his eyes, Mike was maintaining his feigned concern.

'Ah, yes. A problem. An uncontrollable sex-drive? An insatiable appetite for priapic manipulation..? That's not necessarily serious. As your psychiatrist, could I suggest you try to see it as simply a manageable feature of your life? All you need to do is ensure you save your erectile fondlings for intimate – that is to say, more private – moments, when you're sure you're alone…'

'Look, I was not playing with myself. All right? It is serious, ok? I've got a cut. Under my foreskin. A bad cut. And it's painful. Very painful.'

48

Mike's smile faded. 'Ouch…' There was a long pause. 'I can imagine…'

'I doubt it.'

'You're probably correct, maybe I can't…' He was trying to somehow sound solicitous, but it was evidently a struggle. 'Is it deep?'

'Deep enough.'

'Mm.' Mike raised an eyebrow. 'But, erm, how, exactly..?' Daniel's self-respect squirmed. 'How, *exactly*..?'

Last night Helen had danced beside the waves, without needing music. She'd moved hypnotically, to some music in her head. It was magical. Then they'd settled together on a deserted section of beach. She had been responsive to his every move. They were alone under the moon and stars and all had been as he'd dreamed.

'So…' Mike pressed him.

'Well, it was after the dancing. After talking. After kissing. Things were moving on. You know… And she was so relaxed. You know. The usual stuff…'

'And she bit you? Good god, no! She didn't bite you..?' He was trying to contain himself. 'The little viper. Who'd have guessed..?'

'No, no, no. She did not bite me…'

Mike waited again, eyes sparkling.

'We were just touching. You know. Like you do… Petting. That's what the RE teacher used to call it at school. Petting. Gently to begin… then, you know, we were doing things more vigorously…'

'Ok. Yes. Been there, done that. I get the picture.'

'Well, this was different, actually. She had hold of me but there must have been a grain of sand…'

'Oh, no. Jesus.' Just for a moment, Mike was apparently teetering on a ledge, suspended somewhere between genuine empathy and paroxysms of laughter. 'Agh. But you stopped her...' He saw his friend's face. 'No, you didn't, did you…? Why didn't you stop her?'

'Eventually I did. When… I mean, after we had… After I had…'

'But why not straight away?'

'I don't know. I have no idea... Pleasure and pain, I guess. I just let her finish. I mean, I finished and then she stopped...'

'Ah. But when she stopped it was too late? By then the damage...'

'Yes...'

Just for a moment, Mike looked properly concerned: 'Shit, mate.' Then he couldn't stop himself: 'That's torn it, I guess.'

'Oh, yes. That has certainly torn it.'

Had he been alone, Daniel might have shed a tear.

****

He was not going to die of his injury, so Mike could enjoy his friend's discomfiture. After all, he reasoned, Daniel had ejaculated his way through the last couple of years, wreaking psychological damage on females a-plenty so he could hardly complain at a touch of personal suffering. And had Daniel wept for him when he'd picked up an infection and had to go to hospital and have a tube pushed up his most sensitive part? Daniel had not. Had Daniel taken time to support him when he'd been praying the oxytetracyclene would solve the problem and prevent the need for any future intrusive procedures? He had not. So Daniel could sort out his own laceration.

After all, Mike's own world was abuzz with joy, and it had taken long enough. His libido was celebrating and whilst he wished no evil on his friend, Daniel's cut was comedy gold. He intended to enjoy it.

He ate a hearty breakfast with Phil and Carina and regaled them with Daniel's tale. Or, as he put it, 'The tale of Daniel's tail'. They were both much more concerned ('Agh, the poor lad,' said Carina), but they would be. He acknowledged they were nicer people.

He lazed around the port until mid-afternoon, drinking, watching girls and managing to sleep for a while under a tree. Then, since Daniel had been unable to face food or the hike into town, Mike took him back a large packet of crisps, some biscuits and a bottle of water. He didn't even ask to be reimbursed for them. Such largess ought to be appreciated, he thought.

'I am sorry, sincerely sorry, about your mishap, Daniel. Honestly,' he lied.

He watched his friend smoothing oil over his chest, distracted. 'You've been in the sun all day? You'll be ill. And that baby oil just fries you, you know…'

'It's as good as anything, and cheaper. Am I burnt? I think you'll find I am not.'

He almost made a quip about Daniel getting his metaphorical finger burnt last night but managed to stop himself.

'It's been a pretty unexpected twenty-four hours all round, hasn't it? I mean, for a start, who'd have thought Gina'd turn out to have a sex drive like that…'

'I don't want to know.'

'No… But then Helen taking you in hand and doing that to you…'

'Not intentionally…'

'No. 'Course not. Bet she was devastated. I imagine she offered to kiss it better..?'

Daniel closed his eyes. 'Stop it. Now…' There was a long pause. 'She doesn't know.'

'Oh. Manly stuff. You just carried on as if everything was normal. You have my respect. I'm impressed. You just..?'

'Obviously, we did not "carry on". It was impossible. I said nothing much at all. I was in shock, really. And pain. Considerable discomfort.'

'Yes. Quite. So it all ended there? You kissed her a fond goodnight – but not too fondly, under the circumstances, because you didn't want to get excited again…'

'There was no danger of that.'

'… then you staggered away clutching your nether regions and wondering what might become of you and too embarrassed to tell her what had happened?'

'Something like that, I suppose. I got into the sea. 'Thought the salt might help.'

'And?' Mike was loving every moment.

'It stung… I have no idea what she must think of me now. And Dianne… What do I tell Dianne..?' He stopped suddenly, then gazed down the beach and sounded in yet deeper despair: 'Christ! Just when I thought life couldn't get any worse..!'

Mike squinted in the direction Daniel was facing. He could see figures approaching, but nothing distinct.

'You'll have to help me out here, mate. You are freshly perturbed because…?'

'Helen is coming. There. With a guy. That man! Jesus.'

Mike squinted some more and could make out a large figure beside her.

'It's… It's not your nocturnal admirer, is it? You'd recognise him best without his clothes, of course…'

'Yes. Yiannis. What the hell is she doing with him?'

'What an interesting development.' Mike mused. 'You have competition, perhaps? Or, could it be that he is simply using her to get close to you? I have always thought of you as small and unimpressive, if not exactly malformed, but maybe you're special, seen through Greek eyes? Fascinating. It's all very educational and I guess we are in this impoverished country to appreciate their culture and learn about their ways. If he's become obsessed with you…'

'Mike, if you cannot take all this seriously, just fuck off, will you? I'm not joking. This is awful.'

'Is that any way to talk to…?'

'Mike, not today. Don't. Just no!'

'But…'

Daniel's eyes narrowed.

'Enough! For fuck's sake, fuck off! And when you've done that, fuck off some more!'

****

Not just handsome, Kostas had turned out to be both attentive and charming. Breathtakingly so. The morning had not been at all what Helen had expected. Temporarily, his family even took her mind off Daniel and his mood.

Two young girls had met them in the lane – 'Hello, Jeanette, hello!' They spoke in excited English.

'Let me introduce my sisters Cassia and Evangelina,' said Kostas. 'They have been desperate to meet you.'

'And I have been wanting to meet them.'

'Girls, this is Jeanette. And this is Eleni.'

Cassia was in shorts and a new sparkling tee-shirt. She was wide-eyed, with tumbling hair. Evangelina might have been wearing her best blue dress. She too was dark haired, but it had less of a curl, and Helen loved her mouth, shaped like a crescent moon. Jeanette smiled at them and gave a little curtsy. The girls tried to curtsy back. Kostas was clearly pleased. They were possibly ten or eleven years old and treated Jeanette like some princess, gazing at her with awe.

Jeanette looked as pleased as she could be.

The girls led their visitors past a cascade of red hibiscus plants in terracotta pots and a tangle of bougainvillea and into their white house. The inside was a striking contrast, cool and filled with old, heavy furniture. The flooring was marbled.

The dining room was surprisingly dark and dominated by a woman in a chair at the table. Her gaze seemed cold but, after all, Jeanette would be an unexpected prospective daughter-in-law.

'This is my mother,' said Kostas. 'She is happy you come to visit.'

Helen wondered what she must be like when she was miserable. She could have been anywhere between forty and sixty, though her girls' ages suggested she was much younger than she appeared. She radiated the impression that everything in the family revolved around her and always would and her latest burden was to assess her son's new girlfriend wife.

Like so many older women, she wore black. With her lowered brow, she might have been a judge, possibly a hanging judge. She didn't speak or smile, simply stared, piercingly.

'Jeanette!' Kostas said to his mother, introducing her with a quite theatrical sweep of his arm. Then, '*Kái i fili tis, Eleni*!' indicating Helen.

His mother dipped her chin, twice, maintaining her gravitas. Helen imagined it must be like this when you met the queen.

'Hello, Mrs Konstantinidis,' said Jeanette, and held out her hand. '*Kyria Konstantinidis.*' Mrs Konstantinidis allowed her hand to be taken, but as if she was not directly involved in the ritual. It was another royal moment.

Helen smiled and touched hands too.

'*Yássas,*' said Kostas' mother. No more than that.

Jeanette kept a straight face, but her eyes, sparkling with amusement, said to Helen, 'I love her. You've got to adore her, haven't you? Have you ever met such a bundle of fun?'

The walls were decorated with a crucifix, an oil painting of the Madonna and child and several old black and white photographs of couples, none smiling. They were clearly family portraits. Members of the direct line had Kyria Konstantinidis' slight hawkishness, with a somewhat aristocratic forehead and tight lips. Kostas's features were warmer.

In the furthest corner of the room sat his grandmother. They hadn't noticed her at first and it was hard to tell whether she was awake or asleep, slumped in a heap of dark clothing.

'May I introduce my grandmother?' said Kostas.

'*Kalí méra* – good morning,' said Jeanette and '*Kalí méra*' repeated Helen. They both smiled at her.

She half waved a hand. Kostas gave the impression that was to be expected.

He hovered encouragingly and offered both his visitors a seat, so they were facing his mother across the spotless table cloth, which was embroidered with flowers and birds. He stood beside her, the cat delighted with his cream. Helen wondered if he ever broke into a sweat. Probably not. He smiled at her now, the epitome of charm and personability, and she smiled back.

There was good deal of smiling going on but the Konstantinidis women remained stern and silent. It was Kostas who offered glasses of water to his visitors.

It could have been an awkward, exhausting meeting, but Cassia and Evangelina were keen to practise their language skills and they were pretty and sweet and soon led their visitors out to see some sort of hut they were building with bamboo at the back of the house, so everything was much easier.

With Kostas in tow, they then took them back to the beach, to walk and talk and find pebbles that were shaped like anything vaguely recognisable, so they could learn more English words. Afterwards the children swam, laughing in the waves. Helen had relaxed. For a little while, she'd escaped the conundrum that was Daniel.

Only when they were returning to the house to eat did she feel tension returning. The Konstantinidis women were nothing if not intimidating.

However, as it turned out, she need not have worried. Old Mrs Konstantinidis stayed out of the way – Helen wondered if she had been carried off to a darkened room to await the coming of darkness and the spirits – but Kostas' mother had prepared a feast for their guests, which was laid out on a table on the terrace: salad, feta, tomato balls, fried fish, chicken, dips, squid, stewed meat, pasta...

'Egg plant. You like egg plant?' asked Kostas.

'We like new things. We'll try anything new,' said Jeanette. He read nothing sexual into what she said. It was a relief and not like talking with Phil or Mike.

They were encouraged to help themselves. It was fabulous, and there was also wine, which Jeanette only sipped but several glasses of which lifted Helen's spirits.

Kostas continued to talk about anything and everything insignificant; his sisters still hung on Jeanette's every word and followed her every move; his mother maintained her watching brief, observing all from behind her taciturn mask.

As they finished eating and Kostas was asking them about which other islands they'd visited ('You have never been to Milos? It is my home now. It is beautiful...'), a motorbike stopped at the front of the house. Both Helen and Jeanette recognised the new arrival immediately: Yiannis cut a distinctive figure in flared jeans and a baggy tee shirt, his long hair pushed behind his ears and his sunglasses high on his forehead.

'Ah, good,' said Kostas. 'May I introduce... This is my brother, Yiannis. And this is Jeanette and Eleni.'

Yiannis kissed his grandmother and mother and clapped his brother on the back. His sisters rushed to hug him.

He acknowledged the English visitors and spoke with almost grave formality: 'I am so pleased you are here,' he said. 'I welcome you both.' He smiled at Jeanette but held Helen in a long gaze, so she that she had to look away, not displeased, but uncomfortable.

He picked up a plate and began to spoon food on to it. 'The food is good?'

'It's excellent,' said Helen.

'Mama, she is a great cook. You cook, Eleni?'

'Sometimes, yes.' She didn't mention her job back home. Frying bacon and eggs was hardly haute cuisine.

'Mama will love you, Eleni.'

He came to sit beside her.

'I hope she will love Jeanette.'

'Jeanette, yes. And you, Eleni.'

Like his brother, he behaved impeccably but was focused on her, on her alone. She was flattered and wondered, briefly, how she might react if he came to lie beside her and stroke her hair in the middle of the night. She put down her glass of wine.

Away to her right, the hills were bathed in sunlight so their slopes and ridges were sharp and clear. She thought of Daniel again. This family had filled her day but her focus was shifting back to the beach. She had not slept well and the heat, the day's strangeness and the alcohol were beginning to take their toll.

Last evening with Daniel had been awful. Everything had been special at the beginning, but at the end there came a chasm between them. Was Jeanette right and was it always so intimate and then so distant in relationships? Was this what she had to get used to? Surely not. Had she done something wrong..? She'd hoped that with love there'd be no pain and no heartache, only happiness. She didn't want a relationship where she had to pretend; she wanted no more torments; she didn't want to feel alone.

She was distracted by her worries even when Yiannis walked her back through town. ('No, you go. I'd like to stay a bit longer,' said Jeanette. 'I'm very comfortable here. Don't worry about me. I'll be in Kostas' safe hands. And Yiannis is volunteering to be your escort.')

Initially, she made an attempt at conversation: 'What does your father do, Yiannis?'

'No father. There was big problem. He died. Then a new father and he died.'

'So your mother has been a widow twice. I'm sorry.'

'He made many houses… And you, Eleni? Your father?'

'I have no father.'

'Then we are the same.'

'No, Yiannis. I never had a father.'

She didn't want to explain – about her single mum, about the disasters who were her step-fathers or, most of all, about the one who was evil and she could never forget. It was a saga she avoided even with friends, never mind a man she'd only just met.

He didn't ask for an explanation and, as if to compensate for her silence, he talked endlessly about the town and the island. It didn't seem to bother him that her mind was elsewhere, he was full of the joys in his life.

Three quarters of the way along the beach, though, he stopped and said that he had enjoyed his time with her and that he hoped he would see her again. For an instant, she thought he was going to kiss her hand.

She guessed he was turning back there because he didn't want to have to cope with her friends. And perhaps that was wise, because, not far away, Daniel had stood to greet them and she imagined any conversation would prove awkward.

The perfect gentleman, Yiannis simply gave a little bow and said, 'Goodbye, Eleni,' before sweeping a hand through his hair and striding off. She watched him go, thinking again what a lovely man he was, despite Daniel's tale. How could anyone reconcile two such different impressions?

Of course, she didn't have to. Her priority was a relationship which had smouldered for so long, finally burst into flame but then seemed to be extinguished in an instant. More than anything, anything at all, she needed to know why.

****

Daniel might have eaten nothing all day, but the sickness he felt had little to do with the emptiness in his stomach. He'd spent the hours thinking about his pulsing wound but also about the arrival of Dianne and what to do about Helen. Common sense had him by the testicles and with nowhere to run, nowhere to hide, he'd finally accepted that Mike was right. He had to be honest with Helen.

While his world was falling apart, everyone else was enjoying the contentment he wished could be his. There was a Swedish family in the sea, parents with a boy and a girl, playing with a large plastic ball, knocking it up into the air and screaming as they fell around in comic-book splashes. It was unusual to see a family on the beach, but they seemed the picture of happiness. Just along from them, a darkly tanned topless girl and a blond boy from Australia both seemed oblivious to everyone else as they lay together, kissing. The Italians, at the back of the beach, were happily clustered around their cooking pots, excitedly discussing whatever was in there. Mike went to join them and slipped his arm around Gina, who kissed his shoulder.

Yet Daniel was isolated from normality and he couldn't escape the likelihood that Helen would never speak to him again once he told her about Dianne. And what, what, had she been doing with Yiannis?

She came over and sat beside him.

'Hiya,' she said.

She looked stunning.

'Hi…' He watched the departing figure of Yiannis. 'You have a new friend,' he said, feeling pathetic as he said it.

'Yiannis? Yes. I don't know what happened the other night, but he seems really nice. Not predatory at all. He's the brother of Jeanette's boyfriend.'

'Oh. Jeanette has a boyfriend…' At another time, it would have been big news. But not at that moment. 'And Yiannis… Did Yiannis mention me?'

'No.' She sucked in her top lip and he found it captivating. 'You must have meant nothing to him after all.'

'These Greeks… They woo you, caress you then just cast you aside…' It took a huge effort to banter.

'Did he actually say he loved you?'

'Not in so many words. It was in his hands, in his eyes…' He couldn't keep it up: 'Helen, we have to talk.'

'Good.'

He tried to frame the words. The sun was so hot and the sand was so yellow and so dry.

'Last night…'

'Yes?'

'It wasn't you. I mean, you didn't do anything wrong…'

Then it spilled out. Looking anywhere but at her, he explained it all: the grain, the pain, the cut, the horror, the embarrassment, how he found it impossible to tell her.

'I was devastated. I didn't set out to upset you. I just didn't know what to say.'

She gazed at him in disbelief, then she shook her head, all sympathy and affection.

'You silly. Why didn't you tell me? All day, I've been thinking… But it's because I hurt you, and you couldn't say? Just that? It was an accident, I didn't mean to…'

'I know that. Of course I do. And it was my fault, not yours. I should have stopped you. How could you know?'

She put her arms around his neck and kissed him and told him the only thing that mattered was that they were all right.

He adored her – and if only everything else could be resolved so easily. Because there was more she had to know. It was time.

She was so concerned about his cut. 'A doctor? Do you need a doctor? You must see a doctor. There must be one here somewhere…?'

'I honestly don't know.' He took a deep breath. 'But… look… there's something else as well. Something more serious, that's been on my mind for ages. I've dealt with it so badly. I should have told you long ago. Helen…'

Her face changed, her unease palpable. Her eyes registered fear and he felt a sickness it would have been impossible to describe. His mouth was suddenly drier and a new pain hammered behind his brow.

He rubbed his chin, beginning hesitantly: 'There's someone arriving in two days. A friend of mine is coming…'

There was no response but he'd built himself up to this and had to press on.

'Dianne is coming. She lives in London… And we…' This was it. 'We'd been seeing each other before I came away. For about a year…'

There was no vitriol, no flailing fists, not even a question, but he knew her being was wracked by the betrayal. She remained silent, terrifyingly so; then, after some moments, she shook her head again, this time in evident disbelief; and she stood and walked away from him, up the hill towards the next beach.

He felt hollow.

The family in the sea were howling with laughter while the sunbathing Australian ran his hand lightly up and down his girlfriend's arm. The pain from Daniel's cut pulsed hotter still, burning into his core, and he knew he deserved nothing less.

****

Mike had been sitting on the rocks, watching closely. He allowed Daniel a few moments, then joined him.

'You told her?'

Daniel still seemed lost in his own thoughts. He flicked at the sand and stared at the horizon.

Mike studied Helen's back as she disappeared over the hill.

'Did she offer you a plaster?' Daniel's eyes focused on him and blazed fire but Mike was undeterred. 'You could have told her you were going to put it into the hands of your solicitor… But, then again, would it stand up in court..?'

'Mike…'

'I know. I know. Seriously, though, I'd have expected her to be sympathetic to your distress…' Then light dawned. 'Unless… you told her about Dianne, too…'

Daniel remained silent.

'You have told her. Oh. Big hit. And is that it, do you think? Has she gone for good?'

He was thinking of his own chances with Dianne. He was anticipating a nod or a shrug but Daniel offered no reaction.

They didn't speak for a while.

'You know, sometimes there are coincidences.' Mike was using his serious voice. 'It just so happens I have a dilemma too. It's not quite as complex as yours, but it's giving me pause for thought...

'My lovely Italian friends have offered to cook for me, because they're leaving tonight. Yes… Gina's going off without me… Girls can be so calculating… They use us, then they're off and away...'

It was perfect timing for him, of course, if only Helen would forgive Daniel, because Dianne would arrive soon. Out with the old, on with the new.

'I'd no idea they were only here for a couple of days. Anyway, I said that a meal would be good. Just being polite. I couldn't say that it won't be as good as another evening screwing Gina, could I..? But then I found what they were cooking…'

Daniel was showing no interest at all.

'They've not got much money, you see, so they've been fishing. They've scraped shellfish off the rocks and boiled them with tomatoes and onions. And they've caught small fish with a net and cooked them, also with tomatoes and onions: second dish. The problem is, they were short of water so they've used sea water. The stews are likely to prove a tad salty, I have to say.

'So, when we all sit down to eat later, do I have the shellfish or the minnows? I guess you'll have to take a mouthful of the shellfish and suck out the tiny creatures then spit the shells – that's not what I'd fancy, even without the brine. And the other pot has eyes and other bits floating on the surface… So, which to choose? Either is likely to give me a raging thirst and set my upset stomach back days. And I'm sure there's no way I can handle both... Decisions, decisions, eh..?

'Do you have any current thoughts on what to do about your little problem..? I mean with your relationships, not your procreative lesion. Will you be left with a choice, or has the decision been made for you?'

He paused at last.

Daniel rounded on him.

'Is this your idea of a joke? You are seriously trying to say we have a similar problem? Really?'

Mike felt he'd done rather well. He decided to explain his analogy, just in case Daniel was missing the subtlety.

'The thing is... has Helen finally seen you as the cruel deceiver you undoubtedly are? And if you try to hang on to her, will everything ever settle again? Or do you choose the other option: Dianne, who you don't want? In either case, you'll end up thirsting for something better.' Yes, he thought, that was clever. 'In the end, will you have to choose between two possibly poisoned chalices... while I, meanwhile, will merely be choosing between the *poisson* chalices – if you'll forgive me showing off my schoolboy French...'

'Mike...'

'Yes, I know. Fuck off.'

He hadn't expected to be appreciated. He noticed Phil and Carina approaching, and decided he'd leave Daniel to their sympathetic counsel. He waved to them, then set off to the nudist beach to see Helen. He had an idea.

She was easy to locate, sitting obtrusively dressed in the midst of tanning flesh as the strengthening breeze whisked her hair. To reach her, he had to make his way around a couple of low stone circles in which people had set up home and past numerous beautiful bodies stretched out in all their glory. Very nice too.

'Do you mind if I sit here?'

Her gaze was out to sea. She shrugged.

He sat beside her.

Tears were on her cheeks.

'I'm sorry I've fallen out so badly with Jeanette...'

'What?'

'I mean… Try not to think too badly of Daniel. This Dianne thing has been eating him up for a long time…' Silence. 'He just couldn't tell you because he thought you'd have nothing more to do with him…' Silence. 'It was all arranged ages before he met you…' He was trying as hard as he could to sound sensitive. 'He's obsessed with you. Dianne arriving won't change that. He's just stuck in a mess he can't see a way out of.'

She swept her hair back and wiped her eyes on her sleeve.

'And I'm supposed to feel sorry for him?'

'Hardly. I'm just trying to let you know how it is. Men get themselves into awful quandries. We dig holes for ourselves and it's not just because we're all selfish.'

She began to soften a fraction. He could sense it. Her shoulders were not quite so tense. He might yet get his chance with Dianne.

'The two of you need to talk,' he said. 'Properly.'

'Yes, we do…' There was another long silence. 'So, what was that about Jeanette?'

'Dunno. I was hoping you'd think better of me.' He tried to make it sound as though it mattered to him. 'Perhaps I've not wanted to say I was wrong. And maybe I was hoping you might take some advice from me if you think I'm not a totally bad person.'

Her face began to relax too. He was really pleased. I can do this Marjorie Proops, agony aunt stuff, he thought. You just have to aim for sincerity.

They said nothing more, but neither of them moved.

The sea was beginning to be whipped by the growing wind. Grains of sand sped along the beach, veil after veil of them, stinging him and sticking because of his sun oil. It made both of them squint. He put an arm round her shoulders as if to protect her. She allowed him that proximity and he felt he'd done all he could.

He watched a girl to their left who was tidying around her sleeping bag and pack, trying to stop the sand getting into everything. She had long blonde hair, pert breasts with tiny nipples and – he could have gasped – what looked like shaved pubic hair. It seemed to have been shaped into a perfect heart. It was stunning. He had never seen shaved pubic hair before. It was truly remarkable. Incredible! Shaved pubic hair..! She couldn't be English.

As she wriggled into her bikini bottoms, he wondered if she was on her own. There was no second pack beside hers.

He would look for her later, after Gina had caught her ferry.

****

At the end of the afternoon, Helen sat facing Daniel. Despite his tan, there was something ashen about him, as though he'd arrived for a job interview but knew he'd no chance of being successful. They'd arrived early for dinner and settled at the back of the taverna's terrace since the melteme was continuing to blast the island. Daniel was studying her every move whilst she watched the spume-topped waves behind him and ran her finger endlessly back and forth along the edge of the table. There was no conversation. The waiter had brought them a basket of bread and cutlery and a bottle of water and then left them with menus. Perhaps recognising an atmosphere – a silence is a silence in any language – he hadn't yet returned.

Helen didn't know why she'd come or whether she should have come. She found it hard to summon her own feelings precisely. She couldn't begin to imagine what he could say to make things better. He'd said he was pleased she was there and was grateful to Mike for persuading her to talk to him but that was all. It felt like the end.

She was devastated beyond words. They hadn't even slept together, but she loved him. Or had loved him. But he couldn't be in love with her. She was engulfed by a feeling of devastation, as if everything she cared about had died. She'd survived the long horror of her adolescence, when she'd been told lies and had lied herself to help pretend it wasn't happening; but when it was finished she'd vowed she would never accept mendacity again.

He had to be told.

And yet…

Out on the beach, two ducks waddled by, the drake following the hen. Loyal for life? Almost certainly. Two wiry, half-starved cats watched them, but made no attempt to approach. Neither duck, it seemed, feared predators. Helen envied them their confidence.

'I'm not sure there's anything to say.' She looked at him directly. 'There's nothing you can say really, is there? What can you say…?'

They were silent once more. Then the waiter returned.

'Drink?'

'Helen?' He avoided her eyes.

'No. Yes. I don't know… A coke. I'll have a coke. Coke, please.'

'And a beer, please. Henninger beer. Thank you.'

The waiter left.

'Helen, I…'

He halted and she wasn't going to help him.

'I should have told you before, but…'

Tortured, she tried to keep her face impassive.

'This whole holiday thing was arranged ages ago and I really like Dianne, but there is a difference between just liking someone and… And you and I, we're so close now… were so close, I thought… so how could I tell you...?'

'You could have said anything, any time.' Finally, she burst with the righteousness boiling inside. 'You could have done the honest thing. Would that have been too hard?'

'It was...'

'Well, what the hell were you expecting?'

'I don't know.'

Her special holiday was in shards.

The waiter brought their drinks. Almost apologetically, 'Eat?' he asked.

Helen pushed back her hair and gave no response.

'You should eat something. A little?' said Daniel. The waiter hovered. 'Yes, we will eat.' Deadened, she allowed the waiter to lead them to the display case by the kitchen so they could see what was on offer.

Daniel pointed at the sticks of chicken souvlaki; Helen had no interest.

'We'll have two of those. *Thío.*' He turned to Helen: 'Chicken. Is that all right?'

Why should she care?

'*Endáxi.* Ok,' said the waiter.

Helen went back to the table and Daniel followed her.

They sipped their drinks, Helen sitting back and pushing around the cigarette ends and pebbles under the table with her flip flops, Daniel glum. When the meat and the chips arrived, Daniel picked at his, Helen ignored hers.

Mike slipped in with Phil and Carina but without Gina; they just waved a hand and sat at a respectful distance.

Helen and Daniel passed more desultory minutes.

'The thing is, tomorrow I'll have to go back to Athens to meet her,' said Daniel.

'Fine.'

'But I would rather stay here with you. I would always prefer to be with you.'

'Just go to Athens.'

'But...'

It wasn't that she didn't care, rather that she didn't have energy enough to deal with his self-absorption.

'I just don't know what to do. About anything,' said Daniel.

She could find no pity.

'There's a simple solution: I'll go.' They both looked up. Mike had come across to their table. 'I suspect you could do with some time together, my children,' he said. 'Who knows, perhaps you might even manage to sort things out? If it helps and if you wish, I will act as Surrogate Daniel and escort Dianne to Serifos. You can stay here and establish peace, harmony...'

Helen remained unmoved.

'I'm at a loose end now. Gina and her friends have departed. Just like that. A rapid *arrivaderci*, a peck on the cheek and she was gone. I'll never trust an Italian again; I may never trust any woman. I'm not sure I'll recover. However, the

trip might just help me too. I need time away, time to heal…'
He kept his face straight.

Not at all surprised, Helen noted the Mike she'd known for
the past weeks had returned. The new one had been an
illusion, just as she'd imagined.

'Thank you, Mike,' Daniel said. 'That would be great. I'll
make sure I pay you back some day.'

'You will. I'll make sure of that. And if you are accepting
my generous offer, for a start you're paying for my boat
tickets tomorrow and any other expenses I incur.'

Chapter 3

At ten o'clock the next morning, Mike stood on the top deck of the Minos, waving a hand to Daniel in a kind of salute as the ship pulled away. It was running a couple of hours late because of the winds but finally he was heading for Piraeus.

Daniel had bought him his ticket and an undrinkable Nescafé, which must have contained two dessert-spoonfuls of coffee powder; then they'd waited on the harbour wall against which the waves were crashing. It gave Daniel the opportunity to ensure Mike had got his story straight.

'You know what you're going to say?' Daniel was agitated after another night with little sleep and the hot throbbing between his legs.

'It's simple enough. A half-wit could deliver your laments. Trust me.'

'Yes. Ok. Remember: I've got a really upset stomach and couldn't cope with the journey and I'm so sorry to not be there for her. Say it was bad chicken.... undercooked... I've been in a terrible state.... Endless diarrhoea. Don't let me down, Mike.'

'I'm happy to handle Dianne for you.' Oh, yes. 'You concentrate on Helen.'

She'd shown no signs of forgiving Daniel so Mike just hoped his trip back to the mainland wouldn't prove a waste of time. It would be a pity to give up two whole days to court Dianne if Helen decided that Daniel was beyond redemption so he was free again and Dianne fell back into his arms after all. For now, though, Mike would think positively. He was putting his faith in Helen's attraction to his friend and in Daniel's ability to abase himself so completely that she would finally be won round.

Visions of Dianne in distress and requiring his comfort and protection made it all worthwhile. For such a girl, it was a gamble worth taking.

As the ferry left, he leant on the rail and glanced at the bundle at his feet. He had his well-thumbed copy of *Portnoy's*

Complaint to read but also his toothbrush and sleeping bag, because he'd have to spend an uncomfortable night on the ground waiting for Dianne's plane the next morning.

'I'll survive,' he said, 'though naturally, I'm bound to suffer. I'm giving up days of my holiday and I won't get any sleep at the airport – you know how noisy those noticeboards are, clicking over every few minutes. But selflessness is my middle name. I'll sacrifice myself willingly so long as you don't forget all I'm doing for your future happiness, my friend.'

Actually, he knew he could while away the six-hour sail to the mainland comfortably, snacking and drinking; and he could lie out on the deck and catch some rays. In addition, there were always people to meet. It wouldn't match the sheer pleasure of two days with Gina, but she'd gone now anyway; and it turned out that the girl with the heart between her legs had a Canadian boyfriend and wore her other heart on her sleeve. So, he could consider this voyage an investment: you have to speculate to accumulate.

Once on the mainland, he'd need to find a meal in Piraeus before taking the bus to Ellinikon Airport, where international flights arrived, and the tavernas at the port were notoriously basic and grubby. His evening meal wouldn't be a highlight. He guessed he'd end up at a rickety table on a dark street eating cold spaghetti Bolognese, heavy on meat but lacking tomato and flavour. That's how it had been when they first arrived. Daniel had been right: there was nothing at all to recommend Piraeus.

As an alternative and if the mood took him, he could head into Athens, but he'd seen pictures of the Acropolis, which were more than enough for him. Others had told him about the crowds and he didn't want to spend time avoiding crocodiles of tourists trudging around the Parthenon, especially with scaffolding around the site and the city air thick with exhaust fumes. He was in Greece to swim and meet girls, not stare at ruined buildings. Analysing the past was his day job; right now, he was on holiday. In any case, his academic interest was in Wellington's Peninsula campaign, not Phidias and ancient Greek builders. Daniel said he couldn't believe Mike would ever make a proper historian. Mike said that so long as he made lots of women, he'd cope.

As the Minos turned to pull out of the bay and into the surging waves, he reflected again on Daniel's stupidity. Dianne was perfect: what was the boy playing at? Mike would never understand romantics. Still, since Daniel was intent on opening the door for him, he'd endeavour to muscle his way through. To the victor, the spoils.

He squinted back across the water but could no longer make out anything on the land. He hoped Daniel and maybe Phil and Carina were on the harbour watching him go. He'd like to think they cared.

Spray splattered the decks as the boat began to rise and fall. Finding a sheltered corner on the leeward side, he sat on his sleeping bag and decided that this was the perfect time to see if there were any fresh thorns to dig from his feet. He'd brought a needle in his waist pouch, with his money and passport. After that, he'd check out the toilet – and whatever state it was in, it would be the best he'd find before the airport – and see what his bowels could produce today. He'd saved himself for this small luxury, rather than climbing his hill. The fact that he could wait proved he was just about recovered.

He'd also take a turn around the deck to assess the talent – though with care. On one of their earlier sailings, he'd been befriended by a shapeless Norwegian girl in a kaftan who wanted him to return with her to the Arctic to study polar bears. ('You are a lowvely man.' she said, her bangles jangling. 'We will leave a life together.') She'd been so convinced and large that even he was intimidated and it was an encounter he wouldn't forget in a hurry. Of course, on this occasion he would be merely window shopping because even if the boat was packed with sirens, they'd all be heading home. He, on the other hand, now had much to look forward to in Greece.

Indeed, a man transformed, he was eagerly anticipating what might yet unfold. The coast of Serifos passed by and a gull swooped beside the boat and he found himself sighing with contentment. Within days, the numbing tedium had turned into a magic box overflowing with delights.

70

****

After watching the boat pull away, Daniel headed straight to breakfast with Phil and Carina.

It was largely a silent walk. Sensitive to his situation, Carina focused on the fish swimming through the shadows beneath the rowing boats tied up along the seafront. Phil held her hand and picked occasionally at the dried skin on his forehead.

Daniel was in reflective mood, distracted by the old men sitting in the shade of the *kafeneíons*, smoking, reminiscing, lingering over one small drink. They argued often and loudly, in the Greek way, and even when they laughed there was a kind of tragedy about them, he thought. They'd fought through years of hardship, now etched in the lines and wrinkles on weathered faces. They'd doubtless struggled to make ends meet through the wars, then there'd been the communists, then the dictatorship of the Generals. These old people were reflections of Serifos with its unmade roads, malnourished cats lazing in the sun, fishermen's nets being sorted and mended each evening: every day the same. He imagined life on the island had changed little since the ancients sailed these seas and that families had trodden the same tracks for centuries.

Only the island-hoppers were new. Young adults from all over the world congregating each summer to swim and talk and drink and make love on the beach – he winced – and leave transitory imprints: circles of stones to stake their plot on the nudist beach and flimsy bamboo shelters on the main beach.

They brought money but the old Greeks were no richer. Life promised so much and yet… Ultimately, did happiness evade everyone?

He considered his own plight. Even if Helen forgave him and offered her love, Dianne would be stranded in a foreign country, alone with all her woes… He had no answers but enough self-awareness to feel shame.

'Just head this way, if you will, pet,' said Carina. In a daze, he'd wandered past their breakfast bar.

Stavros came across immediately.

'Three today?' he asked, sounding disappointed.

They sat at an empty table.

His wife offered a bright '*Yássas*' and a '*Ti kánete?*' before disappearing inside.

'Orange juice? Coffee? Eggs?' Stavros knew them well. He scribbled the order on a pad – unnecessarily, it seemed – and headed to the kitchen.

'Well..,' Carina said, 'how are things?'

Daniel squirmed again. He closed his eyes and gritted his teeth.

'It seems there's no infection. But it's not healing either… It is very… raw… and sore…'

Phil's face contorted. 'Jesus. I've said it before, mate, I know, and I'll no doubt say it again, but… Jesus!'

'If there's no infection, that has to be good, hasn't it?' said Carina.

'Unless he needs stitches,' said Phil. 'That wouldn't be good at all.'

Carina gave him a withering glare, then turned back to Daniel.

'Actually, though,' she said, 'I wasn't really asking about your… injury, pet. I was wondering how things are with Helen…'

Daniel should have realised her intention, but knew his whole life was public. That being the case, what could be more normal than for his friend's fiancée to ask over breakfast about the state of his lacerated penis?

She gave him a sympathetic smile: 'Any news about Helen?'

He thought about Yiannis. 'I have no idea where she went last night. I didn't see her anywhere.'

'And today..?'

'Your guess about where she is and what she might be doing is as good as mine. She set off early again, with Jeanette.'

He was deep in desolation and Carina and Phil ate with obvious unease. Carina kept muttering 'Ah, well,' obviously unable to find anything else to offer.

The breeze on Daniel's face, the sun through the trees dappling his arm, the blue sky over the water: nothing seemed to matter anymore. Sending Mike to meet Dianne seemed crazy already; attempting to make his life right again seemed no more than a fantasy; hoping that Helen would love him despite everything seemed ludicrous.

And for the first time ever, the white of his fried eggs wasn't crisped.

However, just as they were finishing, Helen and Jeanette arrived. Helen took the spare chair and Jeanette pulled across another from the next table. Momentarily, Daniel was suffused with hope. He managed a smile, trying to make it convincing.

'Hi. I missed you earlier. Are you ok?' He was concerned about Helen, but needed to include Jeanette too: 'Both ok?'

'Fine. Thanks.'

It seemed Helen was going to be as curt as the day before. His optimism dissipated.

'Time for us to go, mate' said Phil.

'People to see,' said Carina. 'Things to do.'

They gave the impression they were fleeing, as if they would otherwise be intruding on others' grief and needed to step away from all the suffering. Daniel knew it wasn't just his heartache, it was Helen's too.

'Drinks? Breakfast?' asked the owner, brightly, of the girls.

'Not today, thank you,' said Jeanette, shaking her head. 'We've already eaten.'

Stavros' bottom lip stretched significantly up towards his moustache. 'No problem,' he said, and left them to what must have registered as communal misery.

Daniel felt sudden panic. They'd had breakfast already? Where? Who had they eaten with? Yiannis? He feared she was lost. She was not, surely? Not totally. That could not be. They must have sat down here with a purpose. What had she decided?

'We've been to see Kostas,' said Jeanette. 'And his brother.'

'I see.'

Sickness. Hopelessness.

'I doubt you do,' said Helen. 'We actually went to get some information...'

'There's a doctor here in town, Danny,' said Jeanette. 'And

we know where to find him.'

'You should see a doctor,' said Helen. 'Unless you're suddenly better?'

Carina, still hovering by the table, waiting for Stavros with their bill, nodded at Daniel, encouragingly.

The idea of abasing himself in front of a Greek doctor – in front of any doctor – was appalling. His natural inclination was to say that it was much better and thank you. But it wasn't, and the worry had tortured him through his latest sleepless night: latent infection, amputation... The mind plays terrible tricks though the silent hours.

Helen cared, though. The black and white world in which he had been stranded was suddenly tinged with colour. It was no more than sepia for now, but even so... He loved everything about her. She was wearing her orange top, her blue skirt. Her lips were pink and moist. She was beside him and he could look deep into her brown eyes. He'd feared that he'd never get that opportunity again.

He was still alive and she was still alive and his heart lifted. It didn't rise far, but a huge swell of emotion spread though him.

'Thank you. It's no worse and it's good of you to... to help.' He wanted to say 'to be concerned' but felt that would make him seem even more pathetic. 'I am very, very grateful.'

'We can find the doctor now if you like.'

Maybe that was best, before fear gripped him and refused to let his legs move? She had done this for him... He got to his feet and dropped a 100 drachma note on the table.

'I don't want to do this,' he said. Then before Helen could interrupt, he added, 'But maybe I have to. Ok...'

Phil, still there and listening, wrinkled his brow. 'Good luck, mate. I'll keep my fingers crossed that it doesn't need an injection.'

Daniel's insides tightened further and he felt sick.

'I'm staying here,' said Jeanette. 'Helen knows where to go.'

A consolation: he had Helen to himself.

They left the others and stood side by side in the road.

'Thank you so much, Helen,' he said. 'I was wanting to

talk…'

'The doctor's is just round the corner. It'll be less than a minute. Come on, let's do this.'

She was practical and distant.

They took the narrow road opposite the short jetty, which led back and away from the harbour. It was just wide enough for one vehicle at a time. She led, and said no more. They passed the bakery and went round the corner, past the souvlaki shop and the shop that sold old-fashioned clothes, beach balls and straw beach mats. Just beyond, there were a couple of very small houses in the same block, set back. They were more terraced than semi-detached.

Helen headed to the first door, where the windows were all shuttered.

'Ready?' she said.

'This it? Not ready at all… Helen… you are doing this because..?'

'Because I'm doing it…'

She knocked and stood back.

'*Giatrós*,' she said.

'Sorry?'

'The word for doctor…'

He wished he could be anywhere else and that he'd sat down with Helen and told her about Dianne on that terrible evening instead of rolling with her across the sand and thinking that all would be perfect as he helped her unfasten his belt and slid his hand up her thigh.

His Great Aunt Harriet used to say that our sins always come back to haunt us and he once had a girlfriend who said it was all karma; but he knew it's simpler than that. Life is just not fair.

****

Helen stood beside Daniel in front of the door with its flaking grey paint. He might have been waiting to mount the scaffold. His demeanour was so desperate, she instinctively took his hand.

He wasn't a bad person, he was a fool.

They were on a concrete terrace. The sun was hot. A van passed behind them; a Greek woman was wandering by with two small children and an old shopping bag; a dog barked from one of the apartments across the road. Time seemed to have stalled; no one answered Helen's knock.

'No one home,' he said.

'You knock this time.'

Daniel was reluctant to relinquish her grasp so she shook his hand away and he moved forward and tapped lightly.

'Harder, Daniel. For goodness' sake…'

He rapped this time, then hastily retreated and seized her hand again, as if that might save him.

The door opened.

The doctor was slight, perhaps thirty years old, with greasy hair falling across eyes which had a smoker's squint – though they were, perhaps, also adapting from the gloom within to the glare outside. He might have just dragged himself from his bed. He wore no shoes, only socks, whilst his trousers and shirt gave the impression they'd been worn for the best part of a month and needed a good wash and the attention of a hot iron. A cigarette hung from his lips.

He sized them up. Finally, '*Boró na se voithíso*?' he said.

Daniel seemed to have lost the power of speech.

'You speak English?' Helen asked.

'*Naí*. A little.'

'Good. Thank you. Are you the doctor? *Giatrós*?' The man nodded, just once. 'We are sorry to bother you' – the doctor didn't respond – 'but my friend has a problem. Could he show you?' He gave an affirmative raise of the eyebrows. 'Daniel. Go on.'

She stretched his arm forward, towards the open door, and Daniel headed inside. The doctor didn't engage with her any further, but followed Daniel into the darkness and closed the door behind them. She had never intended to be part of whatever might happen next.

There was a low wall between the terrace and the road. She sat there to wait.

She hoped all would be well. She felt guilty about what had happened, even though she'd had no idea she was ripping apart his most sensitive skin. It was her guilt that had driven her to Kostas for help. With any medical problem, it was usual in Greece to simply go to a pharmacy and explain it there; but Daniel wasn't going to take down his shorts in front of a Greek woman in a white overall and the assorted customers awaiting their knee bandages and haemorrhoid cream.

As it turned out, Kostas had taken the ferry to Milos and was away on business. He wouldn't be back until later in the day – so it was Yiannis who had given them the vital information.

'Eleni. You come again. It is so good you are here. And Jeanette also. Come in here, please. My mother is with the shops…'

The implication was that she would have been overjoyed to see them, but Helen thought he might well be fantasising.

He waved them forward. His grandmother shuffled out of the kitchen, her face impassive.

'She is happy see you again.' That seemed contrary to all the evidence but he demonstrated the positivity that clearly flowed through the Konstantinidis males. 'You will eat?'

They drank orange juice and coffee and ate toast and honey. Old Mrs Konstantinidis subsided into her chair and it was Yiannis who provided the welcome. He talked about his brother's trip to the bank on Milos; about his sisters who would be so sorry to have missed them; and about the work he was doing, helping to build a new house for his friend. He asked about the beach and how well they had slept and what they were doing today.

He was such a perfect host that Helen found it hard to imagine him drunk and rolling with German women in the moonlight. His charm was more rough-hewn than that of Kostas but was winning and she was struggling to remain wary of him. His face came to life when he laughed and he could not be more different from his stern relatives in the photographs around the room. He was entertaining and treated her with a reverence she'd never experienced before, even from Daniel. His advances were extremely formal and she warmed to them as she warmed to him.

Importantly, though, he knew about the doctor. He told

them where to find him and offered to go with them, perhaps to translate, but Helen explained they needed the information for someone else. Neither she nor Jeanette needed medical attention. They were asking for a friend.

'I will help your friend, Eleni. For you. I go also.' Nothing, it seemed, was too much trouble and he said he could be late for his work without causing any problems.

Helen tried to imagine how Daniel would react if she brought back Yiannis and put him and his injured member into the Greek's care. Judging by her barely suppressed smile, Jeanette was thinking the same.

'Thank you so much, Yiannis,' Helen said. 'We're very grateful for what you've told us.' He was obviously pleased. 'And I'm sure that our friend will be too. I think he'll be alright on his own though, without anyone riding shotgun.' He obviously didn't understand the colloquialism, but appreciated what he clearly perceived to be gratitude.

She was conscious of the fact that she hadn't mentioned Daniel by name.

Jeanette had noticed too. 'Your new admirer was extremely helpful. Our friend will appreciate it...' They were walking back to town. Yiannis had been needed for some errand after all, so they were alone. 'You know, Yiannis has turned into a huge puppy. It has nothing to do with me, of course, but I'm sure nothing would please him more than to be welcomed on to your knee and tickled behind the ears. Or you could get him to sit at your feet. Or encourage him to run off to fetch a ball. Well, maybe he's a bit big for that...'

'Stop it,' said Helen. 'You know better than to tease. He's just being kind.'

'Of course he is... I have to say, for someone who claimed this holiday would have nothing to do with sex, you're attracting them like flies... And, hey, good for you, girl.'

Daniel... Yiannis... Helen had asked for none of this but Jeanette was right; and, yes, it was flattering, in a way.

But she was worried too. Men would always let her down. However her story might conclude, she could not believe there would be a happy ending. Dianne would be here tomorrow and Daniel would be welcoming her. The poor girl couldn't be abandoned. Helen had wanted him forever, but she could never again feel about him as she'd done only a few days ago. And Yiannis? She must be his latest passing fancy. He'd probably be fondling the next naked girl to come along…

After only a few minutes, the door opened and Daniel emerged. Behind him, the doctor was still smoking and inscrutable. Daniel's face was a mask too. It was impossible to know whether he was relieved, chagrined or suicidal. He handed the man a banknote, then shuffled over to her, somehow giving the impression he'd suffered some form of medieval torture.

'Maybe I'll survive,' he said, in answer to her unspoken question. 'Come on, let's go.'

His mood had been transformed and she followed him as he paced back to the seafront. They walked in single file again, but this time he disregarded her totally.

Back on the harbour front, he turned left and into the first taverna, which was empty of customers, and collapsed into a chair.

'I need a beer,' he said. 'Or several.' She didn't point out how early it was.

'So… what did he say?'

'He didn't say much. He doesn't speak much English.'

'But?'

'But I told him what had happened. I don't know how much he actually understood. Then he examined me…' Daniel took a couple of deep breaths. 'Jeez…'

She wondered how Daniel imagined it was for women all the time. For goodness' sake, if ever he'd had to be examined by Dr Jones… She resisted the sarcasm writhing on the tip of her tongue.

'And..?'

'He located the source of my discomfort.'

'He would. With a medical qualification, I'd expect nothing less.'

She had not been offered a personal viewing, but suspected the cut would be livid.

Daniel ignored her tone. 'And then he said there's nothing to be done. It should just get better, he hopes. Given time.

He's written the name of some cream I can get from the pharmacy.'

'Well, that's good.'

'You think so? You would trust a dishevelled nicotine addict to give you health advice?'

She was riled again. She realised she'd actually expected some sort of thanks. His lack of gratitude stung her. He was extremely stressed, but should have managed better than this.

'I'd trust him if that was all there was on offer, yes. He knows a lot more about it than me or you. Did he tell you to see someone when you get home?'

'No. In fact, he didn't seem much interested.'

'Excellent, then. You may not need another doctor. Get over it.' She didn't care if she sounded harsh. 'It'll heal. For now, you can wallow in self-pity and focus all your attention on your girlfriend... who'll be here tomorrow.'

She heard her own bitterness, but why should she treat him like an injured hero? Yes, he'd given her those shivers, made her feel as though everything was melting. She'd have offered all of herself to him with no reservations. He might even have helped her consign her dark times to a deeper place where they would stay forever. She knew all that could have been, but now it was different. It had to be over. Thank God she hadn't slept with him.

Right now, it seemed he'd had enough of everything. As had she.

'Did you think that I just go on holiday to find men?' Like lava from a volcano, anger spewed out. 'Did you imagine we could just laugh this off at the end? What did you think, Daniel? What do you think of me even now?'

'When I met you, I had no plan.' His voice was breaking. 'I didn't know how anything would end. I feel so stupid...' He swung around, desperately. 'Is nobody going to serve us?'

He was still engulfed in his own trauma, his upset, not hers.

'Daniel...'

'I know, I know. I am being pathetic. You don't need to say. That doctor stuff was just really bad. Give me a minute. I need a drink.'

Lost in his own world, he went off to find a waiter, offering her nothing to make amends. She'd thought his main concern would be their relationship and maybe that was why she'd wanted to help him. How stupid she was. It was as clear as day that she'd been so wrong and he was not the one for whom she'd been waiting, the one who'd transform her life. She'd find someone better.

She left before he returned.

****

Dianne lay on the wooden deck of the Ferry Boat Kyclades with her head on her sleeping bag and her towel pulled tight round her shoulders. She was out of the sun and despite the midday heat the wind was strong enough to bite each time the boat altered course and gusts blasted her side of the boat. She wore the jeans and a tight-fitting zipper jacket in which she'd travelled from Heathrow. Mike was leaning against the rail in shorts and a tied and dyed vest, sporting the new sunglasses he'd bought in Piraeus.

They were on that seemingly endless part of their journey, as the ferry chugged down the east coast of Serifos. In reality, it was probably maintaining top speed, but they seemed to crawl for an age past barren hills which tumbled down before dropping precipitously to the sea. There were few signs of habitation, apart from very occasional tiny houses tucked into creases in the landscape. There was no knowing how those people scraped a living, miles from the port.

Mike and Dianne were arriving a day late and after two nights with virtually no sleep he was very tired. If her plane had landed on time, they would have caught their boat and wouldn't have had to sleep in the park in Piraeus before catching the next day's ferry. He thought that if Dianne hadn't been terrified by the pack of stray dogs that had growled around them in the early hours, she might have been in slightly better spirits. As it was, she could hardly have been less impressed by Greece, her adventure thus far and her absent boyfriend.

Mike felt things were going splendidly.

He turned towards his companion. Her initial fury at the non-appearance of Daniel had gradually subsided into a simmering resentment. He suspected – hoped, even – that it would erupt again when they arrived. She was not asleep now, just resting and biding her time: soon, she'd be able to tell Daniel exactly how she was feeling.

She barely cast a glance at the Great Harbour when they sailed out of Piraeus and showed no interest in the islands on their route or the other people on the boat. She'd eaten little and not drunk enough water, though he wasn't going to risk mentioning it again. Her face was grey and her mood darker.

It would be an interesting few moments when Daniel met them. Without doubt, it would be an unforgettable encounter with which he could entertain everybody in the pub when he got home. He was sorry there wouldn't be a film crew on hand to record her fulminations and Daniel's attempts to placate her.

At the airport, she'd come through the arrivals hall flustered and dishevelled, with her usually immaculate hair a mess and her usually perfect makeup needing a touch-up, looking like a woman who'd been travelling all day.

Spotting Mike, she appeared relieved; then, realising he was alone, she looked genuinely concerned. She hurried towards him: Where was Daniel? What had happened? When he explained why he was a reception committee of just one, there burst from her a pyroclastic cloud of wrath.

'What do you mean, he's sent you?'

She was furious. People around them stopped to stare or clutched their cases and hurried quickly away.

'He's not been well, Dianne. His stomach was bad. The journey would have been hard for him.'

'What? The bastard! He invited me to come. Did he tell you that? Now he can't even be bothered to meet me... *His* stomach was bad?' She threw her rucksack at Mike, as if Daniel could be bruised by proxy.

Later, she apologised to him, but never relaxed: she was taut and remained that way and Mike couldn't reason with her. He was doing the decent thing – again – but no matter what he said on Daniel's behalf, he couldn't win her round. Which was perfect. He certainly didn't want her feeling sorry for his friend. He couldn't yet say whether his gallantry in rescuing the fair maiden would produce a positive outcome, but he could allow himself to be hopeful.

Finally, the ship's engines changed tone as they began the turn into Serifos' bay and the boat juddered. There was a crackling announcement in Greek over the tannoy from which he could only make out 'S*erifo! Serifo!*; then there was another thin voice, probably speaking in English, though it might as well have been in Albanian because it was impossible to decode. Mike went over to rouse Dianne.

'Nearly there, Di.'

She opened her eyes which narrowed to remind him not to abbreviate her name. Often, she didn't need to say anything because she had what he termed 'expressive features', though offering that thought to her one night in a London club, intending it as a compliment, had not proved to be one of the highlights in their acquaintance.

When they disembarked, Dianne refused to let him carry her rucksack, heavy though it was, so he did his best to support her down the ramp and on to the quay, where two port policemen were attempting to marshal those wanting to board. Although only a couple of dozen were waiting, they weren't willing to be restrained and pushed forward and though those leaving the boat.

Beyond the scrum, Mike spotted Daniel hurrying towards them. He touched Dianne on the shoulder and pointed. She stood stock still.

Mike decided he'd let them sort this out without his ministrations. He retreated a few steps and leant against a lamp post. Let hostilities commence.

As soon as Daniel was close enough, Dianne stepped forward and hit him across the head with her right hand, then again with her left, which was still holding her handbag. It struck his cheek and stopped him in his tracks.

'You shit! You utter shit!'

A policeman turned as if to intervene, but hesitated. Anyone could see it wasn't the girl who was in danger. Just like Mike, he left Daniel to his fate.

'I know. I know. I just couldn't travel..,' said Daniel, regarding the handbag warily now.

'And if Mike hadn't been willing to come to the airport – what then? What the fuck would I have done?'

Tears of anger and frustration burst out, finally. He tried to put his arms around her, but she stepped back and hit him again, in the chest this time.

'What the fuck would I...?' Her voice trailed away. She was exhausted and maybe no words were strong enough. Daniel, meanwhile, must have prepared some sort of speech, but collapsed under pressure. Clearly he could think of nothing to placate her. She found fresh energy: 'You know this is all new for me. You knew that. I've never even been out of England. Airports... Flying... Have you any idea what it's been like?' Her voice was strident. 'And, what's worse, you knew I could be pregnant. But you didn't come. You sent Mike. You sent *Mike*. You...' She stopped, out of words again.

'I am so sorry.'

Mike barely noticed the slight. Pregnant? Dianne was pregnant? And Daniel knew about it? Mike stared at his friend in disbelief, realising he'd wasted his time traipsing to Piraeus to win her affection. Daniel hung his head.

Sensing he needed to say something to break the awful silence, Mike edged forward. 'Ah. Then, why are we so late? Because we missed the boat... We slept up on the slope in Piraeus, in the little park, on the grass...' His explanation petered out. Clearly, Daniel was in a deep circle of hell and cared nothing for their story. Perhaps he hoped some huge freak wave would come and sweep him away and save him by putting an end to everything.

Dianne meanwhile might have been considering whether to knock him down and grind him underfoot or have done with it and castrate him. There. On the quay.

Daniel tried again. 'Let's talk. Please.' He held out his hand.

She ignored it but set off along the road.

'Thanks, Mike,' said Daniel over his shoulder.

'No problem, mate.' He'd expected to be evaluating his

time with Dianne at this point and wondering whether she'd be snuggling against him soon. As it was, amazed, he simply watched them go.

After thirty yards, they stopped. Daniel lifted the rucksack from her shoulders and slung it on to his own back as they set off again. They didn't seem to be talking.

Mike remained where he was. The boat set off to Sifnos and everyone cleared the area, until only he remained. Not many things in life had left him so utterly nonplussed. He couldn't understand what Daniel had been thinking, what outcome he'd expected when Dianne arrived. And why hadn't he warned him of the impending cataclysm?

The one certainty was that he himself would not be ending his holiday between Dianne's thighs, not if she was pregnant. She was suddenly not so attractive after all.

Never mind. Deep breath. He wouldn't dwell on his setback because there would doubtless be fascinating drama to follow, which, as a student of the intricacies of interpersonal relationships, he would enjoy. It wasn't the end of hope. Things had generally been going well and there might be new girls arriving on a later boat. Gina had changed his mood; he'd decided he should always try to look on the bright side of life… His glass was still half full.

He headed for the shade under the handful of scrubby trees at the nearer end of their bay, where he would slap on some more sun oil and catch up on his sleep. He needed to be in a fit state to savour any developments later and properly enjoy the drama – remaining sympathetic, naturally.

Who knew: he might even manage to meet more Italians too.

****

Daniel took Dianne for refreshments and to meet the moustachioed owner of the breakfast bar, hoping that sitting in the shade might calm her. He was relieved she'd stopped shouting but the mention of the pregnancy had shaken him. He'd continued to dream it would prove no more than a scare. Now, he was unable to think clearly about anything.

It was early afternoon and the tables were all unoccupied. Dianne sat down while he leant her rucksack against the tree, checking around for ants on the trunk. He chose the chair beside her, to try to seem close, but she avoided any contact with him.

Someone had set up two old, battered speakers in the branches over the tables and in a mellifluous drone Leonard Cohen was quietly imploring some lover to *Take this longing* from his tongue. Helen loved Cohen so Daniel wanted to love him too, but his own longing right then had nothing to do with sex. All he needed was a magic wand to make everything all right and Dianne to not be pregnant and not be his problem.

He noticed that for once there was a cloud in the sky, perched over the mountains; but just one, so it was not a symbolic representation of his problems. That would have required an electric storm from horizon to horizon.

Stavros swept out from the kitchen. He was unused to seeing his young customers at this time of day. He stood before them, at first all smiles and a stained white apron, then with eyes narrowed slightly, undoubtedly sensing the mood.

'Hello. A beer, please. A bottle of Fix,' said Daniel. 'Thank you. And… Dianne?'

'I don't know.'

'Anything at all…?'

'Ok. I'll have wine.'

'Are you sure? Would you prefer coke? Coffee?'

'Wine.'

He couldn't stop himself: 'Should you be drinking? I mean… is that wise?' A thunder swept across her features again. 'I mean, yes, wine, of course.' The moustache was waiting patiently. 'Beer and a small carafe of white wine, please. Two wine glasses. And a bottle of water.'

'Thank you,' said Stavros.

He looked at each of them in turn, as if wondering what was going on, this time between his English friend and the new troubled girl with the pale face, but headed back to the kitchen no wiser.

Dianne continued to smoulder, so when he returned, they were still not talking. He put the drinks on the table, added a glass for the beer, two for the wine and another two for the water, and left them to their misery.

Dianne stared at the sea, repeatedly running her hand though her hair, then poured some water for herself and sipped it but ignored Daniel.

This was not as he had imagined it, months ago. It had all gone terribly wrong. In a different universe, by now she would have been telling him every detail of her journey: he could remember well his own first flight ever, to Corfu, and his first experience of Greece, how excited he was by all those people speaking a language he would never understand and by the clean, clear, bluer-than-blue sea. Here in Serifos, he might have expected her to be surprised there were ducks on the beach by the tavernas. She might have been excited by the novelty of the little boats and the locals meandering through the afternoon. She should have been cooing over the cats. And she should certainly have wanted to go quickly to their beach.

But she was pregnant and he hadn't been there for her.

All the while, his brain was hammering out, 'But I Love Helen' whilst his physical ache matched his psychological angst.

He tried again, but knew he sounded pathetic: 'I am truly sorry but I have been ill. I am still not well. Everyone will tell you.' Phil and Carina were primed and he prayed that Helen and Jeanette would hold the line. 'I've been in a shocking state. It's not what you want when you're living on a beach and relying on Greek toilets. It's bad enough here; but I wouldn't have been able to cope in Piraeus… I haven't eaten for days. I've only been drinking water...' Pointedly, she looked at the beer in front of him. 'Until today, in fact… Until now… I've met every boat in case you were on it… I was so worried…'

'You must think I'm an idiot.'

'No…'

'Do you honestly believe I'm going to fall for all this?'

What had Mike told her?

'And, anyway, why avoid me for an extra day or two? Were you trying to pretend everything was all right for as long as you could?' How well she knew him. 'Not coming to the airport wasn't going to make a pregnancy disappear, was it?'

'It's the truth,' he muttered, deeply ashamed even as he said it. 'I was too sick to travel.'

'I've heard.'

She went back to staring at her glass.

'But you are pregnant. Definitely? I mean, you've done a test, have you?' He paused. 'Have you seen a doctor?' Then – and he hoped it was not sounding like an afterthought: 'And is everything all right? I mean, is everything like it should be..?'

He'd no idea what he was expected to ask.

He supposed that in a movie they'd be cuddled together on a settee on a winter evening, the curtains closed and warm mugs of cocoa steaming on the coffee table beside them and she'd be whispering about how excited she was and he'd be stroking her hair and starting plans for a wedding and a nursery… That was how it went.

Instead, a sunbeam had found its way through to their table and was burning his right arm, over their heads there was now a woman singing, presumably about some lost Greek love – '*Mátia mou*' – and Dianne was turning whiter. He feared she might faint.

She didn't answer his questions. She poured two inches of wine into the small tumbler and drank it straight down. Then another.

'What sort of wine is this?'

He tipped a little into his own glass and took a sip. 'Local white, maybe.'

'Quite the expert.'

Bitter. Withering.

She wasn't anything like the tearful lover who'd hugged him at the airport those weeks ago. She wouldn't be.

'I will stand by you, you know.'

He winced. That was right out of a 1960s drama, not at all what he had intended to say. He'd originally planned to meet her and tell her quietly about Helen and say that so much had changed and he never intended to let her down and he was so, so sorry. Of course, he should have known that was impossible and he'd never manage it. He was never brave.

In any case, what would Dianne do on the Greek Islands all alone? He could hardly expect her to just board the next boat and sail away and no longer be his concern. God, what a mess.

He recognised his shallowness and spinelessness and selfishness, but dug deeper into his mine of clichés: 'We could get married if you like. We can work it out.'

Hell, even under duress he should have managed something better than that.

She put down her glass and faced him, her eyes sparkling with disdain.

'Pitiful,' she said. 'Pitiful...'

She pushed back her chair, went across and seized her rucksack. Transformed, she was decisive, as if the alcohol had pumped energy into her veins.

'Come on, then. Show me where I sleep.'

He must have made the poorest marriage proposal any girl could ever have received at a table by the sea, but was still crushed by her response.

As he made to follow her, metaphorically blinking, the waiter appeared immediately. Daniel dug into his pouch and handed him a note.

'Is that enough?'

'Yes. Thank you. *Eínei párapano!*'

Daniel presumed that was a 'thank you'. 'Good. Thanks.'

Dianne was standing on the road in a patch of shade, with no idea in which direction to head next.

'We go this way. Should I take your pack?'

'No.'

He walked beside her, foreseeing two weeks of hell and wondering what it must be like to be trapped in a marriage when you loved someone else.

A man had just clambered from the water. He'd been hunting amongst the rocks and had a small octopus on his trident. He sat on an exposed, dry rock, turned his catch inside out, then began to beat it on another rock beside him, flinging it down over and over again as the ink came out. The creature would no doubt be tenderised and eaten soon.

Daniel sympathised with the squid. That happens to us all, he thought.

****

'Dianne..,' said Jeanette. She was lying at the back of the beach with Helen.

Helen raised her head, followed her friend's gaze, and saw Daniel and his girlfriend approaching, trudging along the edge of the sea. She carried her pack; he was trailing after her.

'I imagine so.'

Jeanette studied the new arrival as she drew closer. 'Pretty,' she said.

'If you like that sort of face.'

'Meow!'

Helen managed a smile.

'Are you really going to say nothing to her?' said Janette. 'I mean, you're not going to tell her what he's been up to? Heaven help me, but I'd be so tempted...'

'What should I say? And, anyway, it wouldn't be fair, would it? It's not her fault. If she knew... He's simply been ill, ok?'

Jeanette put on her disapproving look. 'You've found out what he's like. Despite appearances. Doesn't she deserve to know too?'

'When she's only just got here? Poor girl. I don't want a suicide on my conscience.'

'She seems unhappy already...'

'She'll be wrecked by the journey. And remember, she's just spent a day with Mike...'

'Ouch, imagine that. And a night too. He'll no doubt be accusing her of stealing his condoms before the evening's out.'

Daniel showed her to where they'd be sleeping and Dianne dropped her pack next to his. She slumped on to the sand beside it. In preparation for her arrival, he'd shifted Mike's stuff a distance away. That would give them as much privacy as was possible on a beach.

He stood dithering, seeming unsure about what to do next. Then he squatted next to her and they began to talk.

'He told me earlier he still wants to spend his life with you,' said Jeanette.

'Yeah. He told me too. I told him that boat has sailed.'

'Are you definite? I mean – really? You've decided?'

'There's no choice, is there?'

Her heart was bleeding; she'd not slept properly for three nights and kept waking with sweats and cramps: she didn't want to suffer for a lifetime. She didn't remember her dreams, but they were troubled; and for the first time on the trip, the sand was annoying her during the night, making her uncomfortable, getting in her ears and always collecting in her sleeping bag.

As they watched, Dianne showed no signs of being pleased to have arrived. She hadn't removed any clothes and must have been very hot. Her demeanour suggested she might savage Daniel at any moment.

'I'd guess she wasn't exactly delighted when he didn't turn up at the airport,' said Jeanette.

'We girls can be upset by the most trivial things....'

'We can.'

After a while Dianne did begin to root in her pack, took out a towel and a bikini, changed, apparently without saying anything to Daniel, and strode into the sea, swimming straight out as if she intended to never come back.

Daniel hesitated, then donned his own trunks and waded in after her.

'So, tonight? You're still coming?' said Jeanette.

'I suppose so. I've had no other offers; and the prospect of eating with Daniel and Dianne...' She left it unfinished. 'And who'd want to eat with Mike if they could avoid it...? Maybe only Phil and Carina?'

'Maybe. So let's us go see Kostas... I'm pretty confident Yiannis will be around to soothe your tortured soul... He'll take you aside to whisper Greek nothings, cup his hands gently round your cheeks in the moonlight, then push back your hair...'

'Enough!'

'Your love life is even richer than mine. The duplicitous Daniel adores you... Yiannis is entranced...'

'Stop it. You know it's not what I want. I've agreed to come – give me a break!'

Daniel and Dianne came out of the sea. He had his arm around her waist. Despite the anger she felt towards him, Helen winced, hating herself as she did so. She could still feel his hand on her leg, the softness of his lips, the quivering inside as she'd held him.

How awkward she felt when Dianne came over to them sometime later. They'd seen Daniel wander off into the low dunes with his ground sheet, trailing string behind him, to do who knew what? At Dianne's approach, Helen's practised calm threatened to collapse. Jeanette was aware and gently held her arm.

Dianne was wearing a pretty pink bikini, a stylish floppy white hat which must have been folded somewhere amongst her luggage when she arrived, and a forced smile.

'Hello,' she said.

'Hi.' Jeanette replied. Helen tried to conjure a face that looked welcoming.

'Daniel said you're his friends.'

'A couple of them. Yes.'

'I'm Dianne.'

'Yes. We didn't want to interrupt. I'm Jeanette. This is Helen.'

'It's nice to meet you.'

She sounded tired but was obviously making an effort. She seemed sweet.

'Sit down. Please,' Helen said, sat up properly and moved over so that Dianne could share her towel. It was a bizarre situation.

'I mustn't stay long. I'll burn. Daniel has gone to make a shelter for us, to make everything all right... As if...'

They could see him, further along the beach, towards the headland. He had anchored the ground sheet with rocks on the top of a small dune and was spreading it forwards and attempting to support it with bamboo poles, making a sort of roof that would be three or four feet high. He was struggling and needed help, but no-one was going to offer any.

'It's... mightily impressive,' said Jeanette.

'Oh, yes. And it's going to have bamboo sides. Apparently.'

92

She was lacing everything with sarcasm.

'Well, you made it here finally,' said Jeanette.

'Yes…'

Helen's bitterness spilled out: 'He's a man. You should never expect anything.'

Unexpectedly, she'd found common cause. Dianne was another lost soul, Helen thought. It must have been a shock when he didn't meet her and she was taking it hard. She could empathise with that but did wonder how she might have felt. Perhaps the same way… though before all this she could well have accepted his story.

'If he'd come to the airport, it would have been all right…'

'He has been poorly…' The excuse came out of its own accord. It was only a half-hearted justification because Helen truly didn't feel like defending him.

'Yes… well… We've all had our problems…,' said Dianne.

'You mean you've not been well either?' Jeanette was probing.

'Daniel came out to Greece and left me, even though he knew I could be pregnant.'

It was as if Dianne had been waiting to tell someone. Why would she choose two girls she didn't know? But it happened.

Helen stifled a gasp, but felt Jeanette's hand tightening on her arm. This was not her Daniel, surely? Her throat was horribly dry. Can you trust anyone?

'Well, we didn't know for certain I was pregnant…'

That wasn't a justification. They waited.

'I mean – we thought I might be. And I suppose he couldn't just cancel his holiday in case. I get that. I came out later because of work. But he had to come to the airport to meet me, didn't he? If only to find out. To be there. Anybody would, wouldn't they?'

Yes, anybody would.

'But not Daniel. I thought he was better than that.'

Everyone did.

'That is bad.' Jeanette was stunned. 'Danny…' Whatever her thoughts, words failed.

Helen was still trying to take it in. 'It's hard to believe,' she said, then hastily added, 'but I'm not doubting you... I'd always thought that Daniel was very... moral.' She could have added, 'Until the last few days,' but stopped herself.

'Yeah. Even my mum likes him.'

It was hard for Helen to ask, but she had to: 'What's he said now?'

'He says he'll stick by me but that's what he has to say, isn't it? It's a bit late, really. I want someone who cares about me. I mean, someone who loves me.'

We all want that, thought Helen. Dianne knew only part of the story.

'What have your parents said?' asked Jeanette. 'They must be distraught. But it's still early. Do they even know? Have you kept it a secret?'

Dianne paused for what seemed a long time, as if wondering how to frame an answer.

We're prying, thought Helen. Why should she tell us anything? We've only just met.

Yet it was still as if Dianne needed to talk.

Eventually, 'I've not told my mum anything,' she said.

'I understand,' said Helen, trying to picture the scene if she were to tell even her own careless mother that she was pregnant.

'Me too,' said Jeanette.

'No, I doubt it,' said Dianne. For the first time, her face relaxed.

Helen's face must have registered confusion.

'I'm not pregnant. I never was.'

Jeanette's mouth actually dropped open: 'But you just said... I mean, you've told him you are pregnant...'

'No, I haven't. That's just what he's assumed...'

'Gosh...' Helen's head was swimming. Away on her right, Daniel was tying string to the top of the bamboo supports for his shelter and fastening them to large rocks, to help hold the poles upright. Even at a distance, he looked fraught. She turned back: 'Shouldn't you tell him? Isn't it cruel, to have him think...?'

'He can squirm for a while,' said Dianne. 'I was going to tell him right away. At the airport. I imagined we'd celebrate. Please don't tell him now. Let the bastard stew. It's no more than he deserves.'

Despite everything, Helen felt sympathy for Daniel welling up inside her, but crushed it down. All alone, she'd managed to climb through her horrors with that man who tormented her: these two could surely handle this together. Especially since it had nothing to do with her anymore.

She owed Daniel nothing.

****

When Mike returned from his nap, there were two new girls establishing themselves on the beach near where he and Daniel had been sleeping. He'd no idea what had happened to his rucksack, or to that of Daniel, but assumed they'd be around somewhere. Everything was safe in Greece. Before making enquiries, though, he felt it was incumbent upon him to focus on introductions.

Both girls had radiant smiles, dark eyes and olive skin. 'Hello,' he said. There was a glint in his eye; his rucksack could wait. 'Do you speak English?' Already, Dianne was no more vital for his happiness than yesterday's bruised peach.

'We can a little English, yes...'

'You're Italian?'

Not recently, but back in his positive moments, Daniel had sometimes claimed, 'Hope springs eternal.' Just then, Mike's hope was boundless.

'We are Greek.'

'Wow.' It occurred to him that these were the first Greek girls he had met socially anywhere, never mind on a beach.

And they were lovely. Aimilios was like a doll, with long black hair that reached nearly to her waist. She had tiny features and was exquisite. Agneta's hair was tied back off her face in a long pony-tail. She was not so slim but had a fabulous figure and was remarkably tactile. They were both wearing modest swimsuits. Mike sat down beside them and Agneta rested her hand on his knee: 'And your name, please?'

His weariness left him instantly. What had been wrong with him? He was loving this holiday. Loving it. Especially, he loved tactile.

'I'm Mike.'

He glanced towards the back of the beach, where Daniel and Dianne were sitting with Helen, Jeanette, Phil and Carina. He wondered if peace had been declared between the warring parties – maybe Helen was being signed up as godmother? – but he wasn't rushing over to find out: Aimilios and Agneta had his total attention.

They each had a bottle of yellow Kourtaki retsina, which they offered to share. Agneta passed him hers and, practised, he knocked off the metal cap on a stone.

'You drink, Mike,' said Aimilios. It was a friendly gesture and he was certainly not going to say 'no'. He loved the blend of resin and grape even when it was warm.

He pinned the other bottle in the shallows as best he could with six large rocks, in the hope it would stay fixed there in the wash and cool slightly. He and Daniel had spent the holiday dealing with bottles and melons and rinsing their clothes in a similar way.

'You are very kind, girls,' he said, on his return, when they handed him the bottle again. 'Cheers. *Yamás*, Aimilios. *Yamás,* Agneta.' He took another mouthful. 'So... Tell me all about yourselves.'

'*Endáxi*... Ok. We are from Chriso. It is in Greece, north,' said Aimilios.

'I've never heard of Chriso. Is it small?'

'Very small. Yes.'

'And we are gone,' added Agneta. There was a sudden hopelessness in her eyes and her voice went quieter. 'Forever. No go home now. No family. No friends. Only Aimilios.'

Her friend smiled weakly. Mike waited for more information. None was forthcoming.

'But you'll be going home after the summer? You can't live on the beach in the winter.'

'No. *Athína*. For a job. Maybe,' said Aimilios.

'To Athens. Yes. We go to Athens.' Agneta seemed much more definite.

'But why not go back to…?' The name escaped him for a moment. 'Why not return to Chriso?'

'Because we are here,' Aimilios said, without any sense of joy, and her friend put an arm round her.

'Our families… They say we are bad,' Agneta explained. 'Only bad girls go away. Only bad girls sleep on the beach. People in Greece, people in villages, have old thinks.'

'You mean they are old-fashioned?'

'Our home is very old. The people say we are…' She struggled with the language, 'bad girls…. They say we come for sex and drachmas.'

'Prostitutes? They think you are prostitutes?'

'*Pórnes*. They think.'

It was a situation he could hardly imagine. 'Oh, dear, they've washed their hands of you?' He got blank looks and he tried again. 'You cannot go back?'

They shook their heads.

'We do not want to go home,' said Aimilios.

'But also,' said Agneta, 'maybe my brother come. Maybe I think he finds us.'

'Is that good?' Neither seemed to think it was. He guessed the brother would not be approving of what they'd done. 'It would be hard for you… Which means you have a big problem?'

'Perhaps, yes. He is very angry. He says the family is… *ntrépetai*. They are shameered,' said Aimilios. 'My father not come for us. He not speak to me. But I think my brother, maybe. One island, then another island… My brother comes, maybe…'

'Shameered..?' He thought. 'You mean ashamed. They are ashamed. Yes, I understand. So will your brother want to take you home?'

Agneta shrugged. She didn't seem to know. Mike couldn't tell whether they were just hoping things would turn out well after all, whether they would be doomed to a new life they would have to build from nothing, or whether they might actually be in some sort of danger. Considering his experiences during the summer, it was hard to imagine Greeks were ever violent. Of course, Agneta wasn't talking about any ordinary man; it was a brother obsessed with his family's honour. Who knew what might be in his head?

Mike's imagination took flight. He'd known crazies in England and conjured a wild-eyed man of the hills in the guise of an axe-wielding Aztec priest falling upon the three of them at any moment.

He liked these girls very much though. They were extremely sexy. He could protect them. He felt confident that, whatever happened, no brother could be any more frightening than the twenty-stone number eight who vowed to put him into intensive care on a frozen pitch in a second team match in Pontypridd the season before.

He suggested to the girls that the safest course was for the three of them to eat together that evening. He didn't mention it, but if they decided to take advantage of him amongst the dunes at the end of the night, he would somehow cope.

Once the second bottle of wine was finished, he located his rucksack, swam, dried in the sun, told the still-depressed Daniel he had hot dates for the night, bade a cheery farewell to the others and headed into town with his two latest obsessions. It was really not his concern if Dianne still had a face like thunder, Helen and Jeanette were performing as if in a play and Phil and Carina seemed to be trying to find some way to escape from the tragedy into which they'd inadvertently blundered.

Mike's stomach had settled and there were no more thorns coming out of his feet. In just two weeks he would be home and have new glasses. And tonight he had the company of two innocent Greek girls who would almost certainly be virgins and who he hoped to introduce to life-changing experiences. He felt on top form.

Sauntering along with one either side of him, he felt not a little like a potentate and got admiring glances from the men they passed.

'It is good we meet you, Mike,' said Agneta, all smiles. 'We practise our English.'

'I'll help you practise everything,' he said.

'You are good man, Mike,' said Aimilios.

He laughed and put an arm lightly around their shoulders. Aimilios stepped away to the side and laughed too; Agneta put her own arm around his waist and, briefly, her head against his shoulder.

Oh, well. If necessary, just one would suffice.

The girls wanted to eat in the last taverna, a dark restaurant out beyond the street lighting where he'd never been and where the road was even dustier than in town.

'The food does not cost so much away from town,' said Aimilios.

He found it hard to imagine any prices could be cheaper than in the places around the port, but this was their country and he wasn't going to argue. They probably had little money and it would have to last a long time.

Anyway, he sensed another opportunity.

'Don't worry about money. Tonight is on me, girls.'

Not for the first time, they were confused.

'I will buy the food. For me and for you. It is my treat – my present to you.'

'No, Mike, that is not right.'

'Just tonight, Aimilios. Please. Let me. I am a lucky man to be escorting two such beautiful girls.'

An old man in scruffy clothes and battered brown shoes was sitting outside a small fruit shop. He caught Mike's eye and nodded. Mike winked back, knowing what the man was thinking.

There was no one else in the taverna and the waiter was all around them as they came in. He was unusually portly with scruffy clothes and sweat patches under his arms but extremely pleased to see them and he chatted to the girls as he set up a table for them. Mike had no idea what the others were discussing, and no one tried to explain, but he didn't care. After the flurry of words, the waiter headed for the kitchen and shouted to a woman who shouted back so it sounded as if they were about to engage in mortal combat; but he emerged soon afterwards with free wine and olives. Mike was no lover of olives but wine was always welcome. He shook the man's hand, and filled the three glasses.

He suggested the girls should order the food.

In what seemed no time at all, out came bread, a salad, fried cheese, fried tomato balls and a disgusting dip smelling of fish that Mike avoided. This was not what he might have chosen, but he waved the empty jug for more wine and just picked at the plates before him.

In high spirits, Aimilios and Agneta ate and drank heartily. Mike suspected they'd not eaten well for some time. Soon came chicken and chips, beef in a sauce and more alcohol.

'Mike, this is so good,' said Agneta. 'Thank you. We love you.'

Excellent. He kept pouring drinks and was suffused with a powerful sense of well-being. His tiredness from the trip to Athens had gone. The wine was affecting him considerably, but that was fine too. He knew it was because he hadn't eaten or slept enough for days. But who cared? Their chatter passed over his head, though he felt comfortable and included, like when he'd been with the Italians. The important things were their beautiful mouths and eyes and his fantasies of their naked bodies and a coming night like no other.

He ordered more wine, then the requisite ouzo.

'Girls,' he said, finally. 'I must pay. We should go.' It was nearly midnight and they were still the only ones in the taverna and the waiter was slumped on a chair just inside the building, waiting to go to his own bed. The cook had long since departed. 'I will seek the bill.'

He got to his feet, unsteadily, and waved a handful of drachmas. He could make no sense of what the man said so simply offered him all the cash. The waiter picked through it, removed several notes, handed Mike most of them back along with a couple of coins and said, '*Efharistó polý.*'

'Thank you, my friend.' Mike handed back the coins as a tip, though he couldn't have said whether it was a good one.

'Agneta, Aimilios,' he called over to them. 'Let us go, for it has been wonderful and we have eaten and drunk like a lord... and ladies... indeed, to excess...'

They laughed together and stumbled towards him with their arms around each other. Agneta put her other arm round his waist again and shouted something to the waiter as they headed out into the darkness. He responded with what was presumably a fond farewell.

As they sauntered along the beach towards the port lights, Mike was stumbling and the night was spinning around him but life seemed as good as it could get.

Until his triumph exploded in a jolt that smashed him to his knees.

From nowhere, there came a massive blow to the side of his head. His vision filled with lights. A huge hurt shot right through him as he went down.

Agneta fell with him. She was on top of him so her hair was across his face, then she rolled away sharply and she was all skirt and legs and a rain of sand. Then she and Aimilios were both screaming and there was a man repeatedly kicking Mike, who put up his arms to protect his head so his body took most of the punishment. Drunk and unable to fight back, he could do little to help himself.

'*Málaka*!' the man screamed at Mike, pushing away both girls as they attempted to stop his attack. '*Málaka*!'

'Vasili! Vasili! *Ochi*. Mike, Mike...' Agneta was hysterical.

'*Putánas yié!*' yelled the man, kicking him again.

Mike weighed over sixteen stone and was very fit. He had never been beaten up before but the alcohol and the shock left him defenceless. He had to roll into a ball, foetus-like, trying to turn his back against the feet hammering into him. He felt pain everywhere.

Then the kicks stopped suddenly and there were two men's voices above him, both shouting in a cacophony of Greek. Mike glimpsed a large man with wild hair pushing away another huge figure.

The two girls ran off into the night. One of the men ran after them.

Mike braced for more blows. Instead, there was a hand offering to help him to his feet.

'All right? You are ok?' It was Yiannis. Of all people, it was Yiannis. 'You are Mike? Friend of Eleni? Mike? You are hurt? Your face..?'

Mike wiped his nose with the back of his hand. It was wet, bleeding. He shook his head, to clear his mind rather than to indicate there was nothing seriously wrong with him.

'He's mad. The girls…' Yiannis turned. The three figures had disappeared. 'I go after…'

'Yes. Yes. Go… Thank you,' said Mike who was in no state to help.

'*Naí*. Yes. I go now.'

And he left.

The beach was quiet again. Mike shuffled to the sea's edge and scooped water over his head and down his face. He was shaken. The moon was up and stars were still visible back over the hills but romance had died. Perhaps he was lucky to still be alive.

He sat on the sand. It took some minutes before he could pull himself together, and even then he was shivering. He couldn't remember when he last fought anyone but he'd never lost a fight before, even as a boy. He hoped the girls were safe.

Blinking, he tried to clear the effects of the alcohol and the beating and gradually everything became clearer. Of course, he must have just encountered Agneta's brother…

And Yiannis had recognised him as the friend of Eleni… Eleni? Helen? He was the friend of Helen now?

It had been a quite an evening.

****

Daniel woke before dawn the next morning. At first he was confused because there was no sky overhead; but he was lying under his makeshift shelter, with Dianne beside him. Their heads were up against the sand dune and the bottoms of their sleeping bags were sticking out into the night. The sign he had created from a piece of cardboard and hung from the front corner was a dark shape in his eyeline. It said 'Home Sweet Home' and had a flower drawn in the corner and had been intended to amuse Dianne, but she'd dismissed it with contempt.

Even in these first waking moments, utterly depressed, it felt as though something heavy was crushing the air out of him, making breathing difficult, like a sheet of steel on his chest weighed down with rocks.

Beside him, Dianne shifted. Possibly less than half awake, she stretched and turned on to her side, put her arm across him and snuggled against his chest.

Perhaps more relieved by the normality of it than by any other motive, Daniel found himself responding. He eased himself slightly on to his left side and slid his hand inside her sleeping bag and down her body. His erection was starting, but there was no increase in discomfort. Relief. He knew he shouldn't do it, but he eased open the top of her knickers and slid his fingers down into her moistness. He wanted to offer her some kind of affection, some sort of apology.

As he circled his fingers, though, his pain shot back, searing through his penis, then somehow sharpening up like a hot needle, shooting towards his pelvis. He stopped instantly.

With her eyes still closed but sighing lightly and probably half-asleep, Dianne kissed his chest then moved down her own arm, so that she was able to take hold of him and begin to move her hand up and down, slowly and firmly.

'Ah. Ah. No, Dianne...' He was totally awake now and took hold of her hand, to stop its motion. 'No. Sorry...'

She went rigid, pulled away from him, turned herself on to her other side and lay still, just as he had done with Yiannis. She was fully awake now. Desperation coursed through him. He needed to tell her about the cut and make up some story about how he got it, and soon.

When dawn arrived, he was still trying to decide what he could say.

****

Helen and Jeanette were drying themselves after an early swim when Kostas and Yiannis arrived on the beach. Still in her bikini, Helen felt suddenly embarrassed and wrapped herself tightly in her towel. Yiannis smiled at her; Jeanette gave

Kostas a very pure kiss on the cheek. Then the four of them sat down together.

'All is well here?' asked Kostas.

Jeanette was surprised: 'Yes. Of course.'

'That is good,' said Yiannis.

Neither man said anything more. They appeared content to take in the view and watch the bodies in the sea.

What's going on? wondered Helen. Both had avoided the beach until this point, as if leaving the girls to their other life. Yiannis had not re-appeared with any German women and Kostas always looked far too smart to sit on sand.

'Are the two of you here for a reason?' said Helen.

Jeanette's face said, 'Well, that was direct!'

Kostas took Jeanette's hand. 'We wanted to be sure that you were safe.' He turned to Helen with a concerned face: 'After last night, that you were all safe, Eleni.'

Why wouldn't they be safe?

'Ah, this is Mike?' said Kostas, nodding to their right.

Mike was coming over, carrying himself slightly differently, as if his shoulders were lower.

Helen watched his approach whilst Jeanette assumed her customary indifference, but Yiannis stood to welcome him.

'*Yássas*, Mike. And today all is good?'

'Yes, thank you, Yiannis…,' said Mike, looking anywhere but at the girls. 'Apart from an aching in my kidneys, though that will doubtless pass. But… I owe you many thanks… And drinks…'

They shook hands, quite formally.

Suddenly, Jeanette too was registering considerable interest

There was a redness on Mike's left cheek, below his sunglasses, and a slight swelling around his mouth. Was there a cut across the bridge of his nose? He'd been fighting… Not with Yiannis, surely?

She had never known Mike grateful before and politeness didn't come naturally to him. In addition, he was evidently uncomfortable.

'If you hadn't been there…' he continued.

'It was no problem. I was going home,' said Yiannis.

'What wasn't a problem?'

Yiannis waited for Mike to explain.

'I had a slight problem last night, Helen. Yiannis helped me out. That's it.'

'Come on…'

Prompted, pushed, with only slight embroidery, he recounted the evening's events. He didn't mention the fact that he was hoping for sex, though Helen took that as a given. He explained that he was drunk, the situation Aimilios and Agneta were in, and about the man, who was presumably Agneta's brother; he told them about the attack and thanked Yiannis again.

'Did you find them?'

'No, Mike.'

'A couple of ferries left during the night… Their things have gone too…'

'So – are you really all right now?' Helen asked. She was genuinely concerned but knew what Jeanette was thinking.

'I've a bruise or two. That guy has quite a temper. I hope the girls are safe. I don't know what he hit me with. But, yes, I'm fine. I can't see too clearly…' He laughed. 'But there's nothing new in that.'

He hadn't taken off his sunglasses and studiously avoided looking towards Jeanette.

Sensing her friend might not be able to resist making a biting comment, Helen took control. 'Thank you for what you did, Yiannis.' He smiled modestly. 'If you hadn't come along, Mike might have been in real trouble. You're a sweetie.'

Without any premeditation, she leant over and kissed his cheek.

'Thank you for being our hero.'

Their faces were close. She could smell his skin and, faintly, cigarettes. What in the world was she doing? Her pulse had quickened again. She didn't look across at her friend. She could imagine Jeanette saying she was shifting her affections more often than she changed her tee shirt, whereas really it was nothing, nothing.

Yet Yiannis' eyes held her.

'Eleni,' he said – just that, but he was saying that he wanted her, his voice heavy with Mediterranean magic. She thought he was going to kiss her on the lips. There, with Kostas and Jeanette and Mike watching.

Daniel had never done that in company and she didn't want it to happen now. What would everyone think? She pulled back.

She didn't have the trembling there had been with Daniel, but there was another warmth inside her. It came from an attraction, but also, weirdly, appreciation. This man was handsome and sensitive and more grown up. Despite Daniel's experience that other night, she herself couldn't imagine Yiannis with past lovers, German women or anyone else. It must have been an aberration. She liked him very, very much – and that was all that mattered.

She raised her finger to her lips and touched them lightly. Where did that kiss come from? She'd never done that before. What was happening to her?

When she tore her gaze from him, she discovered that Kostas was watching with interest and Jeanette winked at her.

Above his sunglasses, Mike's eyebrows were raised. 'When she found she wasn't going to be the only pebble on the beach, she became a little boulder,' he said, quietly.

'Mike?' said Jeanette.

'Oh, nothing. Nothing at all.'

Along the beach, Daniel and Dianne had finally emerged from their den and were heading towards them, Dianne apparently as upset as the day before, whilst Daniel seemed woebegone. Helen did not want to thrust this in his face. She had to behave decently, even if he had not. She didn't want anyone, and especially not Daniel, to view her like some giddy girl in a disco on a Saturday night, and she certainly didn't want to feel as though she was such a person. Yiannis was no more than a friend. She edged away from him.

Mike sat down with a 'Mmm!' as if he was taking a ringside seat.

'Make yourself at home, Mike, make yourself at home,' Helen said, though she didn't want to become part of any performance. She created further space between herself and Yiannis.

****

Since Daniel's first visit, Serifos had always been blue and white and sun-baked and perfect. It had been soft sand, warm sea and multi-coloured fish; attractive girls, intelligent friends, charming waiters and a quality of life the vast majority of people in Britain had never experienced; and there had been wonderful, wonderful sex and games. He had rubbed the essence of Greece all over his body and dangled his feet in vats of its hedonistic waters.

This year, with Helen, should have been the zenith of his experiences. Instead, his head was drumming, he had the gnawing pain between his legs, Dianne had arrived and he felt suicidal, locked already into a partnership of inconvenience. She had told him she wished she were back in Tottenham, back with her mum in the tiny house near the football ground on White Hart Lane, with no bathroom, just a tin bath in front of the fire; but they had another two weeks of misery in Greece still to endure.

And just when he thought that things couldn't get any worse... there, for all to see, Helen had been too close to Yiannis, much too close, and she was still too close. How could this be? Yiannis was all wide grins and straggly hair and tight jeans, all ill-fitting shirt and scuffed old shoes, all take-the-tourists-for-sex-for-nothing... How could she..?

'Hi,' said Dianne, to the assembled group. Greetings were returned.

Daniel stared at Helen, and she looked at him directly with neither guilt nor triumph until he had to turn away.

Phil and Carina approached too because it was breakfast time and they were set for town. Daniel was certain he wouldn't be able to eat.

'Hello, pet,' said Carina to Dianne. 'Are you settled in now?'

'I suppose so. There's not much to settle into really, is there?'

'No... Only there's the toilet facilities to get used to. The lack of them, that is. And the lack of a washroom, I guess... And no privacy... Problems if it's that time of the month...

Still…, how is…everything..? You know…. How are… things..?'

She nodded towards Dianne's belly. The baby had become an open secret. Daniel winced. 'Carina..,' he said.

'Oh, sorry, pet. Nothing to do with us, I know. 'Just had to ask.'

'There's no need to be sorry,' said Dianne. She spoke to all of them but she addressed Daniel. 'I'm feeling fine. In fact, I'm not pregnant after all. I never was. It was all… Shall we say it was just a scare. Nothing more. There's absolutely no need for anyone to worry.'

She said it casually and offered no further explanation. Carina's eyes widened, Phil blinked, Mike's emotions were hidden behind his shades, and the Greeks had no apparent understanding of what was happening. All around, though, questions were obviously being framed. Just Helen and Jeanette seemed unsurprised.

No baby? Daniel's heart leapt and then sank again as Dianne turned her back with a 'That's it, really,' and headed down to the sea before anything else could be said. The others sat in silence but, one by one, turned their attention to him.

He was speechless, his world somersaulting. Then things got even worse: Yiannis leant across to rest his hand on that of Helen.

Dianne walked away, weirdly out of focus.

She wasn't pregnant..? So where did this leave them? What came next?

No one spoke.

What could he do?

He licked dry lips and trudged after Dianne like a reluctant schoolboy but baffled and emotionally drained, bile filling his throat.

Out in the bay, the Minos blew its horn and on the quay there'd be a gathering of travellers picking up their bags to leave for the mainland. For the first time ever, he wished it was his turn to go. Seeing Helen like this was a torment and being with Dianne was unbearable. He wanted a consultation with an English doctor and he wanted something to lift him out of this morass. He wanted to escape this misery forever.

Yet all he could do was follow Dianne's footsteps through the soft sand.

2004

Chapter 4

It was August at last. They were truly on their way. Daniel was relishing the hot breeze as the Express Penelope ploughed her way down the Aegean. He was nearly back. Serifos was waiting.

They'd been in Greece for a week. After landing at the new flashy airport in Athens, shiny and built for the Olympics but sadly lacking the rich smell of pine that greeted passengers when they used to disembark at Ellinikon, they took a bus to the little port of Rafina which was quiet and run-down in a very Greek way of which Daniel approved. They stayed on the bustling main square, in a disgustingly seedy hotel with a filthy bathroom. Fortunately, the kids didn't mind at all. Then they sailed to Andros and spent a week in Batsi, but the island was uncomfortably and surprisingly full of Greek families on holiday: it turned out the nation had more money now. The tavernas were full and some even had queues outside.

'Enough, children. Time to be going.' He was pleased for the Greeks but shocked at the transformation.

Since there was no boat connecting the Northern Cyclades to the Western ones, they were forced to return to the mainland and take the bus to Piraeus.

There, came a bigger shock. In a couple of decades it had become a sizeable city, all rush, noise, congestion. The park where he used to sleep before catching ferries seemed to have disappeared completely, buried somewhere under concrete and tall buildings.

And you could no longer just pay as you boarded a boat. You needed to buy a ticket beforehand; and you could only buy a ticket if there was availability. Health and safety had arrived.

The Modern World was taking bites out of the Greece he'd known. People rushed from bus to office block, threading their way as best they could through lines of cars and speeding motorbikes. A whole style of life was gone. The country had joined the EU and the Euro zone: it was no longer just a few marble steps up from the Third World.

Unsurprisingly, prices had rocketed since his last visit. He hoped he'd brought enough money. Cheese pies cost nearly a pound...

At seven in the morning, the Great Harbour was heaving with visitors from all over the world, a huge choking sunny chaos punctuated by shouts, motor horns and whistles. Cars and enormous trucks trundled aboard a long row of huge ferries.

'Lewis, stay close! Jonny, watch him...'

He must have been stupid to think Greece would have avoided all this.

However, as they sailed away he hoped the horrors were behind him. The sea was still deep blue and white caps and deep troughs surged around them and Daniel clung to his dream that the smaller islands might have remained unspoilt...

The Penelope made steady progress, the rumble of her engines constant through the swells. Jonny and Lewis stood with him at the rail for parts of the trip, gripping tight against the roll of the boat and the wind whilst the funnel belched black smoke just as Daniel remembered. The boat seemed so much emptier than used to be the case, and almost everyone was on a seat rather than lying around the decks. You could no longer sit in a lifeboat. This was a clean but regimented new world.

The boys became more attentive as they neared Serifos, baggy tee shirts blustering dry as the Penelope swung round for its approach to the harbour. Jonny, eleven years old, thin and tall, had an arm round his younger brother, who was seven and much shorter. Their blond hair was salty wet after their games in the spray as the deck had risen and plunged on its six-hour journey from the mainland.

As a boy, Daniel's annual week's holiday had been in chilly Bridlington where he'd floated on a lilo on the murky tide, pushing aside scum and detritus; here, the horizon was still a million miles wide, pristine and baking. His children were lucky.

'Pleased to be here, dad?' said Jonny.

Daniel nodded, but he wasn't certain. It was an age since

he'd visited. Twenty-five years was a long time, over half his lifetime. He'd told stories about his stays on the island, but had never imagined he'd return.

He ran his eyes along the island's hills, dotted now with new buildings, and blew out his cheeks: 'It's changed a bit...'

When they sailed into the bay, the three of them moved to the port side so they could see the beaches. Daniel squinted across the water: a line of trees had been planted right along the stretch where he had slept, and the land was less parched, with stretches of green.

His uneasiness was intensifying and he wondered once more if this visit was a good idea. "Never go back!'

He closed his eyes and pictured Helen coming down the beach in the morning, Phil winking at him as he poured her a drink, Helen rubbing her hair dry as the sun set, Mike setting off up the hill to his makeshift toilet as Helen laughed at his haste, Helen walking with her arm around Jeanette, Helen dancing by the waves... Helen... There was always Helen.

'Will it be like Andros, dad? Or will we be able to sleep on the beach this time?'

'Hopefully we'll be ok on the beach...'

'That's what you said on Andros. The room wasn't so bad, I suppose...'

'You just never know,' he said. 'Greece wasn't like this when I came before. Nothing stays the same. When you grow up, you'll find that life always surprises you.'

'I've never slept on the beach,' said Lewis.

'I haven't either,' said Jonny. 'You know that. And I'm older than you.'

From the speakers came blaring information in Greek, then, 'We will shortly be arriving in Serifos...'

'Let's just see what it's like, eh? I bet you'll love it.' Metaphorically, his fingers were crossed. 'We'll sleep on the beach if we still can. Come on – get your rucksacks...'

He hoped this wasn't a terrible mistake.

He shepherded his two boys to the middle deck to collect their packs which they'd left beside the door into the bar. Then it was down to the car deck, as before, where they awaited docking and their release. It was busier than it used to be.

Vehicles revved, the air was poisonous. Some of the foot passengers had suitcases beside them, but most still carried rucksacks and looked like a herd of multi-coloured hunchbacks.

The Penelope didn't go into the harbour, but moored against the sea side of the quay, which was quicker. When the ramp touched land there was the pandemonium he remembered as people rushed to leave whilst those wanting to board pushed forward through them. Plus ça change...

He manoeuvred the boys out of the melee and they halted for a moment. Back on terra firma, he sighed with relief because the old charm hadn't been lost. The port was busier, with a number of smart sailing boats, but was much as he remembered it and the town on the hill was still blazingly white against the barren mountains.

He found, though, that at the end of the quay, where there'd been a taverna that allowed drunken beach bums to pay the next day, there was now a large ticket office; and where there used to be a track over the hill to the beach, there were now concrete steps with sharp white buildings on either side offering rooms to let. There was even a tourist office, offering accommodation lists and telephone numbers. Daniel collected one, then shoved it into his pocket. He didn't speak Greek and they might not speak English. And where were the owners? In Athens, most likely. And where were their rooms? And would the public telephone work? No, he'd have to sort out things himself.

He was genuinely excited, but just praying that his memories wouldn't all be dislocated.

He nodded his sons forward to the steps and up what remained a steep climb over to the beach. They'd arrived in the heat of the day, with heavy rucksacks.

'This is hard, dad.' Lewis was finding the steps especially steep and high because his legs were shorter.

The descent was easier, as there were steps down too, from what had become a scruffy parking area at the top. They passed a 'Sunset Bar' with a terrace, on the left, and there was a sleepy taverna at the bottom on the right. The place had been transformed.

Safely on the sand, they gazed along the shoreline. It was full of holidaymakers. Children ran in and out of the sea. Most families had settled their towels and bags and in some cases food boxes and camp chairs in the shade of the trees. There wasn't a backpack to be seen.

'This is great,' said Lewis. Daniel wasn't convinced. 'Can we go in the water?'

'Yep. After we find somewhere to sleep.'

Clearly, and disappointingly, no one was sleeping rough. Most of the bamboo had gone; and in the middle of the beach, set back but facing the sea, was a well-established, very busy and well-kept camp site. A waist-high white concrete wall ran along its frontage; inside, tents were in designated areas amongst trees which would provide relief from the sun; and concrete paths ran around the site. He could see signs to the toilets and showers, the shop and bar and even bungalows.

'Coralli Camping', announced a painted sign.

One sleepy afternoon decades earlier, sipping beers, he and Mike had discussed how they should borrow some money and buy up some land and open camp sites on Greek beaches. It was too late now, and Coralli was probably making a fortune.

The setting was still beautiful but Daniel had been away a long time. The low dunes at the far end of the bay had mostly been levelled, by time or people, and the soft sand was thoroughly trodden; there was a mess of cigarette butts around the bases of the trees, which were all whitewashed.

He glanced at the headland ahead, which sheltered what had been the nudist beach beyond. That had never had shade, and he knew the children needed to be able to escape the sun. Also, from the boat he'd seen some apartments over there: so he resigned himself to camping.

'We'll have to go in here. Maybe they rent out tents or will know where we can buy one.'

They meandered their way through the site to an office at the back. Outside, there was a car park and a road which probably ran round from the town.

A road… bringing motorists to his beach...

However, the boys didn't complain. Why should they? This was much better than Blackpool.

They went into the office.

No, Coralli did not rent tents. So sorry. Maybe the shop in town might sell them. Otherwise, they could sleep on the concrete. Yes?

Daniel had no idea what that meant, but for one night was prepared to give it a try.

They were directed back into the site and along to the rear, to a stretch of concrete which was raised about six inches. It was fifty yards in length and three yards deep. Behind it was a bamboo wall; trees all around provided extra shade. Others were living there too because rucksacks were in evidence, with sleeping bags laid out beside or in front of them.

'This will be home, boys. Where do you fancy?'

He knew their mother would have accused him of cruelty to their children but Jonny and Lewis were happy with the novelty. They'd be sleeping out at last.

'Down there,' said Lewis, pointing to the far end.

'Jonny?'

'I don't mind. Yes, down there.'

'It's furthest from the toilets.'

'It won't be as smelly then,' said Jonny, triumphantly. 'I want the end spot.' He set off at the best canter he could manage with a rucksack on his back.

They wrapped towels around themselves, changed rapidly into swimming shorts and set off to the beach with the woven plastic beach mats, masks and snorkels they'd bought on Andros. Established under a tree, Daniel rubbed extra sun lotion on to the boys who ran off to splash in the sea. He was confident it would still be shallow for quite a way out. There was more weed than he remembered, but the water was calm and, anyway, they could both swim.

'Be careful, you two! If you drown and die, I'll not speak to you again!'

'Dad!'

He was pleased to just sit and watch. Moments to himself were a treat.

This is it, he thought, after so many years: Serifos!

He gazed around. It was more like a holiday destination rather than a way-station for vagrant youth, yet it was still captivating. There had been changes, but he was genuinely pleased to be back.

His intention was to lie down, close his eyes and conjour once more those images of beautiful young people, attractive girls from across the continents, and Helen, of course: how things used to be. But he didn't get the chance.

'Not many English people come to this island.' It was a woman's voice, obviously American or Canadian – as with Australians and New Zealanders, he found it hard to tell the one from the other. 'Cute kids…'

She was sitting just along from him, out in the full glare of the sun, with an open novel. Her deep tan and dark glasses made her appear Greek and her hair was short, unnaturally black, possibly dyed. She might have been in her late thirties and her body was beginning to fill out. She wore a respectable but stylish one-piece swimsuit in aqua blue.

'Thanks. Yes. Cute? Well, I suppose… It is always different if you live with them.'

She laughed. ''Guess that's so!'

'I'm Daniel. And that's Jonny, and that's Lewis. We're from England. From the north.'

'Hi. I'm Jenny.' She stretched out her hand. 'I used to live in Virginia.'

'And now..?'

'I'm currently living in a small but functional cave on a beach out the other side of town… A bijou residence for the discerning traveller. I sleep there whenever I'm on Serifos. It makes for a cheap break.'

He laughed. 'I used to think Joni Mitchell was singing, 'Carrie, get out of your cave…'

'I think you'll find she was telling him to get out his cane.'

'Indeed… He was probably a teacher…' He had to ask: 'Are you alone?'

'Yeah.' She might have been wondering how much to reveal. 'I do have a daughter, but she's with her dad right now.' He supposed the swimwear was hiding stretch marks, then felt bad for having the thought. It was the twenty-first century and he tried so hard not to be misogynistic. 'My husband and I don't live together… And you? Your wife's around somewhere?'

'We're divorced.' There was the usual silence.

'We're not so different. But you bring the kids with you anyway. That's great.'

'They live with me all the time.'

'Oh! Hard work.'

'Not so bad. They're worth it.'

'Respect.'

Then she was silent, apparently taking it in.

'So, where do you live – when not visiting your cave?'

'In Athens. I teach English.'

'And you speak Greek?'

'My husband's Greek. I've been here a long time.'

They both gazed towards the children.

'Dad, dad!' Lewis, sparkling with water, was shouting. 'Come and see the fish!'

'In a minute?'

'No, dad, now, now.'

Daniel stood up. 'There you go… Duty calls…'

'And I need to get away.'

She started to gather up her things. He was sorry, because he missed talking to an adult. She was pretty too, in her way. Probably too pretty to want to be bothered with a dreary single dad.

'Maybe we'll see you later?' He hoped he sounded suitably laid back.

'Yes. I'll watch out for you. I might be eating up in the square tonight.'

'The square?'

'Up in Chora.' She nodded towards the town on the hill. 'By the town hall.'

Despite his visits, he'd never been there. He'd never moved from the seafront.

'Oh. Chora.' If he'd ever known it, he'd forgotten its name. 'You must be fit. That's a bit of a climb.'

'I've got a bit of a car to get me there.' She laughed. 'But anyway there's always the bus.'

'The bus… Right.'

Of course. Modern visitors had cars. And there was a bus.

Who'd have known?

'New places, eh?'

'In a way…'

'Dad! Dad! Dad!'

'You're needed! Your family is calling. I'll see you, Daniel. Dan?'

'Either is fine. Yes. I hope we might bump into each other. But wherever we end up tonight, I can guarantee we'll be right here tomorrow.' Would she take the hint?

She'd stepped into a loose beach dress, put on a pink baseball cap with crossed swords on the front and slung her small rucksack on to her back in the new way, not over just one shoulder as they used to in England.

'I have a date with a man on a boat in the morning. But perhaps later, who knows…? Bye for now, Dan.'

'Goodbye, Jenny.'

He watched her go, a straight back and a sway of the hips. Altogether classy.

'Da-a-a-a-d!'

'Coming, Lewis. Keep your hair on. And your cap. Put it back now!' He appeared to be trying to catch fish with it.

Daniel became a father again and waded into the sea. Jonny splashed him and then fled as Daniel followed in a thrashing spray, threatening revenge.

Another ferry entered the bay; children screamed as they raced around in the shallows; some young Greeks had begun a game of beach football between the trees and the camp-site and they shouted and laughed; two men were playing chess, lying with their feet in the water with the board just beyond the sea-line; some young women were sitting in the water, reading romantic fiction; and had it not been for the infuriating pat-pat of several couples playing bat and ball, it would have been all good there.

Certainly, it could have been much worse.

Yet he kept glancing around, half expecting an eighteen-year-old Helen to be approaching, pushing her hair back over her shoulder, delighted to see him. Through more brief relationships than he cared to count and an excuse for a marriage that had lasted a decade, he'd never forgiven himself for losing her, for his young man's idiocy. Even in his middle age, she remained a ridiculous obsession.

And he felt her spirit was still alive on this beach. He could picture her. It was as if he could hear her voice on the breeze, even now.

He'd never really known her properly, but had never met anyone he liked so much, no one who even came close. His fantasy remained with him.

*****

Back on Lia Beach, Jenny lay before her cave and read for a while until she was alone. Few other people ever lingered long because the beach was mostly rock and pebbles rather than luxurious soft sand like elsewhere on the island and it had no shade and no taverna, so why would anyone want to stay? Most days, a few souls would wander down, past the derelict farm and along the uneven path, or bounce there on a moped, but they usually left quickly. It was always quiet. She liked it for that reason.

When the last couple had departed, she stripped off and had a final swim, pulled out fresh clothes from the bag she kept in the space under the rocks that she called a cave, smoothed moisturising cream over her skin and changed.

She had never specified to her friends on the staff at school exactly where she stayed, because most of them would be appalled, thinking she was putting herself in danger; and she wished she hadn't told her parents, for that same reason. They'd never been to the coast or even set foot out of Indiana and its vast emptiness and when she moved to the lovely university town of Charlottesville at the foot of the Blue-Ridge Mountains, they feared for her future, if not her life. Going to Greece was a terrifying step further; and on Serifos, they imagined she'd regressed to Neolithic times where she would likely be raped by some primitive or murdered in her sleep.

They begged her to be more sensible, but she explained it wasn't like being in New York and the people weren't threatening and no one carried a gun and she could rest in peace when she turned in for the night. They were shocked by the gross inappropriateness of the phrase. She accepted there was a slight risk, but there was no way she could afford to stay anywhere else. She needed to save every cent she could: her wage was poor, and to have a half decent life she had to supplement her income by working for the Cambridge Exam Board, travelling all over Greece testing oral English for a pittance.

Just in case of trouble – not that there had ever been any – she slept with her Swiss army knife open beside her. It was one detail she generally kept to herself and she had certainly never told her parents.

She was comfortable and she appreciated the seclusion. Two decades of sleeping on beaches across the islands had left a love of the open sky and the wash of the waves. She could do as she liked – and at Lia there were no drunks or late night singsongs to fracture the peace.

At times she had shared her cave with some man she'd met in Athens and invited over, but she soon tired of them and none had been invited again.

Unusually, this time her stay on the beach would be relatively brief. An opportunity had arisen, one it had been impossible to turn down. She'd been offered a free up-grade on her accommodation, which she expected to be confirmed the next day.

When she was ready for the evening, she sat for a while watching the crescent moon rise in the dusky blue-greyness over the sea, then made her way to her old Cortina. Covered in dirt and scrapes, it was parked back from the beach at the side of the unmade road that ran along the coast. For once, it started first time and she drove towards the port before turning sharp right to begin the climb to Chora. The car was well past its best and she nursed it along, driving much of the steep zig-zagging section in second gear.

At the top, the car park ran for fifty yards along a sheer drop of hundreds of feet and there were no barriers. She reversed as close to the edge as she dared, got out, made sure the hand brake was fully engaged, fastened the door tight with twine and then headed down the short slope towards the town.

From just past the bus stop, deep marble steps climbed again through ancient buildings to the picturesque Pano Piatsa Square.

The smells of roasting meat, onions and garlic wafted towards her and it was busy. There was a birthday celebration so the three tavernas by the town hall were crowded. The small metal tables and rickety chairs were almost all taken but she was lucky to find a table which had been vacated at the top end of the square, at the side, at the bottom of an alley which led to the topmost point of Chora, the chapels and the remains of the Kastro walls. She wasn't a tourist in the usual sense of the word and had enjoyed the view many times before so she no longer went up to the town to sightsee, merely to eat.

The waiter knew her – '*Yássou*, Jenny' – and brought olives and bread. She ordered a jug of white wine, water, *horiátiki* and *keftédes*. Her intention was to read her novel as she worked slowly through the salad and meatballs.

She took her battered copy of Henry Miller's *Tropic of Cancer* from her bag but she couldn't concentrate as the two young men on the page discussed the horrors of making love to older women. It wasn't just the songs from the revellers around her that made her concentration wander: she hated reminders that she herself had reached middle age. Her mind skipped back to Dan, who reminded her of John back home, who had made love to her just once many years before in a corn field. It had been a spiky experience, but he was handsome and made the world feel better for a few minutes. Might Dan do that?

She loved sex but holidaymakers were here and then gone tomorrow, of course, and she'd reached an age when brief relationships were often too much like hard work and increasingly she was selective. She'd been disappointed by too many encounters: hearts shattered, expectations unfulfilled, bitter endings, a myriad of spoiled memories and stained skirts. She'd learnt that it all gets better with practice, and one-night stands so often left her feeling empty. Also, she was sick of catching minor infections.

Stelios, her estranged husband, no longer merited any consideration as a lover and she would have torn him from her address book were it not for the fact that with his new partner he held her daughter like some kind of trophy or hostage, damn him. She needed to get a divorce and demand regular access to her child. Sometime soon. Astraea belonged to her too.

She thought about the time she'd spent more recently with Giorgos – was it only last summer? – and she shivered. He'd imagined all Americans were rich. When he found out she was only a teacher, he became increasingly cold and they finally agreed to call it a day. That was just as well, because he never seemed quite clean, somehow. He needed to change his underwear more regularly.

And there'd been Guy in Athens, who claimed to work for the American embassy but really lived off his mother. He said she'd been in adult movies and had escaped to Greece to get away from her latest husband and his friends, who all seemed to be mixed up with organised crime at some level: prostitution, the FBI's investigation of a senator and his missing intern, and a federal enquiry into money laundering. The stories were endless and became increasingly bizarre and she figured Guy was inventing them. Indeed, when she met his mother, she seemed more like an ex-librarian than a one-time porn-star. It was evident that at some point in his life, Guy had become very screwed up. He had magic hands and a tongue that might have fluttered for his country, had oral sex been an Olympic event – but, still, Jenny felt she'd had a lucky escape.

Dan, then? Her food arrived and she moved her fork around, toying with an olive and a slice of green pepper. He was a single dad but handsome enough, even if he was thinning on top. He didn't have the ubiquitous English beer belly. Possibly interesting. An accountant? No, too sharp. A university lecturer? He hadn't said. He could definitely be worth a try, if she could get him away from the kids. He might be ok in bed, even though he was English.

She stabbed a segment of tomato and smiled to herself. She was realistic, always. She knew the presence of the two boys would ensure she'd probably get nowhere. Still, she'd certainly not muddy the waters by encouraging her friend St John when she met him in the morning. He was terribly

English, but thankfully had no expectations, accepted what she offered and had lots of money. She had only ever needed to have sex with him twice. She'd developed a range of strategies to avoid sleeping with him again, but kept him on stand-by, as her financial loan service. She always needed cash.

She sipped from her glass and decided she'd seek out Dan the next day. It could be fun. He could be fun. It was worth a try.

No sooner was her decision made than he was walking towards her, guiding his sons between boisterous tables, past harassed waiters.

'Hello,' he said. 'Fancy meeting you here. As you see, we made it.'

'You didn't walk…'

'Actually, we raced up. There are steps.'

'He's lying,' said the eldest boy. 'We caught the bus.'

'It's good to know I can trust one of you to tell the truth,' she said.

'Jonny doesn't always tell the truth,' said the youngest. 'Like when you've had a biscuit,' he continued, challenging his brother, 'and then ask for another but say you've not had one yet.'

'I don't.'

'You do. Doesn't he, dad? He did today.'

Daniel blew out his cheeks. 'So, let me introduce my sons,' he said. 'This is Jonny…'

'Hello,' said Jonny. 'You're American, aren't you?'

'I am, yes.'

'I've never met anyone American. I met someone from Ireland, and he sounded American.'

'Yeah. I guess he might.'

'And a bit Scottish.'

'And this is Lewis.' Daniel pushed his smaller son forward. 'Lewis, say hello to Jenny.'

'Hello, Jenny,' said the boy. They both seemed perfectly trained. 'I don't lie about biscuits.'

'You lie all the time,' said Jonny. 'You're even lying about not lying.'

'I'm not!'

Jenny wondered if he might become a politician when he grew up. 'Hi, Lew,' she said.

'We aim for perfection,' said Daniel. 'But often seem doomed to fall short.' He was laughing. 'Come on, kids, leave Jenny to her book.'

'No. Please stay. Wanna eat?'

'We ate down at the port earlier.'

'Why not have a drink?'

'They both want ice creams. We climbed right to the top of the town... What a view and you can see forever... Sifnos rising on the horizon like a land of magic... Then somehow we got lost in the alleys on the way down.' He glanced at the boys. 'They need to be revived...'

'Well, how about I get you a drink and you send the two of them off to the shop at the bottom of the steps to get themselves something cold?'

'Great.'

It was a solution that appealed to the boys, who obviously welcomed the freedom. She liked the fact that their father was either cool about releasing his kids into the wild or knew Greece well enough to feel confident they'd come to no harm.

'The Greeks love kids,' she said.

'Yes. It's very different from England. I've been before, of course. It's the first time for them – but they love Greece too.'

He handed Jonny a ten euro note. 'Go forth, my children. For centuries, hunter gatherers have been revered in societies around the world.'

The boys sighed and left.

When his bottle of Amstel arrived, Daniel poured a few inches into his glass, in the Greek way, and sipped it as she asked him about his previous visits to the islands. He told her about his travels years before, the islands he'd loved and where he'd stayed. She'd been around at the same time at the end of the 70s: they could have met back then.

As he talked, his eyes became almost misty. There was a kind of fragility about him, she thought. If he'd been ten years old, she might have pushed the hair back out of his eyes. Of course, he'd have had more hair then. Or if they'd been at a party all night, she'd have invited him back to her apartment, taken off his clothes and led him to bed and he would doubtless have followed dutifully.

Before long, Jonny and Lewis returned in triumph with a handful of change and chocolate Magnums, though in the evening heat the ice cream was already melting and the chocolate was becoming loose around it. Daniel didn't interfere.

Jenny, however, couldn't sit and watch the disaster unfold.

'Hey, can I help you, baby?' she said to Lewis.

'I think you'll find I'm not a baby any more,' he replied, in a very adult way. Then a large lump of chocolate freed itself and fell to the floor and his face collapsed. 'Oh, all right, then. Yes, please...' He sounded desperate.

She managed not to laugh and used a serviette from the plastic rack on the table to cover the bottom part of the ice cream and the stick. It meant Lewis could eat more easily and without the melted streams running over his hand and on to his clothes.

'Thank you, Jenny,' he said, as if she were some rescuing angel. Daniel looked pleased.

'And how about your brother?' she asked.

'I'm fine, thanks,' he said, somehow forcing all that was left into his mouth. She was reminded of the time she'd watched a snake swallow a rabbit.

There were no other spare chairs, so the boys wandered around the corner and sat on a step.

'Alone again,' said Dan. 'I thought they'd never go... No, seriously, you're very good with them. Would you like to borrow them for a couple of weeks? No charge.'

'I'd love to, of course. But would you want them sleeping in a cave?' Once again, she was exaggerating for effect, since it was such a small space that she actually slept on the beach beside it. 'And, anyway, they'd miss their dad...'

'Sadly, you might just be right. I am truly shackled.'

Appearing not at all downhearted, he asked whether they should have another drink, but she suggested they could have one in a place she knew down by the sea, where there'd be room for all four of them to sit and it would be quieter. He thought that was a good idea. She offered them a lift and he said that was even better.

However, he hadn't seen her car. He chatted happily as they made their way back to it. When they got there, he was obviously taken aback but clearly possessed a streak of stoicism.

'Oh. A Cortina. Vintage 1980s. Unique locking system.' He'd seen the twine around the door handle. 'And air conditioning.' He was peering inside at the holes in the floor. 'Do these windows close? Ah, thought not.'

The boys climbed in the back and began rooting around amongst the jumble of towels, clothes, plastic bottles, food wrappers and odds and ends on the seat. 'Relax, boys.' He turned to Jenny: 'They can just settle amongst things?'

'Yeah.'

'No seat belts?' He sounded as though he knew the answer.

'Well, there are some somewhere, but they don't actually work.'

'Very Greek… But how come you have a right-hand drive car with English plates? How does an American end up driving this car in Serifos? I'm intrigued.'

'Donald.'

'Donald?'

'Donald. He said he was a micro-bore plumber from Glasgow. I've no idea what one of those is, but that's what he said he was. He'd driven his car down here and needed cash for it to help him get home. He knew the car wouldn't make the return journey. Anyway, finally he gave it to me, for a few beers and a warm thank you. He was a gentleman. Of sorts.' Actually, she remembered exactly how he'd made love, pinning down her arms and pushing roughly inside, making her scream. It was unnecessary detail. 'He said the car would remind me of his magnificent bodywork and his impressive engine. As it's turned out, it's got a major problem with its exhaust….'

She turned the key and the car leapt forward and stalled.

She tried again, abruptly reversing this time so they were within feet of the sheer drop and Dan gasped; then she swung it round. He grabbed the door handle as she accelerated hard, narrowly missing a Daihatsu that was about to park.

She was laughing, totally relaxed after the wine: he kept one hand on the handle and with the other clasped the seat beneath him.

'Don't mind me. I'm always frightened in cars,' he shouted over the engine's roar. 'Ok… a song anyone?'

They sang Ten Green Bottles as they descended the hill. The children bellowed with gusto and the faster she went, the more excited their voices became. Dan was particularly enthusiastic and sometimes turned round to sing right at them – usually when she was sweeping round the hairpin bends. He only panicked once, on a tight corner when they nearly hit the bus that was coming towards them, but then he apologised and said it was just that he hadn't had enough to drink yet.

He amused her. He was British in a good way.

She drove along to her favourite taverna, beside the sea but along from the port. It stood beside a couple of small hotels and a set of rooms for rent.

'Phew,' said Daniel. 'It's good to be back on the flat.' She knew he'd been terrified and really meant it was good to be stopping. 'Was this built when I used to come to Serifos?' He nodded at the taverna. 'There was nothing down here at all, as far as I can remember.'

'It's a while since you visited.'

'True. You put your calendar on the wall and go off to do the dusting and when you get back years have spun by and half your life is over.'

'I recognise that feeling. Anyway, see what you make of the place, Dan,' she said. She'd turned off the dusty road and parked under a tree. 'It's just about the cheapest place in town but the food is fabulous. And it's a bit more like it was back when.'

'As I said, we have eaten…'

'No problem. We can just drink now but maybe another time you should try the food…'

She chose a table beside the sea. They were under old trees and there was sand beneath their feet. It felt secluded in the dark. There were a couple of tables back across the track, in front of the taverna itself, but the few diners present were all eating on the beach.

'Yep, this is authentic enough,' said Daniel, sounding impressed.

The waiter came across. He pushed his glasses back against his nose, then regarded the far side of the bay, addressing them without any eye contact at all.

'Jenny,' he said, in greeting. 'You wanna eat?'

'We're just drinking.'

He lowered his pad and pen and nodded his head. 'So..?'

'*Krasí… misó kiló, lefkó,*' she said, then to the other three: 'I'm having wine. You guys..?'

'An Amstel… a coke… and..?' said Dan.

'Sprite, dad,' said Jonny.

'Amstel, Coke, Sprite, ok,' said the waiter. He rubbed Lewis's hair, turned and wandered back to the kitchen, casually glancing up and down the road as he crossed it. Lewis smoothed his hair down again, clearly less than impressed.

'Strange guy,' said Daniel. 'Louche.'

'He's cool,' she replied. 'They're not playing to refined tourists here.'

'Cool dude,' echoed Jonny.

Jenny enjoyed the calm and the wine. They were away from the brighter lights of the busy tavernas that were growing up around the port. While the tired boys leant over their bottles and their straws, she watched the sea and Daniel, who sat back, relaxing as best he could on the rush seat of his wooden chair.

'You were right, Jenny. This is more like Greece as I remember it,' he said. 'I can see why you come here. The last time I came, everywhere was like this. I could be back in the late seventies…'

He stopped abruptly. He'd been idly staring around, but his gaze had suddenly become fixed on the restaurant and kitchen across the road. His whole body had stiffened.

'Shit,' he said. He stood up. '1979.' Then he sat down again. 'Wow.' He seemed nonplussed.

Jenny blinked and waited for an explanation.

****

Daniel had been hoping his pilgrimage back to Serifos would have some sort of cathartic effect, that just being there would clear some of his demons. He was forty-seven and far too old to be mooning over a romance that imploded an age ago. He needed to finally find peace of mind.

Whilst booking their tickets, he'd been dubious about whether it would work and had thought about Helen every day before they left home; on Andros, he studied the women passing, just in case one of them was Helen; but once on Serifos, he was definitely in thrall to his memories.

However. Now. This… He might have been in a cheap novel: his throat had actually dried and his body felt ridiculously weak.

As if the action had been choreographed, when he turned towards the taverna's building twenty metres away, Helen emerged. She was unchanged: the same poise, the same figure and hair and face. She might have stepped right out of one of his dreams.

It seemed the years had not touched her at all. She remained nineteen and indescribably beautiful. Still with long hair, still slim, still the same perfect features.

She was wearing an apron now, and wiped her hands on it as she came out of the building and sat at a table beside the door, next to an old Greek woman who was dressed in black and poured her a glass of red wine from a glass jug.

Actually, it was all more like a movie than a novel because the boys and Jenny had become blurred beside him. His heart racing, he was staring down a long tunnel with Helen sitting at the end of it: sharp, defined, and lovely, mouth-wateringly lovely.

What to do?

He found himself standing again.

'I'll just be a minute,' he said.

Without giving a thought to even his boys, he walked towards the girl who'd obsessed him for quarter of a century.

****

Helen's long day was almost finished. She'd been in the kitchen since seven o'clock that morning and would be back tomorrow and almost every day until September was done. Regularly, she worked until after midnight. She was grateful the holiday season only lasted from May until the start of October because she wouldn't be able to function any longer.

At this time of year, work seemed endless; and at this time of night, all she wanted was her bed. Exhausted, she sipped her wine.

Across the road, a man left his table and headed towards them. He was no doubt seeking the toilet. He wasn't Greek. Even at a distance, his shorts, his tee shirt and his sandals announced he was English. She'd direct him inside and round the corner by the fridges and warn him to keep his head down because there was a low beam which caught people out; and he'd register surprise that she was English and be grateful for the help. It had happened a hundred times.

But this man was behaving oddly, moving slowly, diffidently, and although there was no traffic he hesitated at the other side of the road. Then he crossed, warily.

He stood before her, in front of their table, gazing directly at her, not at her mother-in-law. And she knew him. Or, he reminded her of someone: those eyes, that mouth…

'Helen…'

She certainly knew that voice.

His hair had almost gone on top and his face was clean shaven, but he was still slim and had that same charm and sense of vulnerability.

She saw what were new, the wrinkles round the eyes and the high forehead, but it was an old pain that stabbed her.

The past swept back. She could still picture him leading Dianne along the beach to catch the ferry home and recall the devastation when he'd not even bothered to find words to say proper goodbyes to her or even to Jeanette. He lived in her memory as the young man who first gave her belief that men could be decent but then wrecked everything.

He must have stood on the ferry as it left, passing the beach with his arm around another girl as they headed for Sifnos. She should hate him even now.

But she saw the smile she'd never forgotten... and still remembered the lift he'd given, although briefly, to her soul.

Her tiredness left her but her heart didn't leap. It was too late for that. She wasn't delighted to see him. But neither was she angry anymore, because it all happened so long ago. She recognised him but didn't yet know how to respond.

Years ago, she'd wondered what she might do if he ever returned. Her reactions could be dramatic: she could stand, embrace him, kiss him. She could overlook what he'd done and hold him and tell him, without saying anything, that she'd loved him so much. Or, she might tear into him and tell him that she'd never forgiven him and never would and demand to know why he'd come back because everything was finished. Or a weaker woman might see him and tremble because of the hurt he'd caused, and display her resentment, release latent tears.

Or she could sit and say nothing, apparently impassive in the moment. Which is what happened. She had hoped she might if he came back. In the moment, she barely reacted at all.

She could feel her mother-in-law's eyes moving from Daniel to her, but didn't look at the old lady. Inside her head, one memory after another tumbled and tumbled. Much of that long-ago summer had faded from her thoughts, but now it was like when you leaf through the photograph album that's been at the back of the cupboard for decades: vividly, she remembered the sand everywhere; long evenings around drunken tables; watching Mike and Daniel doing whatever they were doing along the beach; holding his hand; that first kiss and his soft touches that one special evening.

She could feel a smile coming, but stopped it, even though that was far from the Greek way, because there had been his mendacity too. And Dianne, of course.

'Helen, I can't believe...' Then he stopped.

It was obvious he'd no idea she'd be there. He hadn't worked out what he might say. The Daniel she'd known had been silent often: but anyone would have planned for a moment like this. He was struggling to put together any words at all.

132

'It's… just… incredible to see you… after all this time. And… and you look...'

Her mother-in-law spoke no English, but his emotions would have been clear in any language. Yet Kyria Konstantinidis said nothing. That was how she was.

'Daniel.' Helen just said his name. It seemed enough.

'Yes. Hello.' His eyes were sparkling. 'I never thought I'd see you again. Ever. I mean, I sort of hoped, but never thought you'd still be on Serifos...'

Was he close to tears? If he started crying, that would be awful.

'Let's take a moment,' she said.

She explained to the old lady that this was an old friend, from when she was young, and led him across the road, to sit at a table there.

Not unnaturally, the woman and the children at the table he'd left were observing the two of them with considerable interest.

'You've abandoned your wife.'

'No, she's just someone I met.'

'Her children..?'

'No, the boys are mine.'

She half raised a hand. The boys waved, then went back to their drinks. Helen had seen the woman before, but was certain she didn't live on the island.

'So, their mother is..?'

'She… left.'

She didn't ask the obvious question but he gave her the answer.

'She decided I didn't love her.'

'It can be hard… But the children…?'

'They live with me; she sees them occasionally.'

'Right.' What to make of that? She looked across at the boys again. 'They must keep you busy.'

He nodded.

'And otherwise?'

It was formal and as if she was talking to a relative who'd left her with debts then suddenly come home. Things could not be as they once were.

'I'm still in publishing... Got married... Got divorced... She left behind the house and two cats and two goldfish and two sons... I should be grateful...' That was it: his life, apparently.

'Mike?'

'I believe he shacked up with a heavyweight wrestler who rippled with muscle and cooked mouth-watering quiche and they moved to San Francisco...'

She couldn't stop herself smiling.

'No, actually I have no idea where he is now or what he's doing... And you..?' he asked.

What to tell him? How much? There was more than half a lifetime but so little. Here she was, still.

'I got married. I have two daughters. They're about the same age as your boys. Yiannis works hard. I cook here during the summer. We go to Athens in the winter.'

Twenty-five years for both of them, summed up in a few sentences. No mention of pains or pleasures, because they would be too personal.

What was he thinking? His breathing was shallow.

'So you married him.'

She could sense his hurt, though what right did he have to be upset? There was no way to make things better for him, and why should she? Anyway, they were different now. Each had a family, each had a life, each had made their choices.

She bit back what would have been a sharp response. 'And Jeanette married Kostas..,' she said instead.

'Ah... You haven't changed at all...' His eyes were watery again and she feared he'd lean over and kiss her. But he went on, 'It must have been a while before you had children.'

'We thought it wasn't going to be possible. Then we had two...'

'And you learnt Greek... Was that hard?'

'Not really. Not when it's all around you. I never went home. It took about eighteen months, I suppose.' She paused. 'Longer to write it. But Yiannis has learnt better English. The girls speak both...'

'Girls. Yes. How apposite...' He paused, then chuckled: 'You know, I can still remember Yiannis lying beside me on

134

the beach. Every inch of him...' His youth returned to his face and she saw him exactly as he used to be.

The young Daniel, for a moment.

Their brief romance should have been a mere footnote somewhere in her history, but he'd been her first love, so it wasn't surprising his ghost had remained, buried beneath the dust of her life as seasons turned. There'd never been anything remarkable about him, yet he'd been so special to her. How she'd trembled on the beach, all childish devotion and adolescent passion and confusions. She'd been prepared to offer all of herself. It had been a once in a lifetime adoration.

The sense of emptiness he'd provoked, she realised, had been dormant within her ever since. How could such a brief romance permeate so permanently? He'd never been remarkable and their relationship had been nothing more than fleeting. And yet...

She hadn't once dreamed of betraying Yiannis but her feelings for her husband had never touched such depths.

They fell silent. A truck drove past and Christos shouted out of the window to her. She waved and noticed her mother-in-law was still watching, as she would, since Daniel was leaning forward across the table, as though he might breathe her in.

She stood up. 'I must get back to the kitchen.'

'Maybe...' That uneasiness again. What did he want to say? 'It's late, I know...'

In every way. She wasn't waiting for more.

'I've got things to clear and clean,' she said, 'for tomorrow.' The old lady was moving inside.

'It was... good... to see you. I mean – it is good.'

'It's a surprise, Daniel.' She was guarded. She had to be. She glanced across at his sons. They were handsome boys. 'Enjoy your holiday. All of you.'

Of course, she knew Daniel would come to the taverna again, but she wouldn't encourage him, shouldn't encourage him: Yiannis would be uneasy because he knew what they might have been to each other.

She hurried after her mother-in-law, preparing herself for the inevitable questions.

****

Jenny was intrigued: a man returning to old haunts with sons
in tow, an English cook who had known him way back, an
electricity between them that was palpable and Daniel's near
silence over his drink afterwards. Was heady romance
brewing? If there was to be no sex with Daniel, he might at
least provide entertainment.

'So, how d'you know her?' she asked.

'I met her on Kamari beach in Santorini. Years ago. We
were very close for a couple of weeks and here on Serifos,
actually…'

'But..?'

'Let's say it didn't work out.'

'Lost love… but it was only two weeks?'

'Something like that.'

There was obviously much more. She wondered how much
alcohol it would take before he spilled the detail. Time would
tell. She could wait.

For now, she had other calamari to fry.

Next morning, she met St John on his yacht at eleven
o'clock as planned. It was Swedish made and thirty glistening
feet in length and if only the owner had been equally Swedish
and six feet tall, all would have been perfect. Sadly, St John
failed on both counts.

He was a fine man, though. Yes, he would go along with
her plan and leave his tent and passport on Serifos. Yes, she
could use the tent for as long as she wanted. No, of course
there'd be nothing to pay. Ok, she could buy him a meal in
Athens sometime. And she could move into the tent whenever
she liked. In fact – and he was obviously hoping for an offer of
availability – perhaps they could spend a couple of nights
squeezed in together before he left?

She'd like to be heading for his tent at Coralli Camping
within the hour, she said, but she thought it was best he slept
on his boat until he left for the Saronic Islands in a couple of
days. She told him she wanted to be alone. Very Garbo.
'Though who knows how I might feel by this evening,' she
added, archly. Hope visibly tingled through him.

She could play him like a harp. Or a double bass. She could twist him so tightly around her little finger that his genitalia were almost pushing out of his nose.

Thus, all was satisfactorily arranged. She drove back to Lia Beach, grabbed her things and moved to the camp site immediately.

Having settled in, she joined the boys and their father on the beach. Daniel was under the last tree, lying with his eyes closed. The boys were in the sea again, this time with a net on a stick, apparently trying to catch fish they could transfer to a sawn-off plastic bottle. They didn't seem to have the knack but were making a great deal of noise, arguing and laughing.

'Hi, Dan.'

'Ah, Jenny.' He sat up. 'Had a good morning?'

'Very good. I've just been moving house.'

He registered surprise. 'Oh. I thought you liked your cave.'

'I do. But I must be getting old. It's hard to resist a free tent for the next few weeks. And showers. And a toilet... So I've become a happy camper. Isn't that the term the English use?'

'It is, sometimes. And you're pitched already?'

'Yep. Sort of. Howdy, neighbour!'

'Hi.' He shook her hand. 'But how come..?'

'It's simple really. I have a friend – well, an acquaintance, an old friend of a friend – who has been here for weeks. Back and forth anyway. He has a boat, but he's been using this site as his base. As you know, when you arrive at the site they take your passport and you pay when you depart and they return your passport... Well, he's been around for months so it'll be cheaper for him to leave without paying; then he'll go to the British Embassy in Athens and say he's lost his passport and they'll let him buy a replacement... It'll save him money. You know the rich always want to do that.'

'It's how they become richer... Although, it sounds perfect for you, if nefarious. Of course, the site owner will be out of pocket...' He's got morals, she thought. Old fashioned and sweet.

'Yeah. But, hey, he does great business in the summer. He'll cope... Anyway, St John isn't going to be using the tent anymore, so he says I can use it and just leave when I want.

I'll go, the tent will stay.'

'Which means you can retire that knife you mentioned?'

British humour.

'Yeah.'

She had no guilt about the owner's bank account. She was certain he'd survive: all he'd be losing would be hot water for her showers and a girl had to get by. He was much better off than she'd ever be unless she came across someone with the wealth of St John but with looks too.

'I have decided we are also staying,' said Dan. 'On the concrete. It is not exactly five-star accommodation, but the kids are happy.'

He inclined his head towards the sea. Lewis had his head on one side too, apparently trying to get water out of his ear. Jonny was tapping him on the top of the head to help.

'I'm glad you'll be around,' she said. 'And you'll get the chance to see Helen again.' Of course, she'd become his reason for staying. She decided to dig a little. 'Is she married?'

'She is.'

'Ah.'

'Ah.'

There was an awkward, lengthy pause. Then he began to talk, almost as if to himself.

'It is so odd. I remember sitting with her just here, long ago. There were no trees then, there was no camp site… Just the sea and the sand. Now…' He sighed. 'Have you seen that hammock strung between two trees over there? Bloody hell, a hammock…

'A wizened old woman used to come along the beach sometimes, all in black with a walking stick, and poke any girls who were sunbathing topless. 'You go after the mountain,' she used to yell, and pointed over there, to the nudist beach. 'After the mountain!' She must be dead now. What would she have made of all this? Christ, what must she have thought of us all then..?'

He paused.

'Anyway, you don't expect to ever bump into the love of your life again, to find her just as you remember her and in the same place where you last saw her. It's…' He appeared to be

138

struggling to sum up the experience. 'It's… amazing. All the things that happened right on this spot, right here... And I'm back again; and Helen is here too.'

They watched the boys for a while.

''Guess you'll be back to Konstantinidis' this evening?'

'That restaurant? Of course.'

She wasn't sure he'd want her around, but she didn't want to miss anything.

'Would you like company? I mean, if you want to just go with the boys, that's fine.'

'No, please, join us. But we usually try to eat early: Lewis gets tired. He's always tired. No matter what I do, he won't rest in the afternoon. Will you be driving down there..?'

She recognised a hesitancy.

'I'll be walking. My car has a pretty permanent spot under the trees just before you get to Konstantinidis'. It's ok there for months if necessary. I never move it off the island… And, anyway, I'm not bringing it here because I don't want to draw any attention to myself… You don't have a problem with my driving?'

'No. No.' But clearly he did. 'I'm just a very nervous passenger... Whoever is driving. It's not you, honestly. I always sit there thinking, 'I could die in this car…''

'No problem.' He was so cute. 'But you can bet your life you won't die in a car… Anyway, we'll walk down together, then? Yeah?' She couldn't stop herself: 'Do you want me to bring bandaid, in case her husband turns up?'

He didn't laugh.

****

Daniel wanted Helen to like him again. Actually, he wanted her to love him again, to leave Yiannis, return with him to England and be prepared to make love to him each night.

Silly dreams.

He prised the boys from the beach to have showers which were quick because the water had begun to run cold. Most campers had got there earlier, and the floor of the toilet block was messy with sand and odds and ends dropped throughout the day. It wouldn't be cleaned until later in the evening. However, their departure was delayed because Lewis needed to use the toilet and the two cubicles with proper toilets were in use. Only the squatties were free and he was not going to use those because 'standing up to poo is disgusting, dad.'

There followed the customary evening ceremony of the application of the after-sun and mosquito repellent, but by seven o'clock they were ready. They were wished cheery goodbyes by assorted twenty-somethings from Germany and Greece and countries around the world who were sleeping nearby and were probably bemused that a man in his forties was established on the concrete with two young children. They probably thought he was an impoverished absent parent fulfilling his parental duty for a fortnight but were too polite to ask.

Daniel hadn't found a tent to buy in town but the boys loved the novelty of sleeping out. Fortunately, he had found three foam sleeping mats abandoned by people who were leaving, so they had a touch of comfort and his hips and shoulders weren't feeling too bruised.

They headed over to Jenny's tent at the furthest end of the site. She could look out over the wall and through the low mesh fence at what was left of the dunes and scrubby vegetation beyond. They found her sitting on a broken camping chair which St John must have left, sipping water.

'Hi, guys. Jonny, you are looking handsome tonight; and, Lew, you look good. Are you both meeting girls later?'

'No, I'm not,' said Lewis, definitely.

'No,' said Jonny, sounding as though it was an arrangement he might quite welcome.

When they arrived at the restaurant, it was quiet. Jenny explained Konstantinidis' was mostly frequented by Greeks, who appreciated the food but especially the prices, and Daniel knew they often ate later. No doubt there would be an influx after nine o'clock.

'You never really saw Greeks on holiday years ago,' he said. 'They had no money, I suppose…'

He looked around, but there was no sign of Helen. Presumably she was busy in the kitchen, with the scary old

140

woman standing guard over her.

He was desperate to see her again. Yes, up close there were tiny lines around her eyes and one or two grey hairs on her head, but nothing like the ravages he felt time had visited upon him. She remained everything a goddess should be.

His group established itself at the same table, close to the water but a different waiter came across this time.

'This is Michalis,' she said. 'Last night it was Andreas.'

'*Kalí spéra*, Jenny,' said Michalis. '*Ti kánete?*'

'*Póli kalá*… I'm very well. *Kaí éssee?*'

'*Kalá.*' Just like Andreas, he ruffled Lewis' hair, and like the cool dude got a scowl in response.

'Eat? Drink?'

'We'll have a drink, then eat,' said Jenny. 'That ok?' The boys were hungry, but Daniel nodded. They could hold on for a while.

'*Krasí?*' Michalis was looking at Jenny.

'Yes. Wine. The usual, please.'

He looked at Daniel.

'One beer, one coke, one sprite, please. Oh, and a bottle of water – *neró*.' He would have liked to ask the waiter if Helen was cooking but would just have to see if she was around later.

'Amstel?'

'Yes, please. *Naí parakaló.*'

The waiter departed.

'So you've just been to Andros?' said Jenny. 'And you had to go back to Piraeus to come here… All a bit of a pain…'

'Yep.' He laughed. Memories of Piraeus were still fresh.

'It was funny?'

'Well, yes…'

The boys had left them to have one last paddle in the sea, so he could tell her about the Piraeus debacle.

They'd arrived late, only to find the last boat had cast off. They watched it sail away. Even the ticket kiosk was closing. They were effectively stranded on the dock for the night and Piraeus was no place to be wandering around after 10 pm with two young children: it was dark, pretty deserted and more than a little threatening. He decided he'd have to find two clean benches on the port where the boys could sleep whilst he stayed awake on watch.

But then a shifty looking man in a well-worn jacket sidled over to them. Daniel half expected him to pull a set of dirty photographs from an inside pocket. Instead, 'You want a hotel?' he said.

'Yes, we do.'

'One minute.'

He made a call on his mobile phone, then waved to them to follow. 'This way. Come now.'

Should they risk it..? Did they really have an alternative?

Daniel told the boys to pick up their packs and they trailed after the man, who led them down various side streets to a hotel which was grubbily brash with a smoky grey glass and steel frontage. It had an illuminated sign: 'Hotel Xtasy'.

Daniel had qualms.

The reception hosted five or six men who were casually propped around, smoking and drinking ouzo or Metaxa. Their guide said something in Greek to the young woman behind the counter and left. The men regarded them, silently.

The receptionist seemed a lovely girl and very out of place. She handed Daniel a key on a phallic key ring,

'One room. One bed..,' she said.

'That'll be fine.'

'Ok. Twenty-five euros. In the room is television.' Her face was concerned. 'Not for the children.'

If Daniel had already got some idea of what sort of place it was, all was even clearer when they reached Room 216. The bed had rich red sheets with a giant heart design whilst all around, on the small wardrobe, on the bed head, on the telephone, on the door to the bathroom, even on the walls, were small stickers of couples in different love-making positions. Jonny was working his way around them, sometimes tilting his head, as if wondering exactly how it all worked...

Jenny was laughing when Michalis arrived with the drinks and a menu. Since the boys were still cooling their feet and watching the tiny fish in the shallows, Daniel could continue...

He'd managed to get the children to sleep in the bed – it

was late and they were tired – then unrolled a sleeping bag for himself and lay on the floor. He listened to the sounds from the rooms around them (reminded of a Leonard Cohen song about lying awake in a hotel with paper-thin walls, listening to a couple having sex next door) but had to resist the temptation to put on the television and find what was on offer there. After all, the boys might wake. It was a real pity.

In his wakeful periods during the night – the screamings and bed rattlings disturbed him more than once – he had time to consider how the years and responsibility had changed him. This place would have been a wonderful discovery when he was young, and Mike would have been in his element. Now, though…

'Poor you,' she said. 'But, hey, Dan, that is one great story. If you hadn't been with the kids…'

'I would probably have gone back to the port and slept on a bench. I sometimes wonder what I've become.'

'Mature?'

'That's a thought. Anyway, I've sworn the kids to secrecy. They are never to tell a soul where we stayed. Especially their mother. I bet you one of them will do a talk on it at school someday. Then the social workers'll be at the door.'

'Certainly sounds like you hunkered down in some kind of brothel? You reckon?'

'Maybe. We'll never know for sure.'

The boys returned and settled around the menus which were in English and Greek.

Michalis returned, notebook in hand.

'Ok. Ready?'

'Two of us will have lamb chops, please,' said Daniel.

'No. Finished.'

'Ah. Shame. What are the big beans like?'

'Big beans. *Gigantes.*' He demonstrated with his thumb and forefinger. 'But tomorrow. Now, all gone.'

'Oh.' Daniel decided further engagement with the menu might prove fruitless. 'So, what do you have..?' He was trying to see what other people were eating. There was a strong smell of fish, but the boys wouldn't want that, and it was always expensive.

'Ok... We have...' And Michalis reeled off a list of Greek dishes, some explained, but all delivered too quickly for Daniel or the children to absorb.

'Spaghetti Bolognese, Lewis? I think that was in there somewhere.'

'Yes, please.'

'Moussaka, Jonny?'

He'd eaten that on Andros.

'Yes.'

'Does that come with anything?'

'No. You want fries?' said Michalis. Brevity seemed his forte.

'Fine. Two moussakas and one spaghetti Bolognese. *Efharistó.* And extra fries.'

'*Né. Pótates.* For one?'

'For two. Thanks. We're hungry... You can share mine, Lew. And a salad...'

'Greek salad? Ok. Local cheese or feta?'

'Feta, I think...'

Jenny discussed her order in Greek, then Michalis headed back to the kitchen.

'I should have warned you about the menu,' she said. 'It doesn't really work here. They cook what they have on any given day. Also, things disappear as the day goes on... and their deliveries are a little intermittent – they come from Athens.'

'The food is good though?'

'Indeed it is. Kyria Konstantinidis has always been the best cook on the island but it looks as if she's passing on her skills to your friend Helen. No fancy starters but lots of healthy food. No burgers... I have to say, though – until last night, I had no idea her protégé was English... I've never spoken to her...'

She looked across, perhaps to see if there was any sign of Helen. Daniel's gaze had been wandering that way since they arrived. He was trying to relax, but finding it difficult. He didn't tell Jenny how he was feeling. He liked her, but suspected he'd become a novelty and she was waiting for the next instalment of the soap opera.

144

Still, across the bay, the evening was offering that pale purity of light he remembered so well. In some ways, this was wonderful. But, oh, for Helen to join them…

They'd finished eating when a motorbike pulled up and a big man climbed off, wearing distressed jeans and an old Wham! tee shirt. Even overweight and with wild hair, Yiannis' features were still recognisable. He went straight into the taverna.

'He's huge. Do you know him, dad?'

Jonny rarely missed anything.

'I did, once upon a time, son…'

'Are we going soon?' asked Lewis. He'd been arranging and re-arranging his Yu-Gi-Oh! Cards for some time, but had begun to yawn and needed to get back to the campsite. It was a long walk for little legs. He wanted to call at the bakery on the way and buy an ice cream 'to keep him going'. Jonny had been playing card games with him, but had become bored and turned his attention to the Swiss army knife his father had bought for him from Barbara's Gift Shop earlier in the day. Daniel watched anxiously as his son whittled a stick he'd found, waiting for him to slice a lump out of some part of his hand or arm or leg.

'We'll need to settle the bill first,' said Daniel.

Jenny's attention was on Lewis. 'Plum tuckered out,' she said, in an exaggerated Texan drawl. 'The poor little critter needs to hit the concrete.'

'Careful,' said Daniel. 'Make fun of him and he might turn violent…'

But Lewis was so tired he didn't rise to the bait.

Andreas emerged from somewhere – he might well have been sleeping since last night or lying around in a drug-induced haze for all Daniel knew – and they paid. He thanked Daniel for the small tip. 'For Michalis,' he said, nodding. Greek honesty.

They were preparing to go and Lewis was already on his feet when Yiannis reappeared. He stood just a moment outside the door of the taverna, then strode towards them.

Jenny immediately turned to Daniel. 'Trouble?' she asked, quietly.

'No, no trouble. Of course not,' Daniel replied, but with much more confidence than he felt.

****

Helen had already settled Lilliana to sleep on her mother-in-law's bed. Downstairs by the window she put an arm around Sophia and her eldest daughter rested her head against her shoulder. She was a lovely girl who would steal hearts when she was older. Helen hoped not many would end up broken.

From inside, she'd kept an eye on Daniel since he arrived. Now, as her husband approached him Daniel stepped forward and offered his hand. Yiannis took it, then sat down with them. She wished she could be a fly on the table.

Yiannis shouted across to Michalis, who was sitting with Andreas. The waiter went over then came inside, opened the fridge and took out two beers, a coke, a Sprite and an ouzo, added glasses and carried them back across the road, his tray balanced at the regulation shoulder height.

She had known all along that there was nothing to worry about but was reassured as she watched the two men at the table talking and drinking together.

Yiannis had been calm after his mother told him about Daniel. He'd come to his wife and she'd told him there was nothing to worry about and he'd nodded. She'd never let him down. He surely knew she'd never be unfaithful.

The old lady was watching Yiannis and Daniel from her seat outside. Yes, visually she was like a crow, but she was actually a sober, loving symbol of calm, stability and continuity. Helen wondered how many Greek mothers back then would have accepted a black girl into their family, as Yiannis' mother had accepted Jeanette and loved her? How many would have welcomed a second English girl too, who pledged to bring up her children in the Greek Orthodox faith, as required at the wedding ceremony, but never would?

What mattered to Kyria Konstantinidis, *yiayiá*, was her family and their happiness. It was because of the matriarch's control of her family that Helen believed Yiannis would deal pleasantly with Daniel, as a friend might. His mother would expect the best from her son and Yiannis would not upset his mother.

He'd insisted on talking with Daniel himself: 'I am your husband, Eleni.' Jeanette often said he was still living in another age, unreconstituted, but Helen couldn't criticise him this time: what man would want an ex-lover hanging around his wife?

Daniel seemed slight and insecure against the vast bulk of her husband and, watching, she felt a pang she recognised from way back.

His return was a complication she'd never expected. Thankfully, tomorrow she could escape. She would be away from the restaurant, the gaze of her mother-in-law, which had been sharp for the last twenty-four hours, the heat of the kitchen and the pressure from Daniel's likely evening visit. It was one of her very irregular days off and she was booked to visit Jeanette and Kostas on Milos and stay the night.

Suddenly, Sophia sat up, rubbed her eyes, kissed her mother on the cheek then wandered out to be with her father. She must have been about the same age as Daniel's eldest and went around the table to stand beside him.

There was chatter, then everyone at the table started to laugh and Sophia covered her face, as if shocked. Helen wondered what she was missing and felt tempted to go and join them, but thought better of it.

Sophia ran back to her.

'Mama, the man said that papa used to lie on the beach with no clothes on.'

'Oh.' She laughed. 'That again. Yes. He was very young…'

'Oh, mama. That's still so bad. Papa! *Tóso agenís*!' Her mouth was open. She paused for a moment. 'Jonny is nice, isn't he?'

She ran back out so she didn't miss anything and pulled over a chair to sit between Daniel's lady friend and his eldest son. She had the wildness, the wilfulness, that was so Greek, but her hormones were kicking in too and she was becoming much more interested in boys. Soon, she would be a young woman.

Helen remembered her own adolescence and gave a customary shiver. Thank goodness Sophia would never suffer like that.

****

Despite her visits to the taverna, Jenny had never before spoken to Yiannis.

He had nothing in common with the effete men she knew in Athens. When he arrived at their table, like an ex-heavyweight boxer intent on retribution, she feared the worst. He reminded her of guys back home in southern honky-tonks, the ones who drank all night, regaled everyone in the bar with their thoughts on music and Mexicans and Dubya and fuckin' John Kerry while they grabbed at the waitresses, and then staggered away in their boots and wide hats to find their wives for as much rough sex as they could manage before passing out. Yet, in contrast, Yiannis proved surprisingly civilised, with beautiful eyes you could slide into and deep creases around them that must have come from smiling – and from smoking, of course. Although he was incredibly large, as if he filled twice the space anyone else might occupy, he was also splendidly dishevelled and not intimidating at all, like a blue-jean clad, scruffy Maharishi.

Importantly, there was something incredibly sensual about him. He would be passionate in the night, huge of hand and confident in body, caressing, probing. She was fascinated. Latching on to Daniel was proving an excellent move.

Yiannis raised his glass, 'And so, it is good to welcome you back, Daniel. We drink to your health. And to your family.' He nodded sagely at the boys, narrowing his eyes as though this was a serious matter. They had revived and were studying him: Jonny paid close attention to what he said whilst Lewis's gaze kept shifting, as if he couldn't believe the amount of hair all over him. 'And good health to Jenny,' said Yiannis.

She raised her glass of ouzo to him: '*Yamás.*'

'*Yamás*,' echoed Yiannis and Daniel.

'*Yamás*,' said Jonny, whilst Sophia watched him, every second. He pretended not to notice, though Lewis was missing nothing and gave up on Yiannis for a while to study the two of them as he sucked on his straw.

'And when did you meet?' asked Yiannis.

'*Mólis gnorísame*,' Jenny said. 'We've just met on the beach here. I live in Athens. Daniel lives in England. We've become friends. Just that... We're both free and single.' She knew how that sounded, but didn't care. When had flirting ever hurt anyone? He was Helen's husband but it was every girl for herself.

'I come to the island often,' she continued. 'I've seen you here before.'

'Yes. Helping mama. And some work on boats. And building...' He paused. 'So, Mike is still your friend, Daniel?'

Daniel had been less talkative than usual. That seemed logical. She wondered what was going through his mind.

'I haven't seen him for many years now...'

'Ah. Yes. People change... But you are happy to find Helen here...' It wasn't a question.

'Yes. And surprised. She hasn't changed at all. She is still so beautiful.' He was taking a risk. Maybe he couldn't help himself. 'You are a very lucky man, Yiannis.'

'Yes. I am. So many happy years. A good wife. A good family. A good life... And we have our girls.'

Sophia smiled broadly. Still, Jonny pointedly ignored her. Lewis continued to observe.

'The taverna belongs to your family, Yiannis?' said Jenny.

'To my mother, yes. My brother lives on Milos.' He turned to Daniel. 'Married with Jeanette.'

'And Helen works here every day.'

'Yes. With my mother. For many years now. My mother sees everything and Helen cooks. She is a very good cook.'

'She is,' said Jenny. 'The Konstantinidis Taverna is special.'

Yiannis beamed, accepting the compliment. He was more relaxed than when he first arrived. His smile, Jenny decided, promised satisfaction.

She wondered what Helen was expecting from this meeting. Sophia kept glancing towards the building and Jenny could glimpse someone – presumably Helen – watching from inside. The old lady was at her table following the progress too. Of course, in Greece the whole family would be involved. If it were a western, they might have been anticipating a shoot-out in the middle of Main Street.

Sophia got up and went around the table to her father. She was opposite Jonny and then his eyes were drawn to her. Yiannis stroked her hair as he talked. She wished she could have cared about Astraea like that but there's no way to account for your feelings. If only Stelios had the charm that was radiating from Sophia's dad. But he hadn't and he was history.

She saw what Helen had seen in Yiannis and guessed many other women had too. Ten minutes together and she was hooked. An Englishman from Yorkshire who worked in her school was fond of the term 'smitten', and she'd made fun of the word. He explained that it suggested obsessive attraction, but she'd thought it sounded like someone being smacked. However, in the case of Yiannis it captured the appeal of his rough edges, the unshaven cheeks and the comfortable clothes. And, of course, he had a kind of easy grace too: Richard Gere's charm, but much more real. She knew she was smitten.

Daniel came to life briefly and explained how he first met Yiannis. Everyone laughed. She imagined Yiannis naked.

'And how long do you live in *Athína*, Jenny?'

Daniel didn't seem to be his focus anymore. Maybe he thought he'd laid down his marker and Daniel was no competition anyway: why would Helen have anything to do with a balding boyfriend from twenty-five years before?

'Gee,' she said, 'it seems an age since I moved to Greece. Fifteen years, I guess… I've an ex-husband with a new partner in Athens. My daughter, Astraea, lives with them… I miss her sometimes. Maybe I don't see her as often as I'd like.'

She looked the world in the eye. Neither man seemed to know exactly what to say. She could sense both Yiannis and Daniel wondering at her admission but it was a reaction to which she'd become accustomed. Was it so strange, really?

This was her life and she could do what she wanted. Hell, Daniel's wife seemed no different. Jenny wasn't looking for sympathy or understanding. She could get closer to Astraea later, maybe. She'd never been interested in little kids and they could suck on that.

Daniel went inside to use the toilet but soon returned. She guessed Helen had avoided him.

A while later, Yiannis said his goodbyes and took Sophia with him.

As Daniel led his group back to the camp site, initially the talk was of love.

'Is Sophia going to be your girlfriend, then, Jonny?' Clearly, Lewis was trying to provoke him. 'She fancies you rotten.'

'Shut up.'

'Well, she does.'

'Well, she wouldn't fancy you, would she?'

Lewis kicked a stone in his direction.

'Enough,' said Daniel. 'Leave him alone, Lew. No wind-ups tonight. Or there'll be no ice cream.'

Lewis said nothing else, but looked as smug as a seven-year-old can.

'They seem a nice family,' said Jenny. 'Yiannis is very... personable.'

'Yep.'

'Damn him?'

'What?'

'Damn him..? It just seemed as if you might add that to your grunt. Just my imagining...'

He didn't reply and she said no more about it right then, because the boys were still there. She had her own thoughts, of course.

'So what about tomorrow?' she said.

He looked questioningly.

'If you have plans, that's fine. But I thought I might take a trip out of town. You ever been to the iron mine? Psili Ammos?'

'I'd never even been to Chora before last night.'

'Well, then? There are three spare seats in the car. But you'll have to do the pushing if it breaks down again.'

'Thanks. Why not? Fancy a trip, my children?' Perhaps he didn't mind her driving after all.

There was grudging acquiescence.

'Don't worry,' said Jenny. 'It'll be great. We can maybe walk a little way into the mine. Creepy stuff! And then a fabulous beach. We might even be the only ones there.'

'That sounds ok, dad,' said Jonny. 'Yep. Let's go. So long as Lewis shuts up.'

'And so long as Jonny doesn't go off behind the rocks with some girl,' said Lewis, ducking as his brother aimed a quite serious blow at his head.

When they'd said goodnight and Jenny was back in her tent, she lay on her sleeping bag holding her cellphone and thinking about the significance of exchanging telephone numbers. Yiannis had given her his number whilst Daniel was away; she'd passed him hers. The fact that it had been done furtively added a frisson of excitement.

It had been a fascinating evening, thoroughly enjoyable. It was worthy of a TV drama and she was keen to know where it would all end. Daniel was crazy about Helen, of that there was no doubt. His yearnings reminded her of some pathetically hesitant character from an English novel. She couldn't identify a similar American hero right now – maybe he was like Nick Carraway – but she knew Hemingway or Henry Miller wouldn't have been sitting around moping, hoping the woman they loved might just spontaneously decide to forgive them. They'd have made it happen.

She was much more impressed with Yiannis. He must be immensely strong, she thought. Obviously, he was a big man, but it wasn't all excess weight and his shoulders were wide and his arms were heavily muscled. Also, she had a thing about men's hands. His were workman's hands which said he was tough and capable and grounded. Yiannis, she felt confident, would fear nothing and tackle anything or anybody and could take what was there to be taken.

She thought of how Daniel and Yiannis had first met, and knew that if she were the one who woke up one night with

Yiannis lying beside her she would likely end up moaning rather than panicking.

As she waited for sleep, she touched herself, imagining the size of his erection and the pressure and roughness of his fingers.

****

Daniel took the boys into town for breakfast. He'd agreed they'd meet Jenny at her car.

Even walking along the beach, even reminding Lewis his sandals were leather and not made for paddling, he was still coming to terms with the strangeness of the previous evening. Helen had stayed away. Naturally, under the circumstances. But if Yiannis wanted to be friends with him, he couldn't understand why and certainly wouldn't encourage it. The man might have been likeable at another time, in another situation, in another life, but not here and not now. Presumably he was making a point, that he had nothing to fear and could trust his wife. The message had been received and understood, even if Daniel found it hard to accept.

He'd slept poorly. Twice he'd woken with a start, his head horribly full of the worst dreams, of Helen and Yiannis making love. It was all so foolish. When he looked at himself in the mirror in the toilet block, he saw a middle-aged man who should have accepted Helen had been lost long ago...

Serifos, meanwhile, remained attractive and, trying to be positive, he reasoned that he should make the most of that consolation. He'd spent years telling everyone it was his favourite place in the world; he'd endeavour to enjoy the day with Jenny.

The breakfast bar that Daniel had once loved had been transformed beyond recognition: it was bigger, with a new owner and a new clientele. Stavros and his cute family hadn't stayed for ever after all. It had become an ugly, brash self-service café for locals, with cheap steel tables and metal chairs, strung with plastic strips across the seat and back. No doubt the food and drink were inexpensive, but Daniel wouldn't be spending time there. Therefore, once he and the boys were approaching the port, Jonny, who loved being thought responsible, ran ahead to the bakery to buy three cheese pies, three yoghurts and a large carton of orange juice.

Daniel and his youngest sat on the side of the small quay, dangling their legs above the water, enjoying the morning sun, watching the little shoals of tiny fish darting below the keels of the fishing boats.

'Will it be a long drive, dad?'

'No idea, son. A few miles, I guess. Though, I suppose however far it is it will seem a long way with Jenny at the wheel.'

'She's good fun, isn't she, dad?'

'Face fixes into a rictus grin…'

'What?'

'Nothing. Nothing at all. Yes, she seems lovely.' He still was far from sure. 'Only, her driving leaves much to be desired…'

Jonny arrived back and they chewed through the pies, then Daniel fashioned spoons out of the yoghurt tops so they could eat from their cartons. They drank the juice, taking alternate swigs as the sun climbed higher. It was time to go.

Jenny's car was parked beyond the small bridge, under the trees, on the sand beside the road and opposite the old Perseus Hotel. She was already there, talking to a man in his 50s who had a huge grey beard. He was wearing garish shorts that flapped around his thin legs and a floral shirt which was under pressure from a bulging stomach. His skin was leathery, tanned deep brown. He must have had years of exposure to the sun.

'Hi, Dan. Hi, Lew, Jonny. Meet my friend St John.' She pronounced it Sinjon, in the upper-class English way.

'Hello there! From England, I'm told?' His accent had a resonance of cornfields, oak-beamed country pubs and flat Home Counties ale. 'Not many people from England make it to Serifos. Splendid place, isn't it?'

'Yes, it is,' said Daniel. 'Splendid.'

'Lovely to meet you all. I'm honoured.'

He shook hands with all three of them. Jonny and Lewis had never before met anyone who was honoured to meet them and offered their hands reluctantly, obviously trying to decide whether this odd old man was to be trusted.

'St John is the man with the boat,' said Jenny. 'It's his tent that I'm borrowing... Soon, he's off to..?'

'Hydra,' said St John. 'It's a beautiful island without any traffic – just donkeys – and the buildings tumble down the hillside to the port. It's where Leonard Cohen used to live. I've always thought I'm a bit like him. From the side.' He turned his head into profile and burst into a song: 'Jenny sweeps you down to her cave where men's dreams linger...'

Daniel remembered Helen used to love the original version, to which St John's parody bore little relation.

'Pure Cohen, eh? Pure Cohen!' St John said, then guffawed.

'You are truly all sexual allure,' said Jenny, her voice heavy with sarcasm. 'If we get utterly bored, you can sing depressing songs all the way home, hon... He's coming with us today, Dan. That ok? You don't mind?'

'It is your car.'

Actually, he was delighted. He assumed St John would sit in the front whilst he would be squashed into the back with the boys and wouldn't have to watch Jenny's erratic manoeuvrings as she wound the car over the hills. If he didn't have to watch, he could pretend they were safe.

'It is good to meet you, St John,' he said. 'It's a pity you're leaving.' They might otherwise have been offered a sail around the coast but nothing is ever as perfect as you'd like, he thought.

'Come on, men. To Mega Livadi!' Jenny bundled them in. 'We'll go the long way round and I'll show you the top of the island too.'

Brilliant, thought Daniel, wincing.

With numerous crashing gear changes, the journey took them forty minutes, though it seemed longer. The road rose, even beyond Chora, and dropped and curved sharply in places: Daniel was relieved he could look out of the side window and only had to worry about what would happen if she took them off the tarmac altogether, rather than panicking about the swerves to avoid occasional vehicles coming the other way and goats meandering out from the verges. The boys coped, though Lewis became quiet and incredibly pale as Jenny braked and accelerated. Maybe they should have given breakfast a miss.

'Do the boys miss their mom?' asked Jenny, casting tact out of the window along with a half-eaten sandwich that must have been sitting on her dashboard for some time.

'Not often.' Daniel's brevity was conscious. Were all Americans so insensitive? He punched the boys' shoulders, in an attempt to make them feel all right.

'And you work in publishing? You've still not really said much about your job.'

'Yep.' He might have gone into more detail if Jenny, at that very moment, hadn't thrown them to the left to avoid a huge ram which had wandered into the road. 'Nothing much to say about it.' He didn't want to distract her.

St John had said nothing since the first corner and Daniel could guess his emotions, gripped with terror and not trusting himself to make any sound because it was likely to transform into a high-pitched scream.

Still, they somehow arrived safely in Mega Livadi, once the hub of the Serifos mining industry.

The road dropped precipitously to the beach, where Jenny stopped her Cortina next to a taverna which had tables on the sand under shady trees. Daniel would have described the car as abandoned, rather than parked. He still had more manners than to ask where she passed her test, but assumed her examiner must have been drunk or blind or both.

They all climbed out sweaty and shaken, apart from Jenny who had obviously enjoyed the drive. St John took deep breaths and closed his eyes as his face relaxed. Jonny and Lewis headed straight towards the sea. The sand had a green hue, presumably from the iron in the local rock; Daniel hoped it wasn't toxic. They took off their sandals and waded in as far as they could go without soaking their shorts. Jenny, meanwhile, struggled to fasten her door with the customary piece of string.

'Have you been on outings with Jenny before?' asked Daniel.

156

St John shook his head. 'On the boat, yes. By car, no. Never.'

'Never again,' was the subtext.

'A drink?' asked Daniel. 'I need one.'

'Definitely,' said St John. He seemed pleased to still be alive. 'Let's all have one. On me.'

Since his new acquaintance was so rich, Daniel found that entirely acceptable.

Afterwards, they wandered to the old iron pier and examined the industrial remains, the buildings, the metal tracks and the cart on rusted rails. It was all such a contrast with the pretty beaches elsewhere. They collected large lumps of quartz that were lying around, glistering in the sun. From a New Zealander on the campsite, Daniel had borrowed *Greek Island Hopping*, a book which claimed to be the Bible for tourists. Its author wrote that the mine's abandoned main building reminded visitors of something you might find in a war-torn banana republic. That much was accurate.

As Jenny had promised, one shaft, which you entered through a large doorway, did lead right through the hill but it was dark and dank and a long walk and you needed good torches – and torches had not been on the list when they were packing.

Anyway, sightseeing was not what the boys enjoyed and it was cold and spooky in the tunnel and Jonny and Lewis wanted to resume their proper holiday.

'Can't we go for a swim now, dad?' said Lewis. 'Down there by the taverna..?'

'We can do better than that, kids. Psili Ammos?' said Jenny.

Lewis looked highly suspicious.

'Psili Ammos is a cute beach and it's much more beautiful than here. It means 'Fine Sand' in Greek. There are trees for shade, low dunes and two tavernas where we could eat.'

'Let's go now then,' said Lewis, immediately full of life again.

'Dad?' Both boys looked at Daniel.

'Dan? Wanna take a look?'

'*The Sunday Times* says it's the most beautiful beach in Europe, I'm told.' St John spread his arms wide. 'And if you can't trust *The Sunday Times*, who can you trust?'

'I suppose.'

'I've sailed into there on numerous occasions, and it's splendid. First rate.' He was interminably pleasant, but a caricature nonetheless.

'You've sold it to me, St John. Let us away.'

It meant another drive. Daniel steeled himself and caught St John's eye. The sailor had agreed to the trip but his look was saying he wished he'd drunk a great deal more while the opportunity was there.

One advantage, thought Daniel, would be that they wouldn't be eating at Konstantinidis'. He couldn't face another evening with Yiannis: that would have seared his sense of loss even deeper into his soul.

****

They drove back to the port – 'Which is actually called Piso Livadi,' shouted Jenny to Daniel, who was in the back again, with the wind battering him though the open window. 'That's Little Livadi. We've just been to Mega Livadi – Megalo Livadi – which means Big Livadi, believe it or not. There's hardly anything there. Crazy, huh? Very Greek.'

'Maybe it was big once,' he shouted, but got no response.

Soon they were out of town again, winding into the hills before descending to Psili Ammos itself, at the other side of the island. The final section was down a dangerous unmade track, all pebbles and ruts, which Jenny negotiated in her wild-cat way. They came to a skidding halt in a parking area behind what turned out to be one of the two tavernas. The air inside the car was heavy with dust and relief.

A motor scooter and three cars were the only other vehicles there.

Jenny led the way around the side of the building and down through the grasses and gorse to the beach, which was truly stunning and almost deserted. The only buildings to be seen were the tavernas: one towards the centre of the curved bay, back amongst trees, and the other, behind which they had parked, could be accessed via some steps from the beach. It had shady terraces with a panoramic view.

The wind was blowing hard and there was a tidal swell; huge waves pounded on to the soft nearly-white sand. There were just four other couples there, spaced far apart. It was a truly beautiful place. The traumas of the drive had been worth it.

Daniel wished Helen was with them, but he knew he'd survive without her. We do, he thought. He had before. We don't die of love, he sighed to himself, rubbing his chin.

'Shady trees again,' he said. They were strung along the beach.

'Tamarisks,' said Jenny. 'Same as on the other beaches. They thrive on salt water. There's something about salt, isn't there? You know, like we lick up saltiness whenever we can.' She winked at St John, who looked pleased but embarrassed. 'And they're whitewashed round the bottom…'

'All the trees are,' said Jonny.

'Yep. It's supposed to keep the ants off them and it helps keep them cooler in summer. Like a suncream. Some people think white bottoms are attractive.' She tapped St John's and he stepped away, looking embarrassed.

A strong breeze had picked up and the sea was angry, raging. With exciting dives through the waves, bodies thrown up on to the shore, shouts and laughter, an hour flew by. Jonny and Lewis played like a pair of otters. Daniel taught them how to body surf: they waded in until they were waist deep, turned their backs to the ocean then threw themselves forward as a big wave swept in so they were carried to the land. He trusted they'd be thrown on to the beach before they drowned.

Jenny was sitting under a tree. She shook her head when Daniel tried to persuade her to join them: 'You guys! No chance!' Seemingly devoted, St John sat beside her, as if star-struck. When he went off to use the toilet in the nearest taverna, Daniel left the water and took his place for a moment.

'Why are you ferrying us around, Jenny?'

'I'm kinda fond of you.'

'We appreciate it. And St John?'

'He's doing me a favour. I'm just returning it.'

'You could have driven around with just him.'

She laughed. 'Yep. That would have been…' She had run out of words. She tried again: 'That would have been great but…'

'Mm. We're actually here to protect you and divert him...'

She put a hand on his bare leg.

'I like you, Dan. I'm always open to diversions, you know…'

It was hard to tell if she was being serious. 'You're crazy.' He glanced at her hair, her face, her body and knew if Helen had not been there and the kids had been at home with their grandmother, he would have responded. But she was and they were and his dreams were about Helen and that was that.

'Dad! Come on!'

He went back to the boys.

Only when Lewis was utterly exhausted did they all dry themselves, though the fine sand had got into their bags, their hair and ears and inside all their clothes. Then they climbed to the higher taverna.

'Better food here,' said Jenny.

The wind dropped as the day ended and the remarkable Greek stillness was all around.

They sat at a large table, the only customers, and Jenny ordered in confident Greek as the roseate evening settled itself over the water. The talking became louder with more jugs of wine. The boys were permitted to have second bottles of fizzy drinks, allowed extra sugar just this once.

All of them were high-spirited, but as the darkness fell Daniel quietened, because he had Helen on his mind.…

After St John had offered to pay and Daniel had said, 'No, we can't let you do that,' and he'd insisted and Daniel had given in without a struggle, they returned to the car. Only one other remained, though the driver was nowhere to be seen. Perhaps he'd hiked over the headland or gone down to the other taverna or was lying further along the beach with his girlfriend.

Jenny laughed her way across the car park. '*Opa, opa*', she sang, spinning.

She stumbled and hung on to St John's shoulder. Then she put an arm around his waist and lightly kissed his cheek and ruffled his hair. The alcohol had obviously heightened her libido. Any sailor in a storm? St John looked suitably appreciative. Daniel wondered if somewhere inside the Etonic persona he had more going for him than might first appear. It was hard to imagine. Of course, his money would be a significant lure, especially if you were Jenny and you were drunk. So many rich men seemed to be surrounded so often by so many attractive women…

She settled herself behind the wheel as Daniel braced himself in the back for what would be a mercifully short drive. He would have buckled in himself and the boys if only the anchors for the seat belts hadn't been broken. Maybe they didn't have MOTs in Greece? He would never have risked their safety in England, especially with Jenny driving and when she'd drunk so much, but he didn't want to have to coax Lewis all the way back along the road. They should be safe. It was late and he doubted they'd encounter any other cars.

'Jeez, St John, you are special,' said Jenny as she started the engine and slammed the car into reverse, 'paying for all that.'

They shot backwards.

Immediately, there came the crunch of metal on metal. They were all jolted back then thrown forward as the engine cut out.

Both boys screamed, Daniel shouted 'Shit!' and St John, 'What..?' Jenny was silent for just a few beats, then groaned 'Fuck! Fuck! Fuck!' as she hammered her head on the steering wheel.

They threw open the doors. St John and Jenny emerged and stood in silence, assessing the damage. Daniel and the boys clambered from the back.

They'd smashed into the other car. If it had looked like a battered old Ford Escort to begin with, it now looked even more ready for the scrap yard. The driver's door was stoved in and Jenny's bumper had smashed into the footwell. It was lucky no-one had been inside.

'Fuck! Fuck! Fuck!' Jenny's range of vocabulary hadn't extended. Her eyes wide, she tugged hard on her hair. 'St John, you have to help me out here,' she said.

'Yes...' He sounded hesitant. 'How? Because..?'

'You just have to, hon...'

'What do you want me to do?'

'Just say you were driving, hey? Say it's your car. Pay them what they want. You know how it works...'

'But...'

'Look, I've got no money. They'll be here soon. If we don't offer them something, they'll get the police. You know that.'

'The insurance will pay...'

'I don't have insurance.'

Daniel, still checking both Jonny and Lewis were fine, stopped, registering the enormity of what she was saying.

'That could prove a problem,' said St John.

'Yeah. So, come on. It's nothing to you. You know how fond I am of you, St John...'

She would never get away with it, would she?

A man was pounding up from the beach, shouting as he came. The noise of the crash must have carried a long way, especially since the wind had dropped. Jenny seemed close to panic. 'Just say "yes", St John... Please! Yes..?'

'Look, just own up. I'll help you out with some cash.'

'St John, look.... I've not passed my test, all right? If they report this, I'm gonna be in deep, deep shit.'

Daniel was slipping into deeper levels of disbelief. 'All Americans can drive. You must have passed,' he said.

'Not me, ok? Not me. But you know I can drive. You know that...' Daniel thought about all their near-misses, about the parking area up in Chora with the sheer drop... 'I can drive but I've just not passed my test. Anyway, I only drive on Serifos, nowhere else... So, St John, waddyasay? Hon..? Please? Please?'

The other driver, furious, was almost upon them, with a woman following. Daniel shepherded the boys away into the night. Jenny and St John could sort this out themselves. He wanted nothing to do with it.

She could have killed them. One thing was certain: she wouldn't drive them anywhere again and no matter how long it took, they were walking back to Coralli. He didn't care how tired the kids were.

He wouldn't go the same way as his parents. He would not die in a car crash.

Chapter 5

It was on Serifos that Helen had come to terms with everything: with herself, with her past, with those long terrible hours she'd feared she would never properly escape. She no longer trembled at her memories – the probing fingers, bad breath, hidden love bites, the secret pain. On Serifos, she'd been transformed.

The Greek sun bleached her past just as it lightened the rocks by the sea. Increasingly, she felt cleansed. And she became more and more alive amongst the old stones and the cool houses, in her skin, in her new culture, amongst olive trees.

She had never needed just an escape. Hope and commitment were what mattered. And, finally, she had won respect to add to the adoration of the man she never thought she could properly love. Now, she had a home.

She had embraced a different way of living, eagerly, impressively as the years passed. The harmonies of Greece permeated her soul. She could sing with Nicos Xylouris when the sun went down and sway to the rhythms of Eleni Tsaligopoulou at gatherings, tossing her hair as the men watched her move. Maturity gave her confidence. She was still slim. Her body was not worn by the passing of so many seasons, not spoiled by the childbearing. She'd been lucky. When she peered into the mirror, her face was hardly lined. She looked like she did when she thought she'd won the heart of Daniel, all those years ago. Only, now she knew more and had confidence too.

She had tamed her husband. She'd built a business. She watched over her girls. Her own childhood and adolescence were hardly even a distant memory.

She'd thought her life on Serifos had healed her. Until now.

'My head is a mess,' she said to Jeanette. 'I truly don't know what to think any more.'

'Well, I'm not sure I can help, but do I want to see Danny. I'm keen to assess this new improved version. There was much room for improvement, wasn't there?'

Jeanette had come back with Helen from Milos leaving Kostas to care for their brood.

The two women arrived on the early morning ferry and headed straight to the taverna, where Kyria Konstantinidis was supervising in Helen's absence, her skin yellow in the dim kitchen as they entered. She kissed Jeanette on both cheeks, asked about the family, then took to her chair by the door, silent and squinting as she watched Andreas wiping dust off the tables outside.

Katerina, who helped with preparation, was peeling onions, chopping tomatoes and frying meats. The air was full of spice and garlic and Helen took charge, fastening on an apron and bustling back and forth, almost immune to the heat after all these years. Jeanette sat to one side.

'You don't need to go seeking him, Jan. He'll be here tonight. Hanging around. Haunting me.' She said it playfully, unusually flattered by the novelty of his attention.

The day away had done her good. They'd driven to Pollonia, walked beside the sea towards Polyegos View, swum in the quiet cove and then returned to the harbour, relaxing in a sea-side taverna through the afternoon. It was quality girl-time and gave Helen the chance to talk honestly. They'd ordered half a kilo of Malamatina, olives, salad and zucchini balls in the Alkis Taverna as small rowing boats danced before them, and Helen started to get her emotions under control. Then they returned to Jeanette and Kostas' villa, behind high walls and under centuries-old fig trees. Kostas had become a successful man and Jeanette's life was good.

When Katerina moved, Helen inspected the stifado.

'Danny sounds transformed.'

'Don't expect miracles. He was never some sort of god, you know. I got that wrong. And he isn't now. He'll be glad to see you, but he's only what he is.'

'Maybe the lady doth protest overmuch.'

'And maybe the other lady believes she knows everything.'

'Touché. But you still think he's attractive, you said as much.'

'Bald men aren't attractive. They're…' She struggled.

'They're… antique… shop soiled… worn…'

'Ah-ha. You've got the hots for a seedy old man now. I guess a change is as good as a rest.'

Once, Helen would have shuddered but the little girl who'd suffered had become a stronger person in this new world.

'I didn't say he's old… Hey, Katerina!' She pointed to the stove.

'*Sygnómi*, Eleni!' Katerina rushed over and lowered the heat.

Helen turned a serious face to Jeanette. 'He's… just… older.'

'So are we all.'

'Anyway, it was long ago. It was a holiday fling.' Who was she kidding? 'Remember what we were like back then?'

'Of course. And your first love meant nothing at all. Who said, "First love never dies"? They've no idea what they're talking about…' She was teasing. 'So I'll just wander along and check him out on that basis.'

But before she moved Yiannis strode through the door, surprising them both, vigorous and smiling. He kissed Jeanette on her cheeks – 'You are more beautiful by the day, Jeanette. Welcome!' – then headed towards Helen with his arms wide.

'My beautiful wife. *I ómorfi gynaíka mou!*'

He wrapped himself around her and kissed her, then stepped back, holding her at arms' length.

'I am a lucky man. *Se agapó.*'

'Yiannis! Let go. Of course you love me. But what are you doing here? You're supposed to be working today. And you smell of sweat. Let go. I'm cooking.'

Katerina was smiling, pretending to ignore his performance.

He laughed loudly. 'See, see Jeanette. So wonderful, so… spirited, my wife. Eleni, Eleni, I miss you.'

'For God's sake,' said Helen. 'I've only been gone a day… Now, I have things to do and you are dirty. Out of my kitchen!' She flapped a cloth at him, unable to imagine what had brought this on.

'You drive me away, but I go dreaming of you.'

After gazing at her for several seconds, as if revering a

precious necklace, he left with an affectionate '*Geiá,*' presumably returning to the apartments where he was working. His mother shoo-ed him out on to the road. He threw some comment towards Andreas, started his bike and skidded away.

'What's got into him?' asked Jeanette. 'I don't have to ask about romance in your life, girl. Has he been watching old episodes of *The Love Boat..*? Ok, ignore me... Anyway, it's time I went to discover things: I'm off to visit Livadakia and Danny. I'll report back.'

She gave Helen a quick hug, bade a breezy farewell to her mother-in-law and headed towards the campsite beach.

Helen checked on the stifado again and the mince for the moussaka, then perched on a chair just inside the doorway. Katerina was preparing fresh batches of tsatziki and egg-plant salad. Across the road, Andreas sat out of the sun smoking, sipping frappé and watching the world go by. It was still and quiet in the mornings – outside the kitchen – and Helen grabbed a moment's peace to think about Yiannis and consider how lucky she'd been in her life. Yes, at times she'd doubted his loyalty but she knew she should be grateful to have him.

****

Jenny adjusted her small inflatable pillow and sighed with contentment. She loved the tent; St John had done well. It was a Canadian model with netting sections at the front and under broad flaps on the top which could be opened so heat was released and cooling air passed through. In addition, it was well-positioned and the trees all around provided full shade much of the day.

She looked at her watch: 11.30. She had caught up on badly needed sleep. She drank from her bottle of water then lay back and stretched out languidly. It had been quite a night. Her cup was full to overflowing.

She would be without her car for a couple of days but St John had been a hero to take responsibility and provide the money to keep her out of trouble. Clearly, he'd hoped to spend the night with her as his reward but, after all, no. Although she loved sex, she had standards and made a point of never selling herself, unless it was absolutely necessary or she was irredeemably drunk.

She began to sort out the tent before it was hit by the glare of the afternoon sun: clothes tidied, tissues into a blue supermarket bag for removal, sand swept to the front opening and outside. After spreading her sleeping bag to freshen over a line that St John had run for his washing between two trees, she took her towel and headed for the showers.

She was tingling and in such good humour that she was happy to sit on the low wall next to the shower block for twenty minutes until it reopened. The owner and his eldest son were opening manholes and struggling to clear the latest blockage in the drains. It amazed her that people still tried to flush paper – and sanitary products – down the toilets. She knew her mother would have been appalled if she'd been instructed to put her toilet paper in a bin, or, worse, had been the one required to empty the bin, especially after visitors. But it was all part of life in Greece. The pipes were so narrow they only coped with liquid. Why didn't foreigners get it?

There was a bad smell in the air but nothing mattered after the night she'd had.

When she sauntered on to the beach much later, after a coffee, bread and honey in the site's snack bar, Daniel was under his usual tree. He seemed proprietorial about his spot but must have been getting there early each day to claim it before others moved in. Whilst Jonny and Lewis read books, he was chatting to an attractive black woman who laughed a lot.

'Jenny. Hi,' he said, in what she thought was a less than welcoming tone. 'This is Helen's sister-in-law, my old friend Jeanette, who lives on Milos.'

'Thanks for the 'old'…'

'And Jeanette, this is Jenny, who has things in common with you. She's American but lives here too. In Athens…'

He didn't mention the previous evening. She noted that she was not named as a 'friend' either. When Dan and his boys had simply abandoned her and St John in the car park and set off back the night before, she'd thought him pretty ungracious. After all, she'd chauffeured them around. She knew he was upset because she hadn't a license but even so... Anyway, she imagined he'd come round; and if he didn't, who cared?

She said hello and sat beside them on her towel.

'You managed to get it all sorted last night?'

He didn't describe what had happened, so they must have discussed it before her arrival.

'Yep. St John is pretty amazing.'

'I am assuming you are unlikely to be incarcerated until later...' She supposed this was a joke. 'So what's happening with your car?'

'It's not bad at all. I mean, it only has to be drivable. It's not a looker. We don't worry about that...' She looked to Jeanette for confirmation. 'There's a guy here who can make it roadworthy for a hundred and fifty euros, and St John's covering that, bless him.'

'It was fit to move?' Daniel was obviously wondering how she got it back from Psili Ammos.

'We got it moving. It would still drive, but it was kinda clanky and slow. I drafted in some local support.'

He didn't delve further but Jonny was listening.

'Yiannis?' he asked, casually, without looking up from his book.

Eyes turned, first to Jonny, then back to Jenny.

She was taken by surprise. 'Well...' She knew she sounded guilty. Daniel looked at Jeanette. 'There's nothing like a local knight in shining armour,' said Jenny. She was desperate to make light of it but wondered how Jonny could possibly have known.

She sensed Daniel had questions but was holding back. Jeanette must have been biting her tongue but doubtless this news would be with Helen within the hour.

Jenny felt trapped. She wished she'd given the beach a miss and gone to see St John, as she'd originally intended.

'He's kind. He's a friend of a mechanic and put me on to him right away, even at that time. Guess I'll owe Yiannis a drink. Two maybe.'

She could brush it aside, all would be well. She was just hoping no-one would ask how she knew Yiannis' number.

'I saw him leaving this morning,' said Jonny, innocently,

still without raising his eyes. 'Yiannis.'

'It must have been last night, sometime, honey...'

'The sun was coming up...'

Although he still looked at the page in front of him, the boy sounded adamant.

'I'm sorry...?'

'I needed the toilet,' said Jonny. ''Thought it was him... He was heading out towards the car park. He's hard to miss, isn't he?'

Jenny couldn't tell whether he was speaking with the innocence of a child or just wanted to stir the pot. Either way, her satisfaction had gone and, no longer full, her cup had become as dry as her throat. There was a long silence. She could think of nothing to add that might even begin to make things seem right.

****

Jenny left almost immediately, struggling through an awkward departure ('I need to go... People to see... Mechanics to advise... St John to thank yet again...') but Daniel and Jeanette were still not free to talk because young ears were still listening. Lewis was lying on his plastic beach mat constructing some sort of miniature building with stones, sticks, bits of broken bamboo and the tree's thinnest roots. Jonny was still glued to Harry Potter and the Philosopher's Stone.

'I think,' said Daniel, 'it's time for a swim.'

'OK, good idea,' said Jeanette.

'I'll come,' said Lewis.

'Nah, not this time, Lew. We're going to be swimming way out...'

He looked to Jeanette for support.

'Yes, that's right.'

'We can have a game afterwards.'

'But I'm a good swimmer, dad. You know that.'

'You are and I do know. But the waves do not... It might be dangerous. And you said you feel tired... You can look after Jonny for me. You just finish that...' He couldn't complete the sentence.

'It's a castle,' said Lewis, his tone suggesting it was blindingly obvious.

'Of course it is. So you just keep working on the... motte and bailey, and give Jeanette and me a moment or two.' He nodded at her: 'Jeanette?'

'Yeah, I'm ready.'

She slipped off her yellow kaftan and they waded in, swimming steadily until they were at a distance from the children.

'Jesus, eh?' said Daniel.

'I wish I hadn't come,' she said, rising with two bigger waves.

'I'm pleased to see you.'

'I didn't mean I wish I hadn't come to see you. I mean...'

'Yep, I know.'

They were working hard, treading water.

'I should be asking you about Kostas and your kids...' They bobbed together. 'But now...! Yiannis... Shit... Will you tell her?'

'I have to, don't I? How though..?'

Daniel's mind was churning as he devised massive plans, instantly: let the marriage collapse, Helen could leave Yiannis and come back to England, somehow he'd manage to afford a place big enough to house four children...

But whilst he could believe almost anything of Jenny, how could Yiannis have done that...? He had Helen, and yet he slept with Jenny. Daniel presumed they had sex. He found it hard to imagine they were discussing the Iraq War until dawn. Even knowing how marriages can stagnate, how pleasure can turn into routine, how eyes can stray, hands can wander, libidos peak and trough; even knowing that marriage bonds can wear into gossamer – even then, he couldn't imagine how anyone would choose Jenny over Helen, even for novelty, even to sample the excitement of an illicit fumble in a tent. He couldn't think of a single reason. Jenny might have led him on, but he had no need to follow. Even if Yiannis was drunk, how could there be an excuse?

He'd become so righteous.

'I couldn't tell her,' he said, finally. 'No matter what I'm thinking, I could never hurt Helen. Not again.'

'Oh, Danny.' Rising and falling in the swell, Jeanette registered the emotions he himself was feeling.

'It's Jenny's fault, you know, not Yiannis'. She's careless and selfish… I suspect she just can't help it.' He was shocked by his own magnanimity.

'That might well be. But Yiannis had a choice. And have there been others..? He was like a newly married twenty-year-old around Helen this morning...'

'Guilt?'

'Probably… Danny, it's great to see you again, and your kids are brilliant, but I wish I hadn't been here today. I wish I'd been somewhere else with Kostas.' She began to kick back to the shore and shouted over her shoulder, 'I wish I'd been anywhere else.'

****

The busy lunchtime was finished. Katerina and her friend Anna were washing up, Yiannis' mother had retired for her afternoon sleep and Andreas was at his table. Helen too could relax for a while.

Inside, Sophia and Lilliana were huddled together over a mess of writing paper. Sophia had decided to test her sister's maths. Sophia was not just pretty, she was very clever. Helen had high hopes for her: she was headstrong but with such fluency in both English and Greek, who knew what she might achieve? Lilliana, a devoted little sister, hung on her words. Helen watched them and smiled. She could sit and watch them all day. Could she allow feelings for Daniel to ruin all this?

Anyway, for now she had to concern herself with life's practicalities because in summer she seized any time she could: her immediate priority was to go and sort the washing. Jeanette would find her there. Andreas and Katerina could deal with any customers, who would probably only want drinks at this time of day. And as always there was warm food in the trays, already prepared.

Sophia and Lilliana bundled together their things and the three of them headed home, to the house where she'd first met Yiannis. It was all theirs because his grandmother had died many years before and his mother insisted on living over the taverna, to be on hand when needed. She had always looked much older than her years but Helen knew there would soon come a time when the she'd need their care. For now, her independence was a blessing; she and Yiannis had their privacy.

The washing was in the machine and she was sweeping the terrace when Jeanette appeared.

'You've been a while.'

'We had things to talk about.'

With a glass of water, they sat at the table, sheltered under the awning.

'So, how is he, really?'

'Well, it seems. He's done a pretty fair job of bringing up the kids on his own, I'd say. They don't often see their mum... He sort of suggested they divorced because he was in love with someone else...'

Helen didn't know that.

'Anyway, they've just moved into a new house, in Leicester. It's nearer to where he works. Some guy who's half Greek and half American who's camping near them has given him a dried pomegranate for good luck, so that's nice...'

In love with someone else...

'He's in educational publishing, which sounds boring.'

But extremely respectable.

'So... what sort of a man is he now?'

'Very decent, I'd say... I like him. Well, I always liked him, but he's grown up. And I like his kids, which is often a sign...' She faded away, uncomfortable, looking across to the hills.

'Something's bugging you. Is it something he said?'

'No.'

'Come on, then...'

Jeanette sipped from her glass, gazing into the distance. The mountains were steep and barren. They'd be hard to climb.

'It's… tricky…'

'Try.'

Jeanette turned.

'It's…'

Helen braced herself, expecting to hear that Daniel was proposing to move to Serifos to be near her; or he'd asked Jeanette to bring a message asking her to go back to England with him; or he was actually deeply depressed and suicidal over her. She'd feared he'd bring problems.

'Is it something terrible? What is it? Jan…?'

Jeanette offered a weak smile. 'Look, I have to tell you. I know I do… But you'll be upset…' Somewhere nearby, a cock was crowing. 'It's not Danny, it's Yiannis…' Was he ill? Or what had he done? 'Little Jonny thought he saw him at the camp site this morning…'

'At Coralli? What was he doing there?'

'… He might have imagined it.'

Helen knew her friend. She knew Jeanette didn't believe that for one moment.

'God. Was he looking for Daniel?'

'No. I'd say not.'

'Good… But he didn't have work there...'

Jeanette's awkwardness was increasing. She turned the glass round and round in her hands.

Helen felt sick. 'Tell me.'

Jeanette closed her eyes and sighed, then whispered, 'He was there at dawn… Look, he could be totally innocent.' That wasn't convincing. 'Who knows what he was up to? It could have been absolutely anything... I mean, nothing at all… But I had to say, didn't I..? I'm sorry.' Jeanette couldn't hide her own distress.

Everything around was closing in. The walls pushed inwards and she found it hard to breathe.

'That makes no sense.'

Jeanette was summoning up her courage. 'Nothing's clear. You need to talk to Yiannis... But... he might have been with Danny's friend, Jenny. Maybe...'

Helen's core was suddenly ripped away, as if a huge pain was burning through her. This happened to other people. It couldn't happen to her. But Jeanette's discomfort told her this wasn't some fantasy.

'He was with her... all night?'

'Well, maybe not. Or there could be a reason.' Helen couldn't think of a single one. 'Most likely nothing happened, eh? He was just there, that's all.'

'He was there. There, with that woman... And where were his daughters..? He left them here? In this house? On their own..?'

A light dawned. Feeling numb now, Helen went inside and returned with a page torn from a notebook. On it were telephone numbers she didn't recognise. She'd taken it from a pocket in Yiannis' jeans as she was sorting the washing. She handed it to Jeanette.

'He hasn't written this, Jan. Who do you think did?'

They both stared at a small piece of paper that seemed of huge importance.

Jeanette shook her head.

There was a mobile number and another which began '21' so it was an Athens land-line and it was written in a woman's hand. Anyway, that was what Helen believed now.

Jeanette put her arms around her and Helen cried.

After Jeanette left, reluctantly but as planned because she had to get the ferry back to Milos to take care of her children, Helen stayed on the terrace, alone in her new awful world, distraught, with a developing fury she'd not felt for many years. She couldn't bring herself to ring the mobile number and knew she didn't need to.

Above, clouds were moving towards Serifos from the south west. Once upon a time, there had been endless sun in summer.

In the house, Lilliana began to cry and Sophia shushed her to try to stop the screaming. Even at a time like this, Helen's life wasn't her own and she went to comfort her daughter.

She was expected back at work but a new batch of stuffed vine leaves wasn't important. Katerina and Anna could prepare them.

She would wait where she was. Yiannis would come home sooner or later.

****

Jenny was not usually one to feel self-conscious and was renowned for her thick skin but she knew when she wasn't wanted. After Jonny's news and the awful silence, she retreated to her tent and left Dan and Jeanette to talk about her harlotry. If she was feeling paranoid, it was hardly surprising because their reactions had been as stony as Lia Beach.

They were seeing her as the Scarlet Letter personified, yet for all they knew she and Yiannis might have just been talking until first light.

Of course, she and Yiannis weren't teenagers.

Despite the backlash, she didn't regret what had happened. How could she, when the sex had been unforgettable? And any fault lay with Yiannis, surely, not her? He was the one who was married, he was the one with kids and he was the one with that huge penis that led him to her tent and then inside. And then inside. She'd welcomed him – who wouldn't? – but why should she be the one tarred and blamed? He'd been called in to rescue her car, not to screw her. He was the one who had done what he'd done and her conscience was clear.

Frustratingly, if Jonny hadn't spotted him, all would have been well. They'd almost got away with it. As a long-time devotee of *Scooby Doo*, she heard a voice inside her head snarling, 'That pesky kid.'

She'd certainly not set out to hurt Helen: she remembered well how she herself felt when Stelios began to test new mattresses. But she didn't dwell on that now: life moves on and girls just wanna have fun. She brushed her hair, donned her pink cap and favourite tee shirt, decorated with the Stars and Stripes and advertising 'Wild Bill's Crazy Circus', and drifted into town.

She lingered over a frappé in a taverna. As usual, she had it with condensed milk and sugar, hating herself for the calories and aware of how fattening it was. She touched her stomach, lightly, and vowed to be more abstemious in future. She couldn't allow herself to lose what was left of her figure; she needed all the help she could get to reel them in.

But she could afford this one treat because she'd burned off a few thousand calories overnight.

Jeanette came past, probably on her way to meet the next ferry, looking distracted and showed no sign of having noticed Jenny, who peered down into her glass. She must have told Helen everything. By now, the cat would be not only out of the bag, it would be shitting on the front porch.

Soon after, St John appeared from the Condilis supermarket and made a bee-line for his boat. Again, she was pleased he didn't notice her. He'd have come fawning round, expecting some reward for his good deeds and she didn't want to sleep with him. His advances had impressed her not at all. Her main objection to their rapid couplings a couple of years before hadn't been his bloated body, nor the even less attractive beard; it was that he had been so unnervingly flaccid.

She sipped the cold coffee and felt a warm glow as she remembered the contrasting firmness of Yiannis as he nuzzled her pussy.

When she'd paid and was leaving, the man himself appeared, his motorbike approaching from a cloud of dust. As she stepped into the road he stopped his Yamaha, beaming, unaware that she was to be the purveyor of very, very bad news.

'Jenny. *Yássou!*' He used the more familiar term of greeting, as well he might since only hours before he had been between her legs while she whispered, 'Oh, my god! Oh, my god!' in a torment of pleasure, trying not to wake everyone on the site. It would be a while before she forgot those tremors, that surging sense that he was giving her everything she wanted but still leaving her wanting more. It had been an age since she'd experienced anything like it.

'*Yássou,* Yiannis.'

She would have liked to invite him for an afternoon treat, but couldn't. 'Yiannis, there's a problem,' she said. Straddling his bike, he looked unconcerned. 'It's not a problem for me. You have a problem…' Whatever he was expecting, he looked amused. How could she soften it? She didn't think she could, because his life was about to change, possibly forever. 'Yiannis, Jeanette knows you were with me…'

His face changed as he processed the information.

'*Gámo!*' He swore, his eyes widened, instantly changed, mightily perturbed.

'She might have told Helen already, hon. They don't know that we slept together, but… they know you left this morning. I didn't tell them… You were seen. I'm sorry. I just had to let you know. It's bad. I know it is.'

He swore again, but more softly. He'd arrived with the dash of Steve McQueen but now his certainty was gone. His lips tightening, he looked haunted.

There was nothing she could do for him. He'd made his bed and would have to lie in it. It had been his choice to have sex in hers, but everyone knows there's often a bill to pay in the morning.

Without saying anything more, he nodded, twitched a forced smile, restarted the engine and abruptly swung the front wheel back in the direction from which he'd come. As she watched him ride away from her, she guessed he'd probably not be coming back, which would be sad, because she wanted to have him again. And again and again.

****

The boys were still reading. Pat-pat went the bats and balls. A large wave rolled in because the Agios Georgios had cut across the bay, blaring its claxon as it neared the quay. Sunlight glanced through the branches. Daniel dwelt upon the news.

Poor Helen.

So many of his friends had split apart. So many of their children had suffered the fallout from broken marriages, as had his own. He looked at the boys and wondered what damage they'd suffered from his divorce. Who could tell what such young minds might be hiding, storing up for later? Would the same happen to Sophia and Lilliana? Or maybe Helen wouldn't leave Yiannis. Maybe it was just the once and Yiannis would beg her forgiveness and she'd be able to pretend it hadn't happened.

But, perhaps, just perhaps..?

Here he was, back on Serifos, dreaming again. John Cleese once put it most succinctly: 'It's the hope that kills...'

Away at the other end of Livadi, Jeanette would have told Helen by now. He still suspected he could never have done it.

Of course, for the boys nothing was amiss. 'Sea, Lew. Come on.' Jonny dragged his brother in, Lewis pretending to resist, saying no, saying he wanted to lie in the shade, then rushing into Jonny with a whoop so they both crashed underwater.

Daniel decided he had to do something, anything, rather than just sitting and fretting.

'Jonny – take care of him!' he said. The surface was like a millpond and shallow and there were plenty of people around. The boys were in no danger; and they were coated in P20 sun screen – a special purchase only available at the airport – so they were well protected. Daniel asked an elderly lady with two grandchildren to keep an eye on them. She was Greek but seemed to understand.

'Don't go any deeper! I won't be long,' he shouted.

'Ok, dad!'

In the sea, they were instantly content. He guessed Lewis was dredging the bottom for lost Spanish doubloons again – which presumably had been washing round Serifos since some galleon went hundreds of miles off course and sank in some huge freak storm in the Mediterranean in the sixteenth century – and Jonny, as ever, was humouring him. It was miraculous how Lewis' perpetual tiredness seemed to disappear when he was immersed in brine.

Daniel went through into the camp site and along the shady paths to their stretch of concrete, taking care to avoid the section where Jenny was living. He didn't want to talk to her right now.

He felt sick for Helen and sick with desire. He found the besom broom which was provided, moved their bags and odds and ends to one side and set about clearing away the sand, grass and leaves that accumulated every day, regardless of their efforts to keep things clean. He sweated and dust rose and just for the moment it seemed therapeutic.

Last night, they'd slept elsewhere. He told the boys to roll up their sleeping bags and took them to sleep on the hill which led over to the one-time nudist beach, and they settled on the inclined track where it was wider towards the bottom. It was a treat for the boys because they had been so good when trudging back from Psili Ammos. It was also much quieter there than on the site itself. A group of young men had just arrived and were spending the night talking loudly, smoking and drinking around their tents.

Lying under the open sky, Daniel was thrown back in time again. Where they lay must have been around the same spot on the hill where he had made a shelter for Dianne when she first arrived that summer long ago. Of course, with the low dunes largely flattened, it was not possible to be precise. However, the sand was still soft, the air was warm and there was a light breeze that didn't penetrate the camp site because of the trees. Briefly, he could imagine it was the 1970s once more.

Despite the trauma of Jenny's driving and the crash and the long walk shepherding the children home, he relaxed.

At first they were silent – until Jonny spotted a shooting star, one of the August Perseids. They had a competition to count how many more they could glimpse, until Lewis started losing and began to pretend there was one after another after another. It had ended with Jonny getting angry, then they were laughing and then the boys fell asleep. Perfect moments.

When the sun rose, they woke and yawned and gathered themselves together. A Greek with long matted black hair and a Def Leppard tee shirt approached. He wanted to warn them they shouldn't be sleeping on the hill.

'Big danger. Scropions. In the rocks.'

'Scropions? Ah, scorpions! Here? Oh, right. Wow. We won't sleep here again. *Endáxi.* Thank you.'

Daniel was grateful they hadn't known before, because it had been a special night.

He thought of a Dave he met on Siros in 1978. Dave too lived for loud music. He was an obsessive Steppenwolf fan ('I'm born to be wild, Dan...') and was one of life's loners though forever seeking a lover. He'd woken on their beach one morning, greeted the day cheerily, climbed out of his sleeping bag and shook it to remove any sand... which was when a scorpion dropped out. He'd spent the night with a new friend after all. And survived, just like Daniel and the boys.

Daniel was aware, though, that there is often some kind of scorpion lurking, and though you might be lucky, it's ready to strike when you least expect it. He laid aside the broom and hurried back to his children.

****

Helen was still on the terrace. Sophia and Lilliana had gone to a friend's house. There was no telling when Yiannis' work might finish because he was able to pick his own hours and nobody ever seemed to mind, so she might have a long wait.

A lizard skittered past, sticking close to the wall. A sudden wind dragged at the towels hanging on the line. Two cats loitered at a distance, knowing Helen often threw them scraps. Not today, though. Everything looked the same, but today was different.

She sat very upright on a white plastic chair, in the shade, holding herself so calmly she might have been braced to meet the Prime Minister, Konstantinos Karamanlis himself. Or she might have been Anne Boleyn, prepared for the executioner...

The distinctive growl of Yiannis' bike came from the beach road sooner than she'd expected. The noise grew louder, there was dust and the final revs of the engine, then it died.

As he walked round the corner of the house and towards her, Yiannis looked sheepish, in such contrast to his performance in the taverna that morning. It had been all show, an attempt to salve his conscience, a way he could try to convince himself that nothing of any importance had happened. It had been an overacted demonstration of pretended devotion, a plunging descent from what she'd once believed him to be.

She trusted Jeanette implicitly and had no doubt he'd been unfaithful. Was this even the first time?

'Eleni…'

That tone. He knew that she knew what he'd done, but he'd deny it, deny it thrice or more.

Had he been back to Jenny? She looked straight into his eyes. He endeavoured to hold her gaze, yet his look wasn't honest.

'Eleni. Jeanette has told you a story. Maybe it is not the real story, eh?'

He tried one of his own. It was a tale about a yachtsman who was offering drinks on his boat because Yiannis had used their car to ferry him and Jenny, Daniel's friend, over from Psili Ammos back to the port. He'd stayed and accepted the Metaxa because he didn't want to insult the man.

He wasn't a convincing Samaritan, but was insistent. Anyway, weren't they friends of Daniel? he asked. Afterwards, he'd taken Jenny back to Coralli, but only that. They had talked, yes, but only that. Nothing else. He opened his arms wide, an habitual gesture, indicating she could ask anything but he'd always be loyal.

But he was not credible, not for a moment.

Still silent, Helen kept her eyes on him. Did he think she wouldn't recognise lies after all these years, that she couldn't see through his gossamer tale? He hadn't carried the scent of the woman back to the house, but might as well have done.

She knew, as well as if she'd been there watching him have sex with Jenny. That, on its own, was enough to break her heart again. But, out beyond that horror, she finally allowed herself to accept what must have happened with other women across the years, that fear which had gnawed at her whilst she cleared away in the taverna or put their daughters to bed.

He responded to her scepticism by changing tack and building up his volume, growing larger, it seemed, remonstrating against the injustice.

'I have done nothing. Jeanette is wrong.' How did he know what Jeanette had said anyway? 'You are my wife. *Sei agapó.* I love you, but you do not listen to me. You are so cold…' He wasn't contrite. It was all her fault.

She remained straight and silent as he played the injured spouse, unjustly accused, unable to make her see reason. Until she could listen no longer.

'We are not free to do as we please, Yiannis,' she said, standing. 'We cannot do what we want, when we want. We have responsibilities. You are not some young man, playing on the beach. You have a family, children… You are my husband… and what have you done..? What have you done to me? What have you done to us?'

He didn't reply.

'I'm going out,' she said. 'I have no idea when I'll be back.'

He found words again.

'Just like that? But, the cooking. My mother… You have a job…' He endeavoured to sound commanding. 'You cannot just go away.'

'You help her, Yiannis, since you're so concerned.'

'And what do I say to my mother?'

'You could tell her the truth. Or tell her whatever comes into your head, Yiannis. I'm sure you can make up something without too much trouble.'

'Lilliana… Sophia..?'

'They're your daughters and they'll be back soon. Pretend you're a loving father.'

She went inside, picked up her keys from the table and strode back past him without speaking. Just for a moment, he looked as if he might block her way but then thought better of it. He simply shook his head as if disbelieving as she swept by, heading round the house to where the car was parked.

Of course, once she was driving she had to decide what to do next.

****

'Daniel.'

He opened his eyes but narrowed them against the four-o'-clock sun. Astonishingly, yes, it was Helen, Helen on the beach. He beamed, stood, took her hand. Then he felt awkward and let it go again.

'It's wonderful to see you here. Would you like to sit down?'

'For a moment.'

She perched beside him under the tree.

Jonny said a polite, 'Hello!' and Lewis paid her little attention. He was watching several small fish and a crab they'd netted earlier which were swimming round and round in their sawn-off bottle. Daniel had told him the distressed creatures must be released back into the wild, but Lewis was delaying as long as possible.

'How are things?'

Her face said, 'Not good,' but the children were listening.

'Ah... Anyhow, I am... honoured.' It wasn't the right word. He knew that.

'Jeanette had to go home. I needed to get away, find some perspective.'

And she had come to him. As if he were someone close. Like a soulmate. Words couldn't express...

'I couldn't talk to any of my friends... I already know what they'll say...' He was so distressed for her, yet so pleased.

She stared back along the beach, all soft sand and holidaymakers and busiest immediately outside the campsite.

'You know, I live on this island and never get down here at all in summer...'

'It's so changed from what it was. I expect it's better out of season when everyone has gone home?'

'It's colder and wetter. These trees drip reddy-brown when there's a downpour. It's dust, I suppose. But the beach is cleaner and quieter. Much nicer, you'd say.'

As if she understood him, which she did. He was becoming renewed.

Right on cue, to ruin the moment, the wind gusted, sweeping sand against them, into their faces, and some loose papers and a stray carrier bag blew past. They both covered their eyes for a moment.

'Nature rough in sand and plastic,' said Daniel, wiping away the grains that had stuck to his sun cream. 'I guess it was ever thus.'

His eyes went back to her. He adored her.

He had been different people in his life. He'd been a little boy in short trousers who liked running and hiding; a teenager who spent so much time avoiding the grammar school bullies; a university student full of the joys of alcohol, entranced by the beauty and softness of girls; and, soon after, the young man preparing to face real life who had met Helen. Since then, he'd been a worker, a husband, a father... but she'd dominated his thoughts, been the treasure at the end of every rainbow since her first smile on Kamari Beach and such a brief friendship.

They sat for a while watching Jonny and Lewis in the water, saying little else. She'd come to him when she needed someone. That was all that mattered.

'I often think of you dancing... in the taverna on Santorini... on this beach even without music...'

She looked at him, perhaps wondering where that had come from, perhaps thinking back, he hoped.

'I love dancing,' she said.

'You still dance?'

'Yes. When I can.'

It was stilted. Maybe he'd never known her well; and he realised that after twenty-five years he hardly knew her at all. Yet his emotions were unchanged.

The boys returned for a drink.

'So,' she said, suddenly more animated, as if making a huge effort to pull herself together, 'how would you all like to come for a drive? See some of the island?'

She was avoiding Yiannis? Perhaps she was making some sort of statement too? Daniel was happy to be used.

'You need somewhere to talk?'

'I'm offering a drive.'

How clumsy he could be. Yet he could think of nothing he'd prefer more than a trip with her, even though Jonny and Lewis looked less than thrilled. They were probably remembering the journey with Jenny, which he wasn't going to mention just then.

'Helen will be a wonderful guide,' he said. 'Will there be a beach?'

'Certainly,' Helen said, directly to Lewis, whose face brightened.

'Will Sophia be coming?' asked Jonny, just slightly too innocently.

'I imagine the girls would love to come,' said Helen.

'Well, it would be best if they didn't miss out,' said Jonny.

'No. You're right.' She could have laughed, but Daniel appreciated her sensitivity. 'They might be with their father, but it's more likely they'll be at their friend's…'

'So… Should we try to find them?' asked Daniel, stupidly, as if Yiannis posed no danger.

'I suppose so. Or the day will be over.'

'Just give us a few minutes to get ready,' he said, desperately keen for the outing to take place, regardless of what the repercussions might be and not wanting her to change her mind. 'We'll be quick.' It would be more seemly if her daughters were there too; but, in addition, if the youngsters looked after each other he and Helen might grab some private time after all. 'We'll need to pop back to base, pack a couple of bags and call in at the toilets. Oh, and, Lewis, please put those poor creatures back into the sea. The sun has made that water hot. How many times…?'

Lewis took his plastic bottle and immersed it in the shallows so the tiny fish could safely swim away whilst Jonny began to collect their things together. Daniel helped him, proud of his sons. They were turning out well. He hoped Helen approved.

However, she was paying no attention to what they were doing. She was thinking, obviously thinking, wearing a tragic frown.

****

Beside her tent, Jenny watched them over the wall. She would have loved to stroll over and find out what had been happening. Obviously, that was out of the question.

As they prepared to move off, she allowed herself a sigh, for Yiannis.

Her father used to tell her that you only live once and should make the most of your time. Since she'd escaped the clutches of Stelios, she'd been endeavouring to follow her father's philosophy. Of course, he'd been talking about extending the range of goods in his hardware store, not sampling as many men as might become available, but philosophy, she would assert, mostly when she'd been drinking and had found someone to warm her night, should not be applied to only the commercial world.

She'd been told by a girl friend that her life was cold and would leave her empty. Perhaps. She told her friend she didn't believe in the happiness of happy families and she missed her daughter only rarely. Her friend told her she was lying to herself.

She bit into a peach. Yiannis had made her back arch and set a fire inside her and she would have screamed with the electricity of it all, had she been anywhere more private. On balance, she figured her life was fine right now, more or less as it was. It was true that everything would have been better if Yiannis hadn't been seen. But still, she thought, as the juice ran between her fingers, that's life, Charlie Brown.

She retained some hope that Yiannis might yet re-appear through the trees and pick up where he'd left off earlier that morning. Somewhere around her left nipple. She touched the exact spot, under her loose tee shirt.

She took another mouthful. The peach was indescribably sweet. All in all, she was having quite a time.

****

Helen had no plan for the outing and no conscious understanding of what, exactly, she was doing or why. After twenty-five settled years, her sandcastle had crumbled. The child, the teenager, the mother: pain upon pain. Is it like this for everyone? she kept wondering. Is this really all there is?

Yet she knew she wasn't doomed by a divine power, some universal fate: her heart had been ripped apart by particular men. Or, rather, by men who were not particular enough. It's a cruel world.

To her left, a young woman had been rubbing oil on to her boyfriend's chest whilst he stroked her leg; beyond them, a father played with his daughter whilst his wife lay on her back and held a German novel aloft, blocking the sun as she read. Everyone seemed content. Maybe everything could all be all right. Unless, of course, they too had hidden tragedies.

She knew her Greek friends would tell her to forgive: the family was what mattered. She knew that the reaction of Yiannis' mother would be automatic: she would defend him in public, but in private do all in her power to make him apologise until his wife took him back.

How could Helen do that? She couldn't behave as if nothing had happened because she would never trust him again.

She was turning to Daniel with irony vibrating through her. Of course, she knew how he felt about her and how he'd snatch the opportunity to be with her and despite their history she needed a sympathetic ear. She knew he'd listen patiently to her torments and it was opportune that he'd arrived on Serifos when he did. Still, Yiannis had been unfaithful and she was turning to Daniel, Daniel of all people...

The boys were soon ready. The four of them and the girls would fit easily into the Nissan Combi – though she needed to manage the pick-up without encountering Yiannis. If the girls weren't at their friends' house, she presumed he'd have left them at her friend Vicki's, assuming Helen would return later and sort them out. He wouldn't want to be burdened with two little girls for the rest of the day: unlike his brother, he left the care of children to his wife.

Conveniently and predictably, when Helen pulled up at Vicki's, the girls were there. Better still, they didn't need to return home since Yiannis had packed them off with their swimming costumes. That was perfect.

Daniel was in the front with her and his sons sat in the back. Sophia and Lilliana clambered in too, giggling, whilst Jonny offered no reaction and Lewis stared away from them, out of the window. Sophia said, 'Hello, Jonny.' Lewis turned then and grinned, and Jonny gave him a huge dig in the ribs; Lilliana, who was only six, whispered something into her sister's ear which made her react with a 'Hey, shush!' Then they were off.

Daniel's fists clenched as Helen negotiated the narrow road up and out of Livadi. 'I've driven before,' she said. 'Relax.'

'I'm a bad passenger. It's a primal fear. I can't help it.'

'I'll drive slowly.'

As if trying to create a distraction from her difficulties in squeezing past other vehicles on the road, he made stilted conversation: 'All these houses with steel rods sticking out at the top... Is it a fashion statement?'

'Not quite. You don't have to pay tax until the building's completed...'

'Ah. And they aren't finished. How very Greek.'

'Very, very Greek.'

Visibly relaxing at the road became easier to drive, he kept turning towards her, looking at her face, her breasts, her legs. She remembered that was how he used to be.

Then, 'This is the road back from Mega Livadi,' he said. 'We've been there.'

She guessed it might have been with the American woman, but didn't comment.

'Don't worry. That's not where we're heading. We're stopping soon,' she said. 'The girls love Ganema.'

'A beach?'

'It is.'

They drove along the coast with Serifos around them in its majesty: towering mountainsides high above; red and grey igneous rock, thorn bushes and the wonder of unchanging baked stone stretching as far as their eyes could see. Drystone walls divided fields and terraces but it was all deserted now. Down a cleft in the hillside there was a strip of greenery and some tall bamboo. Otherwise, all was parched and empty. Way beneath them, the deep blue Aegean shifted listlessly in the heat.

They passed the first cove – 'Vagia,' said Helen. 'No shade.' She pressed on, swept round a bend and parked above a long, nearly deserted beach backed by tall trees. There were just a couple of buildings behind it, almost out of sight. Sophia, Lilliana and Jonny, sure-footed as young goats, bounded down a short, steep drop from the road. Lewis stayed closer to his father, struggling to maintain his balance as the stones slid beneath his feet. Helen offered him her hand, and he didn't refuse. She liked Daniel's kids.

She wondered what Yiannis might be doing at just that moment, though she'd have told anyone who asked that she didn't care.

Once on the sand, which was light yellow and pristine, Daniel lay on his back and thumped his fists down hard, shouting, 'Yes, yes, yes!' He was being ridiculous and for a moment she was reminded of the boy she'd first met on Santorini.

Jonny and Lewis, presumably used to his eccentricities, ignored him and ran off with Sophia and Lilliana towards the end of the nearly-empty beach, hundreds of yards away. Friendship had been established.

Helen looked down at him and smiled. 'I suppose you're registering approval?'

'Serifos as I have always loved it. Unspoiled.' He hesitated. 'Our Serifos.'

Over the years, she realised, Serifos had become different to her, and she didn't respond. It was her home, a place where she worked, not where she played. It was ages since she'd played at all.

They waved to bring the children back, reapplied sun lotion, then released them again.

'Take care, you two,' she shouted to Jonny and Lewis, as they ran off though the shallows. 'There's sand just there but some sharp rocks too…'

'We've become so changed and wise,' said Daniel.

Although they could all swim, the children stayed close to the edge, rolling in and out of the sea, splashing and shouting. It was childish and careless. Helen and Daniel sat under a huge tree with no one within fifty yards of them. She sat on a towel beside him as their children screamed together, sometimes half-swimming, half clawing back and forth in the shallows, part crabs, part breast-strokers, partly like giant browned flat-fish.

Sophia, who had swum since she was a baby, stuck close to Jonny when he went further out. He made up for his relative aquatic inadequacies by making most noise. Lewis and Lilliana finally went their own ways, happy enough drawing shapes in the sand and piling stones.

Daniel kept his eyes glued to the boys.

'Relax,' said Helen, noting his unease whenever Lewis went back to the water. 'They can swim, can't they?'

'They don't know this beach…'

'They'll be fine. It shelves pretty gently and there's no current. Try to chill – as we kids say…'

On a day like this, how ridiculous that she was telling him to relax. She was, though, touched by his concern. Yiannis' care was rougher, he didn't cosset, doting only when the mood took him and often dismissive, almost uncaring. He was a man who had relied on his wife to love and nurture his children. Maybe Daniel was such a contrast because he needed to be a mother to his sons as well as a father; or maybe it was just because he was English. Never having had a proper father, she wasn't in a position to judge.

'Yes,' he said. 'I'm sure they will be fine… Are you… fine?'

'Guess…'

'Maybe nothing much actually happened. Maybe he was just… tempted?'

'You believe that?'

She didn't, and it was clear that he didn't either. They both knew.

She pushed her hair behind her ears and wished that she hadn't, because her eyes had filled with tears. She hoped he couldn't see that through her sunglasses. Blinking, she tried to regain control but he dug into his pocket and handed her a tissue. She dabbed her cheek and looked across the Bay of Koutalas to the far headland, seeing nothing.

'We still love you.'

'What?'

'We still love you. You are still loved. It's a platitude, but true: things will work out and you will survive. Again.'

'We'? He was trying to be kind.

In turmoil, she wanted him to hold her, just for comfort… but the children would see. She could have told him that he'd been her first true love; but how would that help? All she wanted was for everything to be all right again even though it couldn't be because her unfaithful husband was somewhere else. Whatever would she do without Yiannis? He'd stood beside her so long. What she needed was the man who'd seemed a proper husband to her and father to the girls. She needed back the life which had been hers until that morning.

Though, really, she knew things had been so wrong for so long.

Now, yes, she was here with Daniel… but their past was so badly flawed… He couldn't be the answer.

There was no credible way out. She wriggled her toes in the sand, watched the children, felt her stomach churning and held her aching peace.

Her escape to the beach hadn't worked. She was still disorientated, just as desperate.

Chapter 6

The boys were creatures of habit. It was quite natural for them to want to eat at Konstantinidis' that night because it was what they knew. Their world had turned upside down when their mother left and Daniel suspected that since then they'd feared any change. Jonny had been affected more than Lewis, perhaps because he was six when they became a single-parent family and had been more aware of what was happening. Lewis was at an age when you just accept anything and everything, but even so he was always the strange boy in his class who didn't have a mum at home or waiting in the playground and whose dad organised his birthday parties.

Right now, they were simply children who wanted to go to the taverna they were used to and although Daniel tried to avoid spoiling them, he never wanted them to be disappointed. It was about making things as perfect as possible: the endless desire of the single parent to compensate for whatever the children might have missed. Taking them to their taverna of choice hardly compensated for a home without a mother, but if that was what they wanted, they would all go to Konstantinidis' again, probably to the table where they had sat before, and face whatever fallout might occur.

As they were tidying around their patch of concrete and rubbing on mosquito repellent and Daniel was flexing his back – he was definitely aging – Frank came over. He had a tent just five yards or so away. A huge Greek man with the broadest smile, the roughest chin and one of the largest bellies Daniel had ever seen, he was also immensely kind. When he heard Daniel and the boys would be going home whilst he was still on Serifos, he offered them his flat in Athens so they could spend the night in the city before heading to the airport the next day.

'These are my keys!' He handed them over. 'These are instructions to get from the Metro to my home. It is very close to Monistiraki Station.' His accent was Greek with a slight mid-Atlantic twang. 'I have drawn a map. Look.'

They clustered round his notes and his sketch and listened to his instructions about where to turn right by the dress shop and left at the kiosk on the corner. Daniel thanked him and he went back to his tent and that was when the children could protest.

'Dad! You said we could sleep at the airport! On one of those big windowsills,' said Lewis.

'That'll be uncomfortable. Frank is offering his flat. You'll feel differently when the time comes.'

'But it won't be any fun.'

'And, anyway, look how much he smokes,' said Jonny, who was more subtle. 'The place must really smell. I don't want to be in a flat full of ash trays, with cigarette ends everywhere. You know what he's like.'

Daniel did. Frank was unkempt, in a lovable way, but unkempt all the same. And, like so many Greeks, he smoked endlessly. His flat was probably messy and would certainly be heavy with the smell of tobacco. He was friendly beyond belief and obviously totally trusting ('Just leave the door unlocked when you go. I will be home a couple of days after you.'); but should they take up Frank on his offer? It was a tricky one.

It was further complicated by the fact that Frank's dream was to visit the UK to research the American branch of his family. His father, who came from New York, had worked as a steward on a cruise ship but met a beautiful woman in Athens. He jumped ship, married her and, 'They lived happily ever after,' said Frank, their only child.

When their 'ever after' ended and his father was no longer around – Frank was cagey about the details – he had set about discovering what he could about his father's background. His forebears had emigrated from Liverpool in the mid-nineteenth century. There were distant relatives in the States who had supplied snippets of information from over there but he wanted to dig up records in England.

Daniel was pretty certain Frank didn't really have sufficient funds for the trip and was hoping to find a base from which he could research for free. He'd no idea how their tiny house would cope with Frank for just one night, and longer might seem like an eternity. He'd done everything in his power to gently dissuade him from arriving at Heathrow with a small backpack, his sleeping bag and packs of cheap Greek cigarettes.

'Liverpool is a wonderful city. I've only visited a couple of times, though. It's so far away from our new house in Leicester. And travel costs a fortune in the UK.'

Daniel hoped that might do the trick. He felt terrible, especially considering Frank's generosity, but had enough stress coping with his job and two children.

Now, in the face of his progenies' complaints, he would have to find an excuse to return the keys and to turn down the offer of an apartment for the night. Frank, he was sure, was too nice to ever take offence, but it might be awkward and was a task to save for another day.

It was typical that when Frank approached before their evening departure for the taverna, he carried two bottles of beer.

'Drink? These are cold, from the shop.'

'That's a kind offer, Frank, but we're about to go and eat.'

'Ah. That's fine. *Éndaxí.*' He turned to go.

Daniel always felt guilty when discouraging Frank from joining them, which he did regularly, but it occurred to him that it could be useful to have his company this time. They could sort out the apartment business and buy his meal to repay him for his many small kindnesses; and, importantly, his presence might dissuade Yiannis from considering a violent response to Daniel's friendship with Helen. Frank would be happy too.

'Fancy coming with us for once, Frank?' He thought the 'for once' was a sensible touch. 'We're going down to Konstantinidis' – could we treat you tonight? You've been so kind to us.'

The boys liked Frank and looked pleased. Frank beamed.

'Thank you, my friend, thank you. That is so wonderful. One moment. I will put on my trousers and change my shirt and I will be with you in two shakes of a sheep's tail.'

'You'll have to be quick. It's getting late.'

Leaving behind a cloud of cigarette smoke, Frank hastened

to his tent, which seemed far too small for someone of his height and girth. Lewis had joked about how he must get smaller when he got inside, a bit like in Alice in Wonderland, but Jonny had told him to be more respectful. Then they both laughed anyway.

Daniel approached Konstantinidis' with trepidation, even with Frank by his side. He'd no idea what might have happened after Helen dropped them off at the camp site. Would she be there? And would Yiannis be in attendance, would he know about the trip to the beach and maybe think Daniel was the one who told her about his night with Jenny? It could prove more than awkward.

'You've no idea what I do for you, kids.'

They didn't understand. Jonny wrinkled his nose whilst Lewis ignored the comment and ran ahead to claim their customary table.

****

After Daniel, Helen and the boys drove off into the great beyond, Jenny spent an unobtrusive couple of hours reading on the beach until the wind became so strong that she had to retreat to the bar at the back of the camp site for iced tea.

It wouldn't have been hard for her to explain why she then showered, changed and set off towards the port with the express intention of bumping into Yiannis: he was special and they'd enjoyed the most wonderful night she could remember and maybe, just maybe, he might find time for her again? If her clitoris had eight thousand nerve endings, as she'd read somewhere, Yiannis seemed to know his way around all of them. Yet, even so, to go hunting for him seemed absurd, with logic screaming in her ear that he wouldn't want to see her right now – if ever again.

Even Jenny's detractors had never described her as stupid. She had a well-honed instinct for survival, sliding down the side of problems, managing to circumvent unpleasant situations and invariably coming out fine, smelling of bourbon or ouzo: but for once she felt ridiculously carefree. Her Revivalist upbringing could go hang.

Camping does not allow for an extensive wardrobe, but she shook out her long blue skirt with its slit up the side and the white blouse with neat embroidery down the front. She tightened the band of the skirt as far as it would go and didn't fasten the top buttons of the blouse. Before the mirror in the toilet block, she brushed and pushed her hair into place as best she could, applied red lipstick and even a touch of dark eye shadow, put on her bangles and, finally, hung around her neck the blue porcelain eye on a thin chain which she'd bought on Spetses, a good luck charm against '*máti*', any evil she might encounter.

As she walked through Livadi, the restaurants and bars lining the main road were busy and she was aware of the glances she was attracting. Older men looked up from their meals, their thick syrupy coffees or beers and gave long studied glances; married men, out with wives and families, flicked their gaze over her, trying to do it casually; but youths stared too, and she was pleased that she could still get such attention. She wasn't old and withered yet. Where there was interest, there were always possibilities.

'Drink?' A waiter stood in the road just along from the supermarket and bakery, next to a board offering Greek salad, meat, local fish, Greek specials, sweets. 'Or maybe eat? All good.'

He produced a menu, which he offered as he waved his other hand towards an empty table in his busy restaurant.

Maybe it would be best to eat here, she thought. It would be foolish to sail into Konstantinidis'. However, she wanted to be close to the road, in case Yiannis came by, so she chose a table at the front of the taverna where she could see everyone passing.

And, of course, there she could be seen.

It was a restaurant that specialised in fish. She normally chose something cheap like stuffed tomatoes, but decided to treat herself, just this once. She negotiated for a red snapper, ordered a half kilo of white wine – even her husband had been unable to explain why wine was sold in kilos, rather than litres

– and whilst she was waiting for her food she nibbled on the bread.

There was no sign of Yiannis, but within half an hour she'd been approached by several men who asked whether she was alone and whether they could sit with her and buy her another drink. She said no, even to the suave Scotsman with more than a passing resemblance to a young Sean Connery. The attractive waiter, who might have overheard, brought another jug of wine 'on the house', clearly hoping she'd respond to his charm. She was tempted.

'*Póso chronón eísai*? How old are you?' she asked.

'I am twenty-eight years old.'

He was lying. He was young enough to be her son. And handsome as a movie star.

However, her focus was on what might be happening at Konstantinidis'. She'd tried so hard to see last night as an end in itself but longed to feel Yiannis' body against hers again. The positivity she'd felt walking into town was now fortified by the alcohol and if she was going to do anything at all, this was the time; otherwise she might as well retreat to her tent.

Offering her waiter no more than a chaste '*Kali níchta*', she left and set off along the water's edge with hope in her heart and her sandals in her hand, towards Konstantinidis', the final taverna before the darkness round the remainder of the bay. Her heart beat faster.

What she was doing was utter madness. However, in her semi-inebriated state she felt confident that Helen wouldn't rush from the kitchen, out through the diners, to seize her by the hair. Indeed, she didn't think that Helen would even be there, under the circumstances. The alcohol was making her a fool but she hoped Yiannis might be the one present, might take her away, might hold her and touch her and coax her to ecstasy again.

It was after ten and most tables were taken. As she approached, she could see Andreas and Michalis rushing back and forth with plates and glasses as usual. Then they had a heated discussion before Andreas unwound the hosepipe and dampened down the area in front of the taverna, to reduce dust from passing cars.

198

From fifty yards away, she could see no sign of Helen, though there was no way to tell if she was inside.

Similarly, there was no sign of Yiannis.

As another ferry boat docked way behind her a couple of rowing boats bobbed silently beside her and most of the world went about its usual business, she hesitated. She considered retreating to her tent but spotted Dan and his boys sitting at a table with a large dishevelled man and the devil within screamed that all would be well, making her confidence soar. She put on her sandals and strode towards them.

'Hi,' she said, loudly, from some yards away. 'Fancy meeting you guys here.'

They were at a table for four, so she borrowed a chair and settled herself on a corner beside them, not pausing to be invited. Jonny and Lew half-smiled a welcome but there was no warmth from Daniel; the large man nodded at her. She could brazen it out because she had nothing to lose.

'Good meal? The tsatziki never lets you down, does it? Have you tried the giuvetsi? It's a speciality here when they have it, and not too expensive...' It was a slightly slurred monologue. 'What d'yer have, Lew?'

'Spaghetti,' said Lewis. Just that. The kids seemed to be picking up the vibes from their dad.

Daniel's friend remained silent. She looked around for Andreas or Michalis, to order a drink. Presumably they were collecting meals to bring out. She hoped she'd been right and Helen wasn't the one doing the cooking. Still, the alcohol in her bloodstream was flushing out any remaining common sense. Fireworks? Bring them on, she thought...

However, she could not have anticipated what happened next. Almost before she was settled, her evening fractured.

She'd expected the arrival of the waiters or Yiannis or Helen; instead, heading across the road towards them came the old woman who haunted the place. She wasn't zeroing in on them quickly, but came steadily like a dark, threatening vortex, directly towards the table where they were sitting.

Jenny had seen the widow before, often, but only occupying a table by the door, invariably with a glass of wine or water before her and sometimes with a tired head in her hands, looking worn by the world. She remained in her accustomed place all day because that was the Greek way, to go on and on, but never had she come out amongst the diners; never had she done more than stand and hobble a step or two to shout at a waiter or a cook; never had she looked anything but tragic and antique and broken. Now, though, she was transformed, on a mission, apparently unstoppable, like a tsunami of vengeance. Jenny was directly in the path of her visible fury.

The figure in black raised an arthritic finger as she neared, pointing. Jenny experienced a flashback to a movie she'd watched about Salem and witches' curses.

'*Eísai kakí gynaíka.*' The woman blazed at her in Greek: 'You are trying to ruin this family. You tricked my son. You should feel shame. You are not welcome here. Leave now!'

Jenny was not prepared for anything like this. Those at the table were frozen. The other diners were gripped by the unfolding drama: people stopped eating; only a tableful of Australians laughed; Greeks watched as if wondering whether the old lady were Adrastea, returned from mythology to wreak retribution on this American.

Jenny focused first on the finger but then on the old woman's face, contorted with loathing, anger, scorn. Her head swam. She could think of nothing to say. Even drunk, she knew this was truly awful. She should never have gone anywhere near the taverna.

Abruptly she rose and her chair fell backwards. Slinging her bag over her shoulder, she hurried away without looking back. She shed no tears as she stumbled along the road, but there was a terrible sickness inside her, stupidity and frustration blending into a cocktail of toe-curling embarrassment.

****

Yiannis hadn't been at the house when Helen returned from Ganema.

If he was with his mother, she knew he wouldn't be peeling potatoes or stirring pots at the taverna but he would have had to offer some explanation about what was going on. She didn't imagine he'd tell the truth.

Of course, he might be with Jenny and that idea was sickening.

Freed from the ties of work, Helen fed the girls. All evening, Sophia was alive with what Jonny had said and what Jonny had done. She thought Lewis was nice but odd and since he was quieter than his brother both girls tended to dismiss him from their thoughts.

Helen managed to settle them to bed earlier than usual and for once they didn't complain.

Sophia asked, 'Mummy, do you think Jonny would make a good husband? I mean when he's older… He's got really nice skin and blue eyes.'

Lilliana joined in, from her bed across the room: 'He can lift up one eyebrow at a time.'

'They sound like the sort of qualities you'd want in a husband.'

'Qualities,' repeated Lilliana.

'I thought that,' said Sophia. 'He makes me laugh all the time but he's not at all like papa though.'

'No…. Enough for now. Sleep…. Both of you!'

Managing an excuse for a smile, she kissed each of them on the cheek, closed their bedroom door and went off to sit alone with her distress.

When the phone finally rang, she stared at it. Whoever was on the other end rang off then tried again. Helen bit a nail and stared at the receiver.

'Mama, *to tiléfono..*,' shouted Lilliana.

'Phone, Mum,' echoed Sophia.

She picked up and it was her mother-in-law whose words poured out in a pleading torrent. She wanted Helen to come back to the kitchen; she wanted her to forgive Yiannis. As expected, he'd told his mother a version of what had happened. He'd been a fool, said Kyria Konstantinidis, but it's easy for a man to make a mistake when there's a woman like that trying to take him away from his wife. He had done nothing serious. He'd spent time with the woman, which was wrong, but they only talked. Eleni must forgive him. It wouldn't happen again. They all needed Eleni. The family needed her to understand. She should think about the children. She had told that woman she must stay away, that she was not welcome. She wouldn't come back now, sniffing around Yiannis. It was over. Eleni couldn't break up the family.

He was her son and she loved him and had accepted his lie. In any case, she needed to believe him because this affected them all and her grandchildren: what in the world mattered more?

Helen stared into the night and her eyes filled. But, no, she wouldn't allow herself to be held culpable in any way. Those days were gone.

She found it hard to force out the words she had to say, because it all became more real then, as if she had to picture the two of them, Yiannis and the woman; as if by talking about the infidelity she was bringing their bodies together again, hearing each sigh, each gasp, each murmur. But she did it, speaking slowly, a pain in her head and another in her heart.

'He spent the whole night with her. In her tent.' She paused, tormented. 'They slept together.'

It was out. The phrase burnt into her, sounding as sharp and final in Greek as it did in English: '*Kánane érota.*'

There was silence on the line.

'I know this is true,' Helen said, and waited again.

There might have been a sob and a desperate '*óchi*'. 'No,' his mother was trying to say. She might have argued but she didn't. She might have pleaded for him again. She didn't. When she spoke at last, her voice was quiet, cracking and hopeless. It was clear she believed Helen and could only manage, 'I must speak with my son. I love you, Eleni *moú*.'

Helen put down the phone and closed her eyes. Soon, she was sure, Yiannis would be back...

When he arrived, she was outside, listening to the bamboo shifting in the wind. Somewhere out of sight, she could hear a cow tearing at leaves. She looked up into the blackness of the sky, the neverending emptiness of the heavens. She couldn't see most of the constellations because of the light from the

202

house but they were wheeling over Serifos just as they did when she was young. Mars was orange tonight, and the moon had some of its face hidden, but stars were shining as they did millions of years ago. She felt the insignificance so many had experienced before. Her whole story was a click of the fingers in eternity: her hurt as a child, her desertion by Daniel and Yiannis' infidelity had happened and would go like a breath of wind and the universe hadn't noticed. All insubstantial tragedies fade.

Yet she could not deal with this as Kyria Konstantinidis would. Helen knew her mother-in-law's priority would be just the children. Their happiness was important to Helen as well, of course it was, but she herself mattered too. She would not subsume herself for their sake, would not play the hapless victim. If the universe cared nothing for her, that wasn't the end of things, because she could stand up for herself. She'd never been protected by any deity: not by the protestant god of the Wesleyans who'd offered her mother some kind of solace in dark times, nor by the Catholic god of the Greeks. She knew there was no greater power supporting those in need. She would have to deal with her own problems, as she always had.

So Yiannis wouldn't be sleeping in her bed and she wouldn't be preparing food at the taverna tomorrow.

****

Daniel woke to a stunning new morning and couldn't stop smiling at the new day, becoming ever more confident that love would not tear them apart again.

Jonny joined an impromptu game of football at the back of the beach. He was playing with teenagers so was getting no more than an occasional touch of the ball, but was evidently enjoying not being just a little kid for once. Lewis sat on the blue metal bar that ran along the top of the white campsite wall and watched, claiming to be tired, as usual.

Under the tree, Frank was stretched out opposite Daniel on a blue towel that was much too small for him. Between them lay a tiny travellers' chess set. Daniel was losing by two games to one, but the competition wasn't intense.

Earlier, he'd been lying on his sleeping bag on the concrete, watching a lizard try to find a way into his rucksack. Lewis said it kept coming back and was his friend and they should call it Lawrence. Daniel said there were lizards all around, different ones that all looked the identical. Lewis insisted it was the same one. He told his father that sometimes children know best.

Daniel was wondering whether he should check that the packs' zips were all fastened tightly when Frank came towards him, all broad grin and wide belly and long shorts and a shirt with disconcerting underarm stains, and invited him to a chess competition on the beach.

'A competition?'

'Yes. With you and me.'

Playing chess was not something Daniel did at home. In Greece, though, there was endless time to fill and he agreed. 'Why not..?'

Relaxed in the shade, Frank scratched his head before moving his knight. 'I've never seen a girl playing chess,' he said.

Daniel thought about it a moment, then had to agree. 'No. Me neither.' Mike would have said it should suit their love of scheming; Daniel tried to be a modern man. 'Maybe it's too competitive, Frank. Maybe winning isn't so important to them?' Was that sexist too?

There was no response. Either his opponent misunderstood or was more concerned about the threat posed by Daniel's marauding bishop. He withdrew the knight to support his queen, then turned lyrical, 'You know, my friend, this is an island of legends.'

'Really?' Daniel was only half listening, struggling with strategy. Chess had never been his game of choice and he found it hard. He had difficulty thinking more than one move ahead and often simply plumped for whatever seemed best at that moment, with no clear idea of what might happen next. It was the story of his life, really.

'Perseus, who was the son of Zeus, grew up here,' Frank continued, obviously pleased to be able to share his knowledge. 'As you will know, he arrived with his mother, Danae, in a barrel.'

'Who?'

'Danae. She was a beautiful woman – very beautiful. She lived here many years and won people's hearts and the king of Serifos loved her but could not have her.' He smiled his bearded smile. 'She was like your Helen, maybe?'

Daniel laughed. 'Helen came by boat. With me. And I'm a republican. I don't believe in kings. Still, her face could launch a thousand ships, of that I am certain.' It was another allusion which was too complicated for Frank. 'Also, Helen arrived with her friend Jeanette... And to the best of my knowledge, she's never slept with a god, Greek or otherwise.' It came back to him, though, how the girls had been mightily impressed with Yiannis in his youth.

Frank was not to be diverted.

'When Polydectes, the king, fell in love with her, she would not marry him. Years passed. To avoid him, she finally had to go to a temple to be safe. She was rescued by her son Perseus, who had killed Medusa and was waving round her head.' He spun his right arm around his head, grinning. 'Her look still turned everyone to stone – and that's what happened to Polydectes and his court. That is why Serifos is so stony.' He seemed to have run out of myth and brought his narration to a close, in what was becoming his customary manner: 'And they all lived happily ever after.'

'Your point is?' Daniel found it utterly confusing.

'Her spirit is still around the island, my friend. Danae's spirit. The beauty of women haunts you here. It haunts me, all the time.' He was watching two girls in bikinis who were too young, too slim and much too pretty for him.

'You just fancy beautiful girls, Frank. It has nothing to do with legends.'

'No. That is what this island is like. Helen is like a Danae to you. She is someone you want but cannot have, my friend; someone forever out of your touch.'

Daniel hoped not. After their evening at Konstantinidis' and once the boys were asleep, Daniel had told Frank about his history with Helen. The man came across as a great drinker rather than a great philosopher so he hoped there was nothing in what he said.

As he was giving Frank's conjectures some thought and wondering whether he should sacrifice his rook, Yiannis arrived and Daniel's earlier sense of well-being deserted him. Yiannis paced on to the beach out of the entrance to Coralli, throwing back his lank hair, looking left and right. He walked with purpose, his stride as long as ever, but perhaps his head was not quite so high and he looked even more unkempt than usual. He didn't seem like a man whose problems were behind him.

He spotted Daniel, who feared he was about to face a husband's ire. The sand felt rough under his palm as he pushed himself more upright. The sun was suddenly hot on his hat. He ran his hand down the line of his jaw.

Frank, too, had seen Yiannis and must have foreseen danger. He stubbed out his cigarette in the sand. Daniel could sense the muscles tightening under his bulk as he lay opposite him. He was pleased to have Frank as an ally.

How apposite, though, for these things to be happening on just this spot, where Yiannis was playing through the night with those women all those years ago. 'In my end is my beginning…' More and more, he thought that T S Eliot had it right and there must be some sort of cosmic continuum.

'Daniel..!' Yiannis didn't sound angry; shaken, perhaps, but thankfully not stirred to violence. It was a relief.

Daniel relaxed. 'Hi, Yiannis… Sit down?'

'Thank you, no.'

So Daniel stood. He awkwardly held out his hand. Yiannis took it in a builder's grip. Frank, an outsider in the drama, tactfully made a show of concentrating on the chessboard.

'Jenny is not in her tent. You have seen her?'

'No. Not today…' Hell, more Jenny, after everything? What was wrong with the man?

Daniel had just one concern and couldn't stop himself: 'How are things now…? How is Helen?'

Yiannis pulled a face and shook his head.

'She is crazy. Jenny must speak with Eleni today. Eleni must understand.'

206

Understand..? Daniel felt certain that any intervention from Jenny would make more dynamite explode, yet it was not his place to say that.

'Jeanette can help her understand again that I am a good man.' Yiannis straightened his back but might have been talking to himself. 'But Jeanette's son is sick and she cannot leave him. She sits by his bed... So only Jenny can tell Eleni, I think.'

It wasn't Helen who was mad, it was Yiannis.

There was another lengthy silence. Daniel gave a passing thought to Jeanette's boy, but it was Helen who mattered. There would have been phone calls between the two women, yet, clearly, whatever had been said hadn't helped Yiannis' cause and how could it?

Frank rolled on to his back and closed his eyes. None of this had anything to do with him.

The three of them were silent. There was some laughter down the beach and the cicadas provided the usual chorus. It was oppressively hot.

Yiannis, with his eyes fixed on the water, finally came out with an idea, as if it had just occurred to him.

'You must talk to her,' he said. 'You will explain.'

Explain what? Tell her what?

'You can tell her that I did not make sex with Jenny.' A drowning man couldn't grasp for a flimsier straw, thought Daniel, and was he even that substantial? 'You must tell her that children need their mother and father. And you will tell her that Konstantinidis' needs her. We all need her. You must tell her not to go to England. *Se iketévo*, Daniel. Perhaps she will listen to you.'

To England? Daniel hid in his silence. She might come back to the UK...? And Yiannis wanted him to stop her...

'Yiannis... I... I am sure I have nothing to say that could help...'

'You will help, Daniel. You must. Think of the children...'

It was clear he had no idea his wife had spent the previous afternoon with Daniel. Perhaps he hadn't seen his girls and if he'd seen Helen, she'd kept it to herself. What might that mean?

Daniel's brain was jangling: she might actually leave Serifos? He could imagine Frank's eyebrows lifting under his cap.

Daniel took a deep breath and a gamble. 'Yiannis, I saw Helen. Yesterday.' He offered no details. 'I don't think she'll listen to me – whatever I say.'

Yiannis showed no surprise and no sign of jealousy, as if all his senses were dulled. Perhaps he hadn't slept at all.

'But you could try, Daniel. You could try to help us…'

Daniel felt trapped.

Finally, pathetically, 'Ok,' he said. 'I will talk with her, if you want.'

It was an absurd situation: Yiannis was willing to entrust his wife and the future of their marriage to the man his wife had loved, to the man who still loved her.

'I'll do what I can.'

So British. Utterly British. Sickeningly British. Even as Daniel questioned Yiannis' sanity, he wondered at his own… but didn't think he could ever actually go through with it.

****

Jenny had a bad night, her sleep broken regularly by dreams in which a huge balrog flew towards her, jaws wide and talons sharp. She plummeted into a bottomless chasm again and again. Each time, she woke soaked in sweat. Come daybreak, she took paracetamol and drank as much water as she could manage. Her hangover was terrible. She only left the tent to visit the toilet block.

Lying watching shadows of branches shifting on her tent's nylon top, she regained some perspective. Good as it had been – well, better than good, but she couldn't find a truly appropriate word – the night with Yiannis would not be repeated. She should have accepted that straight away, instead of acting like a silly teenage girl just because of his huge cock and the alcohol. She wasn't stupid. It was only sex after all, and there was always sex. Yiannis would make things right with Helen, like husbands do, and if he didn't he'd despise

Jenny and blame her for ruining his life. She knew the routines.

Where had her head been for the past two days? She lay still, listening to the singing insects and people talking nearby and to metallic tapping as new arrivals tried to get pegs to hold in the sandy ground; and she decided to leave. In a bar in Athens, before leaving for Serifos, she'd met a guy called Steve who had wanted to take her to Knossos in Crete, where he'd be working on a new archaeological dig. If he hadn't moved on already, she could tag along with him for a week or two. She winced when he boasted that he had a top of the range trenching tool, but he had smiling eyes and a terrifyingly rich family with a condo in San Francisco. Although she'd been in Greece so long, she was not immune to the lure of the American Dream. Girls, she thought, can't afford to be choosy.

She checked the time and discovered that the morning was almost done. Even feeling as she did, she should eat.

She pulled on a tee shirt, squirmed into a pair of shorts and crawled into the daylight, rubbing her eyes and yawning. She tugged her towel from the line and headed for a long shower.

When she returned, there was a smart, official-looking man hovering around her tent. He was obviously not a camper and didn't look anything like the people who ran the site. He wore an immaculate white shirt, perfectly pressed blue trousers and shiny shoes and was completely out of place. He had a Greek nose, a precisely trimmed short greying moustache and slightly receding but freshly sculpted grey hair.

She heard the German woman from the next tent say, 'She is here,' as she approached, before escaping into her tent, probably familiar with officialdom.

Jenny's first thought was that he was very handsome. Suave, in fact. Her second thought was that she must be in some sort of trouble. Was he investigating the crash? Or was there some problem with St John and his passport and this tent? Surely not, because the owners would have sorted that themselves. It was the accident, then…

The man looked her up and down. The creases in his trousers were so sharp it was surprising he didn't cut his hands when getting dressed.

Still, be casual. Be confident. Don't let the bastards intimidate you.

'Yes?' She flung her towel back over the line.

Briefly, his eyes flicked down, as if he was noticing for the first time how short her shorts were. Or maybe that was her imagination. In any case, he was bound to be looking, surreptitiously or not: it was what men do.

He still hadn't spoken. She waited, running her fingers through her wet hair, then tossing her head back and forth. Was he waiting to see what she'd say next? What was his game?

'Hello. Yes.' He had come to life. 'I am Yiannis' brother. I am Kostas. He has been looking for you. You were not here.' She indicated the towel. He nodded. 'Yes.'

She felt relieved. She wasn't in trouble. Correction: she was not in any more trouble. She would be cool.

'Well, it's great to meet you, Kostas.'

She held out a hand which he took reluctantly, she thought.

'Yes, Jenny.'

'And so, what can I do for you?'

He licked his top lip, hesitating.

'Jenny, because Yiannis helped you… This is difficult for me… Because you spent time together…'

What they had done had nothing to do with Kostas. It should have been Yiannis talking to her. This poor guy was on a hiding to nothing. She sat on the broken camp chair that St John had left. Only inches above the ground, she stretched out her legs. It made her feel less threatened by this awkward man and it would make her seem unconcerned by his visit. There was nowhere for Kostas to sit, but anyway he looked too smart to perch anywhere around. He definitely glanced at her shorts this time, tight round her pubic area, and then away, over her head.

'The family is broken…'

'I met your mother. She said.'

'Yes. Yes. I am sorry about that.'

It was not his place to be apologising. This was so difficult for him. However, he'd started now and she'd wait for him to finish.

'Helen, who is Yiannis' wife…' Jenny nodded. 'Helen needs to know that there has been a misunderstanding and that nothing happened between you and Yiannis. So that the family can stay together. So that this can be… ended.'

She didn't believe Helen was seeking any such confirmation. Her headache was sharp and she was tempted to spit out a response: 'I'm not married anymore, Kostas, and men don't rule my life and this is Yiannis' problem, not mine. What the fuck has this to do with me? Or, actually, with you?'

However, she controlled herself: 'I don't see how I can help you, Kostas.' She watched the German woman, who had emerged and was collecting together her little girl's toys for the beach.

'Helen has to hear sense from someone… Yiannis thinks perhaps you will talk with her?'

She had never heard of anything so weird: that she should go to tell another woman that she hadn't slept with her husband. Why would she and why should she? She could well imagine what Helen's reaction would be. Was there some congenital lunacy in the Konstantinidis males?

One thing was clear: the sooner she set off to find Steve, stolid and American and rich, the better.

****

When Yiannis left the beach, Daniel and Frank resumed their game, though Daniel's concentration was even worse than before. Frank studied the board, wriggling his plump toes in the soft sand and scratching his stubble, evidently waiting for Daniel to say something.

'Life has its quirks,' said Daniel, finally.

Frank nodded, though Daniel was sure the word would be new to him.

'Strange things happen,' Daniel clarified.

'They do, my friend, they do…'

It was then they heard shouting. Daniel was certain he could recognise Yiannis' voice, and could the other be Jenny's...? The breeze had recently eased and the sounds were carrying. No one else on the beach seemed concerned, but Daniel was on his feet immediately. He hesitated a moment until it recommenced, then hurried into the camp site and through the tents.

He discovered high drama. Jenny was on her feet, backed against a thin tree. Yiannis was just yards away in pugilistic pose, apparently howling at her and at the sky; and another man stood between them, a man who looked like a bank manager, his palm raised against Yiannis' chest, restraining him, trying to calm him, in Greek.

Jenny was angry too, screaming that Yiannis could 'Fuck off', that they could both 'Fuck off.'

'You must do this! You will do this!' Yiannis was fierce with indignation.

He was a mountain of a man and inflamed; Daniel, who had never been a man of action, hesitated. But a hand on his hip moved him aside and Frank pushed past. He'd followed Daniel but now strode forward, positioning himself beside the bank manager, calm and assured.

He seemed to be weighing up the figure before him, then, '*Stamáta tóra*,' he said quietly to Yiannis.

It was like a face-off between two grizzlies. Frank was slightly shorter but much the heavier of the two. As if he fought huge aggressive builders every day, he exuded the confidence that usually belonged to Yiannis, who was wild-eyed and breathing heavily but didn't strike.

Daniel, relieved, held out a hand to pull Jenny away from danger. He finally recognised Kostas, who took Yiannis by his right arm and tugged him aside too, speaking a tumble of rapid Greek to his brother. Daniel was still wary, but Kostas had always presented himself as level-headed and mature and seemed to have taken control.

The crisis passed. Looking less like a Greek god and, increasingly, more like a man who hadn't slept for two nights and whose entire world was collapsing around him, Yiannis dropped his fists and stood blinking. All violent intent dissipated in an instant. It would have been no surprise to see tears begin to run down his cheeks but Daniel had no sympathy for him. He'd brought this on himself.

And there was no way he'd plead Yiannis' case to Helen.

Daniel put a protective arm around Jenny despite what she'd done, because she was visibly shaken. Kostas began to lead away his brother. Frank stood back but was ready, in case he was needed again. The German woman zipped up her tent and scurried off towards the beach, no doubt to report all that had just happened to her husband and any audience she could find.

****

Jeanette's son was improving, though she still couldn't leave him because his gastro-enteritis was clearing only slowly, which was why she'd dispatched Kostas to Serifos. For now, she could offer Helen nothing more than sympathy from afar. They'd spent hours on the phone.

'So, what's the latest? I'm still shocked he'd do anything like this…'

'He isn't Kostas. He never was…'

'Oh, Helen…'

'Last night, he said it'll never ever happen again. Of course, he would. He keeps apologising and says it was the drink. He says nothing much happened anyway. But I can see right through him. You would too. He's lying. Maybe he's been lying since I met him. And I know I won't be able to forget. What happens stays with me. You know that…'

'…Therefore?'

'Therefore I sent him back to his mother's.'

'And he just went?'

'Yes. There was no trouble. I expected worse.'

'He didn't…' Jeanette was trying to frame an idea. 'There wasn't any…? He didn't…'

'He was upset. But it was fine. He went quietly.'

'The girls?'

'They're not stupid. They know something's wrong. For now, daddy's working very hard and mama needs a break from the taverna…'

Helen felt her anguish welling up again but she'd vowed to herself she wouldn't cry any more. She'd cried enough. This mess had to be sorted with a clear head, not through a veil of tears.

She moved the phone from her ear. A motorbike was approaching.

'Jan, I have to go. He's back again. I'll ring you later. Thank you.'

'Good luck, girl.'

Helen smoothed down her hair and tried to calm herself. The ache behind her eyes had returned. She was so tired.

Yiannis came in with Kostas, who said hello but paused in the doorway. Helen was relieved he was there.

'Tell her, Yiannis,' he said, nodded at Helen and went out to the terrace, leaving them alone.

Her husband looked as bad as she felt, yet he demonstrated no obvious sense of guilt. His eyes were red and he needed a shower, but he'd adopted the tone of a victim. He wanted her to forget, to move on, but he could go on wanting.

'Eleni…'

'Yiannis, don't tell me you did nothing. *Varéthika me ta psémata sou.*'

'Eleni, I will tell you. It was one time. It will be the only time. There, it is done.'

An admission. Finally. It came as a kind of relief. But that was all he had to offer? Really? Really?

This was no longer the man she'd married. From now on, he would always be another liar, another who couldn't be trusted. She demanded better and she deserved better.

This was the end.

When the home phone began ringing, he ignored it. So did she at first, but the caller was persistent. It rang and rang. Still looking at him, she picked up the receiver, expecting Jeanette to be on the other end, expecting her friend to be checking on her one more time.

'Yes?'

Words came spilling down the wire in a deluge. It was Katerina from the taverna and she was hysterical. Yiannis' mother was ill. She had collapsed. She had chest pains. She had fallen and hurt her head. The doctor was on his way. 'Come quickly! *Grigora!*'

Helen plummeted into another level of hell.

'It's your mother, Yiannis! Kostas! Kostas!' she shouted, and he started in from the garden.

There was no discussion. The siren luring Yiannis into her web was no longer of importance; the marriage was no sort of priority; a stone had been dropped into the pool so that Daniel's reflection was shattered. Just for the moment, only one person mattered.

The girls were at Vicki's, so the three of them rushed to the car. Kostas, always the calmer, climbed into the driver's seat. Yiannis sat beside him. Helen leant forward in the back, trying to control her panic. She put a hand on Kostas' shoulder and squeezed it gently, wanting him to know that everything would be all right; then she rested her other hand on Yiannis' shoulder too, because at that moment it seemed the natural thing to do.

****

Jenny had packed her rucksack by the time Dan and the boys left the beach. She said, 'Hi,' through the trees as they passed, and Daniel came over.

'You're leaving.' It seemed an obvious, disinterested statement.

'Yep. I'll get things sorted with the car first, then I'm gone. I'll be on tonight's ferry. I've an acquaintance who's an archaeologist. He'll be pleased to see me.' He'd promised her a king size bed.

'Such a life.' His disapproval was tangible. 'Travel safely,' he said, without emotion. There was no fond farewell.

'Enjoy the rest of your stay. The tent's yours, if you want it.' There was no reason why she shouldn't be magnanimous. 'If you like, you can bequeath it to the next homeless soul when you're leaving.'

'It's an idea. It would be good to get off the concrete. Lewis's been exhausted all holiday and he'd sleep better in a tent, I imagine. I might feel guilty about deceiving the owner but maybe we'll tell him we've moved in. Anyway, we can think about it.'

It was all very stilted and there was no apparent gratitude and, unsurprisingly, no exchange of addresses, but what had she done to hurt him so badly? She'd driven him and the boys around and then screwed some guy who wasn't his friend anyway which could mean Dan might reclaim his girl. Why the hell did she have to suffer this ice? She might have received at least a muffled 'thank you' in return.

On the other hand, did it matter? Why be piqued? Yiannis was now gone and he'd be a large red tick in her history of top screws, so this visit to Serifos had been more than worthwhile. She had new experiences ahead and there was always a new lover if you needed one.

Her mojo was back.

She hauled on her pack and pulled the pink cap down over her eyes.

'See you, Dan.' She looked across at the boys, who were observing from the path. 'Bye, Jonny. Bye, Lew.'

Each raised a hand and she nodded at them. Daniel offered a half-hearted smile, not even a handshake and no hug.

****

Despite his fear that he could be held accountable for all the tent fees which had accrued from the start of the season, Daniel told his boys they were making the move. The man who swept the paths gazed at them oddly as they struggled along with their rucksacks and arms full of towels and the bits and pieces they couldn't be bothered to pack, but Daniel gave him a friendly smile. Everything could be sorted at the office the next day.

They rested their rucksacks against the stone wall in front of the tent's entrance because there was only enough room inside for the three of them, and arranged the things needed daily – soap bags, creams of varying kinds, books, small toys – in the tent's bell-end, behind where their heads would rest. It was a tight fit but the boys loved it and it was a much better home than the one they'd left on the concrete. Daniel put their dried pomegranate in the hanging pocket above their heads.

'To celebrate our palatial new surroundings, I suggest we spend what is left of the day at Psili Ammos, kids. What do you think?'

He couldn't just sit under their tree, thinking about Helen for hours, hoping and dreaming. Better to invest in a walk then a swim, he thought: and then maybe, if he were lucky, there might be an hour or two with Helen at the end of the day.

'No one's invited us, dad,' said Jonny.

'That's a problem? It's a public beach and not far away. If we could walk back, we can walk there too, surely?'

Lewis groaned. 'It's a long way. There's the huge hill and then the long road. And it goes up and down all the time.'

'It's nothing for fit young men like ourselves. And we can get some food at the port. Cheese pies?' He saw Lewis's face brighten. 'Lay's Crisps as an extra? And a nectarine? Good, eh? Come on. Pack quickly and we shall away.'

Their towels and beach mats, a large bottle of water, a small ball to throw around in the sea, sun cream, books, Yu-Gi-Oh! Cards, the pen knife and two water pistols were crammed into Jonny's rucksack, the original contents of which they piled inside the tent. They stole away before Frank noticed. He was a wonderful man and Daniel owed him a favour but he knew Frank would struggle to walk the two miles or so to the beach and he didn't want to have to spend his time telling both him and Lewis that they were nearly there.

Once they were out of the other end of town, safely past the entrance to Konstantinidis' but still beside the sea, Daniel's spirits soared like a gull. He couldn't be certain that Helen would return to England and to him, but now there was an excellent chance. He could begin to imagine a life with Helen, Jonny and Lewis and maybe her daughters too. It was all beyond those wildest dreams.

He marshalled the boys back along the route they'd taken after Jenny's crash. Leaving the coast, they passed through tall bamboo. There were no cars, even during the day. Daniel knew that Helen lived somewhere close, over there to their left, out of sight. Obviously, there was no sign of her.

When they emerged from the shady lane, they faced a long bend in the road that swung round and rose a hundred feet above them. However, on their right, climbing directly uphill, was a rough track beside an empty holiday home. It meandered through gorse and was stony and steep but to save time and, ultimately, effort, they took it, scrambling up, slipping and sliding as they went. Daniel was encumbered by the pack so Jonny did his best to help Lewis.

It was tricky, but once they stood on the road again, the big hill was almost done – there were only two hundred and fifty yards more to climb – and they could head along the road's undulations to the beach. It was only twenty minutes away.

They rested and took a mouthful of water. The view was spectacular. Beneath them, new white buildings had sprouted, framed by well-watered olive greenery. Others were being planted. There wasn't the three-hundred-and-sixty degree panorama they experienced at the top of Chora, but they looked right down to the port in the distance, to tiny boats and shimmering sea, to the whole bay and beyond. It was Serifos at its spectacular best. The light was sharp and the air was burning. On the horizon, there were islands. By a trick of the light, the nearest, Sifnos, appeared mystically suspended in mid-air because out there the blue sky and the blue sea became one.

'Isn't this magical?' said Daniel. 'It makes you feel it's the most special place in the world. Just look at that…'

'I need another drink,' said Jonny, who was a child and unimpressed.

Lewis sat on a large rock beside the road, looking down at the ground.

'Maybe you'll both appreciate it one day.'

They took another swig from the bottle and Daniel prepared to haul Lewis to his feet. He stopped, though, to look out again, as a whirling sound came over the hills and a helicopter appeared from their left, flying low along the coast but then slowing, circling before hovering over the port. Vehicles were being moved away from the end section of the quay, where the ferry boats moored. Daniel was sorry they weren't down there to watch and even the exhausted Lewis showed interest. A helicopter wasn't a customary sight on Serifos.

It hung for a moment before turning through a hundred and eighty degrees, descending and touching down. Once it settled, two figures ran from it and there was bustling activity, everyone bending forward as the rotor blades continued to turn. A van drove forward... and was that a stretcher being lifted from it and to the aircraft?

'Rock star leaving, dad?' asked Jonny.

'Unlikely... Unless he's fast asleep.'

It took only minutes before the helicopter was airborne again, rising swiftly before swooping up and towards the watchers on the coast road, heading north. Lewis waved, though it wasn't near them. They watched it disappear.

'Imagine being up there, free like a bird, feeling as if you can float for ever if you want, above the clouds, no fears, no worries, no pains...'

'I'm really tired, dad. I just want to be in the sea.'

They set off again, slowly, at Lewis's pace, sweating freely but well on the way to Psili Ammos, where Daniel knew there'd be shade.

They could wait until it was cooler to walk back and they'd be able to eat at Konstantinidis' on their way, even if that caused problems, Daniel needed to find out how Helen was coping. Maybe she'd come to their table and tell him she was coming home to England. For once, he was aflame with positivity.

He smiled at the hills of Serifos and the rocky road ahead and the trudging of Jonny and Lewis. Expanding his chest, he nodded to himself: fantasies can come true.

****

Kostas had offered to stay behind, make arrangements for the business and sort out care for the girls, so just Helen was crammed into the helicopter beside Yiannis. She gazed at the medical paraphernalia all around them and at the old lady's face where she lay on the stretcher. Terrified her mother-in-law wouldn't make it to intensive care, Helen was encased in a paralysing dread she'd never experienced before.

The noise in the chopper was intense and they were handed ear protectors. They could do nothing except watch the two medics working beside *yiayiá*, who was on a stretcher, covered in blankets, not moving, her face colourless. Before take-off she was given an injection, then a line was run into her arm and she was wired to a monitor.

Helen had never been religious and had spent a lifetime saying she had no time for churches and their superstitions but found herself praying silently that the old lady would be spared. Were she and Yiannis responsible for the sickness of this good woman? She felt immense guilt.

There was a chance she would live, because medical care on the island was so much better than in the past. The trainee doctor who ran the new health centre below Chora had rushed to the taverna, checked her, diagnosed her problem and immediately called to get her lifted to the hospital in Athens since there were no facilities for heart-attack victims on Serifos. Thankfully, this was happening in summer – often in winter the helicopter wouldn't be able to land, and there might only be one boat in a week.

Helen knew the old lady would fight because she'd want to see her grandchildren grow up. And, importantly, she was still there to support her. Imagine if she'd been on a plane to England…

The noise from the engine and rotor blades increased as they lifted off and her stomach lurched when the machine pitched to one side to move rapidly away. On any other day, she'd have been terrified to take such a trip. Now, her own feelings were incidental.

The bay, the boats, the blue were a blur filling the entire window to the left; then they steadied and there were the high parched hills beyond, with tiny figures on the road towards

Agios Sostis and Psili Ammos. The pilot swung them at speed directly along the coastline.

Over Serifos for the first time ever, she looked down on its hillsides, grey, pale green and yellow in the summer sun, and its scattered and lonely communities. From the air she saw the aridity but also a size she'd never appreciated before.

And the island was still huge in her soul. Of course it was. She needed this place. She always had. The half-formed plan to leave with Daniel had never been real.

Instead, she was focusing on what mattered. She looked at Kyria Konstantinidis struggling to stay alive, the woman who had been her only true mother, then she looked out again. This was her home and she could never leave.

She realised she was clutching Yiannis' hand tightly. His face was fixed, no doubt with fears, but his other arm was stiffly around his wife.

They had no words to share in such noise, but they were not there to talk, they were there to make sure Yiannis' mother didn't slip away. They were there to ensure she lived to supervise the cooking some more, and they would support her back to good health together.

In those exceptional surroundings, Helen realised it was inconceivable that she might ever have a life without Yiannis. Despite everything, despite what Yiannis had done that night in the tent and whatever he might have done in the past, she couldn't imagine living without him and without the family, without the taverna and without Serifos.

In such a short time, her state of mind had transformed: she would stay where she was, she and Yiannis would work out their problems and all would be well, just so long as *yiayiá* survived.

2019

Chapter 7

Daniel had cheated death, for the moment at least, and the roulette wheel of his world was spinning again after years of desperation. He had another chance. He could drink beer and wine, savour rich sauces and enjoy the warmth of the sun and the sweep of the night sky. He relished his good fortune.

In almost every sense, he was back.

He'd settled himself on a long seat in the middle of the deck under the massive awning, but moved his position each time the boat adjusted its course, to ensure he avoided the sun. He wore a long-sleeved shirt, jeans, trainers and a bush hat and didn't mind the odd looks coming his way.

Greece still had ferries a-plenty but the Adam Korais was one of only two old-style boats still running down the Western Cyclades from Piraeus. He could have chosen a high-speed, which would have delivered him into Serifos in two and a half hours, but he wanted to do things the right way. This, fresh air and breeze and sparkling sea, was how you sailed to a Greek island. It was not the same experience when you were trapped in a hurtling sardine can.

Twenty-first century Greece was so different: less fascinating but so easy to navigate since the country's rough edges had been smoothed down. He booked his journey on-line through Paleologos Travel before he even left the UK and the mini-bus from the Phidias in Piraeus, a clean and friendly boutique hotel, had taken him right to the boat, which departed spot on time. Many passengers showed their phones rather than a ticket, but Daniel was not so technically savvy.

They called first at Kithnos, which, like everywhere else, was embracing the modern age: even the huge decrepit hotel on the port had had a facelift.

Everything seemed improved. In fact, approaching Serifos they were accompanied by four dolphins, playing in the bow wave, sleek grey bodies leaping though the wash. It was the first time in all his years in Greece that had happened. There were so many things still to experience, he thought, still to live for.

More houses had been sprinkled across the Serifos hillsides. He moved forward and leant against the rail to see what else was new as the Korais turned into Livadi Bay, the two funnels spewing black smoke like the old ferries always had: Greta Thunberg would have wept.

Chora at least appeared unchanged, pristine white in the September sunshine, and people around him took photographs. They were mostly young and many were attractive girls with pretty faces and tight bottoms. He still noticed.

The Chinese had selfie-sticks and must have had limitless storage space on their phones. Of course, it did occur to him they might not be Chinese. You had to be so careful nowadays. Anyway, whatever their nationality, they took picture after picture. They hadn't known a time when each print cost serious money, so you shot sparingly and only found out weeks later, when you were home and the films were printed, whether the pictures had been worth the investment. He'd been so proud of his Brownie 127 when he was a child. Had it been twelve pictures per roll of film, or just eight..? You forget.

He went back to his seat. There was an old Greek man sitting opposite, an image from other times, wearing worn clothes and ageless wrinkles. Daniel smiled at him, and the man nodded back. Greece's economy was still under the cosh and the old and poor were suffering the most, as always, everywhere.

With Brexit hanging like an executioner's axe over the UK and set to add decades of austerity, Daniel wondered if the quality of his own life would decline sharply soon. Britain wasn't heading towards a golden future, whatever the nationalists might say. Despite his general sense of wellbeing, he sighed. It had become a habit he was trying to break.

At least he no longer worried about trivialities like whether his savings would see him through until he was coffined and cremated. He had bigger worries and just hoped the lunatics in charge of the Brexit-obsessed government would remember that to stay alive he was not alone in depending upon a battery of drugs from Europe. If the supplies were delayed or came to an end, so would he.

He smoothed some additional Factor 50 on to his exposed skin.

The loudspeaker system crackled instructions about disembarkation and he went down to the lower deck, edging past parked vehicles and other passengers to the luggage racks and his wheelie case. The drivers hadn't started their engines, which was an unexpected treat for his lungs.

When the boat had turned and reversed to the quay, the transom was lowered, sunshine flooded in and the lenses in his glasses darkened. Fresh air. Warning lights flashed and a siren sounded.

Other than that, little had changed: lines were thrown ashore and hawsers were dropped over the bollards on the quay. Within moments, he and the milling throng – around a hundred and fifty strong – were clumping cases down the ramp, trundling ashore amidst the old chaos. Port policewomen blew their whistles and herded the arrivals towards town.

The first buildings beside the road were all new: car rental offices, a new taverna… The old one at the end of the quay which had become a ticket office before the turn of the century had been replaced by a very smart-looking supermarket.

He blinked as sweat ran into his eyes, crossing the road to a wooden seat on a glaring white marina which had been created by pouring a massive volume of concrete into the bay. White yachts were moored before him, where local fishing boats used to bob. It was relatively up-market, but not horrendous. The old Serifos was still recognisable: the colours and the atmosphere of the island. He knew it was going to be all right. Oh, he'd missed it.

He checked his phone, found his email confirmation from Hotels.com, then rose and headed on towards the empty taxi rank, dragging his case behind him. He wondered if the man who used to sit outside the Captain's Taverna producing wooden carvings in the evening was still around. He guessed not. People die.

He had to run a gauntlet of young waiters who were on the

street even at lunchtime, out from a row of new restaurants offering the best fish and the best Greek dishes, the best of everything. They were like the ones who'd been harassing cruise passengers on Santorini for decades, but their relentlessness was a new phenomenon for Serifos.

'Maybe later,' he said to one and then the next and the next.

He would have stopped for a drink, but was looking for Kristina from the Ariadne Apartments, who'd emailed to say she'd meet him... And there she stood, across the road, beside a narrow alley, holding a piece of cardboard with his name on it. She was beautiful, slim, in her early twenties... Once upon a time, though it seemed not so long ago, he'd have longed to make her a close acquaintance.

Now, formally, 'Hello,' he said, offering his hand respectfully. 'I'm Daniel.'

'And I am Kristina. Welcome.' She had a broad smile and perfect white teeth. 'Please, this way. The hotel is not far. Can I take your case?'

He always forgot how old he could seem.

'No, I'm fine. Thank you. I can manage. Please: lead on.'

He followed her slim figure down the alley to a nondescript apartment building, and then inside.

His room, as he'd requested, was at the back with a mountain view. It was simple but perfect for his needs, and cheap. There was a double bed, an old wardrobe and a small, spotlessly clean en-suite. Opposite the bed was a kitchen area, with an antique tiled surround and a small breakfast bar. A sliding door opened on to a narrow balcony.

'I hope you will be happy here.'

'I am sure I shall be.'

'If you have any problem, just ask. I will be cleaning the rooms every morning between ten and twelve.' She handed him his key. 'You can drink the tap water in Serifos. You have seen the restaurants..? Enjoy your stay.' She stopped at the door. 'This is your first time here on Serifos?'

Where to begin?

'Not exactly. I've been before. Many times. I still don't speak Greek... though I should... I haven't been here for
226

maybe twelve years; but I'm so happy to have returned. I love Serifos.' She smiled at him. 'I first came about forty years ago…'

'No! So long! Then you are a real Serifosi… Welcome back, Daniel!'

When she left, he donned his hat again and sat on his balcony. He squeezed himself into a chair in what shade there was and watched the people from the next building busying themselves in their small garden serenaded by the cicadas.

He loved being alive.

He might have stayed there for longer, but he hadn't eaten since his six o'clock breakfast. He drank some tap water – yes, it was good, and would save him money and mean he was not throwing away yet more plastic bottles – then went to the Condilis supermarket, still tight and bustling in the centre of town. After picking up some fruit outside, he squeezed his way round the narrow aisles and stacked boxes to the till with a basket of coffee, milk, cheese and breakfast cereal. They now welcomed credit card payments. He bought bread and cake and fruit juice from the bakery across the road – which, like Condilis, was almost exactly as he remembered it – and returned to his room.

With four weeks' holiday to come, he was in no rush to do anything. He ate a cheese and tomato sandwich, avoiding the heat, then stretched out comfortably on the bed. Before he dozed he sent a text: 'It is still lovely, Jonny. Hot and quiet. You'll adore it. And so will Lara, of course.'

There was an almost immediate response: 'Yes, we will. Keep taking the tablets, dad! x'

Instant communication.

Long flights the day before – including a connection in Frankfurt – and having to get up early for the ferry had tired him, so he slept for several hours. The air-conditioning churned noisily but worked well and the room was beautifully cool.

When he came round, refreshed, he dug out clean clothes for the evening. He could wear whatever he wanted because there was a drying rack out on the balcony if he wanted to wash anything through and, anyway, the house he'd booked for the next week had a washing machine. He glanced in the mirror at his pale face and the long scar across his chest which was also white now but perfectly healed. It was all good enough.

He chose a fresh pair of blue trousers and another long-sleeved shirt because the sun was still high, and did his best to flatten out the creases.

After plastering every bit of bare skin with factor 50 again, he checked his shoulder bag to make sure he had everything he might need: his wallet and phone, mosquito repellent and the required tablets: azathioprine, omeprazole and ciclosporin and calcichew for later. If she were still alive, his mum would have said she could hear him rattle.

Satisfied, he pulled his hat low over his eyes and went to get a beer.

****

Helen looked up from her laptop and watched the lights twinkling in town, across the bay. The night had descended some hours before, but Yiannis would not be home for a while. The spreadsheet on her screen had reminded her that next week she had an English family coming called Daniels and just for a moment the Daniel she had loved came back into her mind, as he occasionally did. Time had passed; his boys would be men now.

She sometimes thought about his stupidity, his indecision and his apologies, and his soft eyes and gentleness. But not often. It's odd how your mind wanders when you're tired though, she thought. Without trying, you carry silly doe-eyed moments round forever, deep in your subconscious, even those from an age ago, and they suddenly catch you unawares.

She stretched her arms above her head, yawned and decided she'd done enough. It was time for bed. She closed down the program, relieved that everything was sorted for the next week because organising room bookings was like endlessly reconstructing a jig-saw, shifting pieces around as circumstances inevitably changed.

Even after ten years, the task needed concentration, but another long day was over. The tables were set for breakfast; the boiled eggs, meats and cheese were in the fridge, ready to lift out in the morning; the cutlery, plates, bowls and mugs were all in place and the fruit was ready to be sliced and diced for the serving bowl. She'd just need to prepare the pastries and get bread from the bakery.

A car pulled up below and she responded with a '*Kaló vrádi*' to the Greek couple arriving back. Being pleasant was important: reviews on TripAdvisor matter. The guests continued on up the steps to their room and she was relieved they hadn't come over to talk.

Since no-one else was around, she sat out on one of the deck chairs on the terrace and for once, for a moment, rested. She caught snatches of music from Livadi and watched the lights on the yachts in the bay. She could manage to find such moments only rarely. Summer months were hard when you were no longer young but overseeing a holiday empire.

She smoothed her dress over her knees and pushed back her hair from her face: all this, she thought, sardonically, and still a beautiful woman. Yet even when she was drained, emotionally so low, she took satisfaction from what she had, from what she'd created for her daughters.

Of course, she always had to be on-site, in case she was needed, so she and Yiannis coped somehow in the room beside the dining area during the summer. Because it was so small, they kept only vital things with them and a couple of changes of clothes. Most of their possessions were with Lilliana in the family house.

Yiannis returned to his wife even later, after the taverna closed and everything was cleared. Helen, who had been in bed for some time, stirred at the revving of his bike; then came his heavy tread outside and the rattle as he opened the door. But she didn't wake fully until he flushed the toilet and the mattress sank as he lay beside her.

She turned towards him, routinely kissing his stubbled cheek as he ran his hand over her hair. It was the complacency of a long marriage, with no energy for passion.

Customarily he fell straight to sleep but for once he spoke.

'Daniel is here,' he said. Just that.

'*Thódos*? Really?' Something lurched inside her. Daniel… She'd never expected to see him again. She was uncertain how to ask about him, not wanting to seem as eager for news as she instantly and shockingly felt.

Yiannis stretched and yawned, offering nothing more.

After a few moments, she discovered the courage to prompt him, her voice light with casualness: 'How strange he should be back after so many years. How did he look?' She paused. 'Is he alone?'

'Yes. But he is different. I don't know. Very smart. Very white. Like Englishmen in movies. You will see…'

She lay still beside him. She hadn't seen Daniel since the day Kyria Konstantinidis was taken ill. Andreas and Michalis told her he'd visited the island intermittently and briefly for a few years afterwards, but either she'd been in Athens, because the old lady had been back in hospital there several times, or she'd been with Jeanette and Kostas. He didn't linger so their paths hadn't crossed.

Was he back because he was missing the island? No, she was wiser than that.

And she was unexpectedly thrilled. She hadn't felt this huge surge of desire the last time she'd seen him, yet now there was a rush of expectation and hope. She could feel the blood in her temples, her temperature raised. Had her life become so dull? Was it because she was almost sixty? Was it merely a desire to feel loved again?

She slept little and when she rose at six the next morning, bleary-eyed and drawn, she felt exhaustion but still a simmering excitement, a sensation that had become alien to her.

However, life couldn't stop because of Daniel. She had work as usual. Before anyone was about, she made pastries and laid out the breakfast buffet, which she covered with cloths, and before eight o'clock she went off in her car to buy fresh bread. When the holidaymakers emerged, she bustled around them. They ate and some lingered. There was sunshine on the terrace and she offered the endless coffee and food that justified in part the 150 euros a night she charged to stay in her

230

rooms. She always had a full house in summer and many of the guests lingered for an hour or two so breakfast stretched from half past eight right through the morning.

Afterwards there was washing up to be done and the laptop to pore over again and schedules to check. Since she also had to help Elira service the rooms, because it was a day with a turnover of guests, there was no respite. Then, later in the afternoon, there were transfers: she made three runs to the ferries to take people who were leaving but had waited on the terrace all day; and she had to pick up the new arrivals, who also needed to be settled in.

Still, she was determined to be at the taverna during the evening, certain that Daniel would be there.

She might have worn her best, looked her best, but Yiannis would be present too, so she'd have to restrain her ridiculous impulses. No makeup.

She did find time to phone Jeanette.

'He's back? Gosh. Interesting.' She could well imagine Jeanette's mischievous smile. 'But an old lady like you can't be going moist at the idea of seeing him? Don't tell me you are...'

'Of course not.'

'You are...! I can hear it in your voice. Pheromones drifting across the water...' She paused. 'You've needed something... Someone... Be careful.'

'I know, Jan.'

'But enjoy... And say hello to him from me. If he's staying, I'll come over in the next few days. I wonder what's been happening to him? It must be... How long?'

'I know I was much younger.' She laughed, but felt the years were just now falling from her. 'Fourteen? Fifteen years? About that. It was when *yiayiá* was so bad, the first time... Maybe I'll see him tonight.'

'Don't forget – give him my love... Control yours...'

Jeanette knew how long her friend had been feeling low.

When Helen parked the car on the road beside Konstantinidis' at nine o'clock, at first she thought she'd missed him. The tables were almost all taken, but there was no one she recognised.

Then she spotted him, sitting alone at the table on the end, on the beach, almost beyond the lights, where he used to sit with Jonny and Lewis. She recognised his profile, though much of his hair had gone; he was wearing glasses and a sharp striped shirt. A hat was on the corner of his table. He wouldn't have known it, but he was staring out across the water towards the apartments she'd just left, on the promontory opposite.

She remained where she was in the car, watching, until Yiannis came to her. 'Yes, he has changed,' he said, through the open window.

'That seems to be the case.' She looked again. 'But haven't we all..? I'm going to say hello.'

Yiannis pursed his lips in acquiescence and nodded. He went back to barking orders at the cooks and the waiters. Sitting at what had been his mother's table, with a glass of beer in front of him, he observed all, thinking he controlled everything. Both Andreas and Michalis were still there, hurrying round, but paying little attention to anything he said. They'd told Helen many times that they'd been doing the job for over twenty years and didn't need a builder to tell them how to do it properly. Even though she'd become a Konstantinidis, they remembered her as a cook, an employee like themselves, and talked to her as they would a friend.

Helen filled a glass with water and made her way towards Daniel. She could feel Yiannis' eyes on her back.

Daniel was in conversation with a young couple at the next table.

'We can't believe there aren't any swimming pools here,' said the girl in a cut crystal accent.

'I mean... we quite like it, but it's very primitive, isn't it?' said her companion.

'Desperately primitive,' said Daniel.

'It just isn't the Amalfi Coast, is it?' said the boy, who radiated Eton or Harrow or Winchester. 'I mean... what's it got to offer? Just scruffy little beaches and small houses. It's hard, working in the City, and you want something special from your vac, don't you? We went to Thailand last July....'

'There's certainly nothing much to bring you back here,' said Daniel.

'Actually, it's quite horrid,' said the girl.

The couple turned back to their food. The man poured two glasses of wine from their bottle, tasted it and grimaced.

'Oh, no! This won't do! It really won't do.' He tried to attract Michalis' attention, but he was ignoring them.

Daniel still hadn't noticed Helen standing beside him.

She pointedly cleared her throat. When he turned, his face came alive.

'Helen. It is. It is.'

He stood and pushed away his chair to embrace her; and he held her more gently than she could ever remember. He caught his breath and bit his lip. 'Oh, my goodness... You are still so lovely...' He took half a step back, holding her arms. She held on to his. 'Of course you are!' he said. 'Of course you would be!'

His eyes filled with tears as she realised that was just what she'd hoped he'd say.

****

'It's hard to know where to start.'

Daniel couldn't take his eyes off her and couldn't stop smiling. He was feeling like he did when they first met. He wanted to offer her everything he had, embrace her, hold her and never let go. However, with Yiannis watching, he simply loved her with his eyes.

'We can sit like this?'

She knew what he meant. 'Yes. He's fine.' Maybe the years had given them total trust.

'He said hello last night.'

Andreas brought them a bottle of retsina and an extra glass for Helen and rested his hand on Daniel's shoulder as he turned to leave.

'Enjoy,' he said, without any sort of smile.

'You've a friend.' She sounded surprised.

'I've not been back for ages, but he remembered me. He's the only waiter who kisses me when I arrive on the island. Well, to be honest he's the only waiter who kisses me anywhere. He does it in a very Greek way, you understand. No sex. No sex at all. Manly stuff. We kind of got to know each other a while back. You were never around…'

'I had some difficult times.'

'Yes...' He didn't probe. 'I needed to see you… Anyway, Andreas and I got on well. I'd come in the morning when he'd little to do. He'd sit at a table with me and drink a coffee. We talked a lot. They say he's a communist but he's the best kind of socialist really. But you know that. He's very decent, very, very decent – if a little stubbly when we're snogging… And he's very clever. His language skills are amazing, but you know that too. To just hear him talking to visitors in German, French, Italian… Yesterday, I asked him why he's still working here and he waved across the water, across the bay, and said, "My friend, I have this. Every day." I asked him what will happen when he becomes old. He said, "In Greece, we do not worry about that. Now is more important…" I understand. I do know what he means. To be that content...'

'Yes. If only….' Before he could comment, she added, 'We all love Serifos… You're not sleeping on the beach this time?'

'I'm definitely too old for that. I'm at the Ariadne.'

'Kristina's place. I know her. And her husband. She's a friend of Sophia.'

'Oh. Married.'

'And much too young for you!'

He smiled. There was a long pause. He waited for her to say, 'And are you content, Daniel?' Perhaps, he thought, that's too big a question.

She took a different route: 'So, come on, make a start. How are you and how are the boys?'

They had to begin somewhere.

'Jonny's fine. Doing well. He has a good job in university administration and a lovely girlfriend. They're joining me in a couple of days.'

He knew that would never be enough, but took a sip of wine and waited.

'That's nice. And Lewis?'

He knew she'd ask and it never got any easier. He composed himself for a moment.

'Lewis died.'

As he spoke, his tears came, as they always did, even after so long. He knew it would happen and there was nothing he could do to prevent it. He struggled to pull a tissue from his pocket and her face threatened to dissolve too.

'No.'

He breathed deeply, steadying himself.

'Stuff happens.'

'"Those whom the gods love die young..." Herodotus...'

'No, it's just further proof that there is no god. No good god, anyway. There can't be.'

It was a conversation he'd had many times.

Helen looked distressed, as she would. Finally, 'How..?' she asked.

The usual question. He filled his lungs and sighed.

'I used to tell him off for being lazy and claiming to be tired all the time... He had leukaemia.'

'Oh, the poor child.' He could feel her wondering when it happened, how long it took, how much Lewis suffered, how they'd coped since.

'When?'

'Years ago.'

He didn't want to talk about any details and she was the epitome of tact. 'But, Daniel, you weren't to know...'

That had been said many times too. It never helped. It was a platitude. Well-meant, but a platitude.

He still saw Lewis lying in the bed, numbed by drugs, lost, beyond this world already.

He took a few moments to collect himself.

'So... So... Meanwhile... your girls?'

That was easier for them both to handle.

'Yes. We're all doing fine. Yiannis' sisters are married, in Germany, but our branch of the family has an expanding business... We have a house up in Chora that we rent out – Lilliana has charge of that. And she helps me with cooking over at Hotel Spiti. You are not to laugh! It's a good name for a Greek hotel. It means "home". It's there.' She nodded at the headland opposite: 'Those lights.' It was the largest complex. 'We do well on TripAdvisor. And Sophia looks after our apartments up the hill.' She nodded again, towards the clusters of new buildings behind Livadi. 'My girls are wonderful. Beautiful and strong.'

As soon as he stepped off the Adam Korais, Daniel decided the view had been devastated by the buildings across from the port, on what had been a barren but romantic spur of land. Yet people have to live, he thought now. Especially Helen. Who was he to judge?

Jonny always told him that as an environmentalist he was far too fickle.

'And Yiannis seems to have control of this place,' he said, looking round the taverna. The once shady trees had been hacked back and there was a wooden roof over the tables. A section of one side had a wooden wall, which would cut off much of the wind but also part of the view for some diners. It was the concept of a builder, rather than of an aesthete, and Daniel felt much of the original charm had gone: but he didn't say so. 'Such success for one family...'

He didn't ask how Yiannis' skills transferred to the hospitality industry but imagined he must have considerable help when it came to the food and the cooking.

Helen read his thoughts. 'Yiannis is the owner and manager. His mother died ten years ago now.'

'I'm sorry.'

'Thank you. I'd grown to love her very much. I thought about leaving but stayed when she had her first heart attack...' He nodded. Andreas had told him the full story. 'We were very close... Anyway, she'd stashed away more money than we ever imagined. She was quite a businesswoman... It meant we've managed to survive the financial meltdown and all the EU throws at us.' She leant forward: 'Having a brother-in-law in the banking business is a great help, and this restaurant does well of course... Then, when it came to the apartments and the rooms, Yiannis had the building skills. It all fitted. Now...' She waved her arm. He looked around the tables and out across the bay, seeing it all as their empire, as if Serifos belonged to them.

'Konstantinidis Inc.?'

She laughed. 'I like that.'

'How very well you've done.'

He said it quietly and sincerely. It gave him enormous pleasure to discover her so successful and fulfilled. He could find no more to say. If he'd added, "You've done so much better than if you'd chosen me," or "You made the right choice after all," he'd have sounded brimful of self-pity, and that was something he tried to avoid.

'Quite a life, eh? I am truly happy for you.'

'Thank you…' Almost formally, awkwardly, she dismissed his felicitations and moved the conversation on – very quickly, he thought. 'But what about you, Daniel? Losing Lewis must have been shattering. I can't imagine… How are you now?'

'It was a long time ago.' He sighed. In truth, it would never be a long time ago. 'I survived. You have to.'

'We all survive somehow.' Just for a moment, she looked her age. 'You seem different though, Daniel. Yiannis said that, and he was right.'

'You mean the lack of hair…'

They both smiled and both took a sip from their glasses. Symmetry, he thought: a girlfriend had once told him it meant togetherness or mutual understanding or love. But maybe it was merely coincidence.

'Your hair is fine,' she said. 'Lovely. Both your hairs, actually.'

Laughing, she was properly young again. He laughed with her.

'Lack of hair is a sign of masculinity. It is because I am constantly exuding male hormones.' He almost added, 'Quite a catch, still.' But he stopped himself, so she could let his comments wash over her.

'What is so different about you, though?'

'I've grown older,' he said.

'We all do. It's not that.'

He had to tell her, of course. It was part of the reason he'd come – to tell her, if he found her. It was not that she could do anything or that he wanted anything from her, nothing she would give, anyway. It was to talk with her, because maybe she'd understand how he felt and what he felt. They'd only known each other for a matter of weeks so long ago, but he hoped that she, out of everyone, would care. He'd idealised her memory but there was no one else in his life, even after all these years, with whom he could share things as he would have liked. Ridiculously, he felt closest to a woman he'd hardly known and no longer knew at all. He might have been inventing their affinity, and the situation was ironic since he hadn't shared things with her as he should have done when they were young, but such was his feeling.

When he told her, she'd sympathise and be pleased for him, he knew, though it was a hard thing to explain without seeming to be seeking sympathy.

He wasn't frightened any more, and had so much to be grateful for. Yet he was sixty-three years old and alone and when he allowed himself to think about it he could feel a cavity at the centre of his being which was deeper and wider than the surgeon had cut.

'Daniel?'

'I've had a strange few years.'

She sat patiently, waiting for more. Cats moved between the tables. Andreas arrived to deliver baklava to the dissatisfied couple on their vac. There was no thank you.

Daniel emitted another sigh, then, 'I had a lung transplant. A double transplant,' he said.

He'd returned to Serifos because he had his health again, after fearing for so long that his end was nigh. He wasn't dying any more – so he'd come just to tell her. There was no logic in his decision but he knew how he'd feel if their situations were reversed. Of course, he couldn't guarantee Helen had anything like the same emotions. She was married, and they'd never been lovers, properly.

'Daniel…' She actually took his hand. It was wonderful.

Without even thinking, he eased his body forward and rested his other hand on hers. It was the simple intimacy he craved, yet he lifted his hand away quickly, realising what he'd done and with her husband watching.

'But you are fine?' she said, as if the contact meant nothing. 'You seem fine. Is everything all right now?'

'I am, as you see, still breathing. For which simple pleasure I am constantly grateful.'

238

'So what was wrong..?'

All the details lived with him as they were bound to.

'I had something called pulmonary fibrosis. It just happened. It's idiopathic: that means there's no definite cause – and before you ask I've never smoked...'

'But they were able to sort it...'

'It's a long story but I went to see a consultant who said I'd die... that there's no cure... that it would be all over... Like that' He snapped his fingers. She blinked, shocked. 'Well, not exactly as simply as that, because I was looking at months, maybe years, of decline. But he offered me no options... I was finished.

'However, this being the twenty-first century, I took to the internet and went looking for a second opinion, like you do. I found a better man. It turned out I could have a transplant, which the first bastard hadn't even mentioned. Without it, I'd have ended up permanently hooked to an oxygen cylinder until the end came...'

She had the stunned look and the need to know.

'Well, remarkably, the man I found is a top, top clinician and surgeon and he said he'd be able to operate. I wasn't bad enough at first – ridiculous as that sounds – but he said that when I was worse but if I was still healthy enough, he'd hope to find me a donor. I know, it is crazy... But also there's another catch: the teams are trained and the beds are waiting in specialist units but there's a huge shortage of organs. After a road crash, the relatives are asked if organs can be used from the victims and the relatives s often say "no"... and another person dies for want of the lungs, or the heart or the kidneys... The government's changing the law at last, so people will need to opt out of organ donation, rather than opting in, which will be better, but meanwhile, people go on dying... and any change would've been too late for me.'

'But..?' She managed a half smile.

'But I was lucky. There was a traffic accident and I was called in to the unit in Manchester... The lungs were a match, a fit... I was a lucky bugger. Some other guy there had been summoned five times but was still waiting. He just had to go home again. Poor sod. You can't imagine the tension, the hope, the fear… My operation lasted ten hours. It was successful and I got two new healthy lungs. Abracadabra: I'm alive once more.' He lowered his head in a semi bow.

This wasn't the moment to tell her about his horrors in intensive care, the wild, terrifying hallucinations, the slow, slow recovery which was still underway, the cupboardful of drugs…

'And you're well enough to come on holiday.'

'But not to sunbathe. The immuno-suppressants I take are strong, which means the rays would give me skin cancer. Staying in the shade is a small price to pay…'

'Just the pallor. Yes, it is. You can fly, even. When did all this happen?'

'Three years ago… Yep, I can travel. If you survive the first year, the doctors reckon you can get back to living pretty normally again. And I am getting fitter.'

'You look honed…' He was glad she didn't say 'emaciated', though he was incredibly thin. It was taking forever to regain the weight shed during his treatments. 'And you'll live a long and full life..?'

'Who knows? But all being well.' Ten years, perhaps twenty, he hoped.

'No wife, though?'

'Still no new wife.'

He would have liked to say, 'I have only ever loved you, Helen.' Instead, 'Yiannis hasn't changed much,' he offered.

'I think you're being kind.'

Yes, even from a distance Yiannis was hugely overweight; the casual biker style that Daniel remembered had been replaced by sagging extra-large clothes. His face was lined and weathered but bloated too. He'd entered the middle age collapse that can happen anywhere but is particularly remarkable in Greece, as if some sixty-year-old men routinely transform into a homage to Metaxa and ouzo.

Yet Daniel was surprised by Helen's comment: he'd expected her to speak well of her husband.

He risked it: 'Is everything OK with you?'

'Everything is fine, like I said.'

240

He hadn't expected her face to be at once so determined to be convincing but haunted by such depression. She was an awful liar. How should he respond?

He attempted levity. 'So you're heading towards a long and happy retirement…?'

'It's not planned yet. But I'm thinking about it.'

They sat together, offering little more of significance as the busy restaurant happened around them and Yiannis observed from his table across the road and the late ferry docked at the entrance to the bay.

It was better than Daniel had dared to dream: Helen, relative privacy, the night. But it was unsettling too. He suspected her head was full of his tragedies and, it seemed, her own.

Yet hope does spring eternal: how much had gone wrong in her life? Might she even have been waiting for him to return..?

As if! How stupid can I be? he wondered.

Round and round life rolled.

****

Daniel and Helen went their separate ways. Because the taverna was busy, there was no opportunity for Yiannis to ask his wife what they'd discussed and when he arrived at Spiti much later, she feigned sleep. He might have woken her, held her and reminded her that she was his, still. Unsurprisingly, that didn't happen. Their familiarity had long ago bred distances. He simply stripped off his clothes and rolled into bed beside her, snoring almost immediately, tired, unconcerned or indifferent. With him, he'd brought the customary smell of a working day and Karelia cigarettes.

She turned so that she was facing away from him. She could usually accept his heavy breathing as a rhythm, rather than an irritation, but not this night.

Relax. Relax.

No, sleep wasn't possible: her thoughts churned, she could find no way to be comfortable and the tee shirt she was wearing twisted. Her head was full of Daniel. And a vague notion of escape.

Poor Daniel: Lewis… and then the transplant. There must be terrible scarring, she thought. She hadn't felt she could ask. And the tablets. A dozen a day, he said, probably for the rest of his life… She turned on to her back. He said he'd returned because he'd always loved Serifos. Of course, he'd really come back because he'd always been obsessed with her... She shifted position again. How does anyone cope, that damaged? Are you just relieved to still be alive? Obviously. And wanting to make up for lost time…?

But not with her. No, no, no. She'd chosen her life.

Yiannis didn't wake, even between sleep cycles. He wouldn't be conscious until morning.

Despite herself, she slipped her hand between her legs and imagined Daniel was with her right at that moment, and she moved her fingers and felt the familiar warmth and the stirring through her core. Her heart beat quickly.

Amazed to find she had feelings again, she took a huge breath and shuddered.

****

Daniel was thinking of Helen too. She'd agreed to meet him the next day and he would never have imagined that could happen. They'd be on a beach together again: no Mike and Jeanette, no Jonny and Lewis or Sophia and Lilliana – just the two of them, after so long.

His air conditioning trundled on, cutting out any noise from neighbouring rooms, and he lay awake thinking of the bow of her lips, the life in her eyes, the shape of her body and even the grey wisps in her hair. It was all special, all of it.

It was almost dawn before he fell asleep at last. For once, there were no nightmares from his time in intensive care, none of those faces leering from under the beds, no long hands stretching from green scrubs, clawing at his face and covering his mouth and nose to stop him breathing. Instead, he dreamed of a deep soft bed and a beautiful woman who gave herself to him totally and bathed his skin in oils and sang and danced for him until he slept in her perfume.

He managed only a few hours' sleep yet woke feeling better than he'd done for many years, so well in fact that he made a decision to adventure. He knew, as the young never seem to do, that he was not immortal, but some wisdom from Mae West was lodged in his head: 'You only live once, but if you do it right, once is enough.'

While he still could, he would take to the hills, though with more circumspection than when he hiked with Mike forty years before.

He packed his small rucksack, had toast and coffee on the waterfront then took the bus up to Chora. At one euro eighty, it was still much cheaper than the transport back home. When he arrived, the climb to the main square was harder than he remembered. Of course, he was using second-hand lungs. They gave him more understanding of how Lewis struggled.

Up there, it was as pretty as ever – perhaps better, with the three *kafeneíons* sporting newly painted and different coloured chairs: pale grey in front of the town hall, yellow across the middle swathe and turquoise beyond. Only the *Kafeneíon Stou Stratoú* at the top end was open, because it had shade, but a settee up against the wall and covered in throws was free and he claimed it. There, he sipped a frappé and drank a glass of water, flapped away the bees and watched the few passers-by.

People meandered along with bags: tourists with cameras and rucksacks and locals with shopping. A small hunched old lady wandered back and forth with a cigarette between her fingers, offering what sounded like caustic advice to any Greeks she passed. Daniel felt certain she'd been there, exactly the same, on his last visit. Maybe she'd been there since the town was built in the fifteenth century.

A young woman arrived to open the central café, which was surprising because it would be bathed in burning sunshine for hours to come so would have little trade. She was wearing a tight yellow skirt, a crocheted crop top and a money belt, her black hair scraped up in a bun. She was beautiful and slim, like a starlet, and he decided she alone had been worth the bus fare; then, thinking of their relative ages, he chuckled and it occurred to him that he hadn't sighed all day.

He looked at his watch. It was one o'clock and time to go because he wasn't certain how long his walk might take. He paid then headed back down the steps towards the bus stop, but at the bottom he cut away to his right, down a narrow road which he hoped would lead at least part-way towards the distant east coast beaches. After a couple of mistakes, he discovered a route between clustered houses and then down a long dirt track, dropping through fields and between hills to a graveyard with a tiny chapel beside it. A road ran to his right, presumably leading to Livadi via a circuitous route. Its metalled surface had been laid recently, no doubt to facilitate the easier transportation of the dead to their final resting place.

Beside the white chapel was a cluster of green bushes round a shallow pool and when he approached dozens of frogs of different sizes sprang away. It was an oasis of life beside the tombs, amongst the dried grasses.

He had read somewhere that the frog was an ancient symbol of the island: the internet was a wonderful source of knowledge. Perseus bade Zeus take away the voices of the frogs on Serifos because they disturbed him, but the frogs had survived whilst their persecutor had not. He who laughs last, he thought...

He took a drink from his water bottle before heading up the slope beyond the chapel. At the top, he found another new wide road leading down. Beside it, what must once have been a goat path tumbled in the same direction. It was barely a track at all, beside a wall and cluttered with gorse bushes and messes of boulders, and he was pleased he didn't need to use it. There wasn't a living soul anywhere and it would be an inconvenient spot to break a leg or to be bitten by a poisonous snake.

Just at that moment there came a skittering through the vegetation on his right. It could have been a large lizard – he had once seen one almost a foot in length – but was it actually a snake? Would a snake make any noise? He couldn't even remember whether it was brown ones or silver ones that were dangerous. Or was it black ones?

He'd glimpsed a snake from his balcony and Kristina told him there were many on Serifos. He was glad he hadn't known that years ago when he slept rough. Traditionally, she said, the locals had burned flip-flops and smeared the blackened plastic around their gardens to keep snakes away, but recently the more environmentally aware had taken to spreading a white powder which had the same effect but needed to be replaced every three weeks.

Of course, no one would do anything to deter snakes on a hillside.

Perfectly safe though, Daniel headed down the empty road towards the reservoir sparkling below. Above him were massive scourings into the hillside, presumably made by some giant cutting machine, and incipient terraces above. Maybe a new development would be born there in the future and the snakes would have to retreat.

The reservoir itself was new and full. Kristina had told him Serifos had experienced dry winters – 'Climate change, Daniel' – and people were worried about water supplies, especially since the island hosted so many tourists. However, the last winter had saved them.

He paused on the bridge that led across to the coast road and watched turtles – or were they terrapins? – in the water below, and there were seagulls on the surface. He loved life.

The hardest part of his trek was done and, incredibly, he'd managed it with relative ease even though he'd been walking for almost an hour in the afternoon sun, the most strenuous exercise he'd undertaken in many years. He pushed back his hat, wiped his glasses and folded his sleeve-covered arms with satisfaction. It was as if everything was possible once again.

Beyond the reservoir, the coast road descended to Psili Ammos, but he'd arranged to meet Helen on Agios Sostis Beach, which was half a mile away, back towards the port. He'd confirmed the geography on his laptop before setting out.

As he walked, his head filled with Lewis again. This was the road along which they had plodded to and from Psili Ammos. He'd have given everything to have his small boy still moaning at his side.

It used to be a tougher route over pebbles and through the dust, before the tarmac was laid, but it had offered more beauty. Then a bus went by, heading towards Psili Ammos.

You no longer needed to walk: the island had entered a whole new age.

He was meeting progress, black in tarmac and loud with an engine's roar.

After fifteen minutes, he took the still-rough track on his left, which ran beside what used to be the old farm and was now a smart villa. Then to his right, round the hill, was Lia Beach, where Jenny stayed; but he kept left, climbing a sandy, rocky track. Here too the scrubland was being cleared on either side and a bulldozer waited silently for a driver to appear to shovel away more of the island's character.

In no time, Daniel was looking down on Agios Sostis. The view was unspeakably beautiful. It was as if a narrow bulge of land had pushed into the ocean. There were two beaches: rough waves rushed down from the north whilst others drifted in peacefully from the south. Opposite him, there was a chapel up on the rock. He wondered who in the world would travel out there to use it. Maybe it was booked by the rich for their weddings.

There were cars parked beside him and a handful more at the bottom of the steep slope. Presumably the people who had driven down there were incapable of walking a hundred yards.

Actually, the place was busier than he expected. The dozen trees on the south-facing side – mostly small and thin – all had bodies clustered beneath their branches. Somehow, he managed to squeeze in amongst the crowd, finding enough space to lay out his beach mat and towel. That had been quite a walk. How well he was doing.

The only one fully clothed, he drank deeply from his bottle and ignored the stares. He was avoiding cancer, but couldn't go round telling that to everyone in the world. And why should he?

He checked his watch again: it was approaching three o'clock, meaning he'd not only survived the hottest part of the day but had even arrived sooner than he'd expected. Helen wouldn't be along for another hour or so. In his pack was a Pat Barker novel about the grim lives of Trojan women captured by the Greeks in ancient times, but he was more concerned with one Greek wife in the present and, anyway, was too tired to read.

He lay back with his hat over his eyes and felt wonderfully at ease. That he was there at all was a miracle. He thought only rarely about the poor soul whose lungs he received, which was best, though his gratitude could know no bounds. He was so, so lucky, stretched out under a tree on a Greek island with the water lapping only yards away. His donor would never know what their lungs had meant to him, what a life they'd given him. He blessed them and their family and the transplant surgeons, the clinicians, nurses and support staff; and he felt he had been blessed too.

As always, though, even as he appreciated his own good fortune, those final images of Lewis returned to his mind. He'd been saved, yet no-one could save his son.

'No one ever said life was going to be fair.' The words jangled in his head and he did sigh – for the treasure he'd lost.

****

Helen phoned Jeanette once more and said her head was a mess and she really didn't know what she was doing.

Jeanette said Helen knew very well what she was doing and she should go meet Daniel as arranged because otherwise she'd spend the rest of her life regretting it.

Helen said that Jeanette might be right but should try to avoid clichés whenever possible.

They both laughed, then Helen packed a beach bag and headed for her car.

When she arrived at Agios Sostis, she parked at the top of the hill. Why were other people so lazy? Why did they drive down and ruin so special a place? She sometimes felt very old; though like Jeanette she'd never been comfortable when they were despoiling beaches as teenagers, even if it was just what you did back then. Hypocrisy runs through us all.

Descending the slope, she spotted Daniel immediately. Everywhere there were girls in skimpy bikinis and boys in ridiculously long bathing shorts, but in the middle lay an Englishman, obtrusively covered from head to foot and apparently asleep in the shade. Her daughters would have said he looked silly and cute.

As if sensing her approach, he sat up, saw her and broke into a huge smile. 'Helen!' Getting to his feet – slightly clumsily – he welcomed her with a kiss on the cheek, which was fine because they were anonymous amongst the holidaymakers. He waved a hand towards his beach mat. 'May I offer madam a seat?'

He turned the mat through ninety degrees and they sat together. There was no opening of hearts, no revelations required, and she was happy to be beside him, watching the waves and a young couple playing in the water. The girl clung around her boyfriend's neck and, underwater, his hands must have been busy. She screeched and everyone was guessing what he was doing, surely; but the couple were oblivious.

You needn't worry if things can't be seen.

'I'm glad you're here, Daniel.'

'I'm glad to be here. It's been a long time... I've spent all these years thinking about you,' he said.

'Young love...'

'Yes,' he said. 'I have...' He ran out of words. 'I have never...' He stopped again.

She laughed.

'I'm sorry. I'm not laughing at you. I'm laughing at us.'

'Yep.'

He pulled his hat lower over his glasses, staring out as people do beside the sea.

'You came back to see me...?'

'To see the island again, of course. It's strange when you're about to die but know that things will still be there when you're gone. If you find you're still living after all, you decide you'd better get yourself in gear and go see places before it really is too late...' He stopped. 'Yes... I came back to see you....'

She was so glad.

Immediately in front of them, the young woman came out of the sea and swept her hair from her face and over her shoulder.

'You're different from the last time I saw you...'

The girl squeezed water out of the hair, shook it loose and turned back to watch her boyfriend. He waded to her, picked her up and carried her back into the sea.

'People change, not just places,' she said.

'That much? Do they?'

'We're never sure what will happen next.'

There was a long silence.

'I love you,' he said.

After forty years he'd said it to her, there on the beach, surrounded by strangers, resting back on the mat on his elbows, with his knees pulled up, behind darkened glasses, in a soft voice, delivering each syllable haltingly, as if the words might explode.

It was what she had been waiting for – for ever, it seemed.

'We never slept together.'

'I know.'

'I know you know. How odd, though.'

'Not then.'

'No.'

He was looking at her directly now. She could see his eyes through the photochromic lenses.

'You were a shit. But I always loved you, Daniel.'

She closed her eyes and lay back. Were they too old for this? It couldn't be normal.

But she felt him lie beside her and this time he took her hand and just for that moment she felt healed.

****

Knowing Helen would be busy all evening, Daniel steered clear of Konstantinidis'. Just fifty metres from it was another taverna and he installed himself there under a traditional bamboo umbrella, which was so much more authentic than Yiannis' wooden roof, and looked over as Andreas and Michalis bustled back and forth. Yiannis stood on the roadside in his supervisory role, chain-smoking and apparently growling at the waiters as they passed.

Beside Daniel, under a neighbouring umbrella sat two drunken British couples. They grumbled at the waiter and left making far from muted comments about 'foreigners'. Daniel felt deeply ashamed, again. He should have challenged them; he should have spoken up for the waiter, who was blameless. But he did nothing, in the English way. Instead, he tried to look sympathetic.

'That's what a far right government unleashes. I am so sorry.' The waiter smiled, perhaps understanding the tone if not the words.

Still, once the embarrassments had left, Daniel relaxed. A bottle of Mythos made him feel better; a second made him positively mellow. The food was good and if only Helen had been sitting with him, he would have been totally content. However, she loved him too. That is what she'd said and that was what mattered. What a day it had been.

Belatedly, he took his azathioprine and omeprazole, more determined than ever to live as long as possible. When his third beer arrived, he phoned Jonny. There was a buzzing tone, then his son answered.

'Hi, kid. How's Athens?'

'Hi, dad... It's polluted. Noisy. Same as, same as. Full of homeless refugees now though. People sleeping on the streets. It's even worse than home. Poor sods.'

'Mm. Otherwise, are you both enjoying it? Lara too?'

'We've only been here a couple of hours.'

'Yep. Of course.' Jonny didn't add anything. 'How is the Apollo?'

'As it always was, really. It's a hotel. Cheap. Cheerful enough.'

'Good. And the Acropolis?'

'More scaffolding than ever...'

And how are you doing, dad? he might have said. Have you seen Helen? What's your hotel like? Have you been to the place we're all going to be staying? What's that like? Are you lonely? How have you spent the day? Is your breathing ok?

Instead, 'Look, sorry, I've got to go,' he said. 'It's getting late. We're at the Acropolis and Lara wants to look round the stalls at Monistiraki and we need a drink. I'm hoping to see Frank! See you very soon, yeah?'

'Yep. See you soon.'

Children grow up and away, he thought. That's how it is. Even loving children. And that's how it should be. Of all the things he had to lament, the uneffusive nature of his surviving son was the least of his worries, though he couldn't help wondering whether Lewis might have been different.

He took his other tablets, waved to the waiter and unwisely requested a fourth beer because for now he must celebrate, not mourn. This day…. after everything – he expanded his lungs – after forty years… such a day… He would move on to ouzos later.

****

For months, Helen had needed to talk with Yiannis. It had become imperative because things had to be resolved, things like the rest of their lives. Now it was going to happen. But first she spent a frustrated evening preparing food. She baked apple pie, cheese pies, *kéik melioú* bathed in extra honey and *nistísimo kéik sokolátas* because there were two families staying and each had children who loved chocolate. She usually adored the sweet smell from her ovens, but for once and understandably her mind was elsewhere. When everything was cool, she filled the fridges and braced herself, waiting.

The preparations had helped maintain some sort of normality but it was a way of living she could no longer bear. Mere existence was no longer enough. Despite herself, she knew she was jealous: she'd never enjoyed the happiness Jeanette found with Kostas. All her youthful drive and ambition were gone, like petals washed away by the waves. The climate was hot but her own existence had become cold; her marriage had long since run its course.

She wanted to warm to everything around her and laugh again. She wanted love and she wanted to make love.

When Yiannis came back, after midnight, she was sitting out on the terrace, prepared. She said nothing as he wheezed up the final steps from their car park and sat clumsily in the deck chair beside her.

'Eleni?'

She looked up at the stars. 'I can't go on like this, Yiannis.'

No reply. Either he was processing her words or it was just that she'd surprised him. It might have been both.

'It is Daniel,' he said, finally, his head still down.

Oh, that was what he would say, excusing himself from any blame, excluding his own behaviour from any discussion. For what seemed an age, so much about him had been lamentable.

She flipped into anger. '*I kalýteri ámyna eínai i epíthesi*, Yiannis?' Her voice sharp, she threw the Greek proverb at him, not caring if they were overheard: 'The best defence is a good attack, Yiannis? Really? Is that all you have? Of course it is. Of course it is…'

He was like a huge discomforted animal.

'Daniel? No, it's not Daniel,' she said. 'We've done nothing wrong. He's only just arrived. But you know what I could say to you. You are so cold with me, but there have been so many names, so many faces, so many sorry nights: Marianne, Vici, that blonde from Sweden, Deborah, Eugenie… You want more..? You want more, Yiannis? We're strangers and you're a poor excuse for a husband. What have we become? All we have in common are the businesses and our daughters…'

He offered nothing.

'I could have left with him long ago. I stayed.' Her voice hissed in the darkness. 'Daniel and I are friends, nothing more.'

She was lying to him but she knew that this moment would have arrived soon anyway, even if Daniel hadn't.

Above them, a stray meteor burned across the sky.

'I will talk to Daniel.'

'You never listen. Jesus Christ. But, yes, you'll talk to him. Why not? You never talk to me…' She looked at his profile and felt no love for him at all. 'I've told you it's not Daniel. Still, talk to him. Do that. But take care, Yiannis, take care. If there's any trouble.…' She paused. 'If there is any trouble, I will never forgive you. Never.'

She stood and looked down at him. 'See him if you want, but you're wasting your time. You are the problem, Yiannis. It's you, no-one else.'

She headed off to their room; he remained where he was. When she looked back, in the chair she saw just a husk of the man who danced and sang at their wedding. He was no longer a man she could love.

****

Daniel slept late. It was nearly ten o'clock when he opened his eyes, but he was retired and on holiday.

In the yard he heard voices and was certain one of them was Kristina's, though she was speaking in Greek. She'd want to come in to clean soon so he needed to get up.

He slipped on his glasses, his one pair of shorts and last night's shirt, went out on to the shady balcony and looked down.

She was standing in the yard, hanging towels on the line and talking to a young woman who was wearing a short grey skirt and a red tee shirt which asked the world to 'Big it up'. She had long brown hair and even from above it was clear her legs were long and brown too. She might have been in her twenties.

Kristina noticed him. 'Hello. You have a visitor. You want she should come there?'

The other girl looked up. She had a lovely face.

'A visitor? Yes. Thank you.' He hesitated. 'Yes, come up now. Do. I'll open the door.' He wasn't going to turn away a beautiful young woman, whoever she was and whatever she wanted.

Rapidly, he tidied the room, squeezing things into the bottom of the small wardrobe and pushing numerous items under the bed. I'm so desperate to create a good impression these days; I must be old, he thought.

He answered his visitor's tap at the door.

'Hi…' It was a pleasant surprise to have a young, stunning girl call on him, even if he had no idea what she might want. He gazed at her, wondering where they might have met before and wishing he could have shaved. Of one thing he was certain: in these days of #MeToo, he wouldn't ask her to sit on the bed.

'Come in, please. Should we go outside?' She hesitated, then dropped her bag on the kitchen surface and followed him to the balcony. 'There is just about enough room for the two of us to sit...' He indicated the chairs. 'Tell me – I feel I should I know you...' She'd still said nothing and her expressions kept shifting: amused, wary, always pretty...

'I'd love to sit down, thank you,' she said, finally. A Greek accent, but perfect English.

'A drink? Water? Coffee?'

'No, thank you.'

The woman on the next balcony nodded at them. He said, '*Kali méra*.' She watched his visitor squeezing past the table and into a chair, then went inside so they had privacy.

'Are you thinking of putting me out of my misery?' She sat facing him, with Chora looking down upon them both. He doubted she was struggling to find the right words; she was toying with him.

'I'm Sophia.'

Of course she was. Sophia. Little Sophia who'd hung around Jonny and was always laughing. He could see it now – she had Helen's eyes and perhaps her nose but nothing of Yiannis in her looks or her build, which was a blessing.

'Goodness.' He stopped himself saying, 'How you've grown,' but was unsure whether there was actually an etiquette when meeting a woman you last knew when she was a child. He placed his hands against his heart. 'Sophia, please forgive me. It's been so long.' She was slim and beautiful and Helen hadn't exaggerated. 'No wonder your mother is so proud of you.'

'Thank you, Daniel.' Her laugh was the same. 'And Kristina is an old friend.'

'Your mother said.'

Silence again. He wondered why she'd come. Once more, though, he didn't find himself sighing. Her visit was a treat.

'Mama said you were staying here...'

'It's great to meet you again...' There was a question behind his words.

She faced the hills for a moment. 'She is so pleased that you are here,' she said. 'She has not been happy for a long time…'

'And I am overjoyed to find her so well.'

Overjoyed? He sounded antique, but Sophia was very Greek so maybe linguistic subtleties would pass her by.

'The thing is…' Sophia paused again. 'I'm not sure how to say this, really… Daniel, mama has been sad…'

'I thought she loved it here on Serifos.'

'She belongs to the island and the people. It's just…'

She stopped. They listened to the chorus of cicadas, which was suddenly very loud. Sophia didn't seem inclined to continue.

'Does this have anything to do with your father?' He knew he should tread lightly and had no idea why he had asked so abruptly or what she might say.

'*O patéras mou einai énas kalós ánthropos*! Daniel, my father is a good man…'

'Yes.'

'But, sometimes…' She faded away again.

She stroked her hair and bit her bottom lip, looking prettier still.

Kristina had gone from the yard and he was grateful the other balcony was now empty so no one was listening.

'Sometimes he has been bad,' she said, quietly. 'We know he's been bad. It's upset mama. It has upset us all.' She threw back her hair. 'He's been with other women, Daniel.' He thought of Jenny. 'There. That's it. He doesn't mean harm but he has hurt mama many times…'

All her laughter had gone. He felt dismay for Helen and when Sophia turned she was blinking and her face had clouded.

Her hesitancy was gone too: 'I came to make sure she is not hurt again, to make sure you do not hurt my mother any more.' Her demeanour had completely altered, she'd become agitated and her voice rose. 'For the last years…'

She left the sentence unfinished. He could only guess what Helen might have been through. He'd never forgotten Yiannis on the beach with the German woman… with Jenny… Do people ever really change…?

Trading, he felt driven to open his heart.

'I love your mother.'

Her eyes flashed: 'Maybe. But love has never stopped anybody hurting others. I have hurt people I loved. I will hurt people again. But this is my mother and she is special. The rest of the world can go fuck itself, it can do what it likes, but you must not hurt my mother…'

Although she'd arrived smiling, she'd become a coil of anger.

'Trust me, Sophia. Time moves us along. Whatever happens, I will never be less than kind. I promise.' He tried to sound strong but could produce nothing more than a wan smile. 'I am too old and too damaged to ever hurt anyone again, believe me.'

She nodded. He couldn't get over how lovely she was and how much more forward than her mother, how Mediterranean.

****

Helen was restless. It was evening and she hadn't seen Yiannis since that morning and hadn't seen Daniel since the afternoon before.

'Drive down and find them,' said her therapist. 'You don't have to have sex with either of them. Unless the mood takes you, I suppose. But not with both at once, obviously. Just go and make sure everything's all right. Set your mind at rest. But keep your head up whatever's said.'

Helen was gazing at Konstantinidis' across the bay, her mobile to her ear. 'You're right, Jan…'

'You've no idea what Yiannis is going to do?'

'If only…'

'I'd help if I could. Kostas could have a word with him, if you want…'

'I just wish you were here, Jan.'

'This weekend. *Endáxi*? I'll be over. I promise.'

'Yes. Great. Can't wait… Thanks… Bye.' She ended the call.

She couldn't wait at Spiti any longer; she couldn't just sit there hoping her life would be magically mended. She changed into a silky dress – she didn't try to fool herself: it was for Daniel – then she set off to the taverna, with no idea of what she would find or what she might say to either Yiannis or Daniel when she met them.

She drove with the radio blaring much more loudly than usual, as if it was a declaration of intent. Amaryllis was singing *Óla Epitrépontai* and she had her windows down for all the world to hear: 'Everything is allowed,' sang Amaryllis. It was perfect for her mood. She would be strong.

As she pulled up at Konstantinidis', Michalis was padding across the road with a trayful of glasses and bottles. He nodded his head back towards the tables on the beach. Andreas was following him, equally laden, but he came across to the car.

'A good time to arrive,' he said to Helen, in English.

'Because..?'

He pointed with his elbow: 'Your husband…'

At a table near the sea, Daniel was sitting with food before him. Yiannis was there too, standing by the table, more animated than she'd seen him in a long time.

She shook her head. No, no, no. Not this and not here. She had a vision of Daniel falling, in slow motion, clutching his chest, with Yiannis the cause. She rushed over, through the tables and the diners.

As she arrived, Yiannis, whose back was towards her, knocked aside a chair then moved round and seized Daniel by the front of his shirt, dragging him up so he was on his toes.

'*Maláka*! *Putánas yié*!' He was blazing with anger.

All dining stopped.

'Yiannis…' Daniel gasped.

'Yiannis!' In contrast, Helen's voice was close to a scream as she grabbed his shoulder to pull him back. 'Stop this now!'

Daniel's face was contorted and his arms were flailing. Yiannis' right hand was free and it seemed he might throw a punch.

'Enough! Yiannis, *tha ton skotósei*! That's enough..!'

He turned to her and, as if coming to his senses, released his grip so Daniel dropped back on to the chair, like a stuffed toy. It rocked backwards, but didn't topple.

Yiannis turned to Helen. 'What? I'll kill him? Kill him?'

His breath was heavy with drink, but she didn't pull away.

'Yes, you could kill him. You want a death on your hands, Yiannis?' Her throat was horribly dry. 'Will that make you more of a man? Will that make you more my man?'

Andreas was back and looking torn, presumably wanting to intervene but not daring; he was resting his hand on Daniel's chair, as if to offer some support, but could do nothing against his employer. Helen and Yiannis stood strangely frozen as the waiter poured a glass of water for Daniel, whose face had turned grey. It was a kind gesture but ridiculously everyday in the circumstances.

Helen wondered, only for a moment, if Yiannis' violence might fall upon her next. But he had never hurt her. Not physically.

With the darkness all around and the fluorescent tubes installed by Yiannis above their heads and illuminating the scene, they might have been on a stage. Their audience was the other diners, all gripped, the tension palpable.

Daniel took a sip from his glass and then, with a hand on the table to steady himself, got to his feet and poured what oil he could on the troubled water.

'It's all right, Helen. Truly.' He was breathing haltingly. 'Thank you, but I am ok. No damage done.'

That didn't seem to be the case. He was unsteady, his shirt pulled and his hat on the floor. He made to pick it up but Andreas rescued it for him.

Helen still faced Yiannis and neither was taking a step back. Two tall young men who might have been Scandinavian had got to their feet just as Helen arrived, presumably to come to the aid of the old Englishman; slowly, they sat down again. Everyone continued to watch.

'Is that it? Do you want to kill Daniel? Quickly, though, not like you're killing me? Is that what you want?'

The look on Yiannis' face shifted to incomprehension. She had control.

'Go…' Her eyes flicked to the right. 'Go now, Yiannis…'

Responding like a chastened pet, he moved away and she followed him towards the kitchen, nodding at Andreas and offering him a twitch of a smile but saying nothing to Daniel. It wasn't the time.

Chapter 8

By next morning, Daniel was relieved to feel much recovered. He stood, proprietorial, in the sunshine on the light blue stone terrace at the front of the holiday let to which he was moving, which he'd found online, advertised as The Best House on the Beach in Serifos. Before him there were eight steps down to a sandy garden area which sloped a further twenty metres to a stone wall and was adorned with pink-flowering bushes. Beyond that was what he had always known as the nudist beach. Thanks to the internet, he now knew it was Karavi Beach and was where Livadi turned into Ramos.

Immediately behind him on the terrace and running along the front of the building was a long stone seat covered in floral cushions and throws, and there were two wicker chairs and two orange canvas ones. Down the side of the house, even more shaded by wooden frames, closely-latticed bamboo and the neighbour's wall, was another long seat, a large wooden table and more wicker chairs.

He was impressed by the size of the place. It had three levels: a cool basement bedroom and bathroom; a living area and kitchen on the ground floor; and upstairs another double room with its own en suite, for Jonny and Lara. It was an airbnb property and certainly the largest and grandest place Daniel had ever stayed in Greece. Its Italian owner lived in Genoa and claimed some sort of distant relationship to Silvio Berlusconi, which, bizarrely, he advertised like a badge of honour.

Surveying the beach as if it was his fiefdom, Daniel decided he'd made a good choice.

He watched a cluster of nudists to his left, lying on the rocks. Judging by their mix of bald pates, grey hair and less than svelte bodies, they might have been there ever since he and Dianne had established a temporary home in the centre of the beach, ringed by knee-high stones, and since Mike ogled the women. The rest of the two hundred metre sweep of the bay boasted just half a dozen conventional sun-worshippers, all more modest in swimsuits. Still, the girls were in the latest fashion, Daniel noted, which meant their bikini bottoms were very Brazilian, with no more than a thong at the back. It came pretty close to nudism.

And Karavi was impressively clean and civilised – such a contrast to how it had been on his first visits, when transient youth drank and loved there for a while in scruffy and careless abandon.

Now, The Best House was one of a line of solid white buildings set just above the sand and there was another row behind them and another to the side. He imagined they must have cost a great deal to build or buy. He had paid over two thousand pounds to stay for two weeks. It was many times more expensive than Kristina's apartment but a treat, to celebrate his continued existence. He'd invited Jonny and Lara to come too because they wouldn't have been able to afford a holiday otherwise and they needed one.

The location was as fine as ever and since the beach still sported no trees, Jonny and Lara could bake down there in the sun all day if they wanted, or they could go over the hill to the campsite beach, officially Livadakia Beach, according to the internet. Who would have known? Anyway, meanwhile, on the terrace Daniel would have permanent shade, could watch the Aegean and read his books.

Yes, this will do nicely, he thought. They will like it, I'm sure. If Helen is all right, it'll be a fortnight like no other.

His nerves had steadied and, thankfully, he'd come to no real harm the night before. Naturally, he was fretting about Helen. Yiannis had stormed off into the night and Helen had driven away without saying anything, but he knew she and Yiannis must have ended up in the same room later. He was certain that under normal circumstances she could look after herself, but it was disconcerting to see Yiannis so angry, so out of control. Yiannis was not the man he'd known.

Everything had moved incredibly rapidly since Daniel's arrival and he prayed that Helen would be safe, yet what could he do to help? He'd decided not to go to Spiti. He didn't want Yiannis' hands around his throat next time. He would never have been a match for him with his own lungs and certainly wouldn't be now. He couldn't even ring Helen because he didn't have her number. Why he hadn't asked her for it, he had no idea. Jonny said that sometimes he behaved as if he was from another age.

Before leaving for The Best House, he'd sought out Andreas, hoping he might know something, but when he arrived at Konstantinidis', with considerable trepidation, the waiter was nowhere to be seen. Fortunately, Yiannis was elsewhere too.

Michalis offered no information of any kind. He didn't seem to want to get involved, which Daniel could well understand. He would just have to bide his time and hope for the best.

He packed his things together at the Ariadne, left saying he'd be back again when his son went home – he'd booked another ten days after that – and wheeled away his case to find a taxi.

That was hours ago. He checked his watch: shortly Jonny and Lara would be arriving on a high-speed. If he remained where he was on the terrace, he'd see the boat thrust its way across the bay, but probably wouldn't get to the port to meet them; so he drank a glass of water and set out in plenty of time. The half-hour walk into town along the beach would be a breeze. He felt healthier than he had in years.

When he crested the hill between the two beaches, he paused. The campsite beach had undergone considerable changes: it had bars, umbrellas and even a water sports section, replete with canoes and paddle boards which required two lines of buoys, creating a no-swimming area stretching into deeper water. It was a disfiguring transformation. Might he have liked it when he was younger? Maybe, though he thought not. Luckily, the bars were towards the further end, closer to the port; beneath him as he looked down was just the end of the campsite and quieter couples and small groups lying beneath the trees.

His mind drifted back and he wondered for a moment if Jenny eventually found a relationship and whether Frank ever made it to Liverpool. Ships in the night.

He remembered too how they'd lived on Livadakia without

shade. No wonder he had damaged skin on his head and arms and back now. His doctor told him it was just waiting for when the moment was right to break out into skin cancer. Such a cheery man.

Dying had been much on Daniel's mind in recent years. There are so many ways to die, he thought. But after all he'd been through, imagine the irony of dying because he used to smother himself in baby oil to save money...

He removed his shoes, rolled up his jeans and paddled along, avoiding families playing at the sea's edge. If he closed his eyes, he could still remember how it used to be: bamboo, an occasional camp fire, scattered backpackers. Now, it was alive with people. According to Kristina, many came from Athens for the weekend.

Obviously, they could afford it, despite the economic plight of the country. Or were these people just the better off? He doubted many playing through the afternoon would be disciples of the Minister for Finance, Varoufakis, and his socialist solutions. He'd not come across anyone with a good word for Prime Minister Alexis Tsipras or his government since his arrival – apart from Kristina, who thought he was good looking. Daniel had always had respect for the man, but would he survive the coming elections? Probably not. The electorate gets the government it deserves and parts of the world seemed to have gone crazy. You only had to look at Trump in the States and Boris Johnson's populist catastrophe in the UK...

He was still waiting with trepidation to find out if the Tories would actually be stupid enough to implement a hard Brexit and lead the country into the economic wilderness with no trade deals. His major fear kept returning: what would happen to his supply of medications which came from the EU? He'd die without them... Being dependent on drugs sharpened your political senses.

Hopefully, someone in the system was stockpiling medicines, though he guessed the self-serving millionaires in the government wouldn't concern themselves at all about the sick millions needing drugs to keep them alive.

It was best to try not to brood. Surely, surely even a Tory government wouldn't kill its own people?

For the moment, other thoughts began to occupy him. Approaching Livadi, he was becoming increasingly tense and as he repeatedly looked around, fearing Yiannis might attack at any moment. It was a ridiculous thought. Yiannis is not a homicidal maniac, he told himself, he is Helen's husband and all will be well. He could hear Jonny whispering, 'Chill, dad, chill.'

Reaching the harbour, he stood in the passengers' shelter on the quay. Waiting with the boys, he used to peer through the small window, looking for their boat to appear on the horizon, but the glass had been painted over and you could no longer see what was coming. Why? he wondered. Why?

He must have appeared concerned when Jonny's boat was late.

'It'll be about ten minutes,' said a cockney voice beside him.

'Right, good. Er... you sure?'

'That's what my phone's showing, mate... You not got the app? Marinetraffic.com...'

'No... OK. Cheers...'

He remembered once being stranded on Folegandros in the 70s when no one had any idea when a boat might arrive, and the locals were short of fruit and even water. Word got around that a boat would be arriving, and locals turned up from goodness knows where to hang around the port for hours until it did, when they rushed forward to grab whatever was available. He still remembered little old Greek women emerging from the scrimmage with a watermelon under each arm. What would they all have given for marinetraffic.com...?

He felt sure the cockney would be proved correct but still stepped out of the shelter briefly to gaze seawards. Old habits die hard.

He was pleased Jonny and Lara were nearing the island. It would be a welcome distraction from his worries to have them around.

****

After the confrontation in the taverna, Yiannis had accelerated into the night, his bike roaring into the distance; more calmly, Helen drove round the bay and up to Spiti.

She headed straight to their room and could do nothing but wait for her husband, who must come eventually. She felt sick with disillusionment and seriously worried about what he might do next.

Lying on the bed, fully clothed and eyes open, she tried to stay calm.

Occasional cheers blew across the water from the other side of the bay where someone was having a party. Finally, around midnight she heard his bike, then his footsteps and his wheeze through the open window as he climbed the steps from the terrace. She stood. She'd intended to maintain an icy silence, but when the door opened a wave of emotion swept over her and she didn't care if anyone heard.

'I suppose the taverna is looking after itself,' she spat. 'We'd be in trouble if I took that attitude up here. Or Sophia and Lilliana gave up on their guests...'

He swept his hair back from his face but kept his own voice low.

'You thought I would kill him?'

'Yes...' It wasn't what she'd expected. 'I thought you might...'

He turned on the light, seeming sober now but hardly penitent. He shifted around the room, as if he couldn't decide what he should do, picking things up and putting them down and gazing around, apparently unseeing, until eventually he too sat on the bed. He gave the impression that she was as much a mystery to him as she had always been, as if life itself was a mystery he'd never been able to fathom. Meanwhile, she looked at him and knew what his every frown meant, every shift of his eyes, every dip of his head. He was clasping his hands as if holding on to what he feared might soon be lost. She realised that he'd rarely ever seemed comfortable with her since they met.

Even at a time like this, when she felt something like loathing for him, she knew he wasn't evil. But he'd let her down too many times. He'd treated her with disdain; he lacked any consideration for her, or compassion, never mind love. They'd drifted way past the point of no return.

He shook his head, lank hair falling over his eyes.

'But, kill him? *Ti eídous ánthropos nomízeis óti eímai*?'

He looked aghast.

So she told him about the transplant.

He sat still, expressionless, for what seemed many minutes but must have been fewer; then still fully clothed he rolled backwards until his cheek was on the pillow, facing away from her. He didn't move or speak...

In that moment, he too was a mystery.

She knew he was awake when it was time for her to rise the next morning, but after such a wakeful night she didn't speak. They had both tossed and turned and she slept for only short periods, waking each time from a nightmare that involved a long, long fall down a dark, dark place into a bottomless sea whilst Yiannis stood above, watching and drinking. She couldn't tell whether he was laughing or crying.

She felt empty.

He continued to feign sleep whilst she showered and dressed and went out to prepare the breakfasts. Much later, as she served and cleared on the terrace, he emerged, descended the steps and rode away without looking towards her, sliding his bike down the steep, rough slope before roaring off round the bend. For an age, she thought, they'd been living separate lives. She watched him speed along the road towards Livadi; he could have been going anywhere, meeting anyone.

Talking with the guests over breakfast was a struggle for her, but it's the proprietor's necessary performance and at least they were all finished and gone long before eleven o'clock.

There was too much crockery for the dishwasher and a mound was stacked high beside the sink but she left it for Lilliana, who would arrive soon. Elira would help her to tidy up if necessary, after the cleaning. For once, Helen turned her back on it all, wiped her hands and rested on a chair. She'd been on her feet for five hours, and the heat had been intense

266

since nine o'clock, despite the bank of clouds appearing over Chora. She was exhausted.

Maybe there would be rain later, she thought. Like the Greeks, she welcomed the relief it brought after the hot months.

Then Sophia's car was approaching round the bay, which was good because Helen needed her support. Her daughter was emotional and often unpredictable but in some ways very wise and would understand everything.

However, as she climbed hurriedly from the car park, Helen registered her urgency. Judging by the look on her daughter's face, she was bringing a new storm.

****

At the port, the Speedrunner docked efficiently, the newcomers surged ashore and Daniel spotted Jonny's white cap and Lara's yellow tee-shirt. He waved and they came over to him. He gave Jonny a huge hug and Lara a hug and a kiss. They both looked tired, but he guessed they'd been out until the early hours of the morning.

'Hi, dad.'

'Hey, Daniel.'

'Pleased to be here, kids?'

'It's good to see you, dad.'

A member of the port police was blowing her whistle in the customary manner, waving her arms furiously.

'OK – this way… Before she swallows that thing…' Daniel encouraged them forward. 'There are changes, Jonny. Even women port police now… But first things first: do you want a drink before we head over to the house?'

Jonny said nothing but looked to Lara for an answer.

'Maybe a fruit juice?' She was struggling with her wheelie case because of the loose pebbles on the road. 'That seems like a great idea…'

'I'll certainly have a beer.' Jonny relieved her of her luggage and immediately walked off with his rucksack on his back, dragging her suitcase with apparent ease. 'Follow,' he called over his shoulder. 'I'll find some shade and claim us a good table.'

He headed towards town at a pace that was far too brisk. Lara gave Daniel a weak smile, and linked her arm through his.

'And off he goes!' she said. 'Never one you can pin down. No thought for others…'

That tone. Something was wrong. Daniel's heart sank. Maybe they'd just had a row? He hoped it was nothing serious because he wanted them to enjoy Serifos and so much wanted to enjoy their company.

'What's happened here, dad?' Jonny shouted back. 'All this concrete used to be sea!'

For the moment, Daniel swallowed his disappointment. 'Improvements,' he said to Lara with a shake of his head. She knew he didn't stride out anymore and was walking patiently beside him.

The three of them settled into shade in the busy Indigo Bar, which was busy with lunch orders. It was comfortable, with grey and white sofas and deckchairs under bamboo sunshades. Padded wicker chairs were set around low stylish tables amidst large potted plants. From a CD player somewhere, a high-quality Spanish guitarist was picking out Ed Sheeran songs, piped through to wash around the customers eating and drinking just two metres from the sea. A handful of small boats were moored nearby, presumably waiting for the few remaining local fishermen to take them out sometime.

Jonny had rested the luggage in the tight space next to their table. Whilst they waited to be served, he and Lara applied extra sunscreen. Young people are so immensely sensible nowadays, Daniel thought. And as if on cue, a middle-aged man with an enormous belly and ginger hair sat down at a nearby table, all lobster-red face and burnt chest and arms and legs.

Daniel found himself hoping the ozone layer had still been holding back some of the harmful rays when he was young and without any protection at all.

'British?' said Jonny, quietly.

'I guess. But the sun won't harm him: Anglo-Saxon exceptionalism. Ah, note the flag of St George on his back…

Tasteful…' The tattoo, in three ugly shades of blue, was a reminder of home. 'However, it's mostly Greeks and Italians and French on holiday here at present,' he said. 'There are only a few Brits. That particular one supports Brexit, without doubt…'

Which will burn us all, he might have added.

'I've brought my EU tee-shirt, dad.'

'Good lad.'

When their drinks arrived, Daniel took a sip, uneasily: Lara looked uncomfortable, though Jonny's thoughts were impossible to gauge with his eyes hidden behind dark sunglasses.

Daniel hadn't expected this meeting to be awkward but said nothing. It is the silence parents learn to adopt. Hopefully, the kids were just exhausted.

'Does it live up to your expectations, then, Lara? I mean Greece in general, but Serifos..?'

'It's just as I expected,' she said.

'Oh.' He'd hoped for a more effusive reply.

'She's seen all this before, dad.'

'Really?'

'YouTube.'

'Of course.' He sighed. 'I keep forgetting that all mystery has gone… So – videos, then?'

'Yes. Sorry. There are dozens of clips.' She pulled her mouth into an apologetic grimace. 'I mean, it's much more beautiful when you're actually here, obviously… It's really hot and quiet and busy, isn't it, and it seems sort of friendly…'

'It is busier than it ever was… But the Greeks come here now. In numbers. With their cars full of family.'

He made the effort to look appreciative of what she'd said. He liked Lara very much. Jonny had made an excellent choice; or Jonny had been lucky that she chose him. They met in a drama group at university, where Jonny was a techie and Lara an aspiring leading lady, and they never looked back. Having spent a weekend together at a Drama Society getaway in York, they struck up a closer rapport, quit the drama scene and their dreams of fame and fortune, moved in together to share the cooking and the cleaning and concentrated on getting good jobs and saving to buy a house.

In that too, they displayed all the maturity of modern youth. Perhaps they had to, with so much student debt stacked against them and living in a world where the gap between the rich and the poor, the haves and the have-nots continued to widen.

'Didn't mean to spoil it for you, dad.'

'Not to worry, Jonny. It won't stop me sleeping tonight.'

He might have added that he had much more to concern him, but this wasn't the moment. However, as if mindreading, Jonny asked, 'Have you heard anything about Helen yet? Does anyone know where she is now?'

'Funny you should say that... She's right here. Well..,' he pointed at Spiti across the bay, 'right over there.' Jonny's eyebrows rose above his sunglasses.

'In that blot on the landscape..?' It could have been Daniel speaking. But through Jonny's disapproval, it was clear he wanted to hear more.

'It's not so bad... I can fill you in later, eh? Suffice it to say that we've talked and enjoyed meeting each other again as new people – I do try to be properly grown up nowadays.'

'So how are things? That sounds pretty downbeat. You don't fancy her anymore, or what? Does she fancy you? Has she put on mounds of weight? Has she lost her looks?'

'Jonny!' Lara looked appalled. It occurred to Daniel that this was the first time she'd addressed him since they arrived. And had Jonny said anything to her?

'Well, it might have happened...' Jonny wasn't letting up. 'You've gone off her? She's gone off you? What about Yiannis?'

Of course, Daniel had no idea how things actually stood. He was in stasis, like T S Eliot's pinned butterfly.

'Don't jump to conclusions, my son. Be patient. For now, just enjoy your beer, savour the moment. This is a holiday. Relax. I don't intend to lay out the details of my emotional life cramped between tables and chairs and with half of Europe listening... Later, maybe...' He turned to Lara. 'More importantly: how is the orange juice?'

It was cool and freshly squeezed and she'd already spotted how much it was going to cost so was intending to enjoy every delicious mouthful, thanks...

Because of the bags, like Daniel earlier they took the taxi to Karavi, where Jonny and Lara made positive noises about the house, the beach and the view before Daniel showed them to their room. While they unpacked, he sat on the terrace with a glass of water, troubled by whatever was going on between them.

Within moments, it seemed, the sun disappeared and when he turned there were clouds across the darkening hills behind him, scudding along on the wind. Sheets of water masked the patches of sunlight left on the tops. He began to collect up the cushions and throws, ready to take them into the house when the deluge hit the coast. Already, there were spots of rain in the air.

Welcome to Serifos, Lara. Welcome back, Jonny. Rain on Serifos in summer... He sighed. Whatever next? Damn climate change. Damn climate change deniers. Damn Trump and Russia and China and India and lunatic industrialists and oil companies and businesses and entrepreneurs and politicians right across the world.

Damn the fact that nothing ever goes as it should.

****

Helen was used to calming Sophia. Even as a baby and toddler she'd been wonderfully affectionate one moment, then kicking out in the wildest tantrums the next; and she'd become an adult with hopes and dreams that the world could never fulfil. Mostly she was perfectly rational, but sometimes she'd be screaming, the next moment crying, the next laughing. Her mother rationalised her outbursts as aeolian furies, signifying little.

However, Sophia was especially overwrought this time, exploding into Greek. She always used her native language when her pulse was racing.

'It hasn't been sorted at all,' she said, all flying hair, raging. 'Something has to be agreed, mama. You two cannot go on fighting. It can't go on like this.' She paused. 'I've done all I can. I can't go on like this either... None of us can go on like this.'

'It's not my fault, Sophia. You know that.'

Her daughter flounced, threw down her bag, tossed her hair over her shoulder and spread her arms wide.

'It's madness. Papa's at the taverna drinking. It's only lunchtime and he's drinking. Goodness knows what he'll be like by tonight. He won't talk to me but I know where all this is coming from. It's Daniel. It is, isn't it? Did you tell him you love Daniel? Daniel loves you, you know. Of course you know. And did you tell papa? You did, didn't you..? It's tipped him past the edge...'

Helen exhaled, wishing everything that was tightening around her existence could be blown away, then she breathed in deeply. When she was a child, in that awful bedroom with the pink curtains and that disgusting breath and those horrible times, her stomach had always cramped and she'd taken short breaths, a way to get through even if she was unable to get away. Now, later in life, it was different. A huge intake of oxygen helped her cope.

She loved Sophia and her good sense and her emotions and she adored both her daughters because they were honest and loved her so much. They were devoted to their father too, of course, despite his faults.

'The problem is his, Soph. Not mine. I don't have to tell you that. Daniel has come back, but he's done nothing wrong and I've done nothing...'

Her daughter pushed the hair from her face once more and there were tears down her cheeks. She looked set to emote again, but instead sat on the chair beside her mother. Maybe she couldn't trust herself to speak now her storm had broken.

Helen wondered what to say next as she tried to focus on Konstantinidis' across the water, unable to see clearly individuals or even tables because of the distance. She was tempted to say that if Yiannis was drinking, there was nothing to be done today; but she didn't know what she'd be able to do even if he were sober. He'd fallen out of love with her; she'd fallen out of love with him. And Sophia knew that.

272

She took her daughter's hand.

'I'm sorry this is making you so unhappy.'

'Oh, I am sorry for you, mama.'

There was a long silence again.

'I might leave him.'

'You can't.'

'I think I can.'

'You can't leave him because you can't leave us... You live here. You can't leave all this... Where would you go..?'

'Really, it wouldn't be what I want. But this isn't what I want either. I think you'll find I can leave if I need to, if I want to...'

Sophia turned to her with desperate eyes.

'Mama, you can't leave us.'

She was stating what was to her a simple truth and it brought Helen down from her tower of self-pity. She could not have cherished her daughter more.

'We'll see,' she said and patted Sophia on the knee. 'It's not over till Demis Roussos sings.'

'Oh, mama, Demis Roussos? Demis Rousos? Really? Why can't you just be normal?' She almost managed a smile.

They watched the scientific survey boat come in to dock and a beautiful blue yacht with three masts moving slowly out of the bay. A lone swimmer crawled past Spiti with long, leisurely stokes, perhaps a quarter of a mile from the beach and apparently oblivious to the huge jellyfish likely to be around him in the warm water. Helen reminded herself how lucky she was to be in such a beautiful place with such children. Lightly, affectionately, she hugged Sophia.

Then she looked over to the taverna once more and felt all positivity slide away.

Sophia must have sensed the change.

'What will you do?'

'I said.'

'But I said it's impossible...'

'I'm going to tell him it's all finished.'

'Tomorrow. When he has a hangover. No... But is it though? Are you certain? And how will he cope with that?'

'That's his concern. We're finished, Soph. And it's not

something I can save for later. I'm telling him as soon as possible, even if he's got a sore head. Let's face it, he's never any different, is he? And I don't want him here anymore. He can sleep over at the taverna. It's up to him...'

She squinted. A motorbike was weaving along the road round the beach at that moment. It was Yiannis, returning home. She was certain of one thing: he wouldn't be staying.

She felt a drop of rain and then the heavens opened. Sheets of water almost hid the mountains. Chora was indistinct. Whilst Sophia leapt up and dashed back and forth, moving chairs and coverings and closing up the glass frontage of the breakfast area, Helen remained where she was. She was wet to the skin in moments, her hair flattened and her clothes clinging to her, but she didn't move.

The bike crashed over as Yiannis dismounted. He left it there and started up the concrete steps, supporting himself as best he could by flattening his hands against the wall at the side, squinting up towards her through the streaming rain. He was very, very drunk. His progress was slow and she expected him to tumble back at any moment. It was amazing that he'd managed to manoeuvre the bike all the way back without hitting a car or a curb or a bin or a tree or losing control on the loose or jutting rocks.

She didn't move to help him. If Jack fell down and broke his crown, Jill did not intend to tumble after.

****

When the storm passed, Daniel found a brush in the cleaner's cupboard and began to sweep water down the steps from the terrace. Then he replaced all the cushions on the seats, fearing he was tempting providence even though the sun had reappeared and the ground was steaming.

He'd just finished when Jonny emerged to join him. 'Showered?'

'Yep. Though I guess I could have stayed out here... Greece isn't supposed to be like this, is it?'

274

'It's September and the world's climate is going to pot, son. Drink?'

'Erm…'

'Beer?'

'Later, certainly.'

'Coffee? We used to buy Nescafés over here. They're Americanos now…' He sighed.

'Moan, moan, dad… What would you do if you'd nothing to complain about..? Yes, why not?'

Daniel went inside to put on the kettle. He shouted up to Lara, but she didn't want anything. Waiting for the water to boil, he and Jonny sat together watching the naked old people on the beach who had sat out the warm downpour and were wringing out their towels.

'They never change, do they?' said Jonny. Daniel looked at him questioningly. 'I mean, everything's moved on, but not the nudists. They were here, just like this, when we were little. We used to think they were funny. Now they just seem sad. They're always old…'

'Not always. And anyway, they've not always been old. I had a couple of summers over here as a nudist… in the seventies… I was young and beautiful.'

'Grim thought… But ok, back then, maybe. Now they're enough to turn your stomach and if anyone should be covered up, it's them. The women all sag.' It was a good job Lara wasn't with them. 'And the men. God, look! They spend most of the day at the edge of the sea with their hands on their hips and their legs apart, gazing into the distance, apparently to make the most of what they have so anyone in the sea can be impressed. And as if! Like you, I avoid Americanisms when I can, dad – but don't you think it's pretty gross..?'

'I have to admit, if you were to tell people that you were staying on a nudist beach, they wouldn't have an image of… Well,' he said, peering towards the rocks, 'of anything quite like that…'

A couple of old timers who had just arrived were settling themselves on towels and mats, unpacking bags and removing clothes. Everything was hanging loosely on both of them too. They repeatedly glanced up at the sky, as if wondering whether this was all a great mistake and they might yet be washed away. Meanwhile, an extremely portly and bald man who seemed to have very little at all between his legs stood on the largest relatively flat rock and stretched his arms towards the sky while a small woman, presumably his wife, sorted things around them.

'Live and let live,' said Daniel.

'I know. But that guy there: shouldn't he be sort of not drawing attention to himself? There isn't much there to celebrate, is there? And it's not even as if he's just been in the sea…'

Daniel laughed. For a generation that was supposed to be having sex all the time with everyone, male or female or even half and half, he thought young people could be amazingly prudish.

He made the coffees and he and Jonny continued to watch the world.

Finally, Daniel had to ask.

'Is everything all right, son?'

'Yes. Why?'

'No problems..?'

'Like?'

'I'm not sure….' Pause. 'Is Lara all right?'

'She just fancied a lie-down.'

'Which is fine… Of course….' He grasped the nettle: 'But is everything all right between you?'

Jonny said nothing, his face non-committal.

'I apologise. It has nothing to do with me. I just sensed… I just wondered…'

Still Jonny didn't react.

'Jonny?'

Nothing.

Daniel waited. Then Jonny stood and turned his back to the sea, semi-perching himself on the low wall at the damp edge of the terrace, so he was facing his father. It was as though he was trying to decide what to say. His unease was palpable.

He watched a series of huge waves approaching the beach.

Finally, 'It's supposed to be secret..,' said Jonny.

'Then say nothing.'

'The thing is…'

He cast a glance towards the open lounge window, as if to check that Lara hadn't come downstairs. Then he returned to his chair, dabbling his toes into a small pool of residual rainwater, looking like a child trying to find a way to confess. Daniel recognised the little boy that was still in Jonny, that had always been in Jonny, through his university career and brief success as an athlete and was still there now, despite his job and aspirations and occasional brash tales of drunken nights.

'It looks like Lara's pregnant…'

'Oh.'

'You're shocked…'

'Yes. No. That isn't shocking. Surprising… Just surprised it's so soon. And surprised at your reaction…' Daniel remembered a boy with a girlfriend from Tottenham and feared what might be coming.

'Mm… Look, I'm twenty-six. Just twenty-six. I'm not ready to be a dad, dad.'

Yes. That. He could empathise. 'We rarely are.'

'Nappies. Rattles. Pushchairs. Baby food… I couldn't cope…'

Daniel sighed. 'People have to cope. What does Lara want?'

Jonny gave a shrug. 'It's complicated… But I can't do this.'

It was clear where his priorities lay.

'I thought you loved her?'

'I thought I loved her. Maybe I do.'

He wasn't convincing.

The sea had become calm, waiting for another squall.

Daniel waited too. It was forty years since he thought he was trapped in the same situation, right in this place, on Serifos. He had no idea what had happened to Dianne since. They hadn't seen each other again after flying home and he'd never forgiven himself for the disaster. Of course, he'd been obsessed with Helen… but had he been as callous as this? He just couldn't decide whether he was worse, because he didn't love Dianne; or whether Jonny was worse because he'd claimed to love Lara. In either case, how could he criticise his son now?

Lara, though, was sweet and deserved so much better.

She came out to join them. Thankfully, it seemed she hadn't been listening.

'All ok?'

'Yes, Lara, all is fine…' He pulled himself together with the finesse of age. 'Happy with the room?'

'You've done so well, Daniel. It's everything I hoped for.' She didn't say 'we'.

Planning all this, he'd simply wanted to make them happy. Now, they were all facing a long, long fortnight. When he'd been the one in the depths of despair and Dianne had been so angry, they'd escaped to the nudist beach to find space and try to work things out. This time they were already there and the house offered no hiding place at all.

****

'It will not end like this. I will not let it happen.' Yiannis was slumped on the bed again. The things he wore were crumpled and his face was haggard. It wasn't a winning look. 'I can change and I will change.'

'You're like a broken record, Yiannis.'

He didn't understand.

'Never mind.'

She was standing at the door, looking out into the light. Both of them were wet through. Helen's skirt and top were sticking to her body; Yiannis was sitting on sheets which were wet now. When he lifted his head, his hair had draped across his eyes and he had to push it back.

'Eleni. I am so sorry. We can begin again.'

Could they, though? Hadn't they been making fresh starts for years? Yet she'd invested a lifetime here and Sophia was right: if she left Yiannis, she couldn't stay on the island. She'd be walking away from all she knew. Did she have the strength for that? When she'd tried before, she failed.

The rain had stopped and hundreds of feet above a peregrine falcon was riding the currents, black against the sky, its huge wings holding it steady. It was often there, always alone, soaring and watching, no doubt hunting. She'd never seen it plunge to the earth, never seen it catch anything before swooping away inland.

Yiannis came across to her. She sensed his movement and her body tensed. He rested a hand on her hip, presumably expecting some response, but she didn't move.

'Eleni *moú*!'

She wondered where Daniel was and what he was doing and whether her life would be any happier, no matter what she did. Perhaps everyone's life became a compromise? Jeanette and Kostas were the only truly happy people she'd ever known: two in all the hundreds, maybe thousands. Sophia and Lilliana were usually content, but they were still young.

That falcon is still alive, she thought.

She shifted away from Yiannis' touch. 'I'm changing,' she said, and began to tug at her blouse. 'I'm not going to steam dry.'

He didn't watch as she stripped with her back towards him and then dressed again.

When she was ready, she brushed her hair briskly into the best state she could and picked up her handbag.

'I'm going out.'

'You are not baking for breakfast?'

'No.'

'We cannot talk?'

'No. We have talked. I'm going out.'

'To Daniel? To see Daniel?'

'I don't know. Maybe, maybe not.'

She wondered how often her husband had lied to her.

Fishing out her car key from the bag, she resisted the urge to say, 'At least I won't be out all night,' even though anger was coursing through her like adrenaline. Instead, 'Don't worry,' she offered, 'I won't do anything you might regret.' His face registered confusion but she wasn't in the mood to offer explanation. 'I don't know when I'll be back but I'd prefer you not to be here.'

Perhaps the idea that she would be coming back placated him. He made no move to stop her but stood by the open window, watching her head down the steps to the car. He looked like a scruffy dog whose owner was setting off for the day and leaving it behind, but made no move to pad after her.

Once outside in the hot sun, she could breathe again.

Sophia emerged from the kitchen: 'Mama?' she shouted.

'I'm going.'

Yiannis was standing with his hand on the door jamb now, seeming much older than his sixty-five years, damp, grey, worn.

Sophia looked at him then repeated her father's question. 'You are going to Daniel?'

'Later maybe.'

'I'm coming with you.'

'No, Soph, I…'

'No argument, mama.'

Helen shrugged. She set off again with Sophia hurrying behind.

Suddenly there was an almighty crash behind them. They both turned. Yiannis was no longer in the doorway.

Helen had no choice. She hurried back, Sophia ahead of her. They paused outside the room, waiting a moment, fearing what they might find inside.

When they entered, however, it reminded Helen of the scene from *One Flew Over the Cuckoo's Nest*. Presumably in frustration or despair, Yiannis had somehow managed to rip the washbasin from the wall so the pedestal too had come loose, toppled and cracked. The porcelain lay beside him on the tiled floor of the bathroom where he sat. From open pipes, water was spurting everywhere.

He said nothing at all, as shattered as the fittings. At another time, she'd have been wrung with sympathy, but not now.

'Drama? Drama won't help, Yiannis…' she said. Then as an afterthought: 'I'll be really pleased when you've got that fixed. And it won't be tonight, will it? We'll see how long it takes. I'll be staying over at the house; I can't live here without a sink. Don't think of coming to join me.'

****

Jonny was adamant they must all go to Konstantinidis' for their first night.

'You want to go, Lara, don't you?' he said.

Daniel was pleased they were speaking again.

'Of course. Is it as special as he says, Daniel?'

'The atmosphere is not what it was…' He was thinking of the roof, the trees that Yiannis had butchered, the new plastic chairs, the lights… and Yiannis' hand at his throat.

'The food's good?'

'It is. As always. And the location and the service. Familiarity does not always breed contempt.'

Obviously, it was a foolish decision to go there. Helen was unlikely to be around to rescue him again; and it seemed ridiculous to die a violent death on a Greek island after surviving imminent death back home. His mortality was still haunting him.

It was an especially stupid move with a myriad of other restaurants from which to choose, but he found it hard to deny Jonny anything, more so after Lewis' death, even though his little boy was now a man. He could have explained his problems, but Jonny and Lara had enough to worry about already.

He decided to risk Yiannis' ire.

They arrived at the taverna early enough to claim their old table. Although it was still light, the moon was rising over the hills across the bay.

'Beautiful,' said Lara.

'I remember all of this now,' said Jonny.

Daniel was pleased.

Andreas came straight over.

'My friend,' he said.

'Andreas – you remember my son, Jonny? He was…' Daniel held out a low arm. 'Not so big, then.'

'Ha, ha. *Yássas*. Yes, small boy then. A Sprite. Now a man. *Megálo*. A beer?'

'Hi. Yes.'

'And this is his…' Should he say 'girlfriend'? 'This is his partner, Andreas: this is Lara.'

'Hello, Jonny, Lara. Welcome.' He smiled, comfortable, taking his time. 'Together again…'

They ordered, working through what they would like and what was actually available and Andreas pushed his glasses to the bridge of his nose before heading back across the road.

'Just the same. Still cool,' said Jonny.

'I like him,' said Lara. Anyone would.

They chatted over their two beers and a coke, waiting for the food.

'You've brought your tablets, dad?'

Yes. Two to be taken with food, two at ten o'clock: as if he would forget.

It had turned into a calm, warm, pale blue, white and golden evening. Fortunately for his state of mind, with no good reason Daniel had decided while walking that Yiannis would not be around after all. He'd cast any logic to the winds, but had relaxed.

However, he kept peering towards the road in case Helen's car pulled up and before long she did arrive. Sophia got out too and together they went into the taverna. Daniel's spirits had lifted.

However, it seemed there was consternation in the kitchen. Michalis came out to serve another table with a face that registered disapproval; and Andreas followed, glancing at Daniel with raised eyebrows, which might have meant anything.

When Helen came over to them, Sophia was still shadowing her. Daniel rose to greet them.

'Hello.' He risked what he hoped would seem a chaste kiss on her cheek and smiled at Sophia: 'It's lovely that you are here.'

He nodded towards a chair and Helen sat with them. Before he could find one for Sophia, she'd said something in Greek to the couple at the next table, received what was clearly an affirmative answer and took one of their chairs for herself. Jonny was awkwardly half sitting and half standing, trying to be polite.

282

Daniel made the necessary introductions: 'Helen and Sophia – Jonny and Lara.' He glanced from Jonny to Sophia. 'Do you two remember each other?' As if it was yesterday, he could picture the two of them huddled together with Lewis and Lilliana, giggling in the back of the car; and the four of them playing in the waves.

'Of course,' said Jonny.

'You are the same but different,' said Sophia, looking at him with what appeared to be approval. 'And hello, Lara. This is your first time on Serifos?'

'Hey,' said Lara, more guardedly, straight-faced. 'Yes, it is.'

Jonny was smiling directly at Sophia. It was the first time he'd seemed cheerful since their arrival. He was not blessed with subtlety and all at once there was a chemistry in the air.

'It's amazing to see you again,' he said.

'You too.'

Daniel was hoping Lara hadn't noticed the magnetism Sophia had brought with her. Could she be oblivious to it though? That was unlikely – it was a grown-up version of what happened when the children first met. She maintained her manners immaculately but it was impossible to know exactly what was going through her head.

Helen recognised the dynamics, he was sure, and she led the conversations, inviting Sophia to comment, asking Jonny what he thought, as if hoping to somehow disrupt the connection between them, playing the responsible parent.

Daniel had thought they'd be focused on their own situation, on Helen's difficulties and the complexity that was Yiannis. Instead, young hormones flooded the evening.

Maybe – and more painful memories piled in upon him then – maybe, like him, Helen felt the spirit of Dianne at a nearby table, observing them, scowling. He'd led a far from blameless life, but the summer of '79 was a nadir and its ghosts would haunt him until he died. If only he could have had his time again.

****

Helen had imagined that when Jeanette finally arrived on Serifos, she'd be able to unburden herself at last and feel some relief, but as they sat together over a lunchtime glass of wine in a bar beside the water that was not the case.

'So, what's happening to Spiti?' Jeanette was keen to know everything.

'Lilliana's taken over, bless her. Soph is helping too.'

'That's why we have them…. And how are you, really…'

'I'm good.'

'As always, as I'd expect. But how are you?'

Helen laughed. 'I'm well. Is that better?'

Jeanette looked her friend in the eyes.

'Yes… I knew you'd be holding up. But it's less well than good, I'm guessing…' Helen knew she had dark rings under her eyes. Jeanette had kept the conversation as light as she could, but Helen had been waiting for the inquisition to begin. 'And Yiannis?'

She deflected the probing. 'He's finally managed to get a new bathroom sink and he's fixing it today. Apparently, for the last couple of days he's been washing in the kitchen when no one's around because there's no water for the shower either. Goodness only knows where he's going to the toilet…'

'Ugh. And I've an image of him trying to sit on the draining board to soap his feet.'

This time, they both laughed.

'He probably hasn't bothered.'

'Is that it, then?'

'More or less. I don't know whether he'll need new taps too...' She couldn't hide behind her veil any longer: '…He wants me to go back. Of course he does. He's pledging to be devoted…'

'How do you feel about that now? About him..?'

'Oh, Jan, I've had enough…'

'Danny?'

'Great. All things considered.'

'And the girls are coping?'

'Yep.'

She was still guarded. There was a door she'd struggle to open for Jeanette right away.

'And Danny's alive after everything. A small miracle, I suppose. He must be a lucky boy.' She could sense Jeanette dancing round her emotions, all tact and concern.

'Indeed. He knows it…'

'And Jonny? It's awful that they lost Lewis…'

'Yes. Truly awful. I can't imagine…'

The conversation stopped. Jeanette's face was troubled.

'And the rest?'

'Which bit of the rest?'

'Whatever you want to tell me, girl, but can't quite decide whether you should or not…'

Helen watched some boys walking past with a football, heading for the all-weather pitch that had replaced the dust bowl further down the road. After desperately waiting for Jeanette to arrive, now she couldn't even begin. Wounds can seem worse when they're exposed to the light: bandaged, even clumsily, at least they're out of sight.

'Maybe it will have to be later, Jan.'

'Surely not…' Jeanette waited, then she said quietly: 'A problem shared….'

Helen peered into her wine. The scene from earlier was still so vivid…

It had nothing to do with Daniel or Yiannis. She'd intended to spend the morning with Lilliana, who was gallantly managing to keep Spiti running. It was safe to go up to Spiti because Yiannis was supervising some roofing work across the mountains in Panagia. Her intention was to sort out the receipts and the booking schedule, to give her daughter some support. However, she had to drive back to the family house because she'd forgotten an important memory stick.

Another nightmare unfolded. As she walked in, unexpectedly of course, Sophia was coming from her room, laughing, with her trailing arm leading out… Jonny. All three of them froze. Jonny dropped Sophia's hand and appeared to want to say something, anything, but instead stood silently, a man now but the picture of a guilty boy, his excitement punctured. Helen and Sophia held each other's gaze in silence, as if Sophia had been caught stealing from her mother's purse.

She'd brought up her daughter to be different to this, to not let herself down, to not let others down. Of all people, Sophia knew better. But if there was surprise on her face, encountering her mother in such a way, she displayed no shame, pushing back her hair and holding her head high. She didn't offer explanations or excuses; she stood there, daring her mother to reprove them.

Helen suddenly felt very old. She herself wasn't perfect, but she would never have been like this. This should not have happened. This of all things. She couldn't condone this: Jonny was on Serifos with Lara and these two should have known better, should have behaved better. A new generation with old ways: Daniel... and now Jonny.... But her daughter was complicit. In fact, her daughter was evidently the instigator. There could be no doubts about what they'd been doing: she caught a glimpse of the bed through the half-open door, sheets ruffled, pillow on the floor; and though the breeze was blowing through the house, it was as if she could smell the sex on them...

'Give me a minute, Jan,' she said, eyes narrowed against the reflecting glare. 'Don't worry – I'll tell you everything, soon... It's just that it's all so awful...'

****

Daniel sat reading in the shade, struggling to keep his mind on the book. He was sure he knew where Jonny had gone and it was heart-wrenching that he'd left Lara in their room alone again. Jonny had been everything to him for so long that it hurt his very core to know he was behaving unforgivably. For days, his son had been cold towards Lara, who'd done nothing to deserve it, and Daniel knew he'd spent time with Sophia just when Lara needed him. He'd even gone out alone in the late evenings. Though she'd said nothing to Daniel, Lara must have been at her wits' end, and Jonny's absences had prompted raised voices when he returned.

As the tragedy unfolded, Daniel could do nothing except wait.

Considering what Sophia said when she visited him at Kristina's, he could have accused her of hypocrisy, but he blamed his son. Jonny was the one whose partner would soon become a mother.

He heard Lara inside, moving crockery around, then she came out and slumped into an orange canvas chair, not even saying, 'Hello'. He understood perfectly. Feeling helpless and having no better idea, he fetched her a glass of water, but she ignored him. He set it down beside her.

Her eyes were nearly closed as though she wanted to shut out the day, powerless in a cruel world. In a feeble attempt to offer some sympathy, he crouched beside her and put his arms round her shoulders as best he could, offering an awkward excuse for a hug.

'Oh, Lara...'

She cried, resting the side of her head against his forearm and wrapping her arms around his, tightly, as if she needed an anchor. Tears welled in his own eyes. The same mistakes, the same pain, the same awful repercussions...

He was in his sixties, yet still didn't understand why life had to be like this.

****

'*Kalo Empeli?*'

'Yes. It's beautiful. And quiet in September.'

Helen worked through the gears and headed up the hill away from Ramos. She was seeking a break from the relentless stress, from Yiannis and from the children's affair. She knew the responsibility she felt about Sophia and Jonny was weighing equally heavily on Daniel, who sat quietly beside her. Maybe they could decide together how to respond.

Just as importantly, there was the not inconsiderable matter of what to do about their own relationship.

Her car topped the long, steep and winding climb above Ramos and before them the Aegean stretched away to meet the sky, shifting, the deepest blue. Instead of spinning right, along the coast, she took the left fork and the road plunged again. When she turned off the radio, the only sounds were the whine of the engine and the bluster of wind through the open windows.

They bounced down a track to a small parking area a hundred metres below.

'This is it,' she said.

There was a beach far below whilst behind them the mountains were high, brown and a burnt yellow, criss-crossed by crumbled stone walls. Tiny white deserted buildings dotted the hillsides.

'Did they really keep goats in all these enclosures?'

'Hardly. They're called *xerolíthis*. They were built to prevent soil erosion many, many years ago. All this "save the world" stuff isn't new, you know.'

'Respect.' Daniel donned his hat, preparing for the descent to the beach. 'As an aside, did you know that 1971 was International Conservation Year? That went well, didn't it…?' He squinted against the glare. 'Is there any shade down there?'

'In the morning, yes, if you press yourself up against the rocks over at the far end. But not now…'

'Ah…'

'Don't worry. I think of everything…'

She pointed with her thumb. There was a large multi-coloured beach umbrella on the back seat.

'Excellent!'

'Are you fit to carry that as well as your rucksack?' she asked.

'An umbrella? Mm? Let me see…. I am old and frail… but, yes, I'll manage. I'm not that old and frail just yet.'

'I'll carry the car keys and the cool box.'

They passed through a small area of bamboo, then slipped between low scrubby bushes, heading for a chapel fifty yards below. In its paved courtyard, they paused, shaded by a tree and a latticed roof. 'This is weird,' said Daniel, pausing for a moment next to two big sinks. 'All this…' He waved at seats and tables fashioned out of concrete and painted as white as the church itself. 'Is this a primitive Greek Orthodox taverna?'

'As if… No, people come here for the Festival of Sotiras: feasting on a grand scale. Everyone welcome… even the English. But that's at the start of August… You missed it…'

288

'Damn.' He took a drink from his water bottle instead. 'The story of my life... I could do with a bacchanalian feast. You?'

'A change is as good as a rest.'

They set off again, moving more slowly downhill and with Helen picking the best route as they skidded on the pebbles underfoot. Daniel followed, using the umbrella to steady himself whenever his trainers threatened to slide.

Dropping off the final rocks, they were wonderfully alone on the lightest of yellow sand. The beach was deserted and she led the way to the far end, to a small section that pushed into the rock and was more private, with cliffs on either side. As she'd said, they'd need to huddle beneath the umbrella to escape the sun.

After cooling their feet in the sea, they established themselves in the most secluded spot, towards the back of the cleft. Daniel forced the umbrella pole into the tiny pebbles and they set large rocks around its base. Even in their protected nook, it flapped in the breeze. Daniel laid out his towel beneath it, slipped into the shade immediately and took another drink from his bottle. Helen paused a moment – awkward in the circumstances because Daniel was still fully clothed – then slipped off her dress and sat beside him in her bikini, conscious of her stretch marks, faded but visible, and of the fact that her stomach was no longer flat. He'd notice. She pulled up her knees, defensively, and wrapped her arms round them.

'Nice?' she said.

He nodded. 'It's lovely here.'

They were close, their upper arms and shoulders touching, totally alone and together.

'I've had words with Soph,' she said. 'Much use that will do. Any bright ideas?'

'No... I've talked with Jonny, every day, but without success. He cares only about himself.' He paused, as if trying to find words. 'Maybe it's just when you're older that guilt becomes a hair shirt. I know mine has become more and more uncomfortable over forty years.'

'It's long past the time for your guilt, Daniel. And, fret as we might, we can't be responsible for Soph and Jonny.'

'I've tried so hard.'

She put an arm round his shoulders.

He put a hand between her legs and round her thigh, and held it tight. It was intimate and she didn't mind at all. It threw her back to the time when she wasn't old and had a lighter tread. A surge of emotion filled her belly, came up through her body and somehow lifted her shoulders and ran into her hands so that she had to spread her fingers, as if her very consciousness was expanding.

'Perhaps just for now, just for an hour, we should forget the children?' she said. After all, it was really why she'd brought him here.

'And Yiannis?'

'Him too.'

The heat on the beach was intense and the only sound through the gusting of the breeze was the splash and tumble as the waves, running strongly, tugged on the pebbles at the edge of the sea. The place was all theirs, as she'd hoped it might be. Way out at sea a yacht was surging along, alone and free. Her eyes followed its course as she held Daniel more tightly. If only they could sail away and leave all the troubles behind.

His thumb stroked her inner thigh as he turned towards her. Her throat felt full. Close to her face, he was all darkened glasses and hat and there were beads of sweat along each side of his nose. She used a finger to wipe them away.

'Daniel...' She stopped and he waited. She took off his sunglasses. 'I'm... I just need to say... I'm so pleased you came back...'

It sounded trite and he didn't reply and that was fine. She was away from Yiannis and his faults and from Sophia and Jonny and their deceit. She could even forget about Lilliana looking after the guests and Elira cleaning the rooms. Alone with Daniel, just then, she was free of her chains.

Leaning forward, she kissed him lightly on the lips. He paused for a second, then kissed her in return. It was a long kiss and his hand moved to her breast and she hadn't melted like this in many, many years. Maybe not since that taverna when she was only nineteen. She'd never forgotten their first kiss, her first proper kiss.

290

And this was not like kissing Yiannis. This was deep as her soul. This made her shake.

Daniel pulled back and when she opened her eyes he was gazing at her. Her mouth was dry. His hand still cupped her breast, which was perfect because he still held her heart. She had no doubts. This was the time for honesty, if ever there was going to be one. Truly, he'd always been her love. Even though she'd never really known him. It was that simple, even after so many years.

She slipped her hand between his legs and up to his groin and moved it gently to and fro.

'I said I'd never do this again,' he whispered.

'It's not wrong.'

'No, not that.' He laughed but without mockery. 'I mean this, on a beach... This. On the sand. Please, Helen, if I say stop, and I will this time if I have to, please stop, right away... I couldn't cope with being sliced open again.'

She threw back her hair and laughed with him.

'Oh, that!'

'No stopping yet though,' he said.

'Oh, Daniel... For goodness' sake, try not to fret.... I'll be gentle with you...'

Chapter 9

It was becoming Helen's habit to lie in bed long after Livadi had come to life, the sun had climbed high and Lilliana had laid out everything for breakfast over at Spiti. She'd not idled like this for decades.

She stretched under her sheet and stared at the crack in the ceiling and the curtains shifting in the breeze.

I am fifty-nine years old, she thought, the businesses are ready-made for the girls and I don't have to develop anything any longer. I've been fooling myself. Those days are gone. And to be himself, Yiannis has never needed me. He can still shout at Andreas and Michalis and drink and smoke all day if he wants, exactly as he has been doing, without me. I've no part in any of that. And Katerina and Anna can do the cooking. Who needs Eleni? Throughout my life I've been confined. I want to be free. I'd like to make love to Daniel daily, if he can manage that. And I want to take long slow showers and read all those books that have been waiting for me so long. I shall listen to more music and dance. If Daniel doesn't want to dance, I'll dance on my own.

Languidly, thinking of the beach, she raised her knees again, put her hands on the back of her neck and arched her back. So, shall I shower now or not?

Jeanette had woken much earlier and gone to swim. When she returned at eleven o'clock, Helen was on the patio, finishing her breakfast in the shade and trying to concentrate on Leonard Cohen's biography, which she'd picked up the day before from Angela at the bookshop. It was a heavy hardback, 550 pages long, and Lilliana had ordered it for her as a treat. Helen was finding it slow going with so much on her mind.

'Eating bread and honey and not even dressed? At nearly lunch time. Bohemian, I'd say… You're taking this Cohen stuff very seriously.' Jeanette sat beside her. 'You're recovering from a late night…?'

Helen dipped her head.

'I'm guessing you weren't with Yiannis… Danny, without

question. I went to bed at midnight. I thought you weren't coming back. I was imagining you'd simply melted.'

Helen popped in her last piece of bread and offered a hint of a smile, like a cross between a femme fatale and a naughty five-year-old. 'I did melt.'

Jeanette beamed: 'Of course you did. I can picture everything… a warm evening beside the sea… waves crashing… romantic words… soft hands… whispered words… deep, slow penetration… eyes closed, rapid breathing, stars and an earth-shattering climax…'

Helen sighed with contentment. 'Mm. Very good. Very close. But not evening. Afternoon. Under an umbrella. But yes, basically…'

She was still shocked at her own bravado.

'Goodness, girl. In the afternoon? On a beach? You could have been arrested. Are you my friend or has a love-fairy switched you in the night?'

'The final age of man… And woman..,' said Helen. 'You just have to, I suppose, while you can. The beach was empty, if very lumpy, but it was indescribably wonderful.'

'And no one caught you? And you lay there in each other's arms until the sun set, then went off to a quiet taverna for a candle-lit meal, though you were too wrapped up in each other to enjoy the food.'

'He ate a lot actually.'

'Of course. A man needs sustenance. I should have known that. Silly me….' Jeanette went quiet, thinking. 'After so long… it was your first time with him… But it was like you'd dreamed…?'

'I'm floating, Jan.'

'I can tell. What's next?'

'Fresh coffee?'

'You need to ask? Thanks.'

As they talked, they watched the tabby cat and her kittens in the garden, the mother licking her paws and washing her ears in the shade whilst her litter frisked with dead leaves in the sunshine. The cicadas were loud and the bamboo shifted when gusts came from the sea. In the distance, vehicles were winding their way up and down the hill to Chora. Life, Helen thought, always goes on, so why should hers not find a new course? Her kittens were grown.

She might have said exactly that to Jeanette, had they not heard a motorbike approaching.

'Yiannis.' Helen's euphoria left her. Instantly, she was anxious again, braced for another, fresh, confrontation.

She hadn't seen him for two days and had been expecting him sometime soon, but even so his arrival sent a shudder through her. With Daniel, she'd been soothed; but she was so worn by Yiannis' moods, his excuses, his endless apologies and pleadings. Still, she'd resolved that her spirit would not die yet and she stayed calm as Jeanette kissed her cheek and picked up her bag to go.

'I'll leave you to it… Is that all right?' Jeanette hesitated, her face registering concern for her friend. 'I mean, are you ok? Will you be safe? I can stay…'

'No… You go.'

Yiannis was already through the house and stepped out on to the patio. Finding Jeanette there, he stopped abruptly. She acknowledged him as she passed – '*Andio*' – and he nodded curtly as she headed for the door. Helen knew that as far as he was concerned his sister-in-law should have no part to play in this.

He allowed enough time for her to leave, then stepped forward. He'd always been a huge man, but this once seemed to tower over Helen. It was as if he was stopping the oxygen getting to her. Still, she endeavoured to remain impassive.

'*Kali spéra*, Yiannis.' Her composure came from the decisions she'd been making. 'Would you care to sit down?'

Whatever he'd been expecting, her cold civility clearly riled him and there was something new and disturbing about him. He looked dishevelled, but that was not unusual. If his clothes needed ironing, that was hardly surprising because she didn't think Lilliana would be doing that, as well as cooking, looking after the guests and dealing with the bookings. No, it was something in his face. It wasn't just his bloodshot eyes: the twitching of his gaze and the pull of his mouth made him seem almost feral.

Nevertheless, maintaining her self-control she waved a

hand towards the chair in which Jeanette had been sitting.
'Yiannis..?'

He didn't move. His eyes narrowed. He had never menaced her before, but his mood was ugly and unexpectedly she experienced a spasm of fear.

'You must come back.'

'I will not.'

'Then I will come here too.'

'No, Yiannis, no! *Óchi – den tha to kánete.*' She shook her head. 'It's over. We're done.'

She had never got used to the way Greek men often smile when they're angry. His face had that look for a moment, then it was as if he could contain his hurt no longer. All muscled arms, he bent down and seized her shoulders, lifting her out of the chair, up, up until she was on tiptoes. It was so like the way he'd grabbed Daniel. His fingers pressed crudely into the flesh on her upper arms. Her throat contracted as she was squeezed and shaken, trying to scream but producing only a desperate gasp. Panicking, she struggled to escape his grip but he was far too strong.

What do you do? What do you do? How do you stop this? She knew. She'd heard it somewhere, sometime, but she couldn't remember how to defend herself. What, what do you do?

He forced her back so she was pressed against the rough wall. The sun was behind him and there was just his face before hers, contorting, perhaps hating her for what she'd done or for everything he'd done. She smelt his bad breath.

Giving up her futile attempts to free herself, she resigned herself to whatever came next. She had no alternative.

Then suddenly there came salvation. Blows were raining down on the side of his head. Jeanette was there, behind him, hitting him again and again with the heavy book Helen had been struggling to read earlier.

'Yiannis, Yiannis!' Jeanette was screaming, hammering him repeatedly. 'Let her go! For Christ's sake, man, let her go…!'

'*Aou!*' he shouted, though it must have been because of frustration, not pain. He loosened his hold and Helen spun to make an escape across the garden. In an instant, though, he held her once more, this time from behind, one arm round her waist, then the other.

'*Óchi! Óchi!*' he shouted. 'No, no!'

She had no idea where Jeanette was, but as he corrected her stumble and actually held her upright, Helen's head cleared for a moment and she remembered exactly what she should do. Bizarrely, it was Sophia who'd taught her. She'd learnt it from a self-defence expert she'd met on the beach. Her arm snaked down until her hand was between his legs and she dug her nails sharply through the denim, not into his testicles but into the soft sensitive flesh at the top of his inner thigh and twisted. Her nails bit deep.

'*Aouch!*' He gasped, released her and stepped back, half stooping.

Immediately, Jeanette was round him and beside Helen, holding the book in the air, as if it were a hammer or a scimitar. At another time, Helen would have been unable to contain her laughter; but right then nothing was funny.

'*Maláka!*' she said, quietly but no longer calm. 'You bastard!'

'Eleni!' He straightened up, the hurt animal again, his face lined with a pain that could only have been psychological. 'Eleni, please...' His eyes narrowed yet further. Would he cry or spring at her again?

'Get out, Yiannis. Just go!' With Jeanette beside her, her strength returned. '*Poté xaná*, Yiannis. Never again. Do you hear me? Never again. Go.'

She was bruised and could still feel his builder's grip on her body, the strength against which she had no chance, and she would never, never, accept physical abuse.

'This is the end. *To télos*. You understand? It's over, Yiannis. Leave here and leave me alone. We are finished!' She was recovered enough to raise her voice.

Jeanette stepped between them, the book raised, ready to bludgeon him with biography.

He looked at the two of them for perhaps five seconds, then pushed back his hair, turned and crashed through the house, knocking over a vase as he went, slamming his way outside.

Jeanette followed him to make sure he'd gone. His bike started almost immediately and he sped away.

When she returned, Helen hadn't moved. Jeanette held her and stroked the back of her hair. Helen had never loved her friend more.

'You ok?' said Jeanette.

'Of course.' She sat down, shaky and very, very tired. 'I'm always all right, aren't I?' She took a moment, then managed a smile. 'Yiannis was in a slightly melodramatic mood today, I thought... What an unfortunate turn for the worse. I'd been full of the joys of spring too... I'm quite glad you were still here. Making sure I was safe?' Jeanette nodded. 'And it's just as well Leonard Cohen was on hand too... If you can't trust a poet to rescue you, who can you trust..?' She paused. 'The Greeks are such lovely people. Greek men aren't like this. Why me, Jan? Why me? How did I end up with a Yiannis like this?'

'Brave girl,' said Jeanette. 'Brave, brave girl... Tote that bale, eh...? I'll make a pot of tea, shall I? Two sugars each...'

****

Daniel was having a quiet time: assimilating all that had happened, metaphorically pinching himself and sighing contentedly for once, and uncontrollably. They'd made love. They'd made love on the beach. In daylight. Who would ever have thought that could happen? With Helen. In daylight. On the beach.

He felt reborn. His mind ranged over every detail from the day before – the loveliness of her skin, her soft gasps, that moment at last... He found himself believing, finally, that they would end up happy ever after. Surely it could happen and it would happen exactly as it should happen.

He got a glass of water and counted out his tablets: ciclosporin, prednisolone, bisoprolol, ezetemibe, co-trimoxazole and omeprazole, each a small miracle. They had kept him alive for a morning like this.

Still, of course, two tormented souls continued to suffer in the house with him. Jonny and Lara ate their breakfast in grim silence, tearing lumps off the day-old bread, spreading on sweet jam and washing them down with instant coffee, as if all of it might choke them.

Difficult as it was, Daniel was trying not to dwell on their tragedy. He sat a little way from them on the terrace, thinking about how he'd sat on this beach as a young man, pretending not to ogle the naked girls as Mike fantasised about what the next evening might bring. How desperate they must have been, how desperate they must have seemed. How young they were.

And how callous he was then. Where was Dianne now? What was she doing? Comptometers had been redundant for many, many years. He hoped she'd found a wonderful life. He imagined he could identify the place where their makeshift house had been, where he'd tried to pretend everything was all right even though Helen was over the hill and spending her days with Yiannis. Dianne had seemed to accept that his disenchantment was because of his cut (self-inflicted, he'd told her) but there had been no love-making, no pleasure at all. If she guessed he was infatuated with Helen, she never said. Perhaps she had to hold her peace, under the circumstances. How grim it must have been.

He'd been so bound up in himself. Then for decades afterwards he'd been so unhappy... Now, though, now... Finally, there was hope; indeed, greater expectations than ever before. Maybe for one day at least he could be positive. The world turns, perspectives shift... He felt vibrant. Jonny and Lara would have to find their own solutions.

That was how he felt on that day in that place after the trip to Kalo Empeli.

'So, do you two have plans for today? Swimming? Chora?' Lara's face was all bottom lip, indicating she just wanted to go home; Jonny shrugged.

With no apparent desire to go anywhere or see anything, they spent their time close to the house, avoiding each other. If one was under the sun umbrella, the other was in the sea or wandering back and forth along the beach or perched on the rocks.

Daniel, meanwhile, was obsessed with his phone, hoping a text would come through. He had Helen's number now, but she told him her phone was for emergencies. She had an old unsmart Nokia. He empathised with her when she said she preferred life the way it once was, but still hoped for a ping and a message.

She would surely be in touch sooner or later but he had to give her space; so he sat on the balcony and tried to read.

When the heat began to diminish around five o'clock, Jonny and Lara disappeared upstairs. Daniel could hear the shower running, but there were no voices, not even muffled ones. How were they coping?

He ran his tongue along his teeth, to the gums at the back where his two missing molars used to be. It was what he did when he was fretting. The dentist had to remove his crowns and the stumps of teeth beneath before his transplant because they could harbour infections and that was the last thing anyone needed post-op. They had to go, but he missed them. As in life, gaps took away so much of the pleasure. He would consider implants if he could afford them and if Helen approved…

If Helen were with him, of course. He shouldn't project too far ahead, really shouldn't. Nothing in this life is certain….

There was no news all day.

He headed towards town early that evening, with Jonny and Lara beside him. On the camp site beach the shadows of the trees stretched out to the water but families still sat together and people were swimming. Daniel took off his sandals and waded through the shallows whilst Jonny plodded at the edge of the sea, regularly sinking into the wet sand until he was forced to remove his canvas shoes. Lara, looking like some devastated Hollywood starlet behind dark glasses, walked to their left, on the deep soft dry sand, in a world of her own. Daniel was reminded of a line from a David Francey song: 'The heart that's breaking never makes a sound.'

As they descended to the harbour, there was a bustle of activity at the office of the Port Police half way down.

'They always get excited when it's time for their beans on toast,' said Daniel. It wasn't funny and he got no reply but even sarcasm would have been welcome.

They had agreed to avoid the Taverna Konstantinidis for

one evening. Both Daniel and his son needed to be sensible and Lara didn't care where they went.

Daniel suggested they should give Taverna Marianna a try. He'd never considered it on previous trips to Serifos. Set back amongst trees, at the very end of the town beach, it was run by an extremely old lady who was revered for her personality and cheese. Helen, demonstrating surprisingly disloyalty to her family's business, said the place was excellent, an original with old-time prices.

They had to pass Konstantinidis', where Andreas nodded for them to stop on the road. He delivered his trayful of drinks to four Italians, then returned, conspiratorially.

'My friend,' he began, 'you are well?'

'I am. *Póli kalá.*'

Andreas looked towards Jonny and Lara, neither of whom noticed. Lara was looking across towards Spiti; Jonny was gazing into the restaurant, perhaps wondering if Sophia might appear.

'And you, Andreas?'

'Yes, yes. *Kalá.* All good.'

There was an awkward pause.

'My friend…, Yiannis is not so good today.' Daniel's brow furrowed. 'He is very unhappy. And he has drink all day. I am telling you because maybe it is good if you do not see him today.'

'You mean it is best if he doesn't see me…'

'Yes, my friend. If he does not see you.'

Daniel had always suspected Andreas knew everything that was happening on the island. Without doubt, he knew all about their terrible triangle.

'We aren't eating here tonight,' he said. 'But thank you for the warning.' Andreas inclined his head and gave a wry smile. 'It's kind of you to think of us.' Andreas nodded again, pushed back his glasses and returned to his work.

'Let us go, then,' said Daniel, trying to sound upbeat but fearing for Helen and wondering how she might be coping. 'To live a long life, man must eat.' Under normal circumstances, he might have added some comment about being hungry enough to eat for two but that would be far from tactful with Lara there.

At the Taverna Marianna, tables were set out on the grass in front of the building. An old man sitting beside the kitchen door wished them what was probably a warm welcome, though it was all in rapid Greek. Kyria Marianna was cooking, but was much more in evidence than Yiannis' mother had ever been, working as the waitress too, fussing back and forth, ungainly and hot. She might have been in her eighties, was heavily built and struggled on bad legs, the left one bandaged. Daniel watched and felt sympathy; Jonny and Lara had probably not even noticed. They would normally have been appalled by the weird old African carvings beside the low wall in front of them, one a skeletal black face with popping white eyes, the kind of crude caricature you might have found in the seventies. However, for once wokeness was not their priority.

Kyria Marianna led them into the kitchen to choose their food and there too it could have been another age: flies were everywhere, with a heavy concentration around the blackened cook pots. Had it been this grim back in the day? Had Daniel's memory played tricks and had they all survived night after night of fly-blown meat? Possibly.

The old lady spoke just odd words of English: salad, fries, beef. Jonny and Lara left the choice to Daniel, who avoided salad for once, selecting stewed chicken and *pótates* in the hope any germs would have been cooked away.

When they returned to their table, Lara scrolled through her phone, occasionally tapping out messages; Jonny had given up on his. He was gazing across the grass to the sea, but evidently daydreaming. It didn't take a genius to know where their thoughts lay: Lara would be telling friends at home about her troubles and Jonny just wanted to be somewhere with Sophia. There was still no conversation.

The deflation that had been simmering deep within Daniel for hours, which he'd sought to quell, surfaced at last. He reverted to his customary sigh. Kalo Empeli had been a fleeting moment. There is so much unhappiness in the world, he thought. If a god is responsible, damn him.

Other diners arrived, talking and laughing and there was the clink of plates, the chink of glasses and clatterings from the kitchen, but when Jonny's phone buzzed on the table it was quite loud enough to get Daniel's attention. Jonny noticed too but hardly glanced at it. Lara lifted her head for a moment, then went back to her texting.

After a few minutes, the phone buzzed again. And again. Still, Jonny did not respond.

The old man came out of the kitchen with a pan of spaghetti, took it across the grass and scraped it on to a large platter for a cat and her kittens, who fed ravenously.

The diners all watched – except Lara, whose focus had moved to Jonny's phone. It seemed she might snatch it up at any moment. Still he pointedly ignored it, and ignored her. His lack of interest was unnatural; her stare was intense.

Finally he broke from his trance and, apparently sensing trouble, silently pocketed his device, still without looking at whatever had come through, his face impassive.

'That was her, wasn't it?' Lara spoke very quietly.

'What? Who?'

Daniel's toes curled.

'I've had enough.'

Lara didn't raise her voice. She might have said more, so much more: Daniel admired her dignity even as he felt her pain. It was not merely that he liked her so much; it was not that his own past continued to echo so that he wanted to make everything right in an attempt to absolve himself; it was also the fact that she was carrying his grandchild. Would she keep it? Only a couple of years ago, the idea of having a grandson or granddaughter would have been a ridiculous dream and when Jonny told him Lara was pregnant, the enormity had taken a while to sink in. But he was realising he'd love a grandchild, and soon, selfish as that might be. For all his positivity about his health, Daniel didn't know how much time he would actually have with second-hand lungs.

Lara stood up without another word and headed into the evening, back towards town.

Daniel pulled out his wallet and handed Jonny a fifty-euro note.

'Pay for the drinks,' he said. 'And the food too, I suppose. There will be more than enough there. I'll see you back at the

302

house. Soon. Do not stay out all night. That poor girl doesn't deserve this.'

He set off to offer some sympathy to Lara, his earlier feelings of elation subsumed in her tragedy.

****

Helen had gone back to bed when Jeanette left. As far as she could remember, she'd never before been in bed in the afternoon; but she was drained, all the energy sucked from her. She maintained a normality whilst Jeanette lingered, but once alone she felt wrecked, desperate for restoration. She showered, then stretched out and slipped into the arms of Hypnos. She was catching up on decades of rest she'd missed and it was a deep sleep, with the most vivid dream.

She was on Livadakia Beach with Daniel, under the clearest night sky. Their bodies were young again and there was sand in their clothes and in their hair. There were shooting stars, one after another along the Milky Way. They drank wine before making uninterrupted love, at first passionately, but then again, slowly, languorously. Only the two of them seemed to exist. Her body pulsed and her breaths were so deep that she couldn't believe there was air left on the island for Daniel; and when it was all over, daylight infused everything around them as the sun rose rapidly across the bay. They were clothed and leant together, relaxing and watching children who had arrived from somewhere and were playing together at the edge of the sea. In amongst them, Lewis was holding hands with Sophia and Lilliana, and the three of them screamed as they jumped over the waves; but then Jonny splashed towards them and Lewis fell backwards and the others didn't notice because they were running off together towards the rocks. Lewis must have been washed away, because she couldn't see him anymore. She leapt to her feet and rushed into the sea where he'd been, looking left and then right. Yet more boys and girls appeared with balls and li-los, but no Lewis. Daniel was standing beside her and began to shout, 'No! No! No!' He gripped her arm and his shouts were so loud that the rest of the beach looked, wondering what was wrong. Daniel couldn't do anything to find his son because when she turned he was back on the dry sand and his body was bandaged tightly and there were tubes connected to a hospital machine beside him, all wires and dials and flashing lights. Two paramedics who had suddenly appeared repeatedly advised him to 'lie still, lie still, lie still'. Only one man went to look for Lewis. It was Yiannis, who was wading back and forth through the water, looking down as though searching for a lost wedding ring. But he stopped when a tall, willowy blonde woman rose from the sea like a mermaid. Giving up the search, he took her hand and left with her, laughing, his motorbike kicking sand as they slithered across the beach, leaving behind the tracks of a giant snake. At first, she felt surprise that he hadn't noticed her and Daniel, but that didn't last because she felt Daniel's arms around her and any fears were gone. There was a new, blinding light; his bandages and the doctors had left and once more he was healthy and mended. Lewis was back too, holding on to his father's leg, and then all their children were back, laughing and laughing, playing in the soft sand. She and Daniel went running into the waves and fell forward into a beautiful blue silence.

Helen woke crying with relief and hope and a deep joy. Everything would be fine.

It was dark and she felt revived. Her panic had gone. Yiannis was not going to be her ending. She had yo-yoed, her torments dropping away. Her future would be fine. No longer did she have to spend hours on the bookings and on emails; she did not have to concern herself with the traders and their invoices and the staff anymore; she didn't have to worry about the bank loans; she wouldn't have to survive on too little sleep. She could put the businesses – and Yiannis – behind her.

She needn't worry because she would retain the love of her daughters, whatever happened. Nothing could change that. They were adults anyway and could lead their own lives and would cope easily enough without her.

Crucially, she would be with Daniel.

There. Yes. She felt much better. This time she was confident that Yiannis would never hurt her again.

****

It was around ten o'clock that night when the shouting began in Jonny and Lara's room. Daniel, washing glasses at the sink, wasn't tempted to intervene. He could do nothing. So long as Lara was safe – and he was certain she would come to no physical harm from his son – the convulsions would have to play themselves out. He recognised the tone of Lara's accusations and valid laments and what were probably desperate self-justifications from Jonny.

Deciding the arguments might go on for some time, Daniel escaped to the beach and the night. He couldn't play the role of referee.

He was still trapped between the breakdown in their relationship and the hopes for his own. His horizons were broadening and he could gaze up at the light twinkling from millions of years ago and for another moment believe the universe is truly beautiful and misery is transitory and all would be well once Helen escaped. This terrible time for the children would pass.

He wondered when Helen would come to visit; she had said it might be late. He fretted over her safety but had to be patient, fearing that if he went to her his presence would make everything yet more difficult. He certainly didn't want to find drunken punches raining into his face and his chest and didn't want to become a medical emergency. Despite the confidence he had endeavoured to portray, his recent brush with Yiannis had left him shaken. The shock had taken a while to register, but was palpable.

I am not a coward, he told himself. It is just that some things are beyond me now.

He might have sent her a text, but knew that could cause problems, like it had for Jonny. So instead he lay back and shut his eyes, listening to the waves. This he loved, this he had always loved... He had lain like this on so many evenings over so many years...

He might have drifted to sleep but was jolted from his reverie. From the house came a smash, then a scream from Lara and some sort of bellow from Jonny. Fearing a new stage in the disintegration of their world, he hurried back, to do what he could.

****

'She threw his phone through the window?'

Helen had arrived after the hostilities had played out.

'She threw it from the house,' said Daniel. Then he understood Helen's confusion. 'I mean, yes, she threw it out of the window. Only she'd just smashed the window by throwing a bottle at him, so much of the glass had gone already. She didn't smash the phone through the glass, if you see what I mean.'

'Still…'

'They have problems which are more serious than a broken window… But looking at it from a practical and personal point of view, I will have an awkward conversation with the owner. I can't imagine he's had guests smashing his windows before.'

'I suppose it's better than if they were trying to knock each other's lights out?' She knew it wasn't her best attempt at humour. 'Can I help? Could I explain to the owner? In Greek.'

'I'd love that… If he were Greek.' He looked up the beach towards the house, which was ablaze with lights. There was a towel pinned over the window of the top room in an attempt to keep out mosquitoes. 'It's an Airbandb: international stuff. Luigi lives in *Roma*…'

'Luigi? Really? *Luigi*?'

'Absolutely.'

Despite everything, she managed to laugh. 'He certainly sounds Italian. What do you think he'll do?'

'If I were him, I'd start by being very angry. When it happened, I'd normally have been furious too – but Lara did it and I can't blame her…'

'Nope.'

She was facing the spur of land which had Spiti at the other end, out of sight from Karavi. Beside her on the beach, Daniel rubbed at a mosquito bite on his leg. She could think of nothing to make the situation seem better. What a mess the children were in.

She loved her daughter but Sophia was in the wrong, whilst Jonny reminded her of a careless young man who destroyed her own dreams. Like his father, he was not some devil incarnate and maybe he'd just inherited damaged genes and would grow into a better person too but that wouldn't help them in the present.

'I don't know what to say.'

'There is nothing that would help, is there?' Daniel took her hand. 'I am hopelessly happy and inexpressibly sad all at the same time.'

Such a weight was upon them.

Their silence was broken by the arrival of Jeanette and Kostas.

'Hey! Hello!' Jeanette shouted as they came down from the terrace. Earlier, she'd called Kostas on Milos and asked him to come over to try to reason with his brother. Usually, he managed a measure of influence over Yiannis, though Helen wasn't convinced he'd be able to work any miracle this time.

He smiled beatifically, as ever. 'Daniel. We meet again!' His manners were unfailingly perfect. 'This is all so difficult.'

'You are the master of understatement,' said Daniel, getting to his feet. They could have been talking about either of the fractured relationships.

'I have not seen you for many, many years, Kostas,' he said, holding out his hand. 'You look well.'

'Thank you.'

'And you, Jeanette, look fabulous. Of course.'

'Of course!' She smiled back at him. 'It's great to see you again. We seem to meet every few decades. Alive and well, eh?'

'Alive and... well... as well as can be expected,' said Daniel. 'Let's get into the light? A glass of wine, perhaps?'

'Thank you, yes,' said Kostas.

Back on the terrace, they were all uneasy as they sipped their drinks: stilted conversation, stiff body language, wine glasses held in cupped hands. Even Kostas wasn't as suave as usual and kept wiping his brow. He'd come from seeing his brother.

'I am worried about Yiannis,' he said to Helen.

'We all are,' said Daniel.

'He needs help. Eleni, perhaps...'

Jeanette winced, all divided loyalties.

'No, Kostas... We've spoken. Everything's over.' She tried to avoid sounding bitter. 'He's hurt me deeply – many, many times, but he's never frightened me before. He's not the Yiannis I married.' She controlled what could have been a shudder. 'He's become unpredictable and I've no idea what he might do next. You can't live with someone like that. You can't talk to them. You know that, Kostas, don't you?'

Kostas was an intelligent man: 'I know it,' he said. 'But you know this is not how we are in Greece...'

'I know, Kostas. This has nothing to do with being Greek. He just is what he is.'

A stray cat had made its careful way along the building and to the side of Helen's chair. It rubbed itself against her leg, back arched and tail raised. She absent-mindedly stroked its head and it rolled over on to its back, flicking playful claws at her hand. It drew blood and she left it alone.

'Tell him you've seen me... Say...' Helen paused. 'Say I'm going back to England with Daniel. Tell him I'm done with Serifos.'

****

After everyone left, even Helen, who went to see Lilliana, Daniel sat alone on a canvas chair on the terrace. Behind him, Jonny called, 'I'm out, dad,' in a voice full of frustration, maybe wretchedness, and the door slammed. Lara was probably crying upstairs. Daniel didn't try to stop his son. Instead, absentmindedly he ran a finger along the line of the scar across his chest.

This is not an end, he thought. We survive. Unless sickness takes us, we all survive. I am still here, against all the odds.

He had made love to Helen on the beach. She said she was coming back to England with him. He would come home in future and the love of his life would be waiting. Or, if she wanted to work, she would be with him each evening, each weekend, every holiday. And they would have all the time in the world.

'Daniel?'

It was Lara.

'Hiya.' He came out of his reverie. She stepped from the shadows and sat beside him, ashen-faced.

He felt he should say, 'How are things now?' but that wasn't a question that needed to be asked. Her dejection would be clear to anyone.

There came a gust along the beach. A towel blew off the drying rack.

'Jonny doesn't want a baby.'

'No.' He hardly dared ask. 'You?'

'I don't know.'

'But Jonny…?'

She misunderstood him.

'No, I don't want Jonny. Not anymore.'

They gazed into the darkness.

'I've tried, but I can't picture myself as a mother and alone.'

It seemed Daniel's fantasy of dangling a child on his knee was not to be, yet it wasn't his place to try to convince her to have the baby. He couldn't begin to imagine the anguish she was suffering already; and the shadow of Dianne was always beside him, of course, so he held his tongue.

'I'm going home.'

'Ah. Immediately?'

'Yes.'

'You'll have to find a flight...' He corrected himself: 'We'll have to find you a flight.'

'There's always a flight. I don't care how much I have to pay.'

'You won't be paying.' He knew she'd want to argue, but he also knew she'd been grateful for this holiday because she'd no spare cash at all. 'This is not your mess. This is Jonny's fault. Don't worry about the cost.'

The cost to you has already been immense, he thought. All he could do was try to atone.

'Thank you, Daniel. I want to go right away. That must be possible…'

There were tears on her cheeks.

'It might be a bit late to make a flight tomorrow. Maybe the day after? I can check ferries and airlines if you like. It is no good trekking to the airport and being stranded there. Shall we see what I can come up with?'

'It's good of you.'

She had always presented herself as self-confident and competent: now, she was simply putting herself into his hands. He ached to do something to ease her pain.

'Would you like to have my room tonight? I can manage on the settee – or out here even.' He should have offered days ago.

'I can't make you…'

'You aren't making me. Please. Let me do something.'

She nodded, offered a wan smile and went inside, presumably to move her things.

He turned back to the shifting waters. Everything is mutable, he thought: Jonny must have gone to Sophia, and Helen was arranging her own imminent departure. And might this be his own final farewell to Serifos? Would there ever be a good time to come back?

When he closed his eyes, thinking he might sleep where he was, the past returned, as so often before. He pictured Mike with sore feet picking his way up the hills and wondered what his old friend was doing now. Then Jenny was driving madly down from Chora as he and the boys sang loudly with the windows wide open. And he saw Lewis, complaining that he was tired as he plodded along the road to Psili Ammos, saying he didn't want to walk any further; and he heard himself being sharp and uncompromising. And he cried.

Deep breaths.

He'd survived his surgery and had a future… He would leave with Helen... Why was he torturing himself? Nothing

310

was going to stand in their way. Life would be better and whatever they might have to face, they could cope. *Que sera, sera.*

He went inside to find a blanket.

****

Helen ran her fingers along the hangers in her wardrobe, then looked at the suitcases lying open on the floor. Most of her clothes wouldn't be suitable for the British climate, which was probably just as well since she'd far too much to carry, but what should she take?

Lilliana was saying little, perched on the bed, pulling at her long hair like a sad waif, watching.

'You really don't think you'll be coming back again?' she said, making it seem like the end of the world, which it was, in a way.

'I won't be coming back any time soon.' She put an arm around her daughter. 'I am so sorry, my angel. I'll phone you every day. Or we can Skype, can't we?'

'I don't want you to run away, mama…'

Helen felt the tearing in her heart again.

'You know I can't stay… Your father…'

She didn't fear for the safety of her daughters but she was worried about what Yiannis might do to her. Only days ago, such a thought had never entered her head but his assault had left her frightened, her nervousness reflected in her occasional glances to the door and the window and in her indecision about what, exactly, she should pack first.

Lilliana, a grown woman, ran her foot back and forth on the tiled floor, just like when she was little and wanting some favour.

'You could stay for a week…'

'No. I need to go as soon as possible. Maybe in the next day or two. Quickly, that's all.'

Daniel had sent an urgent text: Lara was going home and he felt they should leave with her. Money was no object, he said, because it was vital to arrange a quick exit.

How awful that it had come to such a pass.

As if in a Hollywood movie, she opened a drawer, swept up an armful of underwear and dropped it into the suitcase. Then, despite her situation, she knelt down, lifted it all out again and started to fold each item neatly.

Lilliana flounced from the room with the sort of flourish Sophia would have admired. Helen came close to a smile. They would both be fine, once they'd got their heads around what was happening. In fact, they'd both be so busy without her that they'd have no time to mourn. She hoped so, anyway, because Sophia would be without her lover soon enough, when Jonny returned to his home and his job. It would be nothing more than a holiday romance for him. Goodness only knew how Sophia was handling that because her daughter was keeping her own counsel…

Helen carried on packing, but her mind wandered.

After marrying Yiannis, she'd absorbed herself in all things Greek, even struggling through some ancient writings by the Greek philosophers, a brief flirtation because her language skills were so limited and their wisdom proved a hard and dry discipline which certainly didn't help her chop onions. A university professor who visited one summer suggested she should have chosen the French existentialists instead. Maybe Camus and Sartre might have offered some crumbs of comfort in her present plight.

Still, a quotation from Heraclitus came back to her: *Ta pánta réoun kai típota den ménei, óla dínoun to drómo kai típota den paraménei statheró.* "Everything flows and nothing abides, everything gives way and nothing stays fixed."

He was correct, though most of her possessions would have to stay fixed exactly where they were. To take them all would require a small cargo plane. Unable to decide what to squeeze into the case next, this time she was the one who sat on the bed.

She'd spent the day trying to control her emotions but as she thought about Spiti, about the sea and the sky and the beaches and her daughters and remembered a life that had been full of sunshine, tears pricked her eyes. The years had passed, the fish had gone from the seas and her marriage was empty as a rock pool.

She might have spent a long while lamenting her tragedy had Lilliana not returned, this time with Sophia. One sat either side of her on the bed and put their arms around her. They rested their heads on her shoulders and the three of them hugged as they did when the girls were little.

'Thank you,' Helen said. 'Thank you and I am so sorry.'

'I am sorry, mama,' said Sophia, for the first time.

'Things happen. We do what we do...' Sophia would learn.

Later, she drove behind Sophia back to Spiti. There were things she wanted to collect; and her daughter said she'd left her shawl there and wanted to get it before she met Jonny. Helen didn't trust herself to comment.

They found Yiannis' bike at the bottom of the steps.

'*O patéra sou...* Your father's not here, is he?'

'No. He said he has work. He must have walked there this morning. Maybe he's drinking again.'

Helen was struck by the matter-of-fact way Sophia talked about it. This was not the life she'd wanted for the girls and she'd worked hard to make the family a happy one: above them towered the apartments, a symbol of what she'd achieved, whilst across the water twinkled the lights of the taverna. All of this would soon be behind her.

'Sophia... You and Jonny...'

'It's our affair, mama.'

'It's too late now for Jonny and Lara. We both know that.' She wanted to say, 'And you will have to live with what's happened,' but she didn't. Instead, 'But take care, please,' she said. 'He's here on holiday. He'll be heading home soon. You'll be left behind. That's how it is.'

'I will be ok, mama. We'll be ok. I'm seeing him soon. Don't worry about us. Take care of yourself.'

That gave her no confidence, but at least Sophia didn't beg her to give her father another chance. It was too late for that as well.

She headed up the steps. 'I'll just get my bits,' she said. 'I'll be quick.' Lilliana was using their room, but it was so small there was nowhere for anything to be hidden.

Helen didn't know where Yiannis had been sleeping and she didn't care. However, when she opened their door, she

knew he was inside, presumably asleep because the shutters
were closed. She recognised the scent of her husband and she
could hear his laboured breathing. She'd hoped to avoid
another confrontation, but it seemed that would be impossible
because she needed her toiletries. At first she hesitated, but she
braced herself and switched on the light.

The shock was terrible.

'For God's sake, no!'

The moment before she'd been nervous, but in an instant
she was livid, more angry with him than she'd ever been
before.

Yiannis had been asleep and was stretched on their bed
with his arms around a naked blonde woman whose eyes
opened and filled with surprise, then shock and fear and
embarrassment. She threw off Yiannis' arm and sat up,
twisting left and right, presumably looking for something with
which to cover herself.

She might have been in her thirties and they could see she
was a natural blonde. She was slim and Helen hated her all the
more because she had a perfect body.

'For fuck's sake!'

It was quite likely that Sophia had never before heard her
mother swear but she was way beyond caring.

'How could you do this? Yiannis! *Málaka*! This is our
room! This is our bed! This is where our daughter is sleeping!'

'*Je m'excuse! Je m'excuse!*' The woman got to her feet and
frantically grabbed her underwear from the chair and the floor.
She looked dazed now, horrified. Slipping a beach dress over
her head, she seized her sandals and made to depart.

'Go, go, go! Move quickly, before I break you! *Grígora*!
Allez! *Allez*!'

The woman stumbled out into the evening – she must have
been drunk – but Helen didn't give her another glance. Her
gaze was fixed on her husband.

Yiannis was squinting at them, unmoved and unmoving.
He raised himself on to one elbow, but that was all.

'Cover yourself! You have no shame? You really have no
shame? Even in front of your daughter…' Sophia turned and

left them. Helen struggled to find words. 'How could you? Here! How? How?'

'*Éndaksí*. Ok, so no shame. Why should there be shame? You have your man… You are with Daniel… You are going away with Daniel?' One of the girls must have told him. 'That is true, yes? *Eínai alítheia* … I am no different to you!'.

Surprisingly he was remarkably sober, which made it worse.

'This is our bed…' Helen was waving her arms, her fury encompassing the bed and the room and the whole building. 'Here! You did it here..!' Her mind was whirling too. 'How many times have you brought other women into our bed, Yiannis? How many times before? How many times?'

Later, she realised she would have known. If there had been other times, she'd have recognised the signs. But she wasn't rational at that moment.

'Never. I have never.'

She knew his tone and she recognised his look. They'd been together for forty years. She believed him.

'But now you do. All the others, it happened somewhere else, but now it happens here. This is how much you love me, Yiannis. This is how much you respect me…'

'I am not planning to go to England with a lover.' He was on his feet now. How ridiculous men look without clothes, she thought. 'I did not end everything. Do not try to blame me. This is your doing, Eleni. This is all your choice…'

It was not her fault but she wouldn't waste her time telling him.

****

'Today? We can leave straight away? That's good.'

Lara looked as if a weight had been lifted. Daniel offered her a weak smile.

'I can get tickets for the high-speed this evening, nine o'clock. We can stay in Athens tonight – they have rooms at the Athens Gate Hotel – and Aegean have three seats back to England tomorrow: for you, me, and Helen. I'll confirm the tickets, it'll be just sixty euros for a taxi to the airport, and you'll be home by late afternoon. Is that ok?'

She nodded. Helen would be pleased too.

He booked it all using his phone: Android life.

'Jonny is staying here until the end of our rental…'

He watched for her reaction but was uncertain whether she was registering relief that they wouldn't have to spend another day together and that he wasn't travelling with them or disdain because he'd be in their bed each night with Sophia. It had become devastatingly clear that Jonny cared nothing for her or their baby.

She muttered, 'Fine!' then a genuine, 'Thank you, Daniel,' picked up her towel and bag and left, presumably to find shade under which she could endure her last day. He winced, perhaps for the hundredth time, at what a disaster their holiday had become. When he set out, his lungs had been his obsession…

He'd just sent an email to tell Kristina he wouldn't be returning to her apartments after all when Jonny returned from his swim.

'It's all sorted,' he told him. 'We'll be leaving later.' Then he sighed. He was doing that again.

Looking at his boy, he saw himself as he used to be. If for no other reason than that, he'd never abandon him, however crass might be Jonny's behaviour. Yet he wanted to shake him and demand more maturity, more common decency. What would Lewis have thought? Perhaps he'd have said, 'He's your son, dad.' He'd have been old enough to say things like that by now.

Jonny's face was impassive. He shrugged and slumped into a chair.

'Sorry, dad. It's just what I want more than anything.'

'Yes. Freedom, eh? It always comes at a price for someone. "Freedom. We have freedom…"' Jonny ignored him.

They sat in silence, watching one couple and then a second wander down from the hill behind and towards the sea. The first ones took a small beach tent from their bag, set it up facing the waves and disappeared inside. The next two struggled to anchor their umbrella in the soft sand because of the breeze. At another time, he and Jonny would have laughed at their struggles, but they'd stopped laughing at anything. Daniel wondered whether Jonny and Sophia laughed together. He hoped they did.

'It will only take me a few minutes to pack this afternoon. I've been living out of the suitcase,' he said. 'Right now I must away to town to pick up our tickets from the booking office. See you later.'

He squeezed his son's shoulder and went to find a clean tee-shirt.

He spotted Lara sitting under a tree as he traversed Livadakia Beach, though she was oblivious to him as he passed behind her. She hadn't bothered to remove any clothes. He imagined that getting a tan was the last thing on her mind.

She was watching hundreds of small fish taking dolphin leaps together across the bay, silver flashing sparkles in the sunshine. Then they were gone.

He climbed the hill that led over to the harbour, noticing again how much stronger he was becoming. At the top, he made a sudden decision and turned right instead of descending immediately to the port. Ahead, on the promontory above the entrance to the harbour, was the small chapel and cemetery. For the first time ever, he went to look around, lured by the monuments to eternal rest. The transplant had affected him in strange ways.

Presumably everything was set on solid rock and the closely packed graves were shallow tombs. Even from the beach it had seemed less congested forty years ago, though that was bound to have been the case. People continue to die: that was his continual refrain.

It was peaceful beside the chapel surrounded by the customary marble though he had no desire to enter the building, because churches always frightened him, a reminder of his own mortality.

He'd hoped for somewhere to sit and think in the shade but there was no seat and out of respect he couldn't sit on a tomb. An old lady was tidying around a large family plot, removing the dead flowers and shifting away dead leaves, and he had no wish to cause offence.

There was an angel above her, atop the marble, protecting the dead, and there were the usual framed photographs of those interred: all were smiling, smart, so alive – but now gone. We must seize the moment, he thought, and his own recent history had hammered home that message.

Amidst the sacred whiteness, one grave surprised him. It might have stood out as the most impressive, but instead was remarkably shocking. It had a photograph of a bemedalled middle-aged man in uniform, military cap on his head, a severe face with a trim moustache. Yet, although the photo had been left unspoiled, the monument itself was piled over with heaped stone, broken bricks, roofing tiles and general refuse.

The man had died in 1969, the time of the Generals, when Greece was under military law. Was he in charge of the island at that time, an army chief or the police chief? Was this, perhaps, the revenge of the people after his death? Had they signified their hatred of him, at the last? Greeks normally show enormous respect to their forbears: indeed, the old lady was putting fresh flowers in a tin jug beside another monument as the thought came to him. Daniel would have expected the man's family to remove anything that defaced the tomb. What terrible sins had he committed to be left like this? When he'd been interred, the intention had been to gift him a view across the bay forever. Instead, his memory was defiled, his transitory glory faded.

Whatever the reasons, we live, we shine, then none of it matters, Daniel thought.

He intended to be cremated. Before his operation, he'd made that clear to Jonny.

'Burn me, my son, burn me. I cannot do with all that rotting away. And find me a cardboard coffin. Let's be environmentally sound at the last, eh?'

'You'll have years left, dad.'

'Maybe.'

When his time came, he'd love to have his ashes scattered in the sea here. He would add that to his will when he arrived home.

He didn't dwell on his epitaph and wasn't sure his deeds would weigh on the right side of the scales that St Peter or some celestial inspector in a sharp suit with a clip board might be holding. When he wondered what an after-life might have in store, it was without great confidence. He was relieved that he wouldn't be dying for a while. There would definitely be a scary number of minuses on his heavenly account.

Still, he thought, removing his straw hat and wiping sweat from his brow and cleaning his glasses, perhaps I'll be fine. I've tried to atone for what I've done wrong. Maybe if there is a God after all, I'll be allowed to live a long and happy life and at the end I might be able to double down on my repentance and be forgiven. Fingers crossed.

Since there was nowhere to sit in the cemetery, he selected a taverna down in the harbour beside the water where he could watch the boats and sip a beer and say farewell to Livadi properly, maybe for the last time, and think about leaving with Helen. He tried not to think about poor Lara's future.

****

Helen arrived at Karavi Beach in the evening, ready to leave the island, much more ready than ever before. She bumped the car down the steep slope in the dark and swung it round to park at the back of the house, where two suitcases were waiting for her. She'd spent years hauling other people's cases up the steps at Spiti and knew she'd be much more able than Daniel to lift weights, so rather than going straight to the door, she opened the boot and dragged in the luggage beside the two huge suitcases of her own. She'd have to pay for excess weight on the plane, but it was inevitable if you were moving the bones of forty years of your life to another country.

She was almost out of the existence she'd known for so long, she was levering herself away from Yiannis and, although twists in mood kept hitting her as though the menopause was returning, for the moment she regretted nothing.

Sophia and Lilliana had wanted to come with her, to say goodbye, but much as Helen would have liked to spend every final minute with them, she'd no desire for extras at Daniel's house – especially Sophia, under all the circumstances.

She told her, sharply, to stay away. 'Once we're on the ferry, you will do what you like, Sophia. But I'm not having you upsetting that poor girl any more. Not here. Not now. Understand?'

''*Daksi. Né, mama.* Ok.'

She was still Helen's child and hugged her as if she was never going to see her again. It was a new experience for them both; Helen had never before been parted from her girls for more than a week or two at a time.

As she slammed the boot, Daniel and Lara emerged. Jonny hesitated behind them, not following, leaning on the wall by the door, pretending casualness. He half-waved. Helen presumed he was keeping his distance from Lara, though he probably wanted to see if Sophia was in attendance.

Daniel gave Helen a hug, then turned back to his son.

'Jonny!' he said, quietly.

He embraced him, holding him for a moment before returning to the car. Lara had already settled into the back and didn't give them a glance.

'All set,' said Daniel to Helen, climbing in beside her. 'What are you going to do with this?'

'The car, at the port?' Helen rammed it into gear. 'I'm passing it to Lilliana – she'll need it for the guests... Oh, wait. Damn.' She braked and groaned. 'I'm sorry. I need to go back to Spiti. I keep forgetting things. I've left a photograph. I can't go without it...'

'A photo? We have time?'

'Yes. Just about. No problem.'

'It's that important? It's only a photo. Lilliana could send it on. We mustn't miss the boat.'

'It's of Sophia and Lilliana. When they were small. I want it now, Daniel. I'll let Lilliana know what's happening – though she might be at the port already.'

She started the car with the phone to her ear.

'Hi. Look, we're having to call back at Spiti. Where are you..?'

Lilliana was at the restaurant, with her father, who was drinking heavily and had threatened to sack Andreas for trying to talk some sense into him. Michalis had sunk into a sullen silence and was talking to no one.

'OK, we'll drive straight past but pick you up on the way back if you like. Be ready. It'll save you the walk. Does your dad know I'm leaving tonight?'

He did. She'd told him. Hence his mood, no doubt. She prayed he wouldn't turn up at the ferry because she'd no desire to fight with him again.

She leant across and slid her phone into her handbag by Daniel's feet.

'It'll be fine,' she said. 'Don't worry.' Not for the first time, she pushed her doubts aside. 'We'll be out of this in half an hour.' She hoped that was true.

Daniel too seemed uneasy, fussing with the cuffs of his shirt, pressing his glasses against his nose, flattening the short hair at his neck, moving his hat around on his knees, rubbing his chin, eyes fixed ahead. It would be easier for both of them once Serifos had been left astern.

There was only one route with the summer one-way system in place so they had to take it. They came down the main road into town, past the bakery and along the seafront, through the restaurants. The waiters were already busy, hastening across the road from the kitchens to the tables, trays stacked high. When they drove past Konstantinidis', Helen looked straight ahead, not wanting to catch anyone's eye or evoke any more passion from Yiannis. Had he seen them? Beside her, Daniel breathed deeply and said nothing more.

She glanced into the mirror. Lara seemed to be focusing on nothing in particular, which appeared to be her default mode now.

They drove up the steep incline to the apartments in second gear, Helen keeping her foot pressed hard down. The ferries were often a few minutes late, but time was very short.

'You're sure we'll make it?' Daniel was looking at his watch – perhaps avoiding looking ahead as the engine revved loudly and they shot into the darkness, slithering uphill.

'Yes, of course. We'll be able to have a coffee before boarding,' she shouted, joking. The lights of the SeaJet were already cutting across from Sifnos; and, unlike the old boats, these modern ones hurtled between the islands. 'I'll be quick!'

She pulled the car to a halt in the parking area, leapt out in the haze of dust and ran up the steps to the room. Where was the photo? Maybe Yiannis had thrown it out in one of his rages? Or perhaps Lilliana had put it away for safety? No, no, there it was in the top of the wardrobe. She grabbed it and rushed back, thrusting it at Daniel. Across the water, the SeaJet was reducing its speed while the lights on the quay illuminated a cluster of passengers around the shelter preparing for its arrival, and a line of cars and trucks.

Relax. They still had ten minutes or more before docking, unloading and boarding would be complete.

'This it?'

'Yes.'

It was her favourite photograph. The two tiny girls were in pretty dresses, carried small bouquets of flowers and were grinning, in a happier time. Lilliana had lost her front teeth.

'It's beautiful.'

'Yes.'

'Let's go.'

She slipped the Nissan into reverse gear. There was no time to spare.

****

They'd had most of the day to get ready and still they ended up in a scramble to the boat... How typical of life, thought Daniel.

Yet he was within minutes of having Helen to himself. Finally. Any other problem in the world was insignificant. His lungs were working fine and for one of the few times in his adult life he was looking forward, rather than struggling with the present or wallowing in the past. And Jonny would work something out and Lara would cope, because you have to.

He tried to relax. Helen would get them to the boat and it was important that he didn't scream at her driving: she might consider terror unbecoming in a man to whom she was committing the remainder of her life.

He clasped the photograph on his knee. It could have pride of place when they got home.

Opposite, the whole of Livadi was twinkling with life. Spreading from the lights in the restaurants and bars, coloured reflections danced in the water, figures moved back and forth and there were vehicle lights, white, yellow and red. He glanced up at Chora. The bus was zig-zagging its way towards the top and would be full, mostly with young people heading out for the evening. They had their whole life ahead of them. He envied them, though he knew he too had the best of his yet to come. Now, he simply wanted to be home with Helen.

He put his hand lightly on her leg, remembering their nights out long, long ago.

Away on their left, the SeaJet was closer. He patted the tickets in his pocket, checking they were instantly accessible.

After a five-point turn, Helen depressed the accelerator, jerking them out of the parking area and off down the steep incline. Even over the sound of the engine, he sensed a gasp from Lara behind and her hand thrust hard against the back of his seat.

'Seatbelt on, Lara?' he shouted, laughing.

'Have you?'

'We'll be there in just a minute.'

He glanced across at Helen's profile. In his suitcase, he had a brown paper bag with white lettering on the front which read 'Think of Serifos and smile': inside was a white dress in soft cotton and lace which he'd purchased in the Smeraldo gift shop. It was a special present, a thank-you-and-let-us-begin-all-over-again present. He'd give it to her on the ferry and hoped she'd find a way to smile, maybe with relief that they were actually en route; and perhaps she'd wear both the dress and the smile for their meal in Athens much later when they were clear of Yiannis and Serifos and the past.

They sped away. Pebbles crunched and wheel-spin made the vehicle slide for a moment before Helen corrected it. Their headlights cut through the darkness ahead. It was a track she knew well and she eased around to the right at speed, holding the slight skid and straightening up as she moved to third gear.

That was when Daniel saw Yiannis. His bike was in the middle of the road, heading straight towards them, without lights. As usual, he was wearing no helmet, his hair lifting in the breeze. There were no more than fifteen metres between them.

It was one of those frozen moments that most people experience only once or twice in a lifetime.

With his eyes fixed ahead, shocked, Daniel didn't see Helen do anything, though she reacted in an instant. The car slithered as she braked hard, wrenching the steering wheel to the left as Yiannis slithered to their right and into the ditch there, his bike disappearing under him.

The people carrier spun sideways on the stones of the track, turning round as it reached the edge of the drop. There might have been a screech from Lara and maybe something desperate from Helen but Daniel's mind was beyond them, registering the horror of what was happening.

His head had cracked against the side window. The pain was acute.

But they had stopped. The back wheels were over the cliff. Was this it? Was this how they died?

His mind sharpened, though. No, they were still breathing. It wasn't the end.

'Out, out! We have to get out!'

It should have involved each of them gently easing themselves to the ground in turn, to avoid any chance of the vehicle slipping backwards down the cliff, yet they simply flung open the doors and tumbled out. And, miraculously, the car didn't move.

Daniel took the shaking Lara in his arms. She was wracked with tears, as if beyond any consolation.

'We're alive, Lara. We're safe...'

Helen was standing with her hand on the bonnet, looking stunned, but as if she was trying to hold the car in place. He couldn't move to her because Lara was gripping him as if he was all that was standing between her and the plummet to the sea they'd escaped.

There was a sound, shifting pebbles, and he turned the other way. Yiannis was approaching, limping but hastening to Helen, who'd also begun to cry. When he reached her, he said something in Greek, wiped her tears away and took her in his arms. She rested her head against his shoulder and he moved his head so it was touching hers. His hand rested on her crown.

Daniel felt utter despair, a wrenching agony that seemed as bad as moments before when he was convinced they would plunge down the cliff; it was worse, it seemed just then, than when the consultant had told him he would die. This simply couldn't happen again. He couldn't lose her again.

No, no, no.

He heaved his biggest sigh, as if to exhale all the mistakes and misfortunes that had plagued their relationship from start to finish, and shed silent tears of his own.

He coaxed Lara away to a large boulder beside the road, where she sat, crumpled. He stroked her hair, because he could think of nothing else to do, then looked over at Helen and Yiannis again. She still leant against him, her eyes closed.

Daniel couldn't let this be. Yiannis could not take her back.

He left Lara and approached them slowly, still dazed, still conscious of a massive hurt above his right ear. When he touched it tentatively, his fingers were wet. The scalp had split and blood was seeping. Helen opened her eyes as he hesitated and, ridiculously, he held out his fingers to show the blood.

'Daniel…'

She put her hands against Yiannis' shoulders and eased herself away. Gently, with a softness that had not been evident at all in recent times, he made to recapture her.

'No, Yiannis. No. *Ochi.*'

And he stopped.

She came to Daniel: 'Oh, dear.' His glasses were badly bent. She shook her head. 'New glasses, my boy…'

She'd regained control. She touched his cheek and her hand brought that fondness he'd never found with anyone else. There were still tremors through his body, but they didn't matter. He looked into her eyes and saw only love.

He didn't need to worry. It was his time; everything would be fine.

Yiannis looked at the two of them, then at Lara and finally at the car, miraculously suspended over the edge. He seemed completely sober now. There was a long, long pause, which could have meant anything. Daniel didn't take his eyes off him, but he had Helen in his arms. This time, he would fight for her if he had to, whatever the consequences.

It didn't come to that. Yiannis took out his phone, stepped away and began to make a call, turning his back on his wife and her lover.

Across the bay, the SeaJet was reversing and people would shortly be boarding and that sailing would soon be gone, but Daniel didn't care. There would always be tomorrow.

Nothing mattered because at that moment he felt as if he and Helen were melding into each other at last, after everything.

Cheering carried to them across the water from a taverna in town.

Helen kissed his cheek and that was the most important thing in the world. He closed his eyes.

And yet, and yet… The pain in his head was enormous. He had to grit his teeth. Flashing lights were engulfing him, every colour. And there was a demented shrieking inside his skull as if an electric current was bouncing round in there.

He managed to force open his eyes, and gasped.

Reality returned. Terrifying reality. He was still in his seat. He was still in his seat..!

The car was at an angle, its bonnet pointing upwards and it hung there for what seemed an age. He was facing the blackness of the hillside and was conscious of light filtering down from Spiti just above.

Yet they were halted…

Hope. Desperate hope again, even through his pain. Their story would not end in disaster.

But that too was an illusion. The back of the car began to tip until he was looking up at the stars. He had time to register the blueness of the night sky as the moon shone brightly down on Serifos.

Then, punishing him for daring to dream there could be a happy ending, the nightmare recommenced. Everything was in slow motion at first, yet there was no time for Daniel to move at all. His muscles tensed against what was to come, his legs braced in the footwell, his right hand clutching the door handle, his left squeezing the photograph and clenching his seat. There was no time for his intellect to respond, recognise ironies, curse fate. There was no time for goodbyes.

The car dropped, plummeting backwards. He released the photograph, his arms shooting uselessly forward. He couldn't reach the fascia. There was no seat belt to hold him and he was flung back and over.

Somewhere, miles away, Helen was screaming this time and so was Lara. Perhaps his voice joined theirs.

A hundred feet below, they smashed against the only tree, bounced past it, turned over and crashed on to the black rocks that rose from the waves.

A shower of broken glass stabbed into Daniel's neck and face and into his eyes as his glasses were knocked away; then a spear of fresh agony shot through him as his legs broke and there was a final explosion in his head.

He lost consciousness before the car hit the water and the sea claimed them all.

If you enjoyed *Circles on the Sand*, please review it!

A good review is worth a great deal, so if you have time to leave one on the Amazon/Kindle website, it will help others in their choice and make the author very happy!

Just go to:
UK – *www.amazon.co.uk/dp/B0DQR8QHBQ*
US – *www.amazon.com/dp/B0DQR8QHBQ*

If you wish to **contact Keith Brindle** or to know about his future projects or would like to see some **photographs of Serifos** through the years, please visit *www.keithbrindlewriter.com*

Acknowledgments

I've been lucky to have been able to visit Serifos so regularly over fifty years. The island itself has a rare, stark beauty which has always seemed to attract fascinating individuals. The Konstantinidis family is fictitious, as are their businesses, and although none of the characters in this novel is real, many characters' quirks and peculiarities have been borrowed from people I've encountered on Serifos and on my travels around the islands: the Greeks themselves, of course, but also Italians, the French, Germans, Australians, Scandinavians, Canadians, Americans... and the ubiquitous British.

With regard to this book, I need to offer special thanks for the insights into Greek life provided by Andreas Nikolatos on Serifos and Helen Hallaris, the best host you could ever encounter, on Santorini.

I am grateful too to Canadian/Scottish folk singer David Francey for permission to use lyrics from *The Waking Hour*.

Closer to home, poet John Irving Clarke gave me helpful direction at an early stage of the drafting, whilst novelist Peter Rowlands provided much-needed encouragement when I was editing the manuscript. I am also indebted to him for his technical know-how and his endless patience as I prepared it for publication.

Phil Curzons made significant contributions to the final text. A dear friend, he was the bravest man I've known and his willingness to explain pulmonary fibrosis and exactly what it's like to have a double lung transplant were both unnerving and invaluable. How I wish he were still around to read the finished novel.

Finally, I owe so much to my wife, Christine Hallett, for her endless positivity, her insight and her editing and proof-reading skills, without which *Circles on the Sand* might still have seen the light of day but would have ended up crouching in the shadows, simply squinting out at the world passing by. I believe she's helped make it a more confident story: it's more relevant and appropriate because of her advice.

About the author

Keith Brindle lives in the north of England. He worked as a kitchen porter, a postman, a labourer in an engineering works and was at one time probably the oldest and most highly qualified paper boy in Wakefield. After fifteen years as head of English in a high school, he became an education consultant. He was principal examiner for various AQA English Language exams, as well as a senior moderator and senior speaking and listening adviser, and was involved in teacher training. He toured England for many years doing a kind of stand-up routine, explaining to 16-year-olds how to be successful in English exams. Eventually, very, very tired, he decided to focus just on writing.

He's had articles published in the national press and has written for amateur theatre. His poems have been included in anthologies and he performs at live poetry events. In addition, he's written or part-written and edited sixty-four school text books and revision books.

Circles on the Sand is his first novel, though he's currently completing a second one, *Mr Pilgrim's Progress*, which will be available in 2025.

Printed in Dunstable, United Kingdom